The Diamond House

The Diamond House

A Novel

Dianne Warren

HarperCollins*Publishers*Ltd

Published by HarperCollins Publishers Ltd

First edition

HarperCollins Publishers Ltd
Bay Adelaide Centre, East Tower
22 Adelaide Street West, 41st Floor
Toronto, Ontario, Canada
M5H 4E3

www.harpercollins.ca

Library and Archives Canada Cataloguing in Publication

Title: The diamond house : a novel / Dianne Warren.
Names: Warren, Dianne, 1950- author.
Identifiers: Canadiana (print) 20200185616 | Canadiana (ebook) 20200185624
ISBN 9781443445108 (softcover) | ISBN 9781443445122 (ebook)
Classification: LCC PS8595.A778 D53 2020 | DDC C813/.54—dc23.

Printed and bound in the United States
LSC/H 9 8 7 6 5 4 3 2 1

For Sherry Cuthbert

1

The First Wife

For all the years there were children in the Diamond house, and long before a woman named Emyflor Santos lost control of a rogue vacuum cleaner hose, a white hand-thrown teapot sat on a corner shelf in the dining room. It was clearly the work of an amateur: oversized, indelicate with its evident throwing lines, and heavy as a ten-pin bowling ball. The children had a vague idea that it had been made by an Aunt Salina they'd never met. They imagined a woman bent over a muddy potter's wheel, an eccentric old relative back east in the town their parents had come from. They knew nothing of that town. To them, East was a foreign country.

One night, when the rest of the house was asleep, the youngest of the five children, Estella, decided to sneak downstairs and have a good look at the teapot. She knew it had been kept for some reason other than steeping tea, and she wanted to know what that reason was. She descended the stairs in the darkness and turned on the light in the dining room, then climbed on a chair and retrieved the teapot from the shelf. It was so heavy she could hardly lift it. She set it down carefully on the mahogany dining table, trying not to make it clunk. The lid wouldn't budge, so she found a wooden spoon in the kitchen and began to tap carefully around the rim. She was persistent. It finally gave way.

Inside, Estella discovered a collection of old letters and, on top of them, a small velvet bag. When she opened it, she found five black clay beads wrapped in a soft cotton cloth. She removed the beads to have a closer look and saw that each had a miniature white figure in relief on its surface. The figures reminded her of creatures that might keep watch over a mummy's tomb, but they did not tell her much, so she set them aside and turned her attention to the letters. She was only five years old and there wasn't much she could do better than her brothers, but none of them had learned to read before they'd even started school.

As she stared at the glossy teapot and the pile of letters on the table, she thought, *I knew there was something.*

She opened the top letter.

At first, she almost gave up and put it back because the handwriting seemed impossible to decipher, but she stuck with it and the *ABCs* began to emerge, or at least enough of them that she could guess at some of the words. The letter made little sense, but after struggling through it for a second time, she discerned that it was personal correspondence from her father to a woman named Salina Passmore, who was clearly not her aunt and clearly not the old woman she'd imagined. Estella was picturing this Salina and her father walking home together in the pouring rain—there had been a funeral, she'd figured out that much—

when she realized her father was standing in the doorway to the dining room, watching her. She'd been concentrating so hard on the cursive writing that she hadn't heard him coming down the stairs. Without saying anything, she folded the letter, slipped it back into its envelope, and placed all the letters once again in the teapot in the order she had found them. She set the bag with the ugly beads on top, just as it had been, and replaced the ill-fitting lid, although she was careful not to jam it on too tightly so it would be easier to remove in future. Then she climbed onto the chair and put the teapot back on the shelf, aware the whole time of her father in the doorway, and the whole house in darkness behind him.

When she'd returned the chair to its spot at the table, she faced him and said, "Am I in trouble?"

He replied, "Curiosity is a gift, not a thing to be punished. Perhaps I should give those beads to your mother. I imagine they're valuable."

"She wouldn't like them," Estella said. She was thinking, *So, the beads are his to give.*

She waited for him to say more.

Finally he spoke. "You're a smart girl, Estella," he said.

"Yes, I know."

"And handy with a wooden spoon. I'd like to sit and have a pipe, but I think we should likely just go back to bed. Without further ado, as they say."

Estella squeezed past her father in the doorway and he followed her to the staircase. He placed a hand on her shoulder as they climbed the stairs. She took note of the steps that creaked, so as to avoid them the next time.

"Good night, then," he whispered when they reached the top of the stairs.

Third from the bottom. Fifth from the top. Or was it the fourth?

She forgot to say good night before she returned to her room. Her father watched until she was back in bed.

———

THE FUNERAL WHERE Estella's father and Salina Passmore first met in the fall of 1902 was in an Ottawa Valley town called Byrne Corners. It had been an awful day for standing in the cemetery during the committal. The rain was pelting, and it dripped from the brim of Salina's hat, from her eyelashes, the tip of her nose, and she was all too aware of her appearance, given that a young man was standing across the grave from her: Oliver Diamond, a visitor from the West. She knew that his father and brother both worked at the Morris Castings plant, his father in a position of some importance. The elder Mr. Diamond was apparently not pleased that his second son had turned his back on a secure future at the factory and was instead wasting an unexpected inheritance on some folly halfway across the country. Oliver's brother had invested his inheritance in a house and a Morris Castings bond. That was the sensible course of action. Most people in Byrne Corners would have agreed. The daydreamers go west, they believed, or the ones with no other prospects.

To Salina Passmore, this younger Diamond brother was an intriguing prospect. He'd left Byrne Corners before her own family had moved there, when Mr. Passmore had taken up a post at the Union Bank. In the five years since that move, both of Salina's older sisters had found husbands, and one of them, Rose-anne, was already the mother of two noisy toddlers. Salina, on the other hand, had met no man of marrying age who interested her in the slightest. She had nothing against men—as evidenced by her tingling awareness of the young man in the cemetery—but she lacked enthusiasm for the kind of prospect her family wished for her, that is, one who could offer a woman money and comfort. With the constant attention her mother and sisters gave to finding her a husband, Salina felt as if she had already been deemed a spinster, and that being unable to attract a suitable man was the worst tragedy that could befall a woman who was not unpleasing in the looks department and more than reasonably intelligent. The choices they'd steered her toward were all so ordi-nary, and marriage to any one of them would, she was certain, lead to an impossibly predictable life. Perhaps that was the reason the unorthodox Oliver Diamond—or at least the idea of a man who eschewed his father's conventional wisdom—was so appeal-ing though they had never been formally introduced, or even said hello to one another on the street.

It was rumoured about town—and Salina had been listen-ing—that his interest in the West was entrepreneurial rather than agrarian, but no one seemed to know the nature of his ambitions. Something to do with the building trade, or perhaps the farm equipment business, neither of which he knew anything about. Oliver Diamond, they said, had an elevated impression of his own potential. What experience did he have that could possibly be of value in the new frontier? What influential people did he know there? What skills did he possess? None. That's what an unearned inheritance did for a young man. *He thinks he is above working his way up at the foundry, too good for axe heads and frying pans and such,* Salina had heard her mother say to another lady before the subject was quickly changed so they could not be accused of succumbing to the habit of common gossip. Good women of the Methodist persuasion, Salina thought, were happy to yammer away; they just didn't want to get caught.

As the storm lingered above these particular Methodists gathered in the cemetery, the minister led them in verse after verse of "Shall We Gather at the River," and Salina wondered how long this was going to take, and did the minister not know about truncation? She lowered her head against the rain and watched the pools of water at her feet turn slick and spill toward the open grave. Poor Aunt Aideen, she thought, who'd always hated the rain. Salina listened to the voices around her, trying their best to give Aideen a good send-off despite the conditions.

With her head lowered and the brim of her hat hiding her eyes (she hoped), Salina furtively studied Oliver Diamond. She concluded that he was handsome in a lanky way and had an air of confidence that went beyond the extra three inches he had on every other man there. He was, like her, without an umbrella. His shock of dark hair was as wet as a mop just lifted from a bucket, and the rain ran down his face and surely inside the neck of his wool jacket. Still, he stood to his full height and acted as though he didn't care. She could hear him belting out the words—"*Soon our happy hearts will quiver*"—as he sang with the most devout, although Salina detected a hint of irony in his obvious defiance of the rain. A provocative man, she decided, and she resolved to catch his eye when the cause of them all being there was over with and she'd had a chance to return herself to her pre-downpour state of attractiveness.

Please, someone put a stop to this, she thought, *for the sake of preventing pneumonia in everyone here.* As one verse of the hymn slid into the next, her eyes scanned the congregation, and she took note that another young lady—Beatrice Shaughnessy was her name—seemed also to be watching Mr. Diamond. She knew Beatrice from the Young Women's League at the church, where they had disagreed vehemently at one meeting on the matter of suffrage. Beatrice was pretty enough, Salina thought, but she would be better suited to one of Jane Austen's vicars, or perhaps a dairy farmer. She knew she was being unfair to poor Beatrice, but she was well-sick of the service by this time, and the rain, and the minister who didn't know when to call it quits. Beatrice was still relatively put together thanks to the umbrella protecting her hair, and when Salina looked down at her own feet once again she saw that her shoes were probably beyond saving, and the rain had served to weight and lengthen her black skirt so that the lace hem now hung in a puddle. She lifted one foot and it sucked mud like a rubber wellington. She would have to go home and change before the reception. She considered which skirt and shoes she ought to change into. Another black skirt—it was a funeral, after all—but the blue shoes, she decided, with the embroidery on the toe, the ones she would have worn in the first place if the sun had been shining. She imagined herself in the church hall, crossing her ankles just so, and young Mr. Diamond admiring them from a spot close by, where he had strategically positioned himself.

When the hymn was over, the minister finally launched into

the solemn rite of committal, and when that was done Salina looked up and saw that Oliver Diamond was no longer where he'd been standing, and Beatrice Shaughnessy was gazing off in the direction in which, Salina assumed, he had left the cemetery. As Salina dared to scan the grey horizon in search of a disappearing figure, a flash of lightning split the sky and the almost instantaneous clap of thunder caused several ladies to scream, and everyone at the gravesite forgot about piety and went running through the storm toward the safety of the church. Another crack of thunder caused the woman in front of Salina to slip, and Salina managed to grab her arm and keep her upright, and it turned out to be Beatrice. They ran arm in arm until they reached the church steps, at which point Beatrice said, "Oh, thank you, Salina, you saved me from a disaster," and Salina let go of her arm and muttered something about the dreadful day as she wondered which of the two of them Mr. Diamond would have preferred had he stuck around, and whether she would have bettered her chances if she'd let Beatrice land in the mud.

The poor minister found himself alone at the gravesite, and then he too sloshed through the puddles toward the church, where all were now taking refuge. Inside the door, a pile of muddy footwear and wet umbrellas grew, and the bedraggled mourners retired to the downstairs hall in their stocking feet desperate for hot coffee and no longer caring what they looked like because everyone there looked the same. The hall floor was impossible to keep clean with all the mucky hems and pants cuffs dragging across it, and it soon looked as though an army of salamanders had slithered from one wall to the other. Salina gave up on the idea of running home for a change of clothes. With Oliver Diamond absent, there was no point.

The smell of fresh coffee soon filled the hall, while outside the storm continued to rage. Salina was cross that she had been deserted but thought it was probably for the best. In the electric light inside, she no doubt looked considerably worse than she had in the cemetery. She wondered how Beatrice had managed to keep her hair dry in spite of that dash for the church. As Salina stood forlornly watching the door, wishing that it would open but hoping at the same time that it wouldn't, her sister Roseanne appeared and grabbed her arm and whispered, "I saw you sizing up that Oliver Diamond. Don't tell me a man has come along and caught your attention?"

"Don't be ridiculous," Salina said, pulling away from her sister. "He looked like a drowning rat out there. No, I take that back. He must be eight feet tall. It would take an ocean to drown him. Anyway, I wasn't sizing him up. I don't know what you're talking about."

"Everyone saw," Roseanne said. "Don't think they didn't."

She hated the idea of being caught out. And did *everyone* include Oliver Diamond himself?

"That wasn't me," she said. "It was Beatrice Shaughnessy who had her eye on him."

"Beatrice would never go for a man like him," Roseanne said. "She's as likely to smile at a stray dog." Then she hurried off to get in the coffee lineup.

Salina decided she was too completely miserable in her wet clothes to stay for the reception, and she was not about to endure gossip about her desperate need for a husband. When she saw her mother and her sister Edith glance in her direction and then nod as though they were talking about her, she headed for the stairs and the pile of ruined footwear. She jammed her feet into her shoes—they were already on their way to shrinking a size—and stepped out once again into the rain, and who was walking up the boards toward the church door but none other than Oliver Diamond, looking dapper as could be. He'd changed out of his wet clothes into a dry suit, and was carrying an umbrella big enough to keep the rain off a small crowd.

"Oh," said Salina. She could not imagine how unappealing she must look. Her hair. Her face powder. Her bedraggled blouse clinging, and her shoes looking like a pair of turnips just pulled out of the ground. Whatever chance she'd had to attract Mr. Diamond was surely gone.

But he was undaunted by her sorry state and he said, "Miss Passmore, let me introduce myself. Oliver Diamond, at your service." He held up his substantial umbrella in a way that invited her underneath. She thought of ignoring him and stepping around and marching home in her usual independent manner, but there was no chance of a dignified exit, and the rain was still coming down. She was sick of being wet and cold and she did not look forward to getting even more so.

"Oh hell," she said, stepping under the umbrella. "Curses to Aideen McCreary for deciding she had to be buried today of all days. What an inconsiderate old thing."

He laughed in a way that displayed his appreciation for her impertinence.

"Are you making a break for it?" he asked.

"What does it look like?" she replied.

"I was hoping," he said, "that I might have the pleasure of walking you home, but I thought I was going to have to earn it by suffering through at least an hour of church basement small talk."

Now it was her turn to at least smile, if not laugh out loud the way he had. And even though she was still miserable, she felt the tetchiness lifting, because it appeared that Oliver Diamond had come back to the church because of her and not Beatrice Shaughnessy or any other young lady, and he hadn't changed his mind when he'd seen her dismal self step through the door out into the rain.

They began to walk, well-protected by his giant umbrella, which she kept expecting to flip inside out, but it didn't. He appeared to know which direction they ought to go.

"Your umbrella is very sturdy," she said.

"True, it is," he said. "Although not sturdy enough for the winds in the West. An umbrella there is a useless bit of conceit."

Then he said to her, as if he were conducting an interview for the local newspaper, "Miss Passmore, I understand that you have an interest in the processes of clay production."

"Where did you hear that?" she asked.

"About town," he said. "The post office, I think."

She tried to imagine the circumstance that had led to her being the subject of a conversation, or perhaps an inquiry.

"Why do you ask about my interest in clay?" she said.

"Oh, curiosity."

"That's fatal to cats," she said, "in case you haven't heard."

"Good thing I'm not a cat, then, isn't it."

The Passmore home was now in front of them—a stately two-storey brick on High Street, with a unique rounded porch—and they hurried up the steps and sheltered under the roof. Oliver lowered his umbrella and said, "I knew the family that used to live here. Before I went west."

"I hear they ran into financial problems," Salina said. "Our luck that it was available when . . . well, when my father chose so thoughtlessly to uproot us all and move us to a town where cast-iron skillets abound, or whatever else they make at that plant, but you can't purchase a decent pair of shoes."

"I admire a brick house," he said, not seeming to care about skillets or shoes (which was good, since the ones on her feet were such a disaster) and instead studying, even running his hands over, the red-brick exterior of the house. He said, "Built well, built to last," and paused, his hand still on the bricks. He seemed to be thinking. "There is a need for quality in the West," he finally said. "Higgledy-piggledy. That's the way the West is being built. Clapboard shacks everywhere you look. They ship the lumber by train, you know. A necessity. There's barely a tree to be found. A bit of shrub, yes, but no trees as we know them."

"No trees?" she said, not sure where the conversation was going but willing to wait for more clues. "Is it so?" It was hard to imagine a place without trees.

At that very moment a flash of lightning was followed by a loud crack that could be nothing other than an oak tree splitting, although not within their immediate field of vision.

"Well, then," she said, "you don't have to worry about lightning striking them."

"Not the trees, no," he said, "but it's a still a concern when you're as tall as I am," which she thought was a funny thing to say, as though a man could be split down the middle by lightning.

He asked, "Do you like it here in Byrne Corners? Now that you've settled in? Aside from the dearth of decent shoes?"

So he *had* been listening. "It'll do," she said, "but I wouldn't exactly say I've settled in. I have a bit of a wandering spirit." She didn't know why she'd said such a thing that echoed the rumours she'd heard about him. It had just slipped out.

"Do you, now?" he said. "I have myself. In fact, my train leaves tomorrow for the West."

She was unreasonably disappointed to hear this. Why had he bothered, she thought, if he was leaving the next day?

But then he said, "May I write to you?" and the disappointment faded and she felt just a bit of a quickening heart, even as she said, "As you like. I hope you write an entertaining letter, for I'm easily bored."

"I will do my best, Miss Passmore," he said, and then he lifted his umbrella again and stepped back out into the weather.

Salina opened the heavy oak door and went inside. She could hear the wind slapping rain in sheets up against the house. Through the lead-paned window in the door she watched Oliver Diamond walk away down High Street. The factory whistle blew just then. It was a sound she had grown used to, blowing as it did like clockwork to signal the shift changes, but she thought she detected irritation in the way Oliver first looked toward the sound and then turned away from it, and held his umbrella tilted, like a shield between himself and the factory. As he did so, the wind caught it and flipped it inside out, and she saw him struggle for a moment to right it before tossing it over a fence and walking on, head high, to be soaked once again in the downpour.

Salina realized that she was as cold as if she had just got out of an ice bath, and she slipped off her ruined shoes and moved into the foyer, Oliver Diamond being almost out of sight now anyway. She caught her own image in the mirror there and was horrified at her dishevelled appearance. As she walked toward the staircase and the upstairs bedrooms with a plan to repair herself, the hem of her dress trailed across the hardwood floor, leaving mud in her wake. By the time her family arrived home an hour later, she had thrown her footwear in the trash and changed into a fresh frock and the blue shoes. She was not expecting to see Oliver Diamond again that day, but she'd made herself attractive anyway. She felt like somewhat of a new person.

"You disappeared," her mother said, her eyes following the trail of mud that Salina had neglected to clean up. "I thought you might lend a hand at the church hall. I had to ask Beatrice Shaughnessy, who was most obliging. Lovely girl."

"Oh, I shan't give her another thought," Salina said.

It was not at all clear what she meant. She herself did not know, because her mind was elsewhere.

THE FIRST LETTER arrived ten days later, on the very day Salina's white teapot was removed from a backyard kiln. Salina read the letter as she walked to Mrs. Morris's for the unbricking, wearing her pottery apron over her skirt and blouse. Normally, she would have arrived early in anticipation of the magic wrought by the firing, but today she walked slowly, intently reading her letter several times over, and when she arrived at Mrs. Morris's gate she saw that Ruthie Granger was there watching for her.

"Salina, for heaven's sake," Ruthie said. "We've all been waiting. Are you not dying of excitement?"

At first, Salina thought Ruthie was referring to her letter, which she quickly folded and slipped back into one of her apron's many pockets. Then she realized that Ruthie meant the oven, which had been fired on the weekend by one of Mr. Morris's men from the factory. It had been a final gloss firing, which was Mrs. Morris's favourite because she fancied herself a freehand paintress and the gloss revealed her talent at depicting roses and vines and daisies. Her canvas was generally the most basic of shapes, a humble dish or perhaps an ashtray, in Salina's opinion the least ambitious of all the shapes possible, although she wasn't about to say so out loud because Mrs. Morris owned the oven and the shed in which the club worked.

"Quickly," Ruthie said. "Mrs. M. is beside herself with excitement. She thinks she's about to find her masterpiece in the oven."

With the letter safely in her apron pocket, Salina tried to recover from the daze in which she found herself—*Could it be love, already?*—and she turned into the Morrises' yard and followed Ruthie along the side of the house to the back garden, where the others were waiting.

"Finally, then," Mrs. Morris said, not hiding her irritation that Salina was, what was it, seven minutes late?

Ruthie gave her a little commiserative poke in the side. She was the only one of the eight ladies in the club who would dare speak anything remotely like a criticism of their leader, although she would do so only within Salina's hearing. In front of the others, especially Mrs. Morris, butter wouldn't melt, but Salina was happy to have at least a weak and uncommitted compatriot.

The ladies were gathered in front of the oven—more properly called a kiln, but they preferred the less technical term—that Mr. Morris had built at the back of the garden. It stood, fully bricked, like an altar at which they were about to worship.

"Who wants to do the honours now that we are all here?" Mrs. Morris asked.

"Of course that should be you, Mrs. Morris," Salina said, joining the group, trying to redeem herself, and the ladies all nodded, not a word of dissent among them, since they all knew whose property they were on and whose husband allowed such a thing as a pottery oven in the garden.

The firebrick kiln was under a wooden shelter next to the work shed. It was a small kiln with room for just four shelves, stacked one above the other, and a firebox underneath and chimney behind. The size of the kiln placed a limit on the ladies' aspirations, but they were all glad to have any kiln at all at their disposal. Their little club was quite a novelty in town, and considered to be a daring departure from embroidery or watercolour painting. Salina had been invited to join more because of her father's position at the bank than for her artistic talent, which she considered to be quite a bit more obvious than Mrs. Morris's, although that was another opinion she wisely kept to herself.

On this day, a long table had been set up on the lawn to await the unloading, and the ladies formed an assembly line between it and the oven. Once they were organized, Mrs. Morris removed a brick from the oven door and held it up. The ladies clapped, as was expected, and Mrs. Morris made a great show of setting the all-important first brick on a waiting pallet. Then she preceded to remove the bricks in the door until the kiln was sufficiently open for the ladies to peer inside from their various vantage points in the line and see the first hints of the transformations that had occurred inside. *Oohs* and *aahs* were briefly allowed by Mrs. Morris until she recommended the removal of the bricks, continuing this time until the door was completely open and the bricks were stacked neatly on the pallet.

"How is the firing cone?" asked Mrs. Dorinstall—trying too hard, Salina thought, to sound like someone in the know.

Mrs. Morris once again made a ceremony of the process by removing the clay cone meant to melt at the right temperature and signal Mr. Morris's man to stop stoking the firebox and let the oven cool. She held it up for all to see—it had slumped perfectly—and the ladies clapped once again.

Salina thought Mrs. Morris was dragging things out a little too much for dramatic effect, but she finally reached into the kiln and removed the first pot, Mrs. McPhail's small vase with a ring of painted roses spiralling up the side. The ladies complimented the artist as it was passed along the line and set on the waiting table, although Mrs. McPhail expressed her disappointment that she had not managed to distribute the pink colour evenly and the green of the stem had all but disappeared. Salina wondered if the problem might be an uneven firing temperature rather than the quality of the painting, but this was something else that could not be said out loud, as it implied a flaw in Mrs. Morris's kiln.

"It's quite lovely as it is," Ruthie said to Mrs. McPhail, always one to give encouragement.

One by one the pots were removed and the shelves stacked beside the kiln. The stilts that held the wares were dropped in a basket, and the ladies determined that the firing appeared to have been a great success. Mr. Morris's man, they agreed, was getting very good at his job on the side.

They were down to the last few items and Salina awaited the removal of her teapot, the only piece she'd been able to finish for the firing since it had been so difficult to get the various parts made and trimmed and properly attached. Mrs. Morris was taking her time, admiring her own pots as she came across them, until at long last the teapot came out, followed by its lid, and Salina finally had her creation in her hands. She did not remember it being so large and heavy, but still, it was an accomplishment.

"A teapot is a real challenge," Ruthie said. "You should be proud."

"It is, isn't it," she replied, momentarily forgetting the rule of modesty for all but Mrs. Morris. She ran her hands over the warm, white surface, the gently curving spout, the handle she had worked so hard at in order to get the balance right and prevent the pot from tipping too far forward when it was held. She set the lid on and was not even disappointed that a glaze drip prevented a perfect fit, and then she set the pot on the table with the others, and she thought it really was the standout piece. The decorating was subtle, with just a single green leaf painted under the spout and another smaller one next to the handle. She was less interested in painting and the others were better at it, but there was no one in the group who had ever used the potter's wheel to make a teapot with any degree of success.

"It's very plain, isn't it," Mrs. Morris said. "Is that what you wanted? But let's save our comments for our discussion, shall we? For now, let's all have a pat on the back for a job well done. Well done, ladies, don't you think?"

"Well done," they all agreed, patting each other on the backs of their summer dresses with delicate hands and wedding-ringed fingers (all but Salina), admiring their work, the still-warm glazed surfaces of dishes and bowls and vases, the painted flowers shining in the sun. It was alchemy, Salina thought, the many steps that turned simple earth into things of beauty, flawed things, but beautiful nonetheless. She admired the pots all lined up on the table, having emerged for the final time from the fire. There were flashes of ash from the firebox, but these too she loved for the way you could not control them. She felt a sense of goodwill, even toward Mrs. Morris, who was, she had to admit, a competent paintresse in spite of her lack of imagination and her superior nature.

The tea and cakes came out next. Mrs. Morris had a gazebo, well-furnished for her frequent summer luncheons, and the ladies seated themselves for their discussion. It had been Mrs. Dorinstall's turn to bring the cake, and she didn't disappoint with a coffee cake topped with nuts and berries. Each lady chose the best of her clay pieces for what they called their "criticism," which was just, in Salina's opinion, congratulating each other and involved no thoughtful criticism at all, since that would be impolite (excepting Mrs. Morris's *carte blanche* remarks). When it was Ruthie's turn to hold up her piece—a bowl with a pink blob painted just beneath the lip, which Salina knew was an attempt at a peony—Salina felt she could say something at least a little bit constructive because it was Ruthie, and she said, "It was a very difficult subject, Ruthie, the most difficult of any, I would think. Good on you for choosing something so tricky. You could study the Japanese paintings if you wanted to improve your brushwork."

The ladies were silent, even Ruthie.

"I didn't mean that to sound harsh," Salina said. "We all want to improve, do we not? And you can't improve without taking risks. I say bravo to Ruthie."

"Thank you, Salina," Ruthie finally said. "I think you're probably right."

"It's very pretty," one of the other ladies said. "I don't think there is any way you could improve it. It's quite perfect."

Salina felt goodwill dissipating and she thought, *Oh for God's sake, the peony is barely recognizable as a peony, and besides, is anything ever perfect?* But she said nothing further, having been reminded that criticism didn't really mean criticism, unless it came from Mrs. Morris and then you could be certain.

When it was Salina's turn to hold up her teapot, Mrs. Morris repeated her point that it was a bit plain, and Salina herself said that it was heavier than it ought to be, and perhaps she should have worked harder to smooth out the throwing lines. She waited for congratulations on the shape of her teapot but none came. She tried to remain humble, but she had expected someone to acknowledge that a teapot was not easy to make. At least one person might think to recognize that, especially when they were all so free with their flattery.

No one praised the teapot other than Ruthie, who said it had character, and finally another lady filled the silence by saying, "Has anyone ever owned a teapot that poured properly?" Salina was tempted to fill her teapot with water right then and there and show them that it poured perfectly, but she set the pot under her chair and said, "Thank you very much, ladies. How lucky we are to have this group. And Mrs. Morris's pottery shed, of course."

The criticism moved on to the next person while Salina seethed. By the time the discussion got to Mrs. Morris, who for some reason always went last, Salina was ready to abandon caution and say what she really thought, even though she knew this would not be wise. Mrs. Morris held up her finest ashtray, and when it was Salina's turn to speak, she said, with much restraint, "You are becoming an accomplished paintresse, Mrs. Morris. I think you should be quite proud of your ashtray. It's so very plain, and plain is harder than it looks, is it not?" Mrs. Morris scrutinized her with eyes narrowed and didn't say anything in reply. Ladies squirmed in their seats. Salina took a defiant bite of cake, but then she choked on it and Ruthie had to pound her on the back. It was unladylike, but it served to divert attention from Mrs. Morris's palpable disapproval of Salina's *touché*.

When the tea was finished (having been brewed in the Royal Doulton Geneva teapot Mrs. Morris had received as a wedding gift some years previous) and they had been around the circle with their discussion, they packed up their pots and the meeting was over. Salina had brought nothing with her to pack her teapot in, so she carried it home in her hands, carefully, and on the way she passed a child, a little boy, who asked her if she had just bought it at the drugstore (which belonged to Salina's brother-in-law, and was where you bought things like Wedgwood and Royal Doulton in Byrne Corners), and Salina told him that she had made it herself and he called it beautiful. *Booty-full*, he pronounced it, and she said, "Thank you very much, you sweet boy," and in her head she agreed with him. At least someone had said it out loud, she thought, although he did throw a spruce cone at the back of her head when she was walking away from him. If it hadn't been for the teapot she would have chased him down and given him a talking-to.

When she got home, she carried the teapot to her room and set it on her dresser where she could admire it. She had the room all to herself now that Roseanne was married off, and she was glad she did, so she could read once again her letter from Oliver

Diamond. By the time she had read it another half dozen times (and had it practically memorized) the rancour she felt toward Mrs. Morris was gone and had been replaced by a glow that was new to her, and quite overpowering.

She heard mother calling her, no doubt for help with supper, and she started down the stairs after locking her letter in her desk drawer, and then she decided to go back for the teapot. In the kitchen, her mother admired it and asked if it held water.

"Of course it does," Salina said. To prove her point, she gave it a good scrubbing and made the tea for supper in it. The pot was so big her mother's tea cozy wouldn't fit. When it came time to pour, Salina discovered that it dripped from the spout.

"Never mind," her mother said. "I believe they all do that. Has there ever been a teapot that doesn't drip?"

Salina was already examining the spout, trying to figure out where she had gone wrong.

"Is anyone going to pass the meat?" her father asked, as though teapots were of no interest whatsoever to him. Even though, Salina thought, he was the one who claimed he could not live without the requisite amount of tea filling up his hollow legs.

"By the way," Salina's mother said, "I hear you received a letter today."

It was infuriating, the way news travelled in this town. There was no doubt that her mother already knew who the letter was from.

"It was nothing," Salina said. "Just a bit of business."

"Business," her mother said. "I doubt that."

Salina felt the need to change the subject as quickly as possible, and she said, "Roseanne thinks the two of us should make a trip to Niagara Falls. With the children."

"That's nice," her mother said. "But I don't know if the Falls are a place for children. They're very dangerous."

"We're not planning to let them play in the water," Salina said. "And we can tie a rope to them or some such thing."

"That doesn't sound like much fun for them. Father, what do you have to say?"

"I don't think either of you can have much to say," Salina said. "Roseanne is a married woman and I'm perfectly capable of deciding where and when I go. Who knows, maybe I'll meet a nice man on the train and get married in Niagara Falls. I hear they do that there. It could be very romantic. Or I could borrow that woman's barrel—you know the one—and go over the Falls myself for excitement."

Her mother turned pale.

"Mother, I was joking. I've little interest in going anywhere with Roseanne's holy terrors."

"I don't think you're ever just joking when you say a thing like that," her mother said. "Don't forget, I've known you all your life. I wouldn't mind a look at that letter. I must say I'm curious."

"You'll have to stay that way," Salina said before heaping her plate with potatoes.

Her mother finished her meal in silence, as though she were trying to imagine what Salina might be up to, exchanging correspondence with Oliver Diamond.

Afterwards, when the dishes were done and the house was quiet, Salina sat at her desk and penned her first letter to Oliver, enclosing a drawing of her teapot. She did not know where the audacity to do so came from. She was not a pencil artist of any great confidence, although she did keep a sketchbook with ideas for future projects in clay. Beneath her teapot sketch she wrote, *I reveal my modest talent in hopes you will overlook its limitations.* She sat with one ankle tucked behind the other, and she periodically looked down at her blue shoes and admired the colour and the stitching. She felt as though she were talking to Oliver, and she chose her words carefully, with just the right amount of wit and playfulness, or so she hoped. She wondered if a new chapter of her life were beginning, knowing at the same time that it was much too soon to arrive at such a conclusion. She wrote with Oliver's letter open beside her, and when she was done she folded her letter and her drawing and slipped them into an envelope, which she then addressed to "Mr. Oliver Diamond." When she was done, she locked the letter from Oliver in her desk drawer, and went to bed.

——

To young Estella Diamond, there was before and after the teapot. The very night she first looked inside, she felt as though something was different. She couldn't quite grasp what it was, but it had to do with time, which she had previously compartmentalized into the span of her own life, and a second, relatively short and insignificant period leading up to it. Now, she thought it was possible she had not seriously enough considered that period before she existed. The past—especially her father's past— had become a presence, and a very big mystery. Even as the two of them had climbed the stairs in the darkness that night, she'd thought, *Who was he before he was my father?*

They'd returned to bed without waking the rest of the family. Estella heard the bedsprings creak across the hall as her father settled himself beside her mother. Her older brothers were asleep down the hall, two to a room. As the only girl in the family, she had a room to herself. Her mother had decorated it in anticipation of a daughter after the first of the boys had been born, or so Estella had been told: pink-flowered wallpaper, a white chiffonier to match the white iron bedstead, a rose-coloured counterpane with scalloped edging. Estella did not especially care for all the pink delicacy, and she would rather have had dogs than flowers on her walls, but she knew her mother had badly wanted a girl to occupy the room, and so she did not complain. There was that far-off thing called adulthood when she would be able to do whatever she wanted, and she was content to wait until then to exercise her own decorative choices, although she suspected she would not care enough to bother. She planned to have other, more important things on her mind.

As she lay in the dark, the house now quiet around her, she thought about those beads that had been on top of the letters. She knew they were made of clay, and she wondered who had made them and how they had they been fired. Her father's kilns at the factory were huge, the size of a house. How could you fill one of those with such tiny objects as beads? And why had they been decorated with ugly creatures, like imps and goblins in fairy tales? She imagined them freeing themselves from the beads after the kiln was bricked up, running around in the fire and smashing things. Then she began to imagine them running around her room in the dark, and she scared herself and had to switch on her bedside lamp.

She thought of calling to her mother, but instead she got out of bed and crept down the hall and got into bed with Jack and Andrew. She climbed over Jack because she knew he wouldn't mind, and wiggled in between them.

They both woke up.

"Not again," Andrew said.

"I got scared," she said.

They rolled away from her in opposite directions and she was left in the middle with the sheet stretched tight. She tried to be still, but she felt restless. Finally Andrew got up and went to her room, which is what she'd hoped would happen.

When she was alone with Jack, she found that she didn't want to tell him what she'd found in the teapot. He was the youngest of the boys, the closest in age to Estella, and she usually told him everything, but the way her father had watched her without speaking made her think the teapot's contents should not be spoken of. She wondered what he would have told her had they sat in the parlour while he smoked a pipe instead of going back to bed. The decision to return to bed, she thought, was the decision to leave things as they were.

Only they weren't the same. Her father was not the same man.

She found herself squirming to get comfortable until finally Jack said, "Damn it, Nelly, if you're going to stay here, you have to be still."

"Don't call me Nelly," she said, giving him a kick under the covers. Jack was the only one who called her that. She pretended she didn't like it.

"Just count to a hundred and go to sleep," he said, ignoring the kick. He began to snore softly again.

Estella knew there were hunting dogs on the wallpaper in this room instead of flowers. She counted dogs until she fell asleep.

When she woke in the morning to the sound of her mother's breakfast bell at the foot of the stairs, Jack was already dressed and Andrew was pulling on his socks. Andrew saw she was awake and said, "You're a pain in the neck." Then he went down to breakfast, and Jack said, "Just sometimes."

Estella went downstairs, still in her pyjamas. Theo and Mathew were working at the plant now and they had already eaten and left with their father. Estella sat with Jack and Andrew at the dining table, and the three of them had oatmeal porridge and orange juice for breakfast. The boys left for school shortly after, and when they were gone, Estella's mother sat down with her and said, "Andrew says you had a bit of a wander again last night. You must learn to get yourself back to sleep, Estella. You can't keep waking up the boys when they have school."

"Jack doesn't mind," she said.

"Yes, he does," said her mother. "He's too kind to say so."

Estella noticed that the wooden spoon she'd used to get the lid off the teapot was still on the table. Her mother saw her looking at it and said, "I'm not sure how that got there," and she took it to the kitchen along with the empty porridge bowls.

Later, her mother went to the garden and Estella stayed in the house. She sat at the table with her paper dolls laid out in front of her, but she didn't play with them. She kept looking up at the teapot. Every once in a while her mother called in through the door, "Everything okay in there?" and Estella called back that it was. By the time her mother was in the house again, Estella was on the floor under the table, right in the middle, away from the many chair legs.

"What are you doing under there?" her mother asked.

Estella could see only her mother's feet, in stockings, since she'd taken off her garden shoes, a pair of brown lace-up oxfords that had once been her good shoes.

"Thinking," Estella said.

"Don't think too hard. You'll ruin your brain. Do you want some lemonade?"

Estella crawled out from under the table and they had lemonade.

Estella asked, "Why did you name me Estella?"

"It's my favourite name. Don't you like it?"

"You should have called me something else."

"Like what?"

"I don't know. Sally."

"I'm not much for those modern names," her mother said. "Wait and see. You'll like Estella when you're older."

They went to the backyard together. As her mother worked in the daisy bed along the fence, Estella sat on the patio in a wicker armchair and thought about the unfinished business of the teapot. She wished she could take it from the shelf right now and carry it to a hiding spot, but she suspected it would not be a good idea to be caught with the teapot again. She slipped back inside and went up and down the stairs in her sock feet, trying to find the steps that creaked and a way around them. She counted the stairs on her way down and when she hit a creak, she backed up and tried a different spot. She descended ever more quietly, hugging the wall, bypassing the steps she'd identified as the noisy ones.

That night, after everyone was asleep, she practised going downstairs in the dark to get herself a glass of water in the kitchen. No one noticed.

A few nights later, she removed the letters from the teapot again, and she managed to get through the next two before her eyes began to blur from concentrating so hard on the handwriting. Salina's writing was tiny with an even, forward slant. Her father's was easier to understand, more loopy and rounded, like printing. They were both hard to read, though, because she hadn't had much practice with cursive, but she had the stairs figured out now so there was no rush. She put the letters away and went back to bed.

It took her many nights to get through all the letters with the rest of the family asleep upstairs, and when she got to the end she didn't understand what had happened. Who was this Salina person? When she'd figured it out as best she could—that Salina and her father had been married, and that she had died—Estella was back where she'd started with the teapot, and she realized for the first time that knowing more also meant knowing less. The letters, she thought, had changed everything, but mostly who her father was because he had another wife. And if Salina was Oliver's first wife, was she also Estella's first mother? On the one hand, she knew this could not be true—Beatrice had decorated her room when she was born, and called her Estella—but on the other hand, well, it was confusing because she knew the Diamond family only as it was right now.

As she placed the teapot back on the shelf after reading the last letter, the word that stayed with her was "heartbroken." She pictured a red Valentine's Day heart with a crack down the middle, but she suspected there was more to it than that.

ESTELLA AND HER father never discussed the letters. As she grew older, she began to wonder if he knew she had read them. How long had he been watching in the doorway that first night? Perhaps not long enough, and he might have assumed the cursive was beyond her ability. Over the years, she kept expecting there would be some inadvertent allusion to a previous marriage in her parents' conversation, perhaps when they thought the children weren't listening, but none ever came. There was one time in a hotel restaurant when Estella heard her father tell a man named Allen Foster he had been married twice, but that was it. When Estella tried dropping hints now and then, her father displayed no inclination to talk about his first wife.

She could hardly believe it, then, when Salina's name was the last word he uttered, right before he died. Estella was forty-two years old by that time and her father was almost ninety. Her mother had been dead for some years. The whole family was there, Estella, her brothers and their wives—Theo and Gladys, Mathew and Fay, Andrew and Harmony, Jack and Rose—crushed into the hospital room because they knew death was imminent. When Oliver spoke Salina's name, it baffled everyone but Estella, since no one else remembered the supposed aunt who had made the teapot.

That evening, after Oliver's body had been delivered to a funeral home, the family gathered in the dining room to discuss arrangements—*her* dining room now, Estella supposed, because her brothers all had their own homes by this time. It was assumed she was the right one to take notes since she was a teacher, and she was seated at the mahogany table with a pad of paper in front of her. On the table was Oliver's cut-glass brandy decanter, placed there for the men. Estella was the only one of the women who poured herself a glass.

The discussion turned from the funeral to-do list to the meaning of Oliver's final word, spoken with such surprising vigour before he had closed his eyes and slipped away. All agreed he had said the name Salina, although Estella stayed out of it. When her brothers had not much to offer by way of explanation, and when silence engulfed them, she finally spoke up and said that she thought they'd been wrong, and that Oliver had not said Salina but had been speaking to Beatrice.

"I'm sure that's what he said. Mother's name, of course."

"Do you think so?"

"Yes. He might have garbled it, but he was speaking to Mother."

From there, Fay concocted a story that included a tunnel and a bright light.

Estella drank the last of her brandy and poured herself another, drawing a look from Gladys over her new cat-eye glasses.

"I think we should put this in the eulogy," Fay said. "She was the love of his life, after all. What does everyone else think? Is it too personal?"

"No," Estella said. "Let's do it."

She wrote *Eulogy* at the top of a new page and underlined it, and then, *Father's last word.*

Other ideas were tossed around and Estella added them to the list on her notepad. They all agreed that Theo, as the eldest, ought to deliver the eulogy.

"That wedding portrait," Harmony said, pointing to the framed photograph on the wall. "Could we set it on the casket in the church? Would he like that?"

Estella looked up at the portrait. She wanted to say that Oliver was no longer capable of liking anything, in case Harmony hadn't noticed, and then she couldn't stop herself, she began to cry.

The others weren't used to seeing her cry.

"Estella," Gladys said, and she felt Gladys's arm around her shoulder, and along with it a physical loathing for this bit of affection from Theo's wife, who had been in her life long enough that she barely remembered a time before her. She slipped out from under Gladys's arm and rose from the table, thinking, but not able to say, that she was crying for more than one reason: the obvious one, and another that involved a woman they had never heard their father speak of and now never would.

Andrew assumed she'd had too much brandy.

"Maybe lay off that, eh," he said, indicating the decanter on the table.

"Oh, right," Estella said. "Everyone knows women can't hold their liquor."

She grabbed the decanter by the neck and went out to the garden by herself, where she sat in her mother's wicker chair on the patio.

She sipped her brandy and thought about her father. Relief was what she'd felt when he'd breathed his last, the kind of relief that made her want to collapse on the floor, because the caregiving and the fighting and the craziness were over. And then on its heels came guilt, because the last year had been such a challenge to her patience, and she hadn't always met the challenge with grace. She had not been able to get her head around the anger that had been part of her father's dementia, so often directed at her. She was his only daughter, and the only one of his children who knew about Salina. She still remembered the night so long ago when she'd first looked in the teapot, and the feel of his hand on her shoulder as they climbed the stairs together. It was too late now, but she wished that she'd come right out and asked her father more about his first marriage.

She wondered again why he had spoken Salina's name rather than her mother's in his last moments. Perhaps it was just his dying brain going back in time, but was there also a possibility that he had lived all those years in mourning for the real love of his life? If so, it was tragic, but it was also a betrayal of Beatrice. And she wondered if she, too, had betrayed her mother by imagining she might have been a different person had she been raised by Salina.

She had not been a good daughter to her mother in so many ways. Maybe Oliver had not been a good husband in the same ways.

Eventually, she fell asleep with her glass in her hand and the brandy decanter close to empty at her feet. When Theo tried to wake her up because they were leaving, she was in the middle of a dream about white teapots stacked in a beehive kiln with the furnaces about to be lit. The letters were in one of the teapots and she didn't know which one. An oven man was trying to get her out of the kiln as she searched for them, and he kept grabbing her arm. Finally she told him to bugger off and leave her alone.

Which he did. Theo, not the oven man.

She slept the rest of the night in her mother's chair, fretting about the letters, which she had at one time known by heart. The air on the patio stayed warm until morning, even though it was late in the season.

———

Dear Miss Passmore,
I write this from the territorial capital city of Regina after a long train journey west during which I witnessed a great number of extraordinary things. (You see, I am trying to be interesting.) I've been considering

which of these is most memorable, and I have decided it is the Clydesdale horse that I saw escape its enclosure in a moving boxcar and leap from the door that had been left open to provide fresh air for the animals inside. The horse apparently kicked its pen apart before launching itself to freedom, although I didn't witness that particular part of the excitement from my vantage point on the deck between cars, where I myself was catching a bit of fresh air. My last view of the horse was of a black creature from a Greek myth making its way in a gallop across the open prairie, with no apparent injuries. It was a beautiful site, but a memento mori nonetheless, because there is danger and the possibility of a quick end in the wilderness. This is the truth ignored by a romantic way of thinking, is it not? You see, I am not a romantic, in spite of what you might have heard about me.

I have now settled again in my pleasant east-facing room in the boarding house of a widow, Mrs. Gretta Klein, who is an excellent cook, although she perhaps has a more refined taste for sausage than I. Other than her slight overreliance on this Germanic dietary staple—which she lovingly calls bratwurst—she looks after her single gentlemen very well, and she keeps her house as neat as a pin. She does not talk about Mr. Klein, but I believe he was killed in an accident of some kind. I don't know why she chose to stay in the West, but we (her gentlemen) are all very grateful that she did. There are some dreadful boarding houses about the city.

I would like to say that I am glad to have had the honour of accompanying you home after the funeral of your great-aunt. It was most pleasurable, in spite of the downpour. I had been hoping for the opportunity to introduce myself, although of course I wish it could have been under happier circumstances. I send my condolences once again on the loss of your relative. A visit to a cemetery is a reminder to get on with things (whatever those things may be) because time is short.

On that note—and I risk telling you with hope it will be of inter-est—I have made a discovery that will determine my future: this new city in which I find myself sits on a bed of clay. Several months ago, I left the scrapings from my boots on the stoop outside the door of the boarding house. Of course the fastidious Mrs. Klein swept them off into her flower bed, where they did not break down as one might expect, but rather dried into hard balls as the sun shone on them. By nightfall they had hardened into bullets that could not be broken apart. The heavy clay soil here is quite the thing. After a rain, it is near impossible to walk in, and it makes the mud in Byrne Cemetery look like a fine broth. (I hope your shoes have recovered. Mine, sadly, did not.)

Now, as a person with an interest in clay would know, not all clay is refractory, but I have engaged the services of a chemical engineer and we have been testing the deposits in the vicinity. So far, we have discovered three different kinds of refractory clay, and as a result I have invested in the purchase of land. There are four things needed for a brick production plant: clay, fuel, water, and a tempering agent to prevent cracking during the firing process. The first three are at hand, with coal to the south and a running creek on the property. My chemist will tell me what to do about the fourth when he has finished his testing, but we know there is sand in abundance along the Saskatchewan River, not far to the north.

You've probably gathered that this factory is for me an obsession. I understand that the men in my mother's family worked all their lives in factories for the English. My father and brother, as I believe you know, work at the Morris foundry, a fate that I escaped after a brief stint in which I tried to please my father by following in his footsteps. I quickly learned that I resented the factory whistle and its authority over me, and I resented also my father's insistence that his sons do exactly as he did.

But more and more of late, I find myself asking a crucial question: was my disdain for work at the Morris plant an aversion to the work *itself, or was it disdain for lining the pockets of someone else, namely Mr. Charles Morris? Or was it simply that I took a stand against my father's wishes, and determined to prove him wrong that there is only one path in life?*

I am not sure of the answer. My father is a hard man who favours my brother. My mother is an unhappy person in poor health. I do not know where I got my entrepreneurial spirit and I do not see it anywhere else in the Diamond family, which is—truth be told—a family without dreams, and without dreams there is no joy.

I will not go on about this further and risk you thinking that I am a man without joy, because the opposite is true.

I am very glad your father had the good sense to take a post in Byrne Corners. Otherwise, we would never have met. And I also respectfully ask if you would like to go about with me a time or two when I am again home for a visit? And may I call you Salina? Or Sally, if you prefer. Please advise.
Yours in anticipation,
Oliver Diamond

Dear Mr. Diamond,
What a way to begin a correspondence, with memento mori and a reminder that we should all get on with things. I might have reason to accuse you of being morbid. However, you are forgiven, and I did love your story about the Clydesdale horse. I cannot say that I have thought previously of their wild beauty as a reminder of danger lurking. (You have a most serious side to you!) Sometimes when I look at horses in a paddock I imagine myself as one of them, caught between a wild desire for freedom and the comforts in life. (There, I have revealed the serious side of my own disposition, or perhaps I am simply naive, having never lived without comfort.)

Of course you may call me Salina. Or even Sally if you like, although I am not much fond of that particular diminutive. Still, it's better than Hattie, is it not? (I don't know any Hatties. That just popped into my head.)

It was indeed a pleasure to meet you, although I am sorry that the rain interfered with the impression I would like to have made. I assure you that I do not normally go about with water dripping from my hat and the tip of my nose. It was foolish of me to leave the house without an umbrella on such a grey day, but I thought the rain would hold off as a favour to my departed great-aunt. She always said she came to Canada to escape the rain in Ireland. She would have been most unhappy to know she was buried in it. Mercifully, she was under cover, unlike the rest of us.

Your clay city sounds intriguing. I do so hope that your tests and experiments continue to net results. I am sorry that my knowledge of the chemistry of clay is lacking. It is not anything that we discuss at my ladies' club.

And speaking of which . . . what a coincidence that we share an interest in clay! You did say that you had heard of my interest. To elaborate, I am an aspiring potter, although at this moment strictly a hobbyist. We have a small group of ladies here in Byrne Corners who meet twice a week to make bowls and vases and such. Mr. Charles Morris—you already know him as a very-important-man from the foundry—has built his wife a pottery shed in their yard, and he sends a much-less-important-man from the foundry to fire the kiln when we are ready for it. I dare say we could throw our own wood on the fire, but he won't hear of it. I call us the Potted Ladies, but I think I am the only one of us with a sense of humour. The rest take their flower painting very seriously, especially Mrs. Morris, who sticks to ashtrays because they are the easiest to make and have a flat surface for her little paintings.

Please see enclosed a drawing of my most recent teapot. It is white with two green leaves. The decoration is plain. I'm afraid I'm not much of a paintresse, although I do like to think about surface design.

I would be happy to go about with you the next time you are here. Let's say one time and see if it becomes two, or perhaps even three.

May I call you Oliver?

Sincerely,

Salina Passmore

P.S. I am adding this after some thought. It is interesting that your excitement about the future was offset by the story of the horse. I hope I am not being forward when I say that you must be a person led by equal parts practicality and passion. I think this is a good combination for a young man embarking on a business venture and, of course, I wish you the very best of luck. I withdraw my earlier comment about you being morbid.

Dear Salina,

Your teapot is delightful! There is no doubt that you must be the most talented of the Potted Ladies. I cannot imagine any of them being able to top such a design. Do you use a potter's wheel? If so, you are highly skilled for a hobbyist (which you called yourself, perhaps in modesty). I look forward to seeing your teapot in person, and maybe even savouring a cup of good black tea that has been brewed within. How does it pour? That is the test of a teapot, is it not?

As to your observation about horses and a life penned in, I apologize for my dark interpretation of the story of the black horse leaping to freedom. I did not mean to appear morbid and I admit that I sometimes get carried away. I wonder still about the horse and hope that it has been taken in by a farmer who will treat it well. I admire your vision and your propensity for metaphor. At the risk of being forward, I will say that you must be a person of great intelligence balanced by an equal measure of idealism. Surely that is a good combination for a young woman with artistic ambitions.

I have good news on the factory front. My chemist believes we have ample refractory clay on the property I have purchased, and he believes also that with some slight chemical alterations the clay will make bricks suitable for construction. I am now looking for business partners and investors, as the land acquisition has put a strain on my savings and an inheritance from a relative I'd never met. There is a Texan I have heard about, a man named Nathaniel Thick. He is a very successful cattleman looking for opportunities, and if he is as astute as they say he is, he will not turn his back on this one. The amount of building in this city is astounding, and why ship materials by rail when you can make them (bricks, that is) right here? I am imagining the construction of many stately homes such as the ones on High Street in Byrne Corners, all built with Diamond bricks. But of course I am getting ahead of myself.

I am curious about the kiln that Mr. Morris had built for his wife. You mentioned wood. It is wood-fired, then? And what shape? How big is it? I am thinking myself of beehive or bottle-style kilns, which are predominant in England, but the continuous kiln is also a possibility. These can be built up the side of a hill so that the heat gradually rises from one to the next. However, I am not sure if what is called "a hill" here on the Great Plains has a sufficient incline. Coal, of course, is the most logical choice for an industrial fuel source. There are coal deposits to the south that are shipped by train. Did you know they use canals in England? There is a creek close enough, but it is nothing more than a trickle for most of the year and will not be useful at all as a means of transport.

Research! This is a phase that cannot be skipped if I am to be a success, and I have decided to go directly to the source. I am planning a trip to England to see for myself the pottery operations, especially those in the towns of Stoke-on-Trent. Perhaps I can find someone who will take me in as an apprentice. I hope I do not sound like a child on Christmas Eve when I say I am sleepless with anticipation, and of course I will be stopping in Byrne Corners on my way. There are many things, then, to look forward to.

The rain dripping from your hat at your aunt's funeral was most becoming.

Please do call me Oliver, and I am honoured to call you Salina. I think, though, that I should hold off calling you Sally, and I will be sure never to call you Hattie. I aim only to please.
Courteously yours,
Oliver Diamond

P.S. I believe you are too hard on yourself regarding your leaf decoration. I have not yet had the pleasure of examining said leaf, but I have no reason to believe it would not be perfectly attractive. And of course the surface is the canvas, and without it there is nothing, and you have no doubt created a very fine surface in your teapot!

Dear Oliver,
Let me first say that I am enthusiastic on your behalf concerning the trip to England. I think it is wise of you to undertake this research and fully inform yourself of the ins and outs of production. Why not learn from the best? Why not be that ambitious for yourself and the future?

And now for my news: I have been kicked out of the Potted Ladies! Here is what happened.

It was to be a workday in the shed and one of the ladies suggested a challenge, a footed vase, to be made either on the throwing wheel or by hand construction, whichever was each lady's choice. Before we began work, they all removed their wedding rings as usual (all but me, of course) and deposited them in a bowl set on a shelf. It is a bit of a ritual, dropping the rings in the bowl.

My first choice is always the wheel, but Mrs. Morris has only one and I couldn't be bothered waiting my turn today, so I moulded a tall vase around one of the forms we have for that purpose. I had some notion of pinching the lip of the vase into a series of ocean waves and creating a foot to match, but I overworked it and the clay dried out and cracked and a chunk dropped right off. I picked up the dried-out piece and threw it in the slops bucket, and then thought, "Bother," and threw the whole vase in. It was so hot and crowded in the shed, and I could hear the ladies chatting away about this and that and saying nothing of interest, and I felt so uncharitable toward them that I decided to clean myself up and arrange the lunch, since it had been my turn to bring the cakes.

When the rest of the ladies finished for the day and had returned their rings to their fingers, we all seated ourselves in Mrs. Morris's gazebo. As Mrs. Morris joined us, she took the opportunity to say, "Salina, dear, I noticed that you abandoned your project to the slops. Waste not, want not, and clay is a material that can be regenerated with the simple addition of water." I muttered something about the heat and the cracking, and she had the nerve to say that the rest of them had managed, and that flaws in the form can always be disguised later with decoration and a little extra glaze.

What came over me?

I shocked even myself by saying, "Mrs. Morris, the form is surely the most important thing. And if you attempt to make yourself a more interesting form, you're bound to fail once in a while. You may like to paint on the reliable surface of an ashtray, but an ashtray it remains. I suppose you could put a foot on it for a bit of a challenge."

I knew immediately that I had gone too far. I attempted to smooth the waters by saying something about both the form and the surface decoration being important. And then, never one to leave well enough alone, I went on to praise healthy disagreement and asserted that we needed to exercise our brains if we wanted the vote.

Oliver, it turned out that not one of them sees the need for women to have the vote! One lady said she wouldn't know what to do with it if she had it. I looked around the circle for signs that even one lady might see things my way, but there was not one. Not even my friend Ruthie.

(Et tu, Ruthie?)

Quite the silence ensued, with all the ladies looking down at their teacups until finally one brave soul helped herself to a lemon square, bit into it, pronounced it delicious, and made a show of asking me for the recipe. Several others followed, and there was a lengthy discussion about the recipe, which I agreed to write out and bring for them next time. I thought the acrimony to be in the past, and myself forgiven.

However, I had been home for no more than an hour when a note was delivered to my hand by one of Mr. Morris's employees, and signed The Morris Pottery Club. I had been excused, the note told me. I was not a good fit, and brought discord to what had once been a pleasant and agreeable group. They wished me well—and I am certain "they" was Mrs. Morris acting alone since they are all so opposed to voting—and hoped I would find another studio, knowing that there is not another studio anywhere in our district.

And to top it all off, we—the Passmores—had a most ridiculous discussion at the dinner table tonight, with my parents blaming my expulsion from the club entirely on my stance on the vote. It went like this:

Father: "Salina, why do you insist on bringing that up in polite company?"

Mother: *"It is so unbecoming, women marching in public, making spectacles of themselves."*

I: *"I do not see why women are denied the right of electing our government. Father, you've always said we girls are as smart as any boys you might have had."*

Father: *"Probably smarter. Which I see as a problem, and why you should not be allowed anywhere near a polling station."*

Good grief, Oliver, what is wrong with everyone?

After dinner my sister Roseanne came to the house with hopes of convincing me to accompany her and her two children on a trip to Niagara Falls. She's been going on about this trip for weeks and I can hardly think of anything worse. I love Roseanne dearly, but her children are hellions and give me a headache. They live across the back garden and I can hear them even with the windows closed. Her boy Amos is impossible. Well, the trip will not likely take place anyway because Father thinks train journeys are not acceptable for ladies travelling without their husbands or fathers, and he is sure Niagara Falls in particular is teeming with con men.

Yes, I told him, very dangerous con men selling sofa cushions with Niagara Falls embroidered on them.

More dangerous, Oliver, is the lady who went over the Falls in a barrel. Now her I would like to meet. I hear she does talks and sells pamphlets for ten cents.

Oh, I have bent your ear enough with the news of this trying day. That is that. I shall not mention it again.

How are the plans for the factory coming?

I so look forward to your visit, assuming that I have not put you off with this report of my ungracious behaviour.
Sincerely,
Salina

P.S. Regarding your inquiry about Mrs. Morris's kiln, it is not worth speaking of. It is very small, and the poor man from the factory has to feed wood into the firebox all night to get anywhere near the desired temperature, and you seldom get a firing free of ash. Mrs. Morris designed it herself. I'm sure your kilns will be vastly superior. And I would hardly call Mrs. Morris's shed a studio. I don't know where she got such a lofty idea!

Dear Salina,

It is hard to believe that any pottery club in existence should not want you as a member and the Potted Ladies will soon see their loss. I think you are right that no democratic vote on your membership took place. (I assure you here and now that I am all in favour of women voting.) I wonder if this is a case of someone lacking talent being jealous of someone else with an obvious abundance? You can tell me all about it when we meet in person. I am sorry to say that will be somewhat later than what I had originally planned, and I cannot stop in Byrne Corners before I sail. I have tried to find time between business commitments and my departure date, but to no avail.

I will, however, be stopping for a good long visit on my return from England. My mother is not especially well—perhaps you have heard. I hope this is good news (my visit, I mean, and not my mother's illness, which I sometimes think is not illness at all, but is, rather, unhappiness). I do feel we have discovered a surprising harmony in our written exchanges and I look forward to our reunion.

When I see you, I will tell you all about the many developments on the factory front. In short, I have found investors and look forward through the course of my travels to determining the best sort of kilns for what we have in mind, and the most practical way to transport supplies and finished product to the main rail line. For now, that will be by horse and wagon. I am looking into the possibility of a spur line sometime in the future.

There is so much to tell you about the factory and I cannot possibly do so in a letter without boring you.

I will see if anyone—Mr. Wedgwood himself?—can describe to me a practical model for a modest teapot operation. Perhaps, darling Salina, you will be able to start your own pottery club before too long, membership to be limited to serious artists such as yourself.

I have booked passage on the Dominion ship Hamilton, departing Halifax on the 30th of June.

Yours,

Oliver

P.S. Do you think your parents might allow you to accompany me unattended during my stay in Byrne Corners? It is very hard for a young couple to get to know one another when the parents are always hovering in the drawing room, do you not agree? Perhaps I can convince them that my intentions are completely honourable toward their daughter.

Darling Oliver,

I am greatly moved by your assurance of decorum. I have noted that you called me darling Salina, and you will have noted that I returned the endearment. I did not do so without serious thought.

Oliver, there are things you should know if we are going to call each other darling. Forgive my candour. We live in interesting times, do we not? My father saw to it that his daughters were educated, but for what reason, I wonder, since we were all to become the wives of at least modestly successful men, and bear handsome and bright children, preferably a son first, followed by a charming daughter or two. This is an old story, *but I must warn you that it is not a narrative that suits me very well. Although I have not gone so far as to join the suffragists, I admire their tenacity and the drive to liberate modern women from the broom closets of their husbands' houses.*

And oh how I hate it when someone, man or woman, says no to me without giving a good reason, or tells me I can't do something because of my gender.

I look at my two sisters and I see one, Edith, who is conveniently blind to the plight of women because she married a wealthy man who gives her whatever she wants, and another who knows her brilliant mind is wasted and contents herself with thoughts of a weekend excursion to Niagara Falls. This second sister, by the way, is Roseanne, the one I love dearly, and it pains me to write this about her, but she is her own worst traitor.

(There. See what you have gotten yourself into by speaking sweetly to me? You are probably already sorry that you did.)

Here is my true confession. I would like to become something in my own right: a serious designer of fine ceramic objects. I have studied all the books I can find, and I have learned what I can from them. I am sorry no longer to have access to Mrs. Morris's library of books on European china. That is one advantage of the club I had not thought of. There is the Byrne Corners library and of course my family has a membership, but the only books with any mention of pottery are travel books, and they are unsatisfactory, so I am now against a wall, so to speak.

I so admire the determination with which you attack your dream of owning a factory, and at the same time it saddens me because I wonder, how is a young woman such as myself to become what she dreams of being? I envy you that you can go off into the world just to learn when I cannot do the same. Perhaps, when you are in England, you can find out for me whether there are any women in the factories who have achieved renown. I am curious about that.

I am very sorry that it will be so long before you are able to visit Byrne Corners.

This is a love letter. I have bared my soul.

Yours,

Salina

P.S. Please do not assume that I have the vapours. I do not believe in vapours. They are something cooked up to keep women weepy and weak-willed. (I repeat, see what you have got yourself into?)

My darling,

I will take care to avoid all mention of the vapours as I write about my concern for your happiness. I must admit that I have never before thought of "suffrage" in the light in which you placed it. I know, certainly, that the suffragists wish for women the opportunity to become doctors and women of the law, and of course there is the vote, but to think that a woman such as yourself would be hampered in her attempts at artistic fulfillment . . . it seems neither possible nor right in this modern time.

I am trying to think of a path for you, and I wonder if you might embark on a trip of your own. The option of an overseas trip (such as mine) is no doubt out of the question, but perhaps a trip to New York City and the Metropolitan Museum of Art? Might you convince your sister Roseanne of this, as an alternative to Niagara Falls?

I will try to find out whether there are any renowned women designers in the English pottery business. What a good question.

Please take heart, dearest Salina. There must be a way for a talented and eager young artist to find inspiration. I am with you in spirit.

Yours,

Oliver

P.S. I do not expect I will enjoy the ocean crossing. It will be a long haul for this dry-lander travelling alone, without the company of a kindred spirit. I can't imagine that I shall find one among my fellow travellers.

(I believe I mentioned before that I am booked on the Dominion ship Hamilton, *departing Halifax the 30ᵗʰ of June.)*

Dear Oliver,

The cheek!

I am very adept at reading between the lines, and you are surely mad to think that I, a well-brought-up single lady whom you met once previously in a churchyard, should even consider booking herself on a passenger liner to England in order to accompany a man she does not know on a wild goose expedition to visit potteries and industrial plants in the heart of England. You know that a gentleman and a single lady cannot travel together as kindred spirits (to use your words) without shocking the morally righteous.

Shame on you, Mr. Diamond.

I am writing this letter to you without a plan to post it. By the time you read it, the reason will be apparent.

Sincerely,

Salina Passmore

P.S. It is my good fortune that Aunt Aideen chose to name her nieces as her beneficiaries, and I believe she approved of adventure that included ocean crossings since she made one herself.

Dear Mother and Father,

I apologize for the shock of this note, which you will have found on my bed, but I have decided to embark on a grand trip, as liberated young women do these days. I will let you know where I am before long, and I will be very careful and not do anything daring, and I will not jeopardize my reputation. The idea that a young woman should be prevented from seeing the world—or even Niagara Falls, for goodness sake—is outdated, and this is something that I must get out of my system before I settle down to a more conventional life. Perhaps I never will, but you know what I mean. Please do not worry.

Love, Salina

```
MR. WILLIAM PASSMORE BYRNE CORNERS ONTARIO
=YOUR SALINA MARRIED TO OLIVER DIAMOND
ECSTATICALLY HAPPY MORE TO COME=SALINA DIAMOND
```

Dearest Mother,

I must apologize for the regrettable note that I left on my bed, the one that I am sure has caused you a great deal of worry. But you must not worry. You will have learned by telegram that I am now a married woman. I hope you will take pleasure in adding the date of marriage to your notebook of birthdays and anniversaries: June 12, 1903. Is there not something special about being a June bride? Something to do with the availability of flowers, perhaps, although bridal bouquets are not in abundance on a ship, as you can imagine.

I am on my way to Liverpool, England, with my new husband, Mr. Oliver Diamond, who is travelling abroad to conduct research for his brick factory. You might remember Oliver from Aunt Aideen's funeral. His father is John Diamond, who is a manager at the Morris plant. We were married en route by the Captain of RMS Hamilton. Mother, please picture your daughter in the pale-blue gown that you like so much, dancing with her husband, and later with the Captain, for he did ask to dance with the bride, and Oliver agreed on the condition that he return me the minute the music was over (I believe it was a Scott Joplin tune). Please picture your daughter married, and happy beyond measure.

We will be staying for a short time in a very decent hotel in Liverpool that caters to respectable business travellers while Oliver plans our tour. I understand that Liverpool is not far from the historic Potteries of Stoke-on-Trent, which I never imagined I would see. Oliver is taking good care of me (although I don't need taking care of, as you know). One great advantage of being a married lady (and I'm sure there are many more) is that my entry into England was made simple by the fact that I am Mrs. Oliver Diamond, and the authorities required nothing beyond that when we disembarked in Liverpool. Needless to say, Oliver's papers were completely in order, he being a meticulous planner.

Of course my own interest is in the pottery trade rather than bricks. Oliver says there is the possibility of encountering in our travels one of the Wedgwoods, Major Cecil Wedgwood (who has just returned from the Boer War and is the great-great-grandson of the very Josiah Wedgwood) or perhaps his cousin Francis Wedgwood, who is the current head of the family business. I would appreciate it if you would mention this to Mrs. Morris, should you run into her. You may add that your daughter is soon to move in a most illustrious circle in the English pottery trade. I would love to see the look on her face.

Mother, I am no longer the spinster you worried about, and my husband (how I love writing that) is going to build a business that will rival any in the industry. Oliver is an ambitious entrepreneur who has seen great opportunity in Western Canada in serving the building trade.

Please be happy for me. Please keep Father from wanting to hang me from the nearest tree. I admit that I am glad to be across the ocean as I write.

Enclosed is a letter from Oliver to Father. Oliver is a bit of a traditionalist, which I hope will please you.

I will post this the minute we are on dry land.

Your loving and happy daughter,

Mrs. Oliver Diamond

P.S. I would not wish seasickness on any person to whom I am attached. If you would like me punished for what I have done, please be assured that I have been. I cannot imagine that you could think up anything worse.

Dear Mr. Passmore,

I trust that you have learned of the marriage of your daughter Salina to me, Oliver Diamond.

Please let me introduce myself. I am twenty-six years of age. I was born in Ottawa, Ontario, to John Diamond of England and Abigail Diamond (née Cullen) of Ireland, both now of Byrne Corners, and with both of whom I am sure you are acquainted. My father is a manager at the Morris Castings plant and my brother George works there also. My mother is a reformed Irish Catholic and is active at doing good deeds in the community, her health permitting. We are a respectable family and there is little blight on our family tree.

That said, I am somewhat different from my father and my brother. I would describe myself as a more ambitious businessman, and I trust this meets with your approval as a financial man yourself. After receiving a modest inheritance from a relative, I travelled west looking for opportunities in which to invest and I believe I have found one. I have purchased land near the city of Regina, and am building a manufacturing plant for clay bricks. I have found a potential business partner and several other investors, and we have drawn and signed the legal documents that have solidified our arrangement. The West is a booming place with opportunities everywhere, and I believe I am guaranteed financial success and prosperity.

I hope this reassures you that I am a good match for your daughter Salina. We are very happy as newlyweds and she is ambitious for me, and encourages me at every turn that I am proceeding in the right direction. She has the mind and heart of an artist. We are well suited.

We will not stay in Liverpool long. Our plan is to depart for Stoke-on-Trent, where we will settle ourselves in a boarding house run by a Mrs. Wilson, whose husband was a long-time employee at the Etruria Works. I look forward to the magnificent sight of canals and bottle kilns. They say there are four thousand such kilns in the area, which is an unfathomable number. I look forward also to beginning my apprenticeship in the ways and means of running a clay factory.

I know it is after the fact, but I would like to ask you for your daughter's hand in marriage. Perhaps we were impulsive when we were wed by the ship's captain at sea, but we wanted to travel respectably and not in a frivolous manner, and we felt that a tour of the English Potteries together was imperative.

I await your response. I would like to say blessing, but hesitate for fear of sounding overconfident. Confidence is a mark of the businessman, is it not, but it can be dangerous when it comes to personal matters. Of this, I am aware. I enclose an address in Stoke-on-Trent to which I hope you will send correspondence. We very much welcome news from home. Respectfully yours,
Oliver Diamond

Dear Roseanne,

I am sure you are annoyed with me for not telling you my plan before I left, but I was afraid I might change my mind if I spoke of it aloud. I apologize all around for the secrecy. Please do not blame Aunt Aideen and please do not blame Oliver. Even he, as it turns out, didn't guess what I was up to.

In spite of your annoyance, I know you are dying to hear the story so here it is. In short, I slipped out the front door with a small valise and no one noticed. Well, I did run into Mr. Hubbard from the post office on my walk to the train station, and he said, "Going for a visit, are we?" and then he carried on and appeared to have no curiosity whatsoever about where I was going, even though he of all people knew the regularity of my correspondence with Oliver. I thought that he did not possess much in the way of imagination. A woman in the post office would have tried a little harder.

The train took me first to Ottawa and then Montreal, where I had time to brave the French language, find the Morgan's store on Saint Catherine and buy myself a new hat, which was very foolish. All the way to Halifax I worried that I should not have bought the hat. It was the first time in my life that I fretted about spending money.

When I arrived in Halifax, I found a room at a boarding house and spent two days unsuccessfully trying to find Oliver, and it was my own fault because he did not know I was there. (So, you see, you cannot blame any of this on him.) I was able to purchase a small, semi-private 2nd class cabin, and the day of departure, in a crushing queue on the pier, I had my first moment of real fear, that I had been mistaken and Oliver would not be on board the ship. I almost left the line, but a rude woman gave me a push and told me to pay attention or we'd never get on board, and in the pandemonium I dropped my new hat. I tried to bend to retrieve it but I was being pushed forward, hanging onto my bag for dear life, and once I reached the gangplank I had no time to think because it was steep. I kept my eyes on my feet and prayed I would not slip.

When I was finally on board the ship, I followed the directions I'd been given to my cabin, and when I peered in the narrow door, I saw an older lady in a plain frock sitting on one of two small berths, who welcomed me inside. I sat down on the edge of my berth, which was barely a foot from hers, and burst into tears. I told the woman I was crying over my lost hat, but the truth was, I feared that I had done something impulsive and regrettable, and I would never see my family again. She turned out to be a very kind lady—Mrs. Poppy Brenner—and she told me she was on her way home to Yorkshire after twenty years in Canada. Twenty dismal years, she said, without elaborating. She was very effusive in her condolences about the hat, and then she prayed aloud that neither of us would get seasick, stuffed her curly hair into a cotton cap, and lay down to have a nap.

A horn blared and the ship began to move. I decided that I couldn't just lie there in a state of self-pity, so I retrieved my one warm sweater from my bag and pulled it on over my skirt and blouse. I had the last letter from Oliver in my valise and I took it with me, planning to read it again and see if there was any way I might have been horribly mistaken about his date of departure, and I also took the letter I had written to him with a misguided plan to hand it to him in person. As I climbed the three flights of laddery stairs to the deck level, I was plagued by the new fear that if I did find him, he would be on board with a woman, a wife perhaps, whom he had met in the West. Doubt consumed me, and I didn't know if it was because of the grey sky and rolling sea, or because I had made my plans based on very little evidence that Oliver Diamond would welcome my company: one brief postscript in a letter. Perhaps I had seen only what I wanted to.

When I'd mounted the final stair and reached the deck, I stepped outside. The sky was indeed ominous. I could smell the salt, and the gulls looped and screeched overhead as the ship's engines rumbled. There were a dozen or so people about, taking the air, or perhaps avoiding the claustrophobia that awaited them below deck. As the air grew colder, fewer and fewer of them remained. I stood back from the railing and drew my sweater up around my ears, and watched as Canada disappeared altogether into the mist. There were a half dozen slotted wooden deck chairs against the ship's cabin, and I sat in one, not knowing what else to do. A steward in a white uniform came by and suggested that I go below so as not to catch a chill. He had a Scottish accent, and he said it was likely to get rough and he wouldn't want to lose such a pretty girl overboard (he pronounced it garrel).

"Has that ever happened?" I asked.

"Not on the first day out, no," he said.

"But thereafter?"

"Hard to say if it was an accident or the poor wee thing jumped."

I promised not to jump overboard even though I supposed it was a solution to my predicament, and he looked quite alarmed. I then asked if he could do me a favour and tell me whether there was a Mr. Oliver Diamond on board. When he said, "Ah, it becomes clear," I assured him that he had it wrong, and that I simply wanted to deliver a letter to him from a mutual acquaintance, my sister, as a matter of fact.

He took the envelope and I asked him not to read it. He said his discretion was assured and he left, saying that he was going to be keeping an eye on me.

Later, I learned that the steward had found Oliver and delivered the letter, telling him that the sister of its author was on the ship. Confused, Oliver had gone looking for you or Edith. He remembered your given names, but since neither of you still carries the name Passmore and the *booking would surely be under a husband's name, he did not know who he was looking for. Only when he was able to convince the Chief Purser to let him look at the entire passenger list did he find my name and figure out that it was me who had given the steward the letter. By that time, I was lying on my berth with my head over a bucket and Mrs. Brenner caring for me. Thank the Lord that she did not get sick or we would have been in a terrible state in that small cabin. Oliver showed up just in time to witness me heave what must have been the very last contents of my stomach into the bucket.*

And what were my first words to the man I had been so worried would not be on board?

"Just leave me to die," I managed to say.

Mrs. Brenner shooed him away, and told him she would get me fixed up for a caller once the rocking plague had worked its way through. She told him that if he cared at all for me, he would leave without arguing, because no woman wants a man to see her in such a state.

"You do look dreadful," she said after he left, and then she asked if that was my young man, and expressed the opinion that he was handsome for a tall man, and that she normally did not find tall men to be so pleasing about the face.

After two days of the most awful sickness, I was able to sit up without the room spinning and appreciate the news that Oliver Diamond was on board after all, and he had sought me out and promised to return. Mrs. Brenner offered to help me bathe and fix myself up to receive a visitor, and it was a good thing because I didn't have the strength to even brush my own hair, which was in a tangled mess. I was worried that the cabin smelled of sickness, but Mrs. Brenner assured me that she had opened the tiny port and the cabin now smelled only of brine and cod. She managed to get me changed into a clean frock and held her hand mirror up as I powdered my nose.

Roseanne, the next part of the story is the best.

There was a knock at the door, and Mrs. Brenner opened it to Oliver Diamond. In his hand was an envelope, which I knew contained my letter.

"You're feeling better, then?" he asked.

"Much improved," I said. I was sitting on the edge of my berth now, and I indicated that he should sit on Mrs. Brenner's, which he did. Mrs. Brenner left to give us some privacy, although she insisted for decency's sake that the door remain ajar.

Suddenly and to my astonishment, Oliver slipped off the berth and managed to fold and squeeze his long body onto his knee on the floor between us, and he proposed marriage. I did not think about it for longer than five seconds before I said yes. At that point Mrs. Brenner squealed in the hallway, and I called to her to come in so she could share in our good news. Oliver got himself up off his knee, and left the cabin to the ladies so we might talk.

We were married shortly thereafter by the Captain, and I immediately wrote to Mother, and now I am writing to you. These letters will be in the overseas post as soon as we land in Liverpool, and I hope I will be forgiven.

Please, please be happy for me, Roseanne. If there is any opinion that matters, it is yours.

Your loving sister,

Salina

Dear Daughter,

As much as it was a relief to hear from you, do not expect your father and me to forgive you just yet. How in the world did you think you could run off and not tell us? Your father was beside himself with fear that you had been abducted or come to a terrible end. Perhaps both. You have caused us so much worry. How did the anticipation of that worry not stop you—for God's sake—from following a strange man aboard an ocean liner? That was the worst behaviour for a lady, Salina. The worst. That is all I can bring myself to say on the matter.

It is a lovely day here. I have canned the green beans. We opened a jar at supper last night and the beans were a perfect colour and not at all tough.

That young Amos did quite the thing a few days ago. He climbed a tree and couldn't get himself down, and we had to call the fire department to bring a ladder. I don't know what he was thinking to go so high. Luckily, all ended well, although he perhaps didn't think so since his father gave him a hiding.

I have been busy on the planning committee for the upcoming bazaar at the church. I am in charge of the jumble sale and my committee has been collecting items in the church basement. Of course they must be sorted and many of the items have to be laundered. It is surprising to me that people don't take the trouble to launder their used clothing before handing it over. Have they not heard of airing dirty laundry? We have never, in our family, been much for displays of dirty laundry. I do not speak to your father of this matter. It is better to let some things simmer until they have simmered themselves out.

Well, you are a married woman now. I wish Oliver Diamond the best of luck.

Your mother,

Mrs. William Passmore

P.S. The dreadful English weather is not to be taken lightly. Wool is the best fibre for keeping dampness off the chest. I believe that is because of the lanolin, which repels the moisture, thus keeping the wearer of a woollen sweater dry and warm.

Sister Salina,

As usual, you have selfishly thrown us all into a flap, even Roseanne, who is normally far too lenient with you (and her children, but that is another matter). Do you not understand that, from our point of view, you have taken off across the ocean with a stranger? We do not know Oliver Diamond, even if he does come from a good family. And is your marriage even legal? Good heavens, Salina, this is the sort of thing girls named Lizzy do in novels.

And here is what Father is worried about. Someone might as well say it. You claim you are married to a businessman, but so far he does not have a business. He is conducting "research," which sounds fishy. Father has asked around, and it appears that he was trying to drum up money when he was home last, talking up this brick-making scheme and inviting people to "invest" in the business. We fear you have wed a scoundrel, and we fully expect him to ask Father for money now that he has married into our family.

I just do not know what you were thinking to act so impulsively. Were you that desperate for a husband? I would not have thought it. Otherwise, you could have said yes to one of the gentlemen who had the decency to speak to Father. The Frenchman, for example. That would have been a good match, in my opinion, even if he was French.

As far as your interest in pottery making as a vocation goes . . . honestly, Salina.

Your sister,

Edith

Dear Salina,

Don't listen to Edith, who has just shown me her letter to you. I have advised her not to send it, but since when did she ever listen to me?

All right, the truth is, I am angry too. Not that you married your Mr. Diamond, but that you didn't confide in me, your favourite sister, before you left. The very morning of your departure we danced in my parlour to records on the new gramophone, and then hours later you danced off into the beyond without a word to me. And you caused us all such worry. What in the world were you thinking . . . leaving a note that said "Don't worry"? Did you suppose we would take your word that there was nothing to worry about? This is you we're talking about, and you are not very wise sometimes. Suffice it to say that we were all greatly relieved to learn that you are at least still alive somewhere.

I have never seen Father so fuming mad with one of us, and Edith is feeding his anger. Mother and I are the voices of calm, but do not think you are off the hook with us either, and do not pretend you are surprised that Vesuvius has erupted in the Passmore household.

Well, now that I have said my piece I suppose congratulations are in order. I will admit that Oliver Diamond's marriage proposal does sound just a tiny bit romantic, even if you were still green with seasickness. From what I remember of his height, I don't know how he managed to get down on his knee in that small space, but it is admirable that he was willing to propose and save your reputation. That must be one mark in his favour. (I am trying to see the good in what you have done.)

On to other news, since you are not the only one in the world. I finally managed my trip to Niagara Falls. In the end, Mother kept the children while Edith and I and our dutiful husbands took the train and stayed overnight. I was frightened out of my wits to stand at the top of the Falls and watch that water move at such great speed to the edge of the drop, and was thankful that we had had the good sense to leave the children. The shopping was not much. There were not even many charlatans to entertain us. Oh . . . but we did see the woman who went over the Falls in a barrel. She has set up a stand and is selling her life story for a few coins. Her orange tabby housecat is part of her display. She sent the cat over in the barrel first as a test run. She had planned to display this famous barrel (which she designed herself) but her manager ran off with it. Can you believe it? Apparently she is near-destitute. I have enclosed a copy of her story for your reading pleasure. I purchased several, in a feeble attempt to help her out.

I don't know whether to tell you this or not, but Mrs. Morris and her ladies have booked a table at the church bazaar and they plan to sell their wares to the poor unsuspecting public. I imagine Mrs. Morris will price her ashtrays as though she is a great artist. (There is no basis in fact for that. I just thought you would enjoy it.)

I am enclosing the notice that you directed Mr. Ward to publish in the paper. I admit I laughed when I found out you told him to bill Father. Your forgiving sister,
Roseanne

Mr. Oliver Diamond and Mrs. Salina Diamond (née Passmore), both formerly of Byrne Corners, Ontario, wish to announce their marriage on June 12, 1903. The happy couple is now honeymooning in England, where they are undertaking research on the pottery trade. Upon their return to Canada in the fall, they will reside in the city of Regina, District of Assiniboia, where Mr. Diamond will operate his new brick plant as owner and proprietor, and Mrs. Diamond will open a china pottery studio. Mr. and Mrs. Diamond look forward to greeting you as man and wife.

Dear Roseanne,

We are now on the train to London from Stoke-on-Trent somewhat sooner than planned. Although it was an education in itself just to see the Potteries and I was inspired in ways I cannot begin to explain, our stay there was less than satisfactory for Oliver's purposes. To put it plain and simple, there was no welcome mat placed for him at any factory doorstep. Our landlady, the kindly Mrs. Wilson, put an end to our bewilderment about what we had done wrong by explaining that the factory owners are very protective of their trade secrets and the rumours about town positioned Oliver as a young upstart from the colony, in other words, from their marketplace. Needless to say, this was a great disappointment for Oliver, who has been out of sorts that our tour has so far not lived up to his expectations.

In spite of this rebuke by the factory owners, I have met the most interesting woman, a designer with the name of Mrs. Decker-Jones who aims one day to be an independent, which is a term for pottery artists who work in their own studios outside of the factory system. (It is a term I have fallen in love with, incidentally. Independent.)

Here is the story of my escapade with Mrs. Decker-Jones.

She had heard—I suspect from our Mrs. Wilson—about my aspirations to become a designer. She sought me out and directed me to meet her in the dead of night at the Etruria Works, with strict instructions not to tell Oliver, which should have been frightening but it was not. Instead, I was filled with excitement and felt a bit like the woman with her barrel at Niagara Falls. I left Oliver sleeping (as were the factory managers— the reason for the strange hour) and walked along the canal on a path lit only by the occasional gaslight, past the original home of the very Josiah Wedgwood, to our meeting place across the canal from the factory. Then, with the help of an oven man on his night shift, she took me into the Works and revealed the purpose of this subterfuge, which turned out to be an unauthorized tour of every aspect of production: from the design room to the slip house and the pottery shop, to the ovens and the packing rooms. What I could see was limited by darkness—we carried only one lamp—but you cannot imagine what a privilege it was, and as we moved from room to room, she opened my eyes to the plight of women who work in the Potteries. With the exception of the printers and paintresses, they do the menial jobs it is believed they are suited for and suffer the physical consequences of lead poisoning and endless, repetitive work. Did you know there is a thing called "wrist-drop" suffered by the dippers? (Of course not. Why would you?) It is a kind of paralysis. The great injustice of it all is that these women are poorly paid and not protected by the unions as their brothers and husbands are. This has drawn the attention of the great Emmeline Pankhurst, who visited this town just a few years ago, but I know what you and everyone else in Byrne Corners think of the suffragists so I will say no more about that.

Here, Roseanne, is a part of the story I am not proud of, but I am telling it anyway because it is you. Just before we left the Pottery, Mrs. Decker-Jones's friend the oven man handed her a covered basket, the kind you might carry to the shops. I did not think to wonder what was inside as we walked away from the factory, and I was about to thank her and take the street back to Mrs. Wilson's when she stopped under a gaslight and removed the cloth cover from the basket to reveal its contents. It was full of black clay beads, made and decorated in the famous Wedgwood Jasper style, each with the bone-white face of a different hideous creature. She told me that they had been created by her in secrecy and fired in a Wedgwood kiln with the help of her oven man. I had never before seen anything like them. I removed several of the beads to examine more closely the tiny subversive faces, and just at that moment Mrs. Decker-Jones was distracted by the sound of male voices approaching in the darkness.

There is no explanation for what I did next. When she turned toward the voices, I slipped the beads in my sweater pocket. Then the voices faded, and Mrs. Decker-Jones turned back to me and said, "I wish you all the best, Mrs. Diamond. If I am blacklisted here, perhaps I will emigrate and seek you out, and by then you will be an artist of some renown. One never knows."

As she walked away, I felt as unable to call after her as Lot's wicked wife. I tried to tell myself they were only a few small beads from a basketful and she would not notice the missing ones, but that is no defence at all of my transgression against a woman who had done me a great favour. And to top it off, I seem to have offended Oliver by not confiding in him. He is horrified by the thought of me walking alone in the dark, and I think he is jealous that I managed to get a tour of the Etruria Works without him. He is trying to be a good sport, but I believe I have wounded his pride. And of course I did not tell him how I acquired the beads and let him believe they were given to me. In addition to being a thief, I am a deceitful wife.

As punishment for it all, I have contracted a bit of a cold in the dampness, and the air here is dreadful anyway with all the clay pits and thousands of ovens burning coal. I'm sure our new landlady in London, Mrs. Russell, will fill me with lemon tea and provide a good stash of wool blankets, although I find wool to be unbearably itchy and am planning to leave every woollen thing behind when we depart for home.

Don't worry. I will be back to good health in no time.

Here is something I hope you will pass on to Mrs. Morris should you run into her. Two Sundays ago, Oliver and I attended church in Etruria, and who was sitting in the family pew but Major Cecil Wedgwood. You need not tell Mrs. Morris that he didn't give us the time of day after the service, but instead you might say that we left the church together, which is almost true since we followed him out. I told Oliver that the war in

Africa has no doubt affected his desire and ability to be hospitable.

Did I say that Mrs. Russell's rooms in Kensington Court are very close to the new Victoria and Albert Museum, which I have been told has an extensive collection of ceramics from all over the world? When I am over this illness, I expect to be spending many days there. Oliver is planning to visit the Fulham Pottery in London, where he believes a distant cousin may have worked. He has been in touch with a man who has been employed there since he was a boy and thinks he might remember the Diamond name. (Oliver has not fessed up that the cousin is on his mother's side.) Did I tell you that he brought a container of his own clay with him in hopes that someone will fire it into a brick for him? I don't quite see the point.

Oh, that sounded a bit mean. The truth is, I cannot get excited about bricks when there are teapots to be imagined. Still, we are in this together.

Please share this letter with Mother and Father. It is such a long one and has played me out. On second thought, don't. Or perhaps read it aloud to them and leave out the part about their daughter being a thief.
Your sister,
Salina

P.S. Oliver has contacted a doctor whom he wants me to see when we arrive in London. My husband is very attentive, overly so, I think. There is no need for him to fuss, but I will see this doctor for his peace of mind.

Dearest Salina,
Roseanne has shown your mother and me your last letter and we believe an immediate return to the sensible weather of Byrne Corners is prudent. You might think you have just a little cold, but if you do not take care of it, you will end up with a lifetime of grief like poor Aunt Aideen.

Weak lungs are on your mother's side of the family. I fear you may have inherited them, and if so, England is no place for you.

Your mother wants me to tell you that you are not to give another thought to anything but convincing Oliver that it is time he got you home to us. I am sure Mrs. Russell knows what she is doing and is no doubt an expert when it comes to caring for those who have fallen to the effects of the English weather, but there is no one like a mother when one is ill. Have you seen the doctor? What is his opinion regarding your condition?

Your mother says that you are not to leave all your woollen clothing in England just because it itches. You will be glad to have it on the crossing.

Here is a bit of advice from me. As far as your husband's brick business goes, leave the trade to him, Salina. You are a married woman now. When you return, you will have a home to think about and you will soon be blessed with children, God willing. You will be busy enough for one life.

On a lighter note, I am enclosing the letter that you sent to the esteemed Mrs. Morris and she delivered back to us in a huff, telling us that we do not know how to raise polite daughters. I thought you would enjoy her annotations.

Love,

Father

P.S. You make me proud, even as it is wrong to encourage you. And regarding those beads: as you said, a few beads among a basketful.

Dear Mrs. Morris,

I thought you and the other pottery club ladies might be interested in my current travels, since I find myself in London, England, studying the china of the British Potteries. I am truly inspired, and hope I will remember all that I am learning for my own future projects. I hope, also, to be able to share what I have learned with some of the local potters' clubs in Canada. I humbly offer my services. [**Oh, what an arrogant girl.**]

Do you know about the Wedgwood factory? I met Mr. Wedgwood himself, a fine gentleman who has a desire to visit Canada someday. When I told him about the ladies' club and your little backyard kiln, he was most amused. [**You know full well I am familiar with the Wedgwood name!**]

I realize that I neglected to send you and the other Potted Ladies my recipe for lemon squares, as requested. Here it is. It is a very simple recipe, but one that always pleases. [**This recipe is as common as muck. I do not remember a single request for it.**]

For pastry:
1 cup butter
½ cup sugar
2 cups flour

For topping:
1½ cups sugar
¼ cup flour
4 eggs
zest and juice of 2 lemons

1. Prepare the pastry layer by blending together the butter, sugar, and flour.
2. Press evenly into a greased 9×13 inch baking pan.
3. Bake for 20 minutes in a moderate oven.
4. Prepare the topping by whisking ingredients.

5. Allow the topping to rest before whisking again and pouring over the base.
6. Bake again until the custard is set (20 minutes).
7. Cool and sprinkle with icing sugar.

Please give my best to the other ladies. How are your ashtrays coming along? I do not believe Mr. Wedgwood makes ashtrays, but perhaps I am mistaken.
Yours truly,
Mrs. Oliver Diamond (Salina)
[You, my girl, have much to learn about respect for your elders. I will not relay your best wishes. I would prefer simply to forget all about you.]

MR. WILLIAM PASSMORE BYRNE CORNERS ONTARIO
=REGRET TO INFORM THAT SALINA DIED EARLY THIS
MORNING FROM PNEUMONIA INTERMENT BROMPTON
CEMETERY FULHAM ROAD LONDON HEARTBROKEN=
OLIVER DIAMOND

———

THE EVENING OF Oliver's arrival back in Byrne Corners, he made his way to the Passmore home. On the long crossing from Liverpool, he had become consumed with the idea that he was to blame for Salina's death, and that she would still be alive if he had not brazenly implied that she might join him on the *Hamilton*. He thought he ought to return the letters she'd received from her family and, in an act of full disclosure, he was planning also to present the Passmores with the letter that had enticed Salina to run away and purchase her overseas ticket. Who better than her family to decide once and for all whether he was responsible for what had happened? His letter was the evidence. The Passmores would be his judge and jury.

Roseanne, who happened to be looking in on her grieving parents, answered his knock at the door. He knew immediately it was Roseanne because Salina had told him they favoured one another. Oliver introduced himself and handed her the small bundle of letters. It was difficult for him to look at Roseanne because of the resemblance. He could not tell what her feelings were toward him.

She ran her hand over the letters, which were tied with a ribbon, and said, "Was this one of her hair ribbons?"

He replied, yes, her favourite ribbon, and then he got to the point and said that he thought the Passmores should have their letters back. He explained that one of his own letters was in the collection and he was quite sure that letter had brought about the tragedy of Salina's death and the misery they were all now living. He quoted himself—*It will be a long haul for this dry-lander travelling alone*—and said he did not know what the Passmores would do with him, but he would accept whatever punishment they thought appropriate, for Salina would never on her own have come up with the idea of travelling to England.

"I place the ball in your court," he said. "Do with me what you will."

Roseanne had taken her eyes from the letters and was now looking at him.

"You appear to like a good cliché," she said.

"In your own time, of course," he said. "I will await your verdict."

He had not imagined what would happen beyond this point, so he wasn't sure what to do. He decided he ought to leave, but when he took a step away from Roseanne, she said, "Stop."

He stopped.

"You must be a fool, Mr. Diamond. Either that or you did not know my sister well enough. Perhaps both are true."

"Beg your pardon?" Oliver said, not sure that he had heard right. He was struggling to find a context for what Roseanne had said.

"Are you asking us for dispensation?" she asked. "If so, I don't understand why."

"Not at all," he said. "The opposite, in fact."

"My God," Roseanne said, "the ego on you."

He was now truly confused, because he did not see that ego had anything to do with what he had said.

"Do you wish me to take back the letter in question?" he asked.

Roseanne said, "Oh no. You don't get away that easily. Come inside and we'll see what happens."

He did, although with much more trepidation now, and was directed by Roseanne to wait in the parlour. He imagined that he looked wretched, having just stepped off a train, and he wished he had taken the time for a haircut and a change of clothes.

Edith was summoned. She arrived in minutes, delivered by her husband in a new motorcar, and the Passmores gathered in the dining room, seemingly ignoring the fact that Oliver was in the house. The door to the parlour was open a crack and he could hear the murmur of their voices, but he could not make out what they were saying. He kept thinking of Roseanne's words: *you did not know my sister well enough.* Was it possible? They had been married such a short time, but he felt he had known her intimately since her first letter. He wanted to tell them that his life had been made full by Salina and empty by her death, but how could he say that when there was little doubt she would still be here if he had never written to her? Not just the letter that had enticed her to join him, but any letter at all. And what should he tell them about Salina's last days? Would they like to know about the cemetery where she was buried? That he had dried his Canadian clay to a powder and scattered it on her grave so as to leave a bit of her homeland with her? He was sweating through his wool jacket and wishing he had not come, or at least not before he'd bathed and had a good night's sleep.

After an eternity, Roseanne came to the parlour and led him to the dining room. She directed him to an empty chair at the table, which was covered with a perfectly ironed white cloth. Oliver's letter was open in the middle of the table, along with others in his own hand: the ones he had written to Salina from the West. When Roseanne saw him looking at them, she said, "We found them in her desk."

He nodded, and waited to be introduced. He knew who Salina's father was from the bank, but he had not met her mother and sisters. No formal introductions came.

"We've read the first letters many times, of course," Roseanne said. "And now the one you believe is so important."

Mr. Passmore was staring up at the ceiling as though he were puzzling over a chess move and the answer might be in the plaster.

He was smoking a pipe, and Oliver wished he had one too, so he would have something to do with his hands.

Roseanne said, "It's possible, Mr. Diamond, that you've overestimated your significance in this matter. Salina was not a woman who could easily be persuaded or taken advantage of. She was too old to have 'run away from home,' so we can only assume she did exactly what she wanted. Is that not how you see it?"

"She had wild ideas," said Mrs. Passmore. "It was her artistic temperament."

Oliver could not fathom what he was hearing. The Passmores appeared to be blaming Salina.

"Far too independent," Mrs. Passmore said. "We should have nipped it a long time ago."

Roseanne said, "I don't know about nipping, but I think we can all agree that her pluck was her downfall, considering what has happened."

She turned to Oliver. "It appears that she adored you," she said. "Perhaps you can enlighten us as to why."

Oliver had never in his life felt so greatly at a loss for words. He said the first thing that came to mind. "If she adored me, I can only say that I adored her in return. I will always adore her. She was my wife."

Mrs. Passmore seized on this. "Was she?" she said in a pleading way. "Was she really your wife? Because I believe you were married by a ship's captain rather than before God."

Oliver wished he could lie and say they had been married by a chaplain, but he was pretty sure the ship's captain had been mentioned in a letter, and besides, he had come here to be honest, and so he said, "I am very sorry. The ship's captain was the best option."

"Did you love her?" Edith asked. The words were spoken as though she thought it was her turn to ask a question, but she didn't really care what Salina had done. He remembered that Salina had written of Edith in a less than flattering way. Thankfully, those letters—Salina's to him—were in his valise and not in their possession.

"Yes, of course," Oliver said, trying to answer with dignity for Salina's sake. "She was the love of my life."

Roseanne said, "Then I think you were likely in over your head and we should have some sympathy for you."

Again, Oliver did not know what Roseanne meant or what he should say in response. He was overtaken by the memory of a ship's steward trying to tell him that a young lady was looking for him, and the panic he had felt when he realized the steward was talking about Salina. He'd really had no idea she would find her way onto that ship. He began to speak, not entirely sure what words were about to come out of his mouth.

"Perhaps I was in over my head, but not through any fault of your Salina's, and there is no need to send an ounce of sympathy my way unless you are sending it to a grieving widower." He waited for someone to say he was hardly that, since he and Salina had not been legitimately married, but no one did. He said, "We—Salina and I—had developed the habit of being playful in our correspondence, and my words in that letter were meant to be just that, playful. I did not know that Salina would join me without telling you. In fact, I was quite terrified when I learned that she was on the ship. I did not know what to do other than immediately propose marriage, which I had been planning to do upon my return, with your blessing."

As he spoke, he felt as though he were there again, kneeling awkwardly before Salina in her tiny cabin. He'd been trembling as he asked her to marry him. He was trembling now, and he tried to hide it just as he had then.

"I did not expect to see her on that crossing," he said. "I truly did not. I was as surprised as you were by what she had done."

Mrs. Passmore pulled a lace hanky out of a pocket of her frock. Silence followed as she dabbed her eyes, until Salina's father cleared his throat and said, "I don't imagine quite to the same extent."

All eyes turned to Mr. Passmore. These were the first words he had spoken since Oliver had been called to the table.

"Hubris aside," Mr. Passmore said, now turning his gaze to Oliver, "assigning blame to you, or anyone else for that matter, would be saying that Salina's death resulted from either scandalous behaviour or her complete lack of sense. The latter is probably closest to the truth, but I see no need to sully her reputation either way." He tapped his pipe on the table and said, "No one could lead that girl down a garden path unless she wanted to go. As far as I'm concerned, she was married and abroad on her honeymoon, and she was taken from us by an unfortunate illness. Now someone make the tea."

Oliver tried to focus on Salina's father but the room had begun to list. It reminded him of the ship moving with the swell. He thought he should speak but he didn't know what to say, and as he tried to decide—*thank you* did not seem right—the faces at the table became blurred and he felt himself becoming faint, and he feared he might slip off his chair. He broke into a sweat and clutched at the seat with both hands trying to hold himself upright, but the next thing he knew he was lying on the kitchen floor with Roseanne and Edith waving striped tea towels around his face, to give him air, he supposed, but they made him feel tangled in a clothesline hung with laundry.

"I'm fine, I'm fine," he said, brushing the towels away and managing to struggle to his feet and sit once again in his chair, embarrassed now that the spell had passed. He remembered Salina saying in one of her letters that she didn't believe in vapours. Was that what he'd just had, an attack of the vapours?

"I don't know what came over me," he said, sweat beaded on his brow.

"Relief, I dare say," said Edith, handing him a damp cloth with which to wipe his forehead.

Roseanne boiled the kettle on the stove and made tea in Salina's white teapot. By the time it had been poured all around, the linen cloth was spotted with sepia-coloured drips, which Mrs. Passmore dabbed with her hanky. The pot made a heavy clunking sound on the wooden table as Roseanne set it down, and she said, "It's really not a very good teapot, is it?"

Mrs. Passmore gave her a disapproving look, as though it were wrong to criticize Salina's handiwork, but then said she had to agree.

"It was her first, though," Oliver said. "She had ideas for others. I'm sure she would have corrected the flaws." When he lifted his cup to take a sip, he burned his lip and he said, "At least it keeps the tea hot." He set his cup down to let it cool and said, "She wanted to attend an art school."

Mrs. Passmore sighed. "An art school," she said, and he wished he hadn't mentioned that.

He said, "You do not blame me, then. For the carelessness with which I wrote that letter."

Roseanne said, "I think you've missed the point," but Mr.

Passmore held up his hand and said, "We choose not to blame anyone, and let's call that the end of the matter."

The evening soon after came to a close. Edith's husband was called to collect her, and Mrs. Passmore suggested that they deliver Oliver to his parents' home on their way since he appeared to be unwell. He declined, and told them he needed the fresh air. In the Passmores' foyer, he caught a glimpse of himself in the mirror and he looked dreadful. His face was covered with stubble. His eyes were bloodshot. His hair was standing on end. It was a wonder Roseanne hadn't thought him a tramp and shut the door on him.

As he walked along the quiet streets, he mulled over their reaction to Salina's flight and why they did not blame him. Was it possible that no one was to blame, as Mr. Passmore had said, and Salina had simply been taken from them by an unfortunate illness? He did not know the answer. When he arrived back at his parents' house, he found it already in darkness. He fell into his bed and slept through the night for the first time since Salina's death.

OLIVER STAYED IN Byrne Corners for two months before he returned to the West. His mother really was unwell and her illness was not, as he had suspected, all in her head. When she died there was another funeral in Byrne Cemetery. The Passmores did not attend. Oliver stood next to his father and his brother George and he tried to gauge how his mother's death might affect his father. He and Salina had had only a few months together; his parents had been married over thirty years. He studied his father but it was impossible to say one way or the other. He wasn't sure how he felt himself about his mother. She had been so much in the shadow of his father that he had hardly known her. Who exactly was she? A good woman, a good wife, but other than that, he couldn't say. His mind wandered from the words of the minister and he found himself perusing those gathered in the cemetery, remembering the day he had first spoken to Salina. He felt oppressed by a heavy shadow even though the sun was shining.

After the service, he was approached by a young woman who introduced herself nervously as Miss Beatrice Shaughnessy. She said she was sorry about the loss of Oliver's mother, and then she said in graver tones that she was very sorry also for the loss of Salina, who had once saved her from a slip in the mud in the middle of a violent thunderstorm in this very churchyard.

She said, "When I heard that you and Salina had been married, I thought, 'What a lucky man is Mr. Diamond.' She was so pretty and so unconventional, two traits that I myself could never lay claim to. How can anyone ever replace her?" Then her hand went to her mouth and she said, "Oh my. I've spoken out of turn," and she hurried away to join an older couple that Oliver took to be her parents. The father was looking at him as though wondering what his daughter could possibly have to say to Oliver Diamond, even though it was his mother they were there to remember.

As the days passed before his planned return to the West, Oliver found himself thinking about Beatrice Shaughnessy and her kind words about Salina. He inquired discreetly and found out that she was unattached. She was young, younger than Salina had been, and he thought she had asked a very good question when she'd said, "How can anyone ever replace her?" Any woman he married in future would have to accept his love for Salina as something that could not be replicated. Did Beatrice Shaughnessy understand that? Beatrice had been wrong, Oliver thought, when she said that she herself was not pretty, although pretty was not what had drawn him to Salina. When he ran into Beatrice shortly after on the street in front of the tailor's, where she had been picking up her father's new suit, he told her he was leaving in the next few days, and he impulsively asked whether she would mind if he wrote to her. The suit—a dignified grey wool—hung over her arm, and she nodded and said that she did enjoy having pen pals and would welcome a letter.

"A pen pal," he said. "Exactly. I shall try my best to be a good correspondent, then."

He watched her walk away, shifting her father's suit to the other arm, and he remembered Salina telling him that he'd better be entertaining if he was going to write to her. He could not imagine himself trying so hard ever again.

On the eve before Oliver left for the West, Roseanne and Mrs. Passmore unexpectedly knocked on his father's door and presented him with all of Salina's letters: the ones from him that had been in her desk, and even her letters to her family and their replies. By way of explanation they said, "She belonged to us before the letters. It is clear that, from the first letter, she belonged to you."

"You'll notice we kept the hair ribbon," Roseanne said, "since it was her favourite."

In addition to the letters, they gave Oliver the white teapot, because Salina had written to him of it and sent him a drawing to show how proud she was of her accomplishment, in spite of its dripping spout.

Oliver was overwhelmed by their generosity and did not know what to say.

Mrs. Passmore said, "Truthfully, I do not want these reminders in the house. I wish to remember happier times."

"As far as the teapot goes," Roseanne said, "we have the legacy of tea stains on the tablecloth. We advise you to avoid white linens, if they have use for such things as table linens in the West."

The two women declined an invitation to come inside, and Oliver understood that the Passmores were now done with him. He set the heavy teapot at his feet and absently tucked the letters inside as he watched Roseanne and Mrs. Passmore walk away, arm in arm. When they were out of sight, he picked up the teapot, and it seemed logical to leave the letters there. He fetched the others that Salina had written to him, and he sat on the edge of his bed and put them all in order, although he couldn't bear to read them. When he was done, he retrieved from his valise the velvet jewellery bag containing the clay beads Salina had been given by the designer with the double-barrelled name. He could not see their appeal at all, nor could he imagine why anyone had bothered to make them, but he'd bought Salina the jewellery bag in London, and she had been delighted when he'd presented it to her, as though he understood that the beads were precious.

He put the letters and beads—all that remained of Salina—in the teapot.

Early the next morning he stepped from the train platform up into his passenger car with the teapot in hand, because he had not known how to pack it safely at the last minute. Since the seat next to him was free, he placed the teapot there, and as the train left the station he indulged himself with the melancholy thought that he had expected to have Salina ever after by his side. At that moment the factory hardly seemed worth it, and he felt no enthusiasm for his return.

He travelled west with the teapot on the seat beside him when it was free, and at his feet when it was occupied. The ill-fitting lid bounced right off the pot on one especially rough section of track, and Oliver used his shoe to tap it securely into place in spite of the glaze drip, effectively sealing the letters and Salina's beads inside. When he took the teapot with him to the dining car and a porter asked whether he wanted his tea prepared in it, he had to admit to himself that it had taken on more meaning than a teapot warranted. Still, he was paralyzed at the thought of leaving it unattended.

He passed the hours on the journey thinking about what might have been. The miles clacked by and he thought it was likely the last such trip he would make, because he had no reason to return to Byrne Corners. His mother was gone, and his father and brother thought he was a fool. He tried to be sociable in the dining car, and even met a businessman at dinner who was a good investment candidate, but he had no stomach for business talk. Besides, he thought, what sensible person would go into partnership with a man who could not, it seemed, be parted from his teapot?

In his head he wrote letters to Salina, until somewhere along the way he realized he was addressing Miss Shaughnessy, telling her all about Salina and the fire she had brought to his life. He tried penning his thoughts—he had promised a letter, after all—but he quickly realized how inappropriate it was to write to Miss Shaughnessy about Salina, while at the same time it seemed impossible to write of anything *but* her. He gave up on the idea of corresponding with Beatrice Shaughnessy altogether, but somewhere west of Winnipeg he began to think about the future and the fact that a man did need a wife, and there were not many single ladies to be found in the West. What harm was there, he wondered, in writing a polite letter? He had met Salina and Beatrice at funerals in the same churchyard, and perhaps that meant something. Perhaps, he thought, Salina's spirit had been nudging him in Beatrice Shaughnessy's direction.

What could it hurt, he wondered, to write a letter?

Once he was back in Regina and settled again in Mrs. Klein's boarding house, he wrote a short note to Beatrice telling her that he had arrived and was finally shed of the travelling dust, and he provided a bit of description of the uncompromising western sky, saying that she would know what he meant if she were ever to see it. Her first letter to him was also brief. She was delighted that he had remembered she liked pen pals, and she wrote, "Most pen pals become bored with writing after a few exchanges. Please don't apologize if this should happen in our case." Another simple and courteous condolence on the death of his mother, and his wife: "Such a tragic loss for you and her family. The death of a parent is one thing, but it is especially hard to see God's logic when someone as young as Salina is taken. We must trust in His higher understanding, must we not?"

Oliver did not think so, but he didn't say as much. Miss Shaughnessy's thoughts were those of most good people, and he wrote back without commenting on God's mysterious ways, and described instead the city in which he now lived and his plans for the brick plant. A further correspondence ensued, although not one as bold and electrified as his exchanges with Salina. Before long, Oliver realized that he was once again courting a woman by mail.

He was apparently good at it. His exchange with Beatrice continued for six months, at which time Oliver proposed marriage, and she said yes, but with conditions. She would not, she said, announce their engagement until a full year after Salina's death had passed. She expected to be married by a church minister, and she would not agree even to that until she had her father's approval. She did not say so explicitly, but she made it clear that she was not about to head west on a train to marry a man she knew only by mail.

As a result, Oliver returned once again to Byrne Corners to court Beatrice formally and in person while the factory construction neared completion without him, under the supervision of his partner, Nathaniel Thick. With his interest torn between the West and his new fiancée, Oliver endured a month in the house of his father, a good number of suppers at the Shaughnessy table, and nightly strolls up High Street with Beatrice while the whole town watched. He suffered through a painful conversation with Beatrice's father in which he did his best to assure him of the future success of his business and the integrity of his intentions toward Beatrice.

At that point, he felt he had to pay a visit to his former in-laws and give them his news, and when he knocked on the Passmores' door, it was answered by a young boy with flour in his hair. Oliver was taken to the kitchen, where Roseanne was helping her mother make pies with the last of the winter's apples. Oliver told the two women that he was getting married again, and Roseanne said, "So we have heard. I'm not sure what Salina would think of your choice, but I suppose you should not be deprived of a wife. Regardless, it is no longer our business, if it ever was."

"But thank you for the courtesy," said Mrs. Passmore. She was wearing a flowered apron and was rolling out pie dough while Roseanne peeled the withered apples. The boy was now under the table playing with long curls of apple skin.

Oliver was not invited to stay for tea, and he showed himself out.

His wedding to Beatrice took place soon after, and on the very evening of the ceremony the newlyweds boarded the train and headed west. It was not soon enough for Oliver. He'd felt the eyes of the whole town on his every move, and the Morris factory's shift-change whistle pierced his ears each time it blew. His father had shamed him at the wedding by telling Beatrice's parents to expect the couple back in Byrne Corners before the year was out, and his brother George told him not to come asking for money when his so-called business failed. Was that really what they thought of him?

As soon as the train was out of the station in Byrne Corners, he felt a sense of release. He realized that the city to which he was travelling with his new wife—Beatrice, and not Salina—was now his home. He thought about a house full of children who would never know of Byrne Corners and the Morris plant, and would instead grow up with their own family name on a factory sign. It was Diamond and Thick at the moment, but one day it would be Diamond and Son. Or Sons, plural.

He settled into his seat on the train, desperate to get back to the West and begin the life he had imagined. Or, rather, reimagined, since it was bound to be different without Salina.

BEATRICE SHAUGHNESSY-NOW-DIAMOND sat quietly by Oliver's side in the passenger car and admired the green velvet seats and the car's polished oak railing. She thought the train was a very civilized way to travel to what was probably a very uncivilized destination, in spite of Oliver's assurances. She had a new set of Royal Albert dinner china for ten packed in a crate in the baggage car, a gift from her parents, purchased from the drugstore in Byrne Corners. Beatrice had no idea who the ten people were that her parents expected to dine formally at her table, but the red-and-black daisy pattern was modern and she approved of it, even though she'd let her mother choose because she knew about these things and Beatrice did not. Beatrice did not know much about what she was doing or where she was going. She trusted that Oliver would take care of her, in spite of what had happened to Salina, whose illness could not have been prevented by anyone but herself. Women, Beatrice believed, had a duty to be sensible, and Salina, for all her admirable qualities, had not been that.

Once they were on their way Oliver began to talk about his business plans. Beatrice listened as he went on about clay pits and levigation systems, and what his chemists were telling him about fritting and tempering, without trying very hard to understand because she did not see that she had much of a part to play in that side of their lives together. As Oliver talked, she worried about the china and whether it was travelling safely, and she worried also about the marital relations she and Oliver had not yet had, the ones that would result in the children she had always pictured herself with. Her mother had prepared her by alluding to her wifely duty, but Beatrice did not exactly know what this duty entailed.

As the train passed through the pastoral landscape she was used to and into the ruggedness of Northern Ontario, she prayed that she would make a good wife and mother and learn quickly how to keep a household befitting an important businessman of the West. She had been forewarned by Oliver that her marital home did not yet exist. He had rented them rooms in an appropriate boarding house while he undertook to build them a grand new house on a lot that he had already acquired. He would build it, he said, with his own bricks. He did not ask her what she would like in a house. He seemed to believe he knew what a married woman would want.

From Salina, she supposed. They must have made plans.

As they passed into Manitoba after a night in upper and lower sleeping berths, Beatrice wondered how she would stack up to Salina, about whom they had not spoken since she had awkwardly expressed her condolences in the churchyard. It was as though they had an understanding that they would not speak of Salina. She had been one of a kind, Beatrice thought, but—God rest her soul—not likely a woman who would have adapted well to being a homemaker. A free spirit and a suffragist, if you could believe gossip. Beatrice was determined to adapt as well as any woman to the role of wife and mother. She would have that over Salina, even if Salina would always be Oliver's first love. She, Beatrice, would offer him stability and a well-kept home. Beautiful daughters and industrious, handsome sons. For luck, she tapped the wooden panelling beside her not once, but twice, and then once more, just in case.

"What was that about?" Oliver asked, and Beatrice grew self-conscious, because to imagine children was to acknowledge what she would have to do to get herself in the family way. When Oliver noticed she was blushing, he rested his hand on her forearm and patted it, as though he knew what she was thinking and was telling her, *Don't worry, there's not much to it.* They travelled for a time with Oliver's hand on her arm, and then he went back to his notebook and the columns and figures he was working on, about which she could think of not a single thing to say.

When they pulled into the station in Winnipeg, Oliver announced that they were having a night off the train. He had booked them a room and a table for dinner at the Royal Alexandra, a brand new hotel built by the Canadian Pacific Railway. It was a honeymoon gift, he said, a night of extravagance before they settled into their modest living quarters and he turned his attention once more to the brick factory. The hotel had been told they were newlyweds. They had prepared lamb dinner with potatoes and mint sauce, for which Oliver had acquired a taste in England. There were flowers on their table in the hotel's dining room, and more flowers in their room.

That night, Beatrice learned how marital relations worked, and she wasn't much impressed. She found it all quite mortifying for the both of them, but she was glad to have it over and done with, a necessary step to becoming the wife she was determined to be. Oliver, she supposed, was used to the humiliation because he had been married before. No doubt, in future he would expect more of her by way of participation, and she would try to comply with whatever his wishes were. They didn't speak much over breakfast, although he did reach across the table and squeeze her hand. She wondered if he was disappointed in her. She wondered if he wished she were Salina. If so, she could forgive him. She believed that in time she would replace his first wife, and that his memory of her would fade. Beatrice was a practical woman and did not believe in worrying about things over which she had no control.

The next evening, they arrived at their destination. Nathanial Thick met them at Union Station wearing his cowboy hat, and Oliver introduced them.

"You must be the Texan, then," Beatrice said, trying to sound like a wife who knew about her husband's affairs.

"Always proud to be called a Texan, ma'am," he said, and he looked as though he might have gone on with a story or two, but Oliver was already guiding her toward the new Model T Ford parked outside the station doors, with "Diamond and Thick" stencilled on the driver's side. Beatrice was concerned about leaving the china behind at the station, but Nathaniel said that he had arranged for the delivery of their baggage.

"Things are well?" Oliver asked anxiously as they settled in the car. Beatrice was in the back seat holding her hat on her head even though they had barely begun to move.

"Right on schedule," Nathaniel said. "Bit of a delay with the trolleys but nothing to worry about." Nathaniel turned to Beatrice, who was now holding her breath as well as her hat as they gained speed. She had never travelled so quickly on a city street. The signs of construction were everywhere, and the car often bounced when it hit a mound of dirt. Beatrice supposed this was the heavy clay soil Oliver had told her about.

"We're glad to have you here," Nathaniel Thick said to her, "to keep this man happy so he can attend to business on our behalf. A lot rests on your husband's clear head."

She did her best to nod knowingly in spite of the bouncing, and said, "I will keep him fed and satisfied," to which Nathaniel laughed heartily, though she wasn't sure why. She thought perhaps he was being cordial in the exaggerated way of people from Texas. It was obvious that he and Oliver knew each other well, which spoke to the life he had here, the one she knew so little about. She was happy to have this sense of Oliver's life and her own future unfolding as they jostled around in what looked to her to be an entire city under construction.

When Nathaniel stopped the car in front of a two-storey house on a residential street, Beatrice thought, *This is it, where I will become Mrs. Oliver Diamond.* She could see that a woman she presumed to be the landlady was waiting on the stoop.

"Mrs. Diamond, welcome," the woman said, once Beatrice had been helped out of the car by Oliver.

"Yes," she said. "That is I. Thank you."

She didn't wait for Oliver's arm, and she walked up the boards to greet the landlady.

IN THE DAYS after their arrival, Oliver went to the plant with Nathaniel while Beatrice unpacked her bags and tried to get used to the idea that this was now her home. She placed a few of their wedding gifts about to see if that would help: a lace tablecloth, a crystal cream-and-sugar set, a pink china flower vase. The rooms had come furnished, and Beatrice did not think much of her landlady's taste in decorating. The painting above the chesterfield was dark and brooding—a deer running for its life from the hounds—and she especially did not like the stoneware teapot on the sideboard. She tried to remove the lid but it was solidly stuck in place, and when she picked it up, she found herself weighing it in her hands as she might a bag of potatoes in the shop. It was impossibly heavy, and unattractive, with no redeeming value that she could see. She was considering hiding it in the sideboard and replacing it with a colourful china peacock she had unpacked when she heard someone at the door. She turned around and saw that it was Oliver. As he came in, he was saying something about finding her walking shoes, but when he saw that she was holding the teapot, he stopped mid-sentence, and in that moment Beatrice remembered that Salina had been in the Byrne Corners pottery club, and she understood that the teapot was hers.

"This is lovely," she said, not sure how else to describe it politely.

"It's not the best example of a handcrafted vessel, is it," Oliver said, and then he added, "Salina made it. I leave it to you—if you would rather I throw it out, I will do so."

Beatrice set the teapot back down on the sideboard, trying to avoid the inevitable clunk. It had been only a year since Salina's death, she thought, and it behoved her to respect her memory. "Of course we will not throw it out," she said. "Although there's no need to make the tea in it, is there. We have other teapots. I believe we received three as wedding gifts. We'll treat it as a museum piece."

Then she looked around for a place to put the china peacock and decided on the kitchen windowsill.

"Now then," she said, turning to Oliver, "what were you saying about walking shoes?"

He said that he wanted to take her out to see the plant.

They travelled from the city along a well-used country trail that took them to Oliver's property. The factory yard resembled a huge excavation site cut into the surrounding hills, and as they drove toward the new buildings, Beatrice saw the brick kilns Oliver had told her about. She counted six of them. She could see why they were called beehives: the shape, but also the number of men working around them. In fact, when they got out of the car and walked closer, she saw men everywhere, even on the roof of a long wooden building, where they were hammering shingles into place.

Oliver explained that this building was the heart of the operation, from one end, where trolley cars brought clay from the pits, through to the other, where the raw bricks were stacked and taken to the kilns. He took her inside and up a narrow staircase leading to his office so she could have a look at the works from overhead. The office had windows on all sides, and a catwalk was suspended under the rafters so that every aspect of production was visible. As Oliver led her along the catwalk, he explained what she was seeing below them: a giant pug mill, which looked to Beatrice like something you might see in a bread-making plant; the mould shop; the drying tunnels; the network of conveyor belts and trolley tracks that connected the shops and work stations. It was sometimes hard to hear with all the hammering on the roof, but Oliver leaned close so she caught most of what he was saying, and she was amazed that he—or any man, for that matter—could bring such a complicated production into being.

When they'd finished their tour of the building, they descended the stairs and stepped once again into the factory yard. Oliver took her next to see the kilns, and they were able to walk inside one so Beatrice could see the overhead construction that created downdrafts of heat during the firings. Then he showed her the warehouse, where the finished bricks would be sorted and loaded onto skids for transport. Horses had been purchased, he said, and would soon arrive from Ontario by train to pull the trolley cars and transport the finished bricks by wagon to another warehouse in the city, near the railway tracks. He pointed out the new barn that awaited the animals.

"I know nothing of horses," he said, "but Nathaniel has hired a man to care for them and train them to the harness."

Later, they walked out into the quarry hills, and Beatrice wondered how she might describe adequately in a letter home the strangeness of the clay deposits, which did not look at all as she'd thought they would. She'd expected a rust colour, like the bricks in Byrne Corners, but instead, variegated seams of pink and blue-grey ran through the cut banks. She felt as though she had gone back in time, and she half expected a giant reptile to step in front of her with its teeth bared. There was something disturbingly prehistoric about these hills, she thought. She asked Oliver what happened when it rained and he told her the clay sluiced like thick cream. After a windstorm, he said, you might find arrowheads exposed in the surrounding fields. He had found many. She was quiet as they walked then, no longer thinking about dinosaurs, but of a time much more recent. Although it hardly made sense, she felt as though they were trespassing.

As they looped around and the buildings came back into view, Oliver said, "The West is a new land now, Beatrice, and you can't argue with progress, can you."

She didn't know whether you could or not, that was Oliver's business, but on the way home in the car, she was overtaken by a wave of homesickness. She was unsettled by this wilderness, and she felt a longing for quiet, conventional Byrne Corners, Ontario, and the house she had grown up in. Although she admired Oliver's determination, she wondered if perhaps she should not have replied to his first letter, and this thought, too, unsettled her because she did not want to be unhappy and believed discontent was something you brought on yourself. She had once been to a lecture with her parents where a fiery speaker from Chicago said that God wanted His flock to be prosperous, and anyone who wasn't had only his own insufficient faith to blame. He had lost her by appearing to blame poverty on the poor—what had happened to charity?—but she did agree that happiness was of your own making, barring dire circumstances.

When they got back to their boarding house she said she thought she had best lie down, she was feeling a bit poorly. She drank the cup of tea Oliver made for her and assured him that she would be herself again the next day, which she was. She vowed never again to let nerves and homesickness get the better of her, because she was a fortunate woman to have been there to pick up the pieces when Salina died and Oliver Diamond's life fell apart.

She was much better prepared the next time she accompanied Oliver to the plant, a month later when the first bricks came out of one of the beehives. They stood at the open door to the kiln, Nathaniel Thick beside them in his suit and cowboy hat. She was not wearing walking shoes that day; she had dressed up for the occasion. One of the oven men wheeled a trolley from inside the kiln, and Oliver donned insulated gloves and removed a still-warm brick from a stack and declared it the ceremonial first brick. There were at least a hundred workers and their families there, and Beatrice was introduced many times as Mrs. Diamond, the owner's wife.

When the paper came out the following day, she sent a clipping home to her parents, along with a letter.

Dear Mother and Father,

As you can see, Oliver is on the front page of the newspaper! The plant is up and running, and we removed the first brick from one of the kilns with all of the workers there to celebrate with us. Oliver is very proud of that first brick after years of planning and hard work. He and his partner, Nathaniel Thick, hosted a wonderful picnic afterwards for the workers and their families. It was quite the thing to see . . . Oliver serving corn and potato salad at a cookout.

The bricks from Oliver's plant are different from those you are used to. They are a warm yellow colour, and not the red brick you see in Byrne Corners, but striking all the same. This is due to the iron content, I am told, and residue from the coal furnaces. You will see when you come to visit.

Oliver has shown me the plans for our new home—to be built with Diamond bricks, of course—and it looks very much like a house you might see on High Street in Byrne Corners, with a front porch just right for a swing. A swing is one of the first pieces of furniture I intend to purchase. You can look forward to taking your tea in the fresh air when you come to visit, although it will have to be in the summer or you will not survive.

I have other joyous news as well. Oliver and I are happy to announce that we are expecting a child in the spring. I am feeling well, just a bit of the morning sickness, but Oliver is very attentive. I hope the house will be ready by the time the baby arrives and that you will make plans to visit and meet your first grandchild. The train is a very fine way to travel.

Speaking of travel, the Daisy china has not been unpacked since its journey west. However, I aim to put it to good use when the Oliver Diamonds are settled in their new home. I remember you saying, Mother, that proper china separates the wheat from the chaff, and I dare say that will be especially true here in the frontier.

I hope you are both well.
Your daughter,
Beatrice

P.S. I do miss home, but as Oliver says whenever I am a bit blue, the future is here in the West. I'm sure that he is right. He is very clever about these things.

2

The Oliver Diamonds

Oliver Diamond was known to be a family man. Although he was an esteemed member of what was referred to as the city's business community, he had no interest in private clubs or golf courses or the men's spa at the YMCA. He was in his office high above the brick works at six every morning, and every evening at six on the dot he sat down to the supper Beatrice had prepared, expecting his children to do the same until they got married and moved into their own homes. Sometimes he would return to the plant for a few hours in the evening, but unless there was an emergency he was always home again in time to have a cup of tea with Beatrice before she went to bed. If the youngest children were already asleep, he looked in on them. If Estella was still awake (and she often was) he sat on her bed and talked to her for a few minutes, about the book she was reading or what she had done that day. Sometimes he asked her what plans she had for her life when she grew up. In answer to that question, she always said, "Run the factory," and Oliver would say, "Very good, then," before he went downstairs to join Beatrice in the parlour.

Oliver's unquestionable devotion to his family allowed Beatrice to overlook his ambivalence in the matter of the Sunday service. Most husbands in his position sat in the pew with their wives every week, but Oliver went to church with Beatrice only sporadically: on Christmas Eve and Easter Sunday, perhaps to the Thanksgiving service. At his insistence, the children were given a choice about whether to accompany their mother each week, and one by one they all chose not to after being bored silly enough times, but they did not argue on the occasions of Oliver's attendance, when they were told to put on their best clothes. They knew that if their father was going to church, they were too. The United Church minister always welcomed them boisterously and said something predictable like, "Look what the wind blew in, the entire suit of Diamonds," and the other congregants gathered and told Beatrice what a good-looking family she had. She was so pleased by the fuss that no child, not even a teenager, begrudged the inconvenience of having a perfectly good Sunday hijacked, and Oliver's status as upstanding was affirmed in spite of his hazy beliefs. After church on these occasions, the family would arrive home to the aroma of a perfectly timed pork roast, and they would have dinner together at noon rather than six. In the first years, Beatrice used her good daisy china for these special Sunday meals, but as the family grew in number she became worried one of the children would break a plate or a bowl, and so she arranged the dishes and the matching tea set attractively behind the glass doors of her china cabinet and there they stayed. Her parents would be disappointed, she thought, if they knew that neither she nor Oliver felt compelled to host the elegant dinner parties they had imagined when they'd purchased the china.

Oliver's life—through the first decades of the business and the arrival of the children, through two world wars and the difficult years of the Great Depression—comprised two things, the brick plant and his family, which is why Beatrice could not have been more dismayed when he announced, at seventy-four years of age, that he was going on a fishing trip with a group of businessmen he knew. The Diamonds—which by then included the boys' wives and a dozen grandchildren—were all at the house for Sunday dinner, the regular six o'clock kind. There was no question of using the daisy china now, there were far too many people. The only one missing on this day was Jack's wife, Phyllis, who had moved home with her parents. Temporarily, according to Jack, but Beatrice suspected the first divorce in the Diamond family was pending.

"A fishing trip?" Beatrice said. "Have you lost your mind, Oliver?"

He ignored the question and said, "Jack here wants to come along."

No one was going to ask Jack if he had lost his mind. They were all too worried it might be true. He'd spent months in an overseas hospital after the invasion of Normandy in 1944, followed by a full year of recovery at home once he was shipped back to Canada. Now, more than five years later, he was still plagued by headaches and what looked like a complete lack of ambition.

"I believe it might be good for both of us," Oliver said. "Theo, I have every confidence you can run the plant for a week. Time you tried it on."

Theo and his wife Gladys exchanged a look that said they had spoken about his position at the factory, but if they thought it was time he was given more responsibility, they didn't say so.

The fishing party drove north on their way to a remote lodge, but they'd been delayed leaving the city and darkness fell when they were still several hours short of their destination. They decided to stop for the night at the village of Lake Claire, which was not much more than a few small businesses stretched along the shore of an immense body of water. They booked rooms at an old hotel—The Travellers—that had been there as long as the village, and in the dining room they struck up a conversation with a local fishing guide and entrepreneur named Allen Foster. Foster told them he was planning to build twenty rental cabins along the lakefront, the first real commercial development at Lake Claire other than the hotel.

"Twenty *eventually*, that is," he said. "Ten is probably all I can manage for now. The bank's been a bit difficult. They're not sure people will travel this far."

Oliver laughed and said he knew a thing or two about banks. There was something about entrepreneurship they didn't understand, that gambling was a necessary part of winning.

"Tell that to my credit union," Foster said. "And maybe my wife, although she at least sees the potential. Lenora. She's a friendly sort, an asset. She'll do well with the tourists."

As Foster talked on about his plan, and his other assets besides Lenora, Oliver's companions lost interest and drifted upstairs to their rooms. Only Oliver stayed at the table with Foster.

As he listened, he thought about Nathaniel Thick, a man of means who had taken him seriously when the brick plant was just an idea, one that far exceeded his own available funds. He felt affection, nostalgia even, for the early days of the factory and for his old friend, and he almost expected Nathaniel to walk through the door and join them at the table with a ledger and a roll of blueprints. It had ended badly with Nathaniel because Oliver had been so intent on claiming the business in its entirety for his sons. His decision to force his partner out the way he had was one of the few in his life that he regretted. He wondered now if there was something he might do help Allen Foster, with himself in the role of Nathaniel Thick. He and Foster talked into the evening, until the woman who ran the dining room began to turn off the lights and they realized she was waiting for them to leave.

The next morning the fishing party, including Jack, continued farther north, but Oliver stayed on at The Travellers. Every day he went out on the lake with Allen Foster in his fishing boat. Foster sat in the stern with his hand on the tiller and steered them across the open water, and when he slowed to cruise along the shoreline of a bay so clear you could see the fish on the lake bottom, he talked to Oliver about his plans for the rental cabins. Oliver had grown up in a place where hunting and fishing were common—the Ottawa Valley—but he associated fishing rods with subsistence and men who smoked their catch or stored it in ice houses for the winter. Foster had a different clientele in mind, family men with wives and children. The war was over, he said, and young men were settling down, finding jobs, buying houses. No one, young or old, wanted to relive what the country had been through in the last twenty years. There was a market for happiness, and he believed that if he could build affordable family holiday cabins, Lake Claire would provide the rest. Oliver listened carefully, and he became convinced that Foster was on to something.

When they were having supper at the hotel one night as the week drew to a close, Oliver decided it was his turn to talk, and he asked Foster if he would consider brick for his cabin construction. He was thinking about the yellow face bricks that had been stockpiled in his storage sheds since the war, when Diamond and Sons had been declared a war service industry and had switched its operations solely to the production of firebrick for the boilers of ships. After the war, Oliver had discovered there was a lucrative industrial market for firebrick and he had continued with its production. The construction bricks produced before the war were still sitting unused.

Foster had not, of course, considered brick; he'd based his figures on plywood and lap siding.

"Give me until tomorrow," Oliver said.

He stayed up late into the night sketching diagrams and working out columns of figures and what he might get in return for a storehouse of brick.

The next morning he presented Foster with a proposal: bricks and bricklayers for his original plan of twenty modest-sized buildings—cottages, he called them, not cabins—plus a loan that would ensure the installation of a septic system and running water. In return, Foster would repay the investment over time and provide cottage rental for two weeks every summer for the entire Diamond clan, five cottages, one each for Oliver and his four sons and their families. He told Foster that he had a grown daughter as well, an unmarried teacher, but she could stay with him and his wife. He was not sure that she would ever marry, he said. Teachers sometimes didn't.

By the time Jack and the fishing party collected Oliver again, he and Foster had struck a deal and their agreement had been roughed out on paper. Oliver knew enough about contracts to believe their lawyers would say it was an unusual deal, but not unfeasible. It was complicated somewhat by the fact that Foster did not actually own the land, which had been leased by his father from one of the nearby Cree bands, but it was a ninety-year lease with plenty of time left on it. Oliver proposed that the agreement stand for as long as Foster held the lease and owned the cottages, or for the next twenty-five years in the event that he sold them. Foster agreed.

On the return trip south, Oliver did not disclose what he had done. Once he and Jack were home, he gathered the family together and announced that he would be easing into retirement from the plant, that he had sold the stockpile of construction bricks in the storage shed to Allen Foster, and that he had negotiated an annual Diamond family vacation in exchange for his investment in Foster's cottage development.

No one said a word. Beatrice, Estella, Jack, Oliver's other three sons and their wives—each was as stunned as the other. Oliver had never before indicated that he wanted to retire from the plant. The family had never been on a vacation, and as far as they knew Oliver had no interest in outdoor pursuits of any kind. He was not a man who could be easily taken in, but they couldn't help but wonder what had happened in the past week, and whether he had been bamboozled by this Allen Foster. Oliver was an entrepreneur, not an investor in the ideas of others, and especially not in the scheme of a man he had met by accident in a northern hotel dining room.

When Beatrice found her voice, she said, "Oliver, I hope you do not expect me to join you in a forest full of wild animals, and possibly murderers hiding from the law. That is not my idea of a vacation."

"No, Beatrice," Oliver said, "I do not expect that. Picture instead an idyllic cottage built from Diamond bricks, with a view of the lake, a modern bathroom, and window screens to keep the mosquitoes out. That is more what I have in mind."

Beatrice was still flummoxed. The other Diamonds remained silent.

Estella was the only one whose interest was piqued, even though she was as surprised as everyone else by Oliver's announcement. She had arrived at her career as a high school mathematics teacher somewhat indifferently, but it had led her to an organization called The Teachers' Recreation Society, which owned several school buses, one equipped for cooking and the others outfitted as sleeping dorms for single men and women. The summer before, Estella had signed on to an especially adventurous camping tour down the American west coast to the remote beaches of the Baja Peninsula south of Tijuana. She'd been so inspired by the wild beauty of the ocean that she'd bought some paints and brushes and tried, without much success, to become a watercolourist. She'd almost fallen for a physics teacher on that trip, before she found out he had lied about his single status and had a wife and kids at home. Afterwards, she wasn't sure whether she'd been smitten by the teacher or seduced by the Baja coast; she might have confused the two. Because of this, she arrived at a possible explanation for what had happened to her father: he had fallen under the spell of this place called Lake Claire, and because he was a businessman, he had developed a business interest as an excuse to return.

She wanted to see Lake Claire for herself, and the next time Oliver headed north to meet with Allen Foster, she convinced him to take her along. Beatrice didn't object, thinking that someone needed to go and report back on this Foster fellow and the scheme he had cooked up. Estella managed to get two days off school by pleading a family emergency, and when she told her mother this, Beatrice said an emergency was not far from the truth.

It was late fall by this time. Estella and Oliver arrived in the village after dark. Oliver had booked them into The Travellers, where they met Foster for breakfast the next morning in the dining room. Estella could see the lake through the trees from the restaurant windows. The village was situated on a large bay, and a prominent rocky point jutted into the bay at the north end, the direction in which Foster held his lease, her father explained. She could not tell how big the lake itself was because it disappeared into the horizon to the west. A young boy cleared their dishes away when they were done eating. Shortly after, she saw a school bus collect him from the sidewalk in front of the hotel. She assumed that his parents owned The Travellers.

After breakfast, Foster took them out on the lake in his boat. It was the first time Estella had been in an open boat, and as the nose dropped and the boat picked up speed, she pulled her coat around herself and shoved her hands up into her sleeves. She wished she'd brought winter mittens with her. They didn't stay out for long on the water because of the cold—they even encountered ice in the shallow bays—but Estella saw the wilderness appeal of Lake Claire, and she liked Foster. He was not as rough-and-ready as she had expected him to be, and she learned that the cottage development was to be a family affair. He and his wife and three kids lived in a town an hour to the south, but they were planning to move to the village for the summer months and might eventually live there year-round.

At supper that evening, again in the hotel dining room, Estella listened as Foster and her father talked. Oliver was speaking to Foster in an unusually reflective way, she thought, lamenting that all he had done since he had come from Ontario was work, and now he saw his sons doing the same. He said that he had always admired hard work and had provided well for his wife and children, but there were other things he had denied them. He had never taken his wife on a proper holiday, for example. He himself had been to Europe when he was a young man, but they had never been anywhere together, not even to the Rocky Mountains. He had not encouraged his children to seek adventure, he said, although his boys Jack and Andrew had found more than they bargained for when they enlisted. He told Foster that they had almost lost Jack, and he wondered if he had made a mistake by burdening his sons with his dream instead of encouraging them to create their own. When he suggested that Jack and Andrew had perhaps seen the war as a way out, Estella wondered for the first time if he blamed himself for Jack's injuries and the years Andrew lost away from his family. He was feeling his age, she thought, even though he looked as fit as a man ten years younger.

Then suddenly he was talking about his first wife. Estella had never before heard him talk about Salina.

"I was married for a brief time to a woman who wanted to be an artist," Oliver said to Allen Foster, almost as though Estella were not present. "She wanted to be a designer of fine china. Of course, that was a different kind of dream, and I fear that I did not take it as seriously as I took my own, even though I encouraged her."

"I suppose the artist in her had a hard time settling down to marriage," Allen Foster said, assuming that the marriage had ended in divorce.

"Oh no," Oliver said. "That wasn't it. She died."

"I'm sorry to hear it," Foster said.

"A lifetime ago, really," Oliver said. "All in the past now."

Then he turned to Estella and said, "Those clay beads in the teapot, you remember the ones."

"Yes," Estella said. It was disconcerting to be talking about the teapot, even hearing the word *teapot* out loud.

"We were in England and she had met a woman, a pottery designer who later became quite famous, and this woman invited her alone on a private tour of the Wedgwood Pottery. When I found out afterwards, I must admit that I was jealous, and even annoyed, that she had managed to get to the inner sanctum of the Wedgwood plant when I had been unable to, but they were two artists and they shared an ambition that had nothing to do with business. The designer made the beads. I didn't know at the time why my wife admired them so. To my eye, they were ugly things, but she saw them in a way that I did not."

He stopped talking, and Estella didn't know why her father had chosen to tell the story now, in front of a stranger. After all those years, he'd so easily said "my wife" and meant someone other than Beatrice.

The silence was broken when Allen Foster said, "Well, this is it, isn't it," providing an ending for the story.

And then it was as though Oliver had never mentioned Salina.

"So, what do you think of our grand plan, Estella?" he asked.

She felt as if she were being catapulted into a new conversation when she was still thinking about the last one, the story of Salina the artist and her father the businessman. She said, "What about naming each of your cottages after an artist? Tom Thomson, Emily Carr. The Group of Seven."

Her father was immediately enthusiastic, since the suggestion was an indication of Estella's endorsement. When Foster said, "Why not?" she agreed to come up with twenty cottage names for them. There was an art teacher in her school she could ask, a woman whose *plein air* paintings of the prairie landscape graced the walls of the staff room. Estella admired her ability and wished she had more of it herself.

Their empty dinner plates were still on the table and the same young boy appeared and took them away, asking if they would like pie—"It's included," he said—and they said yes, cherry pie all around. As the boy set generous servings of pie and ice cream in front of them, Estella thought for the first time in a long while about her father's other life, before he became the Oliver Diamond who married Beatrice and had five children and built a successful business out of nothing but a clay deposit.

After Foster had left and she and Oliver were climbing the stairs to their rooms, she said, "I've never before heard you talk about your first wife." She dared not look at him as she spoke and looked, instead, at the floral-patterned carpet on the stairs.

"Is that so?" he replied. "Well, there's nothing to speak of. All in the past."

It was the second time he'd said that—*all in the past*—in less than an hour.

When they came to their rooms, he said good night and waited until Estella was safely behind her locked door, and then she heard him unlocking his own room across the hall.

She put on her flannel pyjamas and got under the covers, reaching in the darkness for the extra blanket at the foot of the bed because the room was cold. As she pulled it up over herself, she wondered what—or whom—her father was thinking about at that very moment, and whether he regretted that he had not taken Salina's dreams as seriously as he had his own. When he'd confessed that, Estella had had a little moment of *déjà vu* because of the way he'd dashed her dream of running the brick factory. In Salina's case there had been no consequence because she had died, but there had been a consequence when he'd not taken his daughter seriously, and that consequence was her career as a mathematics teacher—a perfectly good career, but not a dream career. She could still hear his voice when she had asked for a job at the plant, not thinking there could be any answer but yes: *You were five years old, Estella . . . surely you didn't think I was making you a promise about your future.* In fact, she *had* thought he'd made her a promise, but she'd realized at that moment that her future was somewhere other than the plant. The sign "Diamond and Sons" meant what it said.

She had believed—and still believed—that she was in some way her father's favourite, but she'd never really got over that he'd said no to her without considering her proposal. He'd said he wanted her to continue with her education, but then he hadn't questioned her choice to go to normal school and the local college instead of going away to a good university, perhaps in the East. If her parents believed she had the potential to become the family genius, they hadn't done much to encourage her, and they might as well have let her join her brothers at the factory. She wondered if her father would admit he'd been unfair if she were to get up right now and march across the hall and ask him. She no longer thought about working at the plant, but still, she'd have liked to know, just as she'd have liked to know more about Salina. It was easy for her father to say *All in the past*, but was that ever true?

The room was freezing cold. Even with the extra blanket she was shivering, and she wondered if the hotel had any heat at all. She rolled over and sank into a dip in the middle of the bed, which somehow made her feel warmer. When she finally drifted off, she was jolted awake again minutes later from a dream in which there was an earthquake and Salina's teapot was rocking and threatening to tumble from its shelf. At first she thought the dream had woken her, but then she realized a radio was playing Hawaiian music in the room next door.

She lay there listening, trying to see in the darkness, and wondered what would have happened in her dream if "Ukulele Lady" hadn't woken her up. She waited for the sound of someone rising next door—bedsprings, footsteps, a toilet flushing—but there was only the radio. She slipped her arm out from under the covers and knocked on the wall but there was no response. The radio played until morning, as though whoever was in the room had forgotten all about it, and Estella barely slept.

They left Lake Claire the next morning, and when they got home in the late afternoon Oliver immediately drove out to the plant. Gladys had dropped in to show Beatrice a new quilt pattern, and Estella assured the two of them that Allen Foster was neither shifty nor feckless, and was instead a family man and an entrepreneur with a good idea, as far as she could see. Besides, she said, when had anyone been able to take advantage of Oliver Diamond? She told them they'd be ecstatic when they saw the lake and the brand-new Lake Claire Bungalows. Beatrice said she could not imagine herself being ecstatic about a cabin in the woods, but since the finished project was a long way off she could let the matter rest and hope that nothing would come of it except perhaps a few more fishing trips for the men.

"Estella," she said, "look at this pattern Gladys found. Maybe the two of us could make a quilt."

Estella had no interest in sewing or quilts, and it was clear Beatrice did not expect a response.

THE COTTAGE CONSTRUCTION began the following spring. Oliver tried to encourage Jack to assume the foreman's role for the bricklaying, but he wasn't interested, and so Oliver took it on himself. When he was preparing to go north for the Victoria Day weekend, he asked Estella if she would like to come along once again, she assumed because he saw the usefulness of having an advocate. She was more than happy to oblige.

Allen Foster had set up a bush camp at the building site, and Oliver was to stay with him in his tent, which had Beatrice shaking her head—the idea of Oliver Diamond in a tent! Oliver suggested that Estella stay at The Travellers—she could take his car back and forth from the site to the village every day—but she, too, insisted on staying in the camp with the men, and pointed out that, of the two of them, she was the experienced camper, not to mention significantly younger than he was. The week before the trip, she went out and bought herself a pair of Red Wing boots, wool work socks, and long underwear because Allen Foster had warned them it would be cold. She also bought her own white canvas tent and sleeping gear. Her mother was mortified by what Estella was planning to wear, and by the idea of her sleeping outdoors, and so close to the building crew, even if her father was going to be there. She used the word "disgraceful."

"Those look like men's boots," she said, frowning at the pile of gear on her parlour floor.

"Exactly," Estella said. "They don't make them for women. Anyway, stop worrying. It's not like it's my first time camping."

She got a bit of a shock, though, when she realized that Foster's idea of camping was a little more rustic than what she was used to. He and his men—three of them—had cleared a spot in the bush and pitched their tents there, then built an open fire for cooking and keeping warm. There was no picnic table, just a few planks over a couple of upright logs upon which their cooking utensils rested. There were no toilets. "Plenty of bush for privacy, just don't go too far and get lost," Foster joked when Estella asked.

Oliver tried once again to get her to go to The Travellers.

"I will if you will," she said, and of course Oliver wasn't going to the hotel, so they both stayed. She put on her wool hat and her mitts, and she got her new tent out and strung it on the poles Foster had readied for her, respectfully placed a short distance from the men's tents. Then she blew up her air mattress and rolled out her sleeping bag, and by the time she was done, it was already getting dark. When she came out of her tent to join the others, she saw that one of the men was cooking over the fire. For supper they ate rabbit and canned potatoes and peas, and they sat on camp stools close to the fire in order to stay warm. Estella wondered if she would be expected to wash dishes, but they all took care of their own and the cook rinsed the pots. In a way, it was as though she wasn't there.

It snowed that first night, and Estella was so cold in her tent she wondered if she'd make it until morning. As she lay awake in her inadequate sleeping bag, worrying about whether her septuagenarian father was warm enough, she couldn't get the picture of the rabbit on a spit out of her mind. It had looked too much like a rabbit. She got up and put on every bit of extra clothing she'd brought with her, and still she couldn't sleep. She didn't stop shivering until morning, when the men got a good fire going for breakfast and she had her hands around a mug of hot coffee. If her father had spent an uncomfortable night, he didn't say so. They all sat by the fire, the new snow melting within the ring of its warmth, and Allen Foster said to her, "Cold night. Hope you have a good sleeping bag."

Estella tried not to let on how miserable she'd been.

There were six of them around the fire, Oliver and Foster and Estella, and the three men who were helping with the construction, who paid little attention to her. She assumed they were local. Oliver and Allen Foster rolled out the drawings of the cottage development on their knees and discussed the placement of the various buildings, the two-bedroom cottages along the lakefront, and the smaller ones behind, nearer the road to the village. Foster said he was thankful Oliver had convinced him to include running water and a septic system because it would be a lot harder to install once the cabins were built. They raised their coffee cups to indoor plumbing, and Estella wondered if there was something stronger than coffee in them. She noted that, to Foster and his workmen, the cottages were still cabins.

After breakfast, the men went to work clearing bush from the building site, and Estella walked toward the village along the water's edge, the sound of chainsaws cutting in and out behind her. The ice on the lake was breaking up, and she saw that it had splintered into needle-like crystals that were piled all along the shore, and the water was lapping and washing the crystals back and forth. They tinkled like wind chimes with each lap of a wave. She pulled her wool hat tightly down over her ears, and she eventually came to the public beach. There was not a soul on it. The lifeguard's chair had snow still piled around its legs, and behind it was a half-finished building with a wooden deck, a new change house, perhaps. She could see a marina or fishing pier down the beach, and beyond it was a small railway station. The village was across the road. The whole place, including The Travellers Hotel, looked deserted.

She wasn't sure what to do. She walked along the lake, the crystals tinkling the whole way and the icy wind stinging her cheeks. When she came to the fishing pier and the railway station, she turned around and walked back toward the lifeguard's chair again, wishing she hadn't come so far from the campfire. She crossed the frozen sand, her feet numb in her Red Wings, and climbed the steps to the deck of the unfinished change house, where she tucked herself against a bare plywood wall to get out of the wind. If she waited a while, she thought, the sun would be higher and the air might warm up.

There was a boardwalk from the village to the beach and she heard hollow footsteps coming toward her. A boy wearing a winter parka came into view from around the side of the building, and he was a carrying something. He climbed the steps to the deck and handed her what she saw now was a Thermos. When he tipped his parka hood back, she recognized the boy who cleared tables in the hotel restaurant.

"What's this?" she asked, trying to keep her teeth from chattering.

"Hot tea," the boy said. "My mom sent it. She seen you walking and said it's too bad you come on such a nasty weekend, and then it snowed, and you must be cold."

Estella took the Thermos and poured herself some tea, trying not to be critical of the boy's grammatical errors, and then she placed the Thermos at her feet.

"Well, thank your mother very much," Estella said. "I think she might have saved my life." She wrapped her hands around the cup and took a sip of the hot, sweetened tea and immediately felt the chill diminish.

"What's your name?" she asked the boy.

"Peter," the boy said. "Peter Boone."

"And you're what . . . ten years old? Grade five in school?" The boy nodded.

She wasn't sure how to introduce herself to a child. Her nieces and nephews all called her "Auntie."

"My name is Miss Diamond," she said, sounding, she thought, like the schoolteacher she was. She told him where she lived, to the south, in Regina, the provincial capital.

Peter Boone said that he had been there, to a boxing club.

"Really?" she said. "There's a boxing club? I didn't know that."

"Yes, Miss," he said. "I've been there to a camp for boys with promise. That's what they said, that I showed promise. My uncle paid. We got to see a Golden Gloves bout at the club, but the contender got knocked out in the third round. They said he was off that night. He got food poisoning, they said, from eating Chinese food. Chinese duck, I think they said."

Estella studied Peter Boone and tried to imagine him as a boy with boxing promise. It was hard to tell under his winter coat, but she remembered how small and thin he was from the hotel.

"You do boxing?" she said. "A young boy like you?"

"Yes, Miss," he said. "I have a training program. I ordered it through the mail."

She pictured the back of a comic book and the ad with a skinny man on the beach surrounded by bullies. What a peculiar boy this was. It was funny, the way he called her Miss, like a little English boy from a private school, when he was the farthest thing from it, and likely went to a one-room school in the bush and took a peanut butter sandwich for lunch.

"Where do you go to school?" she asked.

He said the name of a town she hadn't heard of. "On the school bus," he said.

She nodded, remembering the bus that had collected him from the hotel. She finished her tea and put the empty cup back on the Thermos.

"Well, Mr. Boone, I'd best be getting back to camp. My father is helping with the construction up the way."

"I know," he said, and she wondered how.

"You can walk with me if you like," she said, "and scare the bears off."

They walked down to the water, and when they stopped to

look at the ice crystals lapping back and forth along the shore, he returned once again to the subject of boxing and told her that when he grew up he was going to be a professional.

"Lightweight, they say, unless I grow, but I probably won't. My dad was only 160 pounds. He died in the war."

"I'm sorry to hear that," she said. "Two of my brothers were in the war, although they both came back." Then she said, "You want to be a boxer like Joe Louis, you mean?" and he said, yes, like Joe Louis, but more like Billie Hughes, because he was a lightweight.

Estella didn't know who Billie Hughes was.

A Canadian, he told her.

Then he said that his uncle drove him into Prince Albert once a week, to a boxing club there. Between times, he trained in his room at the hotel. He and his mother, he said, lived at the hotel.

"What do you do," Estella asked, "to train to be a boxer?"

Footwork, he told her. And different punches, like jabs and hooks. And he went running every day.

"But you're only ten years old," she said. She'd never heard of a ten-year-old training like that.

"Yes, Miss," he said seriously. "But you have to start young. I'm planning to grow, but if I don't there's bantamweight, 118 pounds."

He was so serious. She couldn't laugh, although she wanted to. "You must be good at boxing, then," she said.

"Yes, Miss. I am. Them at the boxing club said so."

When they were at the end of the public beach he said, "I know a different way. It'll be warmer. I run this way sometimes." He cut into the bush on a narrow trail that Estella might not have noticed. The trail was wide enough for only one person so she followed him, wondering about the possibility of bears, but distracted from fear by the beauty of the new snow, heavy on the branches of the spruce trees. The trail was so narrow that the boy often brushed against a branch and the snow fell, and the branch sprang back, free of the weight. They walked without talking now since they were single file, and Estella hoped the boy knew where he was going.

He stopped abruptly and said, "Just ahead, the trail will come out right by your camp. You'll see it. I'd best be getting home. My mom will be wondering." And he squeezed by Estella on the trail and went back the way they'd come, carrying the Thermos. Estella was left standing alone in the bush.

"I'll see you again sometime," she called. "Thank your mother for the tea."

"Yes, Miss," he said, and she thought again of an English schoolboy, only one with deplorable grammar.

She stood alone, surrounded by trees and snow, and wondered if Peter Boone could possibly have played a trick and left her stranded on a snowy trail to nowhere. But then she heard voices, and a chainsaw started up, so she carried on and, sure enough, the trail left the bush not far from the camp. She could see the construction site, with fewer trees standing than when she'd left. One of the men was lopping branching off a fallen tree with an axe.

She wasn't cold anymore. The tea and the walk in the bush had warmed her up. Her feet were still numb, though, so she sat on a log by the fire while Foster and her father discussed pipes and trenching, and her father made notes on his pad of paper. Later, she heard them talking about boats and outboard motors and the potential for a golf course, and she thought this must have been what her father was like when he was planning the brick factory with Nathaniel Thick.

That evening, Allen Foster handed her a ledger and asked her to check the figures. She sat by the fire and went over the columns, adding and subtracting numbers until she was sure they were correct, and then she handed the ledger back. She thought she saw a look of pride on her father's face.

At bedtime, Foster handed out extra blankets he'd come up with, and Estella slept well.

THE NEXT SUMMER, Estella passed on the Recreation Society camping trip to the Maritimes that she'd been looking forward to, and instead travelled to Lake Claire every weekend with her father from May until freeze-up. She became the project's unofficial bookkeeper and her mother's reassurance that Oliver wasn't going to kill himself accidentally with an axe, although Beatrice still disapproved of Oliver taking his daughter into the bush with only men for company. Sometimes she went for walks on the trails in the bush and more than once saw a bear, which she didn't tell her mother. The Diamond siblings were all good swimmers thanks to the lessons they'd had at the YMCA, and once the water in the lake warmed up, she went for long swims by herself along the shore before heading back to the camp to warm up in front of the fire. When she and Oliver got home after one of their weekends at the lake, Beatrice always said they smelled like a campfire. She threw their clothes in the wash as soon as they were in the door and sent Estella upstairs to shampoo her hair so it wouldn't be ruined by the smoke.

On one such occasion they were at the dinner table on a Sunday evening in June with Mathew and Fay and their two youngest, one of them a sixteen-year-old girl named Caroline, who clearly thought Estella was out of her mind to want to sleep in a tent. Oliver and Estella had just returned from the lake, and Estella had not yet had a bath. When Beatrice mentioned her hair for the third time and said that she was going to have to wear a wig for the rest of her life if she didn't start talking care of it, Estella told her mother to stop talking about her as though she were the same as age as Caroline.

"I'm almost thirty years old, in case you haven't noticed," she said. "I think that makes me an adult."

"I won't take that as an insult," said Caroline, "but I agree with Nana. How can you stand having no running water?"

"Not to mention the workmen," said Beatrice. "It's disgraceful, if you ask me. I don't care how modern you think you are."

When the meal was over, Estella began to gather plates and cutlery and leftover food, all the time wishing that her mother would stop thinking she had some special kind of virtue and needed protection from strange men. She wasn't sure what she'd done to make her mother think she might fall from grace so easily. She'd been virtuous all through the war, even as she went dancing with other single teachers and resisted the advances of soldiers and airmen who begged for secret engagements and all that went with them. One of Estella's friends had fallen for it and found herself pregnant, and she'd lost her teaching job while her fly-boy fiancé had disappeared. To give him the benefit of doubt, he might have died in the war, but why had he never written, not once, after he left? In spite of her mother's apparent lack of trust in her judgment, Estella had been a lot smarter than her friend. As she dumped a load of cutlery in the sink in the kitchen, she wondered if she should have gone to a hotel with that married physics teacher in Mexico, as he had suggested, and given her mother something real to worry about.

She called her goodbyes from the kitchen when she heard everyone going to the door, and then she filled the sink with dishes and soapy water and waited for her mother to come and wash so she could dry, which was how they always did the dishes, and had done them for the last twenty years.

When Beatrice came into the kitchen carrying the dessert plates, Estella said, "Why don't I wash and you dry tonight?"

"Why mess with a good system?" her mother said, and edged her away from the sink, saying, "Come on, scoot over."

When the dishes were done and put away, Beatrice said she had a bit of a headache and she was going upstairs to have a bath, if Estella didn't want the tub first.

Estella told her to go ahead, she had work to do for school the next day.

Oliver left to make a quick trip out to the plant, and Estella found herself alone in the dining room with a pile of math quizzes on the table in front of her. There was a girl in her grade eleven class—Cora Hamish was her name—who had not gotten a single question wrong on a test all year. In addition to being a math whiz, she played the piano and was constantly winning competitions at the Conservatory and getting her name in the paper. Estella always looked forward to grading Cora's tests in hopes of finding her first mistake. Once, in the staff room, Estella had said, "The absence of failure is not good for a teenager."

"You're just mean," one of the other teachers had said to her. They all thought Cora Hamish was on the road to a brilliant career. If not as a concert pianist, then something else. A brain surgeon or an architect.

She found Cora's quiz in the pile and graded it: 100 percent. Estella couldn't even find a place in her method to deduct a point or two.

As she went through the rest of the quizzes, she wondered about another piano player, the one who had propositioned her in this very dining room on the night of her parents' thirty-fifth anniversary party. She couldn't remember his name, or if she had ever known it, but he probably *was* a concert pianist by now. He'd been arrogant enough to get what he wanted.

Well, good luck with that, Cora, she thought. She did not believe Cora had enough of that same brand of arrogance.

She looked up from her grading when she heard Beatrice coming down the stairs. She had her nightgown on and her book in her hand.

"Feeling better?" Estella asked.

"A little, yes," Beatrice said. "I think I'll make a pot of tea." Then she again insisted Estella's hair had the whole house smelling like smoke, and said, "I still cannot understand why you want to be with your father and those men."

"Maybe you'd like me to become a nun," Estella said.

"I think nuns are expected to be Catholic," Beatrice replied, and Estella was reminded that her mother did, on rare occasions, display a sense of humour.

Beatrice went to the kitchen and was there for a long time. Estella had heard the water running, but not the kettle whistling.

She was about to go and check on her mother when she came back to the dining room and said, "Oh. Estella. You're here," as though she had been looking for her.

"What's up?" Estella asked.

"The strangest thing has happened," Beatrice said.

"What is it?" Estella asked.

Instead of answering, Beatrice walked right by her and went back upstairs.

That was odd, Estella thought.

When she was finished grading, she went to the kitchen and saw that Beatrice had filled a cooking pot with water instead of the kettle. It was still boiling away on the stove, and when Estella looked inside the pot, she saw her mother's book floating. She turned off the burner and set out some towels on the counter for the book, thinking her mother must have accidentally dropped it but not sure why she would have walked away and left it there. She stood in the kitchen studying the soggy book on the counter, perplexed by the incident. When she heard her father at the door, she scooped up the book and dropped it into the garbage. Later, she took the bag out to the bin in the alley.

The next morning she dressed and left for school, and when she got home at the end of the day her mother asked if she had seen her book, and Estella said no, and the book wasn't mentioned again. She was unsettled by the possibility that the book had not just accidentally fallen into the cooking pot. She wondered if something was wrong with her mother. She'd recovered from the vague nervous illness she'd had when Jack was wounded, but maybe it was Oliver's cottage project, and she was not dealing well with being alone in the house when Estella and her father were away.

The next time Estella and Oliver went to the lake, Estella called Jack—who was on his own now, Phyllis had left him for good—and asked if he would stay with Beatrice for the weekend.

"Tell her it's for her cooking," she said. "She knows you can't boil an egg."

She decided, too, that she ought to take more seriously Beatrice's worries about the men in the bush, even if they were unfounded. There were a lot of men in the camp now that the building was underway, and she would likely have the same worries if she had a daughter. She enlisted her father's help to assure Beatrice that the workmen were all perfectly respectful, which was the truth, and Beatrice seemed relieved to hear Oliver say it. Before they left, she handed Estella a scarf and told her to tie her hair up, it might help protect it from the smoke.

A few hours into the journey Oliver stopped for gas, and he got out to chat with the young attendant while Estella stayed in the car. The attendant filled the tank and then washed the windows, and when he leaned over the hood on the passenger side with his squeegee, he winked at Estella. Immediately, she heard her father say, "Hey, hey, mind your manners," and she thought again of the hired piano player at her parents' party, and how her father had told him in so many words to keep his hands off the boss's daughter. She could almost hear him doing the same with the workmen in the camp.

When Oliver got back in the car she said, "Did you put the fear of God in him?"

"Probably," her father said.

"I am old enough to look out for myself, you know," she said.

"True," Oliver said. "Probably."

He started the car and they were on their way again.

—

IT WAS IN 1939, when Estella was fifteen years old, that Oliver had hired the piano player. The Diamonds were not in the habit of entertaining, but Oliver had decided to throw Beatrice a surprise party for their anniversary because the Depression appeared to be over and he thought everyone needed an excuse to celebrate. The oldest three Diamond brothers were married by then, so Oliver had enlisted Jack and Estella to help with the preparations, although it was mostly Estella, because Jack had no useful opinions when it came to food or music or who should be invited.

On the day of the party Theo and his wife Gladys were to get Beatrice out of the way for the afternoon by saying they needed her to babysit their two children for a few hours. They were then to take her to a salon for a hair appointment, present her with a new dress (chosen by Oliver with Estella's help) and her best shoes, collected from her closet, and tell her Oliver was taking her out to a restaurant. Oliver would pick her up in the early evening, then pretend he had forgotten something, and when they arrived at the house, Beatrice would find it filled with party guests: couples from the business community and her church and clubs, and of course the whole Diamond family.

As Beatrice walked in the door to a chorus of "Surprise!" Estella watched her mother and tried to tell if she'd guessed what Oliver had been up to. If she had, she was a good actor. She looked positively stunned until one of the grandchildren said, "Are you really surprised, Nana?" and then Beatrice said, "You mean there's no restaurant? You sneaky people!" and she began to circulate among the guests, greeting every single one of them, all the time expressing her amazement that Oliver had managed to do it all without giving a thing away. Estella waited for her mother to get to her and ask what part she'd played—quite a big one, Estella thought—and compliment the new outfit she'd bought all on her own, a skirt and pale-blue sweater with pearl buttons, but it was taking forever for her mother to get through all the guests.

When Estella grew tired of waiting, she placed herself against a wall in the dining room so she could watch the musician who had come with the piano her father had rented for the evening. He was young, not much older than Jack, and was a music student at the College. Estella knew her mother had played the piano when she was a girl in Ontario, but she had never suggested her children do so, perhaps because the first four of them had been boys and she'd given up by the time Estella came along. Estella wished she hadn't. It seemed to her that the musician was able to make magic out of the long row of black and white keys. He hummed to himself as he played popular songs by the likes of Glenn Miller and Larry Clinton and Bing Crosby, and he kept looking up at Estella. He was making her nervous, so she moved around the room until he couldn't see her anymore, but she could still watch him.

Once all the guests had drinks in their hands, the caterers brought trays of hot and cold finger food from the kitchen and laid it out on the dining room table, which had been pushed against the wall to make room for the piano. Before Oliver invited people to eat he made a speech. The musician stopped playing and everyone fell silent as Oliver spoke about thirty-five years of marriage and how Beatrice had always stood by him, through good times and bad. The last decade had been especially hard for everyone, he said, but the brick business had survived the Depression, and his sons were grown up, and he had been blessed with wonderful children, and now grandchildren. He made a toast to Beatrice and the family she had raised, and her many years of support and loyalty. Everyone raised their glasses and toasted Beatrice, and then the future.

By this time, Estella was annoyed that her mother had not yet sought her out, and she hadn't had a single compliment on her new outfit. To top it off, everyone and his pet donkey had earned a mention in her father's speech except her, when she had been his co-conspirator and Girl Friday since Jack had turned out to be hopeless. She'd chosen the flower arrangements, gone with her father to select invitations, helped make the guest list, and addressed every envelope, including one to his old business partner in Texas. Since her father didn't have a mailing address for him, she'd even gone to the library to track down the address of his company's head office in Houston. It all made her so irritable that she looked at the teapot on its shelf in the corner and thought, *What about Salina, shouldn't she get some thanks?* She knew from the letters that Salina had been Oliver's first champion, even before there was a Diamond brick factory.

After Oliver's speech, it was obvious that everyone wanted to hear from Beatrice, so she reluctantly took the floor to thank him, and then thank everyone for coming. Estella was jarred out of her bored annoyance when she heard her name. "I know Estella had something to do with this," Beatrice was saying. "Estella, wave your hand so people can see you." Estella waved even though it made her self-conscious, and then her mother said, "Oh, what a lovely outfit, Estella. That's new, isn't it," and she wanted to die on the spot. When her mother quit talking and the party started up again, she considered sneaking upstairs to her room for the rest of the evening, but that possibility soon dissipated when the grandchildren were put to sleep upstairs, one of them in her bed.

Once the children were settled, Estella's sisters-in-law and the other women moved into the sitting room and the men gathered in the parlour, where her father was serving brandy from a cut-glass decanter. Estella was still watching the musician from her spot in the dining room. When he took a break, he swivelled on the bench and saw that she was there. He looked around to make sure he wouldn't be overheard, and then he suggested that the two of them slip outside together. It was the first time a boy had said anything like that to her. What did he have in mind? It couldn't be good.

She walked away from him with her face burning, and went to hear what the women were talking about. Nothing of interest— their children mostly, the scamp who'd got himself in a pickle the week before by taking the milkman's money, the little Shirley Temple who had decided to lop off her curls with her mother's sewing scissors.

"Estella," one of Beatrice's friends from the church said, "you're getting so grown up. What plans do you have for the future? Girls seem to be planning careers these days, rather than their weddings."

She'd always assumed she'd go to work at the plant, as had her brothers, in spite of its name being Diamond and Sons.

"I'll do something at the brick plant," she said. "Wherever Father thinks I'm needed."

"She's very good at school," Beatrice said. "Better than any of the boys were."

Estella knew what was coming next, the story of how they'd discovered she could read when she was only five years old. Sure enough, Beatrice told them how Estella had picked up Oliver's newspaper and read an obituary aloud to them, and it turned out to be the obituary of a child, and Estella had put the paper down and asked, "Is it true that children can die?" It always sounded as though that was the point of the story, but really her mother was bragging that Estella had learned to read so young.

She left the women and saw that the piano player had helped himself to a plate of food and was now sitting on his bench eating. His eyes followed Estella as she tried to find a spot out of his line of vision. Then Jack came to stand beside her and he nudged her in the ribs and said, "Ooh, Nelly's caught someone's eye. Better watch out."

"Shut up," Estella said, and once again she felt herself blushing. The whole family was out to embarrass her, she thought as she followed Jack to the parlour. The French doors were open and the two of them stood together in the entrance to the room. The men by now had had several drinks and were discussing the possibility of war in Europe. The non-aggression pact between the Soviets and the Germans had just been signed, with all indications that Hitler was up to something. One of her father's business colleagues asked if he was worried, having sons who were the right age for military service, especially Jack, who wasn't married, but her father said King George wisely did not see the need for Canadian casualties in a war aimed at putting Germany in its place, in spite of Mackenzie King's announcement that Canada would support Britain if it came to that.

"It will not happen," her father said, and Estella was relieved, because there was so much talk about war in the news.

Then Jack himself spoke up and said that a war might be just the thing to fix the economy.

Estella couldn't believe it, that anyone could think war was a good idea. "Since when do you know anything about the economy?" she asked Jack, but he shushed her because he was listening to the conversation.

She persisted and said, "You can't really think a war would be good for the country."

It was as though she hadn't said anything at all as Jack left her and found a chair among the men, who began to argue about Canada's responsibilities toward Britain. The room was full of smoke from their cigars and pipes and cigarettes. Estella's feelings were hurt that Jack had just walked away from her, without giving her opinion any consideration at all.

From where she was standing, she could see into the dining room. The caterers were now clearing away the food, and the piano player was back at work, playing "Indian Love Call," a popular song from the movies. He periodically glanced up at her, and she grew curious. Did he think she was pretty? Interesting? Someone he'd like to get to know? She got brave enough to stand near the piano again, and he asked her if she wanted to try a few chords. She sat down on the bench beside him, and he taught her a simplified version of the bass line of "Heart and Soul," and they attempted to play it together but Estella couldn't get past the first few bars without getting mixed up. She kept looking at his hands instead of her own. Before she knew it, she felt her thigh touching his on the bench. When she kept hitting the wrong keys, he picked up her hand and placed her fingers in the correct position.

Her father appeared by the bench. He had a cheque in his hand.

"I think the lesson is over for the night," he said, dropping the cheque onto the keyboard. "No need to stay any longer. I believe the caterers have gone. Estella, you can go and see if your mother needs anything in the kitchen."

The piano player collected the cheque and quickly took his leave, as though he were the boy caught stealing the milkman's money. Estella felt like a twelve-year-old.

"We weren't doing anything," she said to her father after the musician was gone.

"Oh, I know that," he said, "but he was a bit cocky, don't you think."

How was he cocky? she wondered. All he'd done was what they'd hired him to, with a little piano lesson thrown in.

When she tried to join her father and the other men in the parlour to see how the war discussion was progressing, her father said to her, again, "Estella, go to the kitchen would you, and see if there's anything that needs doing there. Your mother would appreciate it."

By this time Jack was in the thick of the conversation. Estella knew there was nothing that needed doing in the kitchen—that's what the caterers were there for—but she went anyway because it was obvious she had been dismissed. Clearly war was not an appropriate topic for women, and apparently that's what she was now.

Her mother wasn't in the kitchen. Estella found a tea towel and wiped down the counters even though the caterers had left everything spotlessly clean. When she looked out the kitchen window, she saw that the piano player was still there, standing in the garden with a cigarette, and she threw the tea towel down and went out the back door and asked him if he had a smoke for her. She led him to a dark spot behind the garage so they wouldn't be seen. As he lit a cigarette for her, he said he'd been hoping she would see him and come outside.

"Well, don't get your hopes up for anything else," she said as she puffed on the smoke, trying to act as though she knew what she was talking about and smoked cigarettes all the time.

He began to hum "Heart and Soul," and then he sang the first few lines about falling in love and stealing a kiss, and she said, "What do you think, you're Larry Clinton or maybe Clark Gable now?" She thought she was being funny, but she had no experience with boys. The piano player stopped humming, and then he stepped closer to her, and he dropped his cigarette and stubbed it out under his foot. She knew what was coming and she didn't resist. He tipped her chin and then he kissed her full on the lips. It was so dark she wasn't sure how he found her mouth. He tasted like cigarette smoke. She felt his hands on her waist, and when they moved down and began to lift her skirt, a little at a time, almost imperceptibly, she pulled away.

"Stop it," she said, not knowing what else to say.

He left then. Just walked away, out the gate and down the alley. She could hear his footsteps on the hard-packed clay on the other side of the fence. Maybe her father was right. He was cocky.

She went back inside, remembering the feel of his lips on hers, his hands on her hips. When her mother smelled the smoke, Estella told her that she'd been visiting with the caterers before they left, and they'd been smoking in the yard. Beatrice expressed the opinion that they shouldn't have been, but then she was distracted by a woman in a coral dress looking for directions to what she called the powder room. There was no powder room in the Diamond house, Estella thought. There was an upstairs bathroom.

The party broke up soon after, with everyone leaving in good spirits, saying how wonderful it had been to have a reason to be happy again. Oliver and Beatrice stood together in the foyer to say goodbye to the guests, and when there were only Diamonds left, Gladys and Fay prepared to retrieve their sleeping children from the upstairs bedrooms, but Beatrice said, no, let them sleep, and she sent their parents home without them.

Estella was not ready for bed, and besides, there was a child asleep in her room. She wasn't sure what to do with herself. She noticed the piano's white keys shining under the dining room light and she had the crazy idea that she would magically know how to play both parts of "Heart and Soul" if she tried. She wanted to sit down on the bench and bang it out as loud as she could, whether she hit the right keys or not. Of course she would never do such a thing. She could imagine the disapproval. She wondered what it would have been like to grow up with the rebellious Salina as a mother instead of Beatrice, and then she felt guilty for thinking of Salina twice now on the night that had been so carefully planned to honour her mother.

Before her parents went to bed, they had a cup of tea in the parlour and Estella heard them talking about Nathaniel Thick in Texas, from whom Oliver had not heard.

"It's understandable," he said. "A long way to come for a party. I don't think he would bear any hard feelings." Then he added, "It couldn't stay Diamond and Thick forever, could it."

Estella hadn't known there was a time when the company had been called anything other than Diamond and Sons.

When just she and Jack were left downstairs, she told him what their father had said and asked him if he had known the plant was once called Diamond and Thick.

Jack shrugged, and she thought again that he was no longer interested in what she had to say. She had become his little sister, just as she had always been to the others. He went upstairs, and Estella made herself a bed on the couch.

In the morning, she was wakened early by a three-year-old niece poking her face with a kitchen spatula. She got up and helped her mother give the children their breakfast before their parents came to collect them, and after they were gone the rental company collected the piano. Except for the elaborate bouquet of flowers on the dining table, the house looked as it had before the party. When just Beatrice and Estella were left in the dining room, her mother said, "You're turning into a young lady, Estella. Everyone remarked on it. And I believe you caught the attention of that musician your father hired."

There was a pause, and then Estella knew what the real topic of the conversation was going to be. Her mother had noticed the piano player watching her the night before, or, more likely, her father had told her about the two of them on the bench. She began with a series of warnings: A girl's reputation can be ruined in an instant. You have your whole life ahead of you so don't get distracted by young men who have no intention of putting a ring on your finger. Don't trust any man with a wandering eye. On and on, with no useful information about what Estella really wanted to know and wasn't about to ask. She didn't even know what words to use. She struggled to think of a way to escape her mother, and it came when her father entered the room. He tried to leave again when he realized what his wife and daughter were discussing, but Estella took the opportunity to say, "We're not talking about anything important," and she left the room instead. She heard her mother say, "I think I made my point" as Estella fled to the backyard.

She walked out to the alley and then up and down the length of it. She didn't know what point her mother thought she had made with that speech about rings and intentions. She was fifteen years old. She'd rather have a boyfriend with a wandering eye than one with a ring. She decided her mother didn't know what she was talking about. When she thought enough time had passed, she went back in the house and avoided her for the rest of the day.

A week later, a letter arrived from a woman named Betty Ellen Thick in Texas, and Oliver received the news that his former partner had passed away several years earlier. Estella was surprised that her father seemed to be so affected by this news as he hadn't seen the man for many years, since before she was born. When she had the house to herself she went on a search and found the letter in his writing desk.

Dear Mr. Diamond,
I am sorry to inform you that Nathaniel died by his own hand seven years ago. The Great Depression laid him very low. He never spoke unkindly of you, although I'll say right here, Mr. Diamond, that I believe it was a dirty trick you pulled up there in Canada. Nate did not see it that way and always said, that's business and I'm a businessman.

My congratulations to you and your wife on your long and happy marriage.
Sincerely,
Betty Ellen Thick

Estella wondered, what trick?

The next morning at breakfast, while they were eating corn-flakes, she told Jack what she'd read in the letter. It was Sunday morning and Beatrice was at church. They assumed their father had gone to the plant.

"It's like that, isn't it," Jack said.

"What is?"

"Business. You don't get rich by being the man everyone likes."

"But people do like Father," Estella said. "And we aren't rich. It's not like we live in a manor house. We don't even have a pow-der room."

Jack finished his cornflakes and then picked up the bowl and drank the milk that was left. After he'd set it down again, he said, "I asked Theo what happened between Father and that Nathaniel Thick. He said there was something called a shotgun clause in the original agreement that allowed one partner to set a price and force the other out. They'd both agreed to the clause, so there wasn't anything illegal about it. It could even have backfired and Nathaniel Thick would have ended up with the business, but Father counted on his partner to walk away, and he did. There. Now you know. Are you satisfied?"

Just then Beatrice came in the front door, and the shotgun clause and the house's lack of a powder room were forgotten. Beatrice stood in the door to the dining room looking blanched, the hat she always wore to church in her hand.

"Can it be true?" she said.

Jack said, "Can what be true?"

"That war has broken out in Europe."

Jack immediately went to the radio and turned it on. An announcer was talking about the German invasion of Poland. Jack said he was going out to the plant to tell his father in case he hadn't heard, and Beatrice sat down on the sofa and stared at the radio, still holding her hat. Jack left, and then he was back a minute later because the car was gone and he had no way to get to the plant.

"Never mind," Beatrice said. "He'll have heard. Everyone's heard."

"Canada's not going to war," Estella said. "There's no point. Father said that."

"I think we will learn otherwise," said Beatrice, and it was odd to hear her mother say something in opposition to what her father believed.

But it turned out that Beatrice was right.

WITHIN DAYS, BRITAIN and France declared war on Germany, and it didn't take long for Mackenzie King to announce that Canada was at war. Then Jack came home with the news that he and Andrew had gone to the Armoury and enlisted in the Reserve.

Beatrice just stared at him, as though she could not believe what she had heard.

"But Andrew's married," Oliver said. "He's a family man."

"Well, that's what we've done," said Jack. "It's war. The rules are different now."

"You're eighteen years old," Oliver said, his face colouring with anger. "What do you know about the rules? What is wrong with the two of you?"

Jack tried to say that there was little chance of them doing anything other than learning to clean weapons and march around the parade grounds at the Armoury, but Oliver kept repeating that he was eighteen years old and knew nothing. Estella covered her ears to block the sound of their raised voices, and finally Beatrice spoke and told them both to stop, and no more was said.

For a time, it looked as though Jack was right. They were given uniforms and weapons and they went to the Armoury every day, but no news came that their regiment was being called into service. But then word did come, and off they both went, first to a training base near home, and then to Nova Scotia, where they eventually boarded the *Empress of Russia* bound for Britain. Oliver and Beatrice were in disbelief. Two of their sons had gone off in uniform, possibly to see active duty in Europe, and one of them was married. It was as though the world had been turned upside down again just when they thought it had righted itself.

It was shortly after her brothers' regiment left for Britain that Estella made her case for a job at Diamond and Sons. It was 1941 and Canada had been at war for two years. Estella was seventeen years old and about to finish high school. Diamond and Sons was now producing firebrick for warships, and Estella decided that she should join the war effort too. Women everywhere were donning overalls and learning to use industrial equipment. She could do the same.

She was not expecting the reaction she got when she asked her father for a job. He was sitting at his writing desk, as always in his tweed suit, and he gave the impression that Estella was wasting his time when he had little to waste.

"I'm good at math," she tried, thinking he was objecting to his daughter working in the clay pits, or the pressing shop. "I could learn to do the books."

Oliver shook his head and barely looked up from the papers on his desk.

"You don't just *learn to do the books* like in the old days," he said. "You go to school and become a bookkeeper or an accountant."

"But this is wartime," she said, remembering Jack's words. "The rules are different now."

"They are, are they?" her father said, finally looking up at her. "And what am I supposed to do with Colin Barrett? Let him go, to make a place for you, a girl who doesn't actually need a job?"

She thought back to all the times he'd indulged it when she'd said she would one day run the brick factory. She reminded him of it.

He said, "You were five years old, Estella. You tell five-year-olds about Santa Claus and the Easter Bunny. Surely you don't think I was making you a promise about your future. Now forget this nonsense. I have work to do."

"Well, what about Salina?" she said, before she could think better of it. Then she stuck out her chin and brazenly quoted from one of the letters, words that he had written: *"To think that a woman such as yourself would be hampered . . . it seems neither possible nor right in this modern time."*

He stood from his chair and she thought he was going to leap across the desk at her.

"Go upstairs," he said. "To your room. And do not speak to me of her again."

She didn't move. It was as though she'd forgotten how to move, until he said, or rather shouted, "Estella. Did you hear me? Go. Now."

She left the room in tears and ran into her mother on her way up the stairs. Beatrice wanted to know what was wrong but Estella pushed past her and threw herself on her bed. She stayed there crying until her mother came knocking to tell her it was suppertime. When Estella said she wasn't hungry, Beatrice said, "Estella, you know we don't tolerate histrionics in this family. You are expected at the table."

She went downstairs and sat at her place. She was determined not to speak to her father, perhaps ever again, but when he said, "I admit I was a little hard on you," she couldn't help it and she began to cry once more.

"Estella," he said. "Please understand. This war leaves us without two of your brothers and God knows what will happen to them. I am not going to let it deprive a smart young woman of an education."

"I agree with your father," Beatrice said.

That was the end of it.

When Estella finished high school, she pulled a career out of a hat and applied to go to normal school to get her teaching certificate. Since the Royal Air Force had taken over the teacher training building on College Avenue, she had to walk downtown every day to a temporary site, the old Sherwood Department Store. The only good thing about it was that the streets were filled with young servicemen. She began to go to dances on Saturday nights with some of the other girls from school. When one of the servicemen she danced with asked her if they could be secretly engaged, she laughed and told him she knew what he was up to, that is, he was looking for the fringe benefits of engagement without having to buy a ring, and he could forget it. She developed a reputation as hard to get, but she was a good dancer so she was never without a dance partner.

The war dragged on in a way that no one had thought it would. Jack and Andrew were still not home, although neither had they seen active duty. Harmony, who'd found out she was pregnant after Andrew left, had given birth to their first child, Andy. He was already walking and talking. Estella graduated from normal school and got a job teaching high school mathematics, with a plan to study for a bachelor's degree during the summers, in mathematics, she supposed. Everyone had hope that the war was coming to an end because the Luftwaffe raids were over and the threat to England was already diminished. When the Germans were defeated at Stalingrad, the family was sure Jack and Andrew would soon be home, but another year went by and still they were overseas. In a letter, Jack wrote that he was getting bored, and he joked to Estella that she was right and war was not all it was cracked up to be.

Then came the Normandy invasion, and a telegram saying Jack was missing in action. There was no word about Andrew or where he was. The whole Diamond family gathered in their parents' house every day and waited for news. Estella went to school but she rushed home as soon as the bell rang. Oliver left Theo and Mathew to supervise the plant's operations, and he waited with Beatrice. A week later, another telegram arrived saying that that Jack had been badly injured and was in a hospital in France. The telegram didn't say much about his injuries, just that they were serious. Then Andrew's wife Harmony finally heard that Andrew had survived the landing on Juno Beach and had continued with his regiment into Europe.

Once the Diamonds learned that Jack and Andrew had both been at the front—and Andrew still was—they thought about nothing else. Estella had little interest in her students or their grasp of mathematics. She waited for news with the rest of family, and at the same time dreaded that word would come saying Jack had succumbed to his injuries, or Andrew was missing, or dead. Harmony knew only that Andrew's regiment was somewhere in France, driving the Germans back. Although there was talk of victory, it was almost a year after D-Day before an end to the war was declared, and the family heard, finally, that Andrew was alive, and Jack would in all likelihood recover.

Andrew came home in 1945. He was introduced to his son, and went back to work at the plant as though nothing had changed. When Jack came home six months later, it was as though everything had changed. To Estella, he hardly seemed like the same person. When her school year ended in June of 1946, she changed her plan to take classes all summer and instead assumed Jack's care, to save her mother all the trips up and down the stairs, which she didn't seem to be able to make without stopping to catch her breath. The doctor called it fatigue due to the stress of worrying about her sons in Europe. He found nothing physically wrong other than slightly elevated blood pressure, and he suggested that she had perhaps had a nervous breakdown. He prescribed a sleeping pill.

One evening, when both Jack and Beatrice were resting, Oliver told Estella how much he appreciated her help.

"I wonder," he said, "if you would consider taking a leave from teaching in the fall. Jack is going to need care for some time. It's too much for your mother."

A leave from her job. It seemed like a lot to ask. Still, she said, "Of course," because it was Jack.

When fall came again, Jack was not much better. Estella was granted her leave from teaching, and she cared for him with the help of a visiting nurse. She read poetry aloud to him; he liked Robert Service and British sonnets, Wordsworth and Keats. Gradually, she coaxed him out of his bed every day to sit in the garden for fifteen minutes, and to perhaps walk around the block with her. She convinced him also to wean himself off the morphine he'd been taking, and to join her and their parents at the table for meals, just the noon meal at first, and then eventually all three. She managed to squeeze in a few mathematics classes at the College, but other than that, everything she did was for Jack.

Finally, after almost a year of convalescence, he was able to go back to work at the plant. Oliver started him as Colin Barrett's accounts assistant, two days a week. When Jack was ready to work full time, Oliver gave Colin a generous retirement package and Jack took over from him. Estella tried not to harbour any resentment toward Jack. She was the one with the knowledge of numbers, she thought, but she knew Jack needed the job, and that his integration back into the world was precarious. He met Phyllis not long after and they were married in a private ceremony.

Once Jack was back at work, Estella returned to teaching because she didn't want to stay home without purpose. A full school year had passed while she was caring for Jack, and she realized she had missed the classroom. She was lucky enough to get placed in her old school, where she knew the staff and the students, at least the ones who hadn't graduated while she was away. That fall she learned about the Recreation Society and its buses from a flyer on the staff billboard, and the next summer she went on the first of her camping excursions, to the Black Hills in South Dakota. In the summers that followed she travelled to Santa Fe, New Mexico, and then took the trip to the Baja Peninsula. The next summer Estella passed on the tour of the Maritimes—by then her father had discovered his passion for the project at Lake Claire—and the summer after that she missed a trip to the Florida Keys. Then she lost track altogether of where the Recreation Society buses were going, because she didn't care anymore. They had been replaced by a bush camp on Allen Foster's lease.

When she first went back to teaching after her leave, the staff had a party for her, with cake in the staffroom at lunch. One of the teachers dropped a little rum into their coffee mugs, and the principal said, "My eyes are closed. I did not see that."

When his back was turned, Estella dropped a little more in hers, and accepted that rum in her coffee mug at school was probably the best she could do in honour of Salina's rebellious legacy.

———

THE DIAMONDS MADE their first trip to Lake Claire by train, or at least most of the family did. Oliver and his sons delivered their wives and children—two of them now grown and married—to Union Station, and then carried on to the lake in Oliver's big Oldsmobile sedan with a trunk full of canned goods and breakfast cereal, and a list of supplies to be purchased in the village. Estella, who was used to travelling with her father, reluctantly found herself at the station with the other women, plus fourteen nieces and nephews and the baby and pair of toddlers who had made her a great-aunt.

Her sisters-in-law were dressed fashionably for travelling. In their suitcases they had new cottage clothes, chosen from pictures in magazines since none of them had any experience with beach wear. Even Gladys, who was now in her forties, had a stylish new bathing suit in her beach bag. Estella's teenaged nieces—Caroline and Val and Geraldine—were all wearing pedal-pushers and pastel-coloured canvas sneakers. Estella knew about the two-piece bathing suits that were packed away in their luggage, and she wondered what her brothers were going to say when they saw their girls on the beach with their midriffs on display. She understood teenagers since she spent most of her life with them at school, and she knew the three girls had every intention of showing themselves off, hopefully to boys with slicked-back hair and ducktails, who looked like Elvis or James Dean.

At the station, Rose kept to herself. Her engagement to Jack was new and had come not long after his divorce from Phyllis. She was a quiet person, and it was obvious that she found the pandemonium to be a bit of an ordeal. She was to share a cottage with Estella and her parents, and Estella wondered if Rose even wanted to be there, although she could wonder the same about Beatrice, who still thought she was travelling to a cabin in the wild woods. Estella suspected Rose's reserve was not fear of the woods but rather fear of the Diamonds; they did not always understand how intimidating they could be.

There were several young children among Estella's nieces and nephews, and some of them carried plastic pails and beach toys.

The teenagers stuck together and pretended they were old enough to be travelling on their own. When the call to board came, they all filed from the station to the boarding platform, where the baggage car awaited their luggage. Estella watched her sisters-in-law shepherding children up the steps into their passenger car, and she thought she herself was like Rose, not sure she even wanted to be here. She boarded the train behind the others as they stowed their hand luggage and negotiated seats and travelling partners, and worried that the opening of Allen Foster's cottages would be the ruination of Lake Claire, at least for her. It was not just the Diamonds who were heading there. She'd seen the billboards appearing as far south as Regina, with a robust-looking family of four—the parents, a boy, a girl, the lake behind them—and the slogan: *Foster's Lake Claire Bungalows. Come visit. Come home.* She did not want Lake Claire to be home to people from anywhere and everywhere. She half hoped that a conductor would come along with an announcement that there was something wrong with the train, everyone off. She knew she was being ridiculous. What good were the cottages with no one in them?

The Diamonds jostled and shuffled around until they were all at last seated. Beatrice sat next to Gladys, facing two of the children, with a table set up in between. The train had not left the station before Beatrice had the cards out for a game of Old Maid, a game Estella detested because one or another of the children playing never failed to point out that she was, in fact, an old maid. The other two sisters-in-law—Fay and Harmony—sat together surrounded by the remaining children, except for the teenagers, who sat at the back of the car away from everyone else.

Estella sat down next to Rose and took out her book, *Anna*

Karenina, which she was counting on to last the whole two weeks. The density of the novel seemed more important now than it had when she'd selected it. Rose already had her knitting out. Estella wondered if she felt deserted by Jack, forced to travel with the family circus while he got to ride with the men. If so, Estella could understand. After all the times she had been her father's travelling companion, she suddenly wasn't.

It was ten o'clock in the morning when the train left the station. It went first to Saskatoon and then farther north to Prince Albert, where they had to change trains for Lake Claire. The stop in Prince Albert was a long one, three hours, and the family stored their luggage in lockers as directed by Oliver and ventured away from the station for a quick supper. Estella took them to a nearby café that she knew about—she and her father had eaten there several times on their way north—and they ordered grilled cheese and Denver and clubhouse sandwiches. After supper, Estella suggested a short walk and almost everyone followed her as she led them around the block. She was wearing her Red Wing boots, the ones Beatrice hated so much. Her sisters-in-law were in leather flats. Halfway around the block Harmony complained that she was getting a blister. The air was cooler this far north, and when they all got back to the station they retrieved their bags from the coin lockers and found their sweaters and blankets for the children in case they fell asleep.

"I hope we've brought enough warm clothing," Gladys said. "Is there a place to buy things in the village, Estella, in case we need extra sweaters?"

There wasn't really. A local woman was planning to open a shop—Dot's Beach Hut, it was to be called—which would sell bathing suits and T-shirts and kangaroo sweatshirts with "Lake Claire" printed on them, but as far as Estella knew it was still just an idea.

By the time they boarded the train again for the last leg of the journey, it was evening. Estella tried to make conversation with Rose and then she gave up and returned to her book. The children were fighting over the windows because they were in the bush now and the scenery was a novelty. Her niece Caroline sat down across from her and Rose with a hairbrush and dramatically brushed out her long hair.

"I hope it's not too dull at this lake," Caroline said.

"I've never been bored there," Estella said, looking up from her book and watching Caroline draw the brush from her part and down, first one side and then the other. She was pretty, and well aware of it. After she finished with her hair, she stuck her brush back in her purse and said, "I wanted to stay in the city but Daddy doesn't trust me with *the boys*. If I do meet a boy at the lake, I might need you to talk to him or I'll never get out."

"I don't think that's my business," Estella said, "to talk to your father about boys."

"Just remind him how old I am."

"You can do that."

Caroline gave her the same look she sometimes got from her students and said, "You used to be our fun aunt," and then she got up and moved.

Estella tried to imagine what Caroline would appreciate about Lake Claire other than boys on the beach. After all the trips in which Estella had slept in her tent and sat around the fire in the evenings with her father and Allen Foster and the work crew, she was about to hand Lake Claire over to people whose experience would be completely different. People who would move into the finished cottages with running water and shower stalls and never know what had gone into building them, or what the lake looked like in early spring when there was still ice in the bay, and glistening crystals lapped back and forth on the shore as the air slowly warmed and they melted. Everything was about to change, and there would be no going back. What if all these Diamonds on their way to Lake Claire were a mistake? She tried to read her book but it was hard to concentrate.

It was one of the children who soon after smelled smoke.

Estella could smell it too, although she didn't believe it was anything to worry about. This was the bush, after all, and people built fires, Cree and Métis families who had camps in the summertime. But then the smell grew stronger, and you could see smoke through the windows, wisps of grey along both sides of the train. When the wisps turned into long black plumes trailing from the engine to the caboose, Theo's daughter Goldie jumped up with her month-old baby in her arms and screamed, "Fire!" The baby started to cry, and then all the children were screaming. The train was already squealing to a stop when someone thought to pull the bell cord. Estella ran to the next car and found a young porter, who was on his way with orders to see to the passengers. Smoke was now building in the air outside the passenger cars and beginning to seep inside through the windows.

The porters got everyone in the two passenger cars off the train, and there they were, the Diamonds, all twenty-three of them, along with the other passengers, standing between the bush and the tracks. Everyone could see smoke coming from the engine ahead. The conductor and porters and brakemen and even some of the male passengers went to work to figure out the source of the fire and what to do about it.

It didn't take long until it was out—it had looked worse than it was, the conductor said—but the train was going nowhere. The passengers had all got off in a hurry without taking much with them, and they were soon miserable, swatting at mosquitoes and shivering in the chill that came quickly when the sun went down. Estella felt badly that they were frightened, especially the children. They were scared of wolves and bears, of sounds they heard in the growing darkness. The cracking of a branch. The *huff huff* someone claimed to have heard. She tried to reassure everyone, but to them she was just Estella. What did she know about the bush?

The conductor seemed to be the one in charge, and he eventually turned his full attention to his passengers, some of whom appeared to be terrified of this unknown outdoors. He allowed them back onto the train long enough to retrieve sweaters and blankets and jackets to protect themselves and the children from the insects and the cold, but he wouldn't let them stay onboard. They all sat in the growing darkness, having been warned that under no circumstances were they to go into the bush. Estella could see the train staff conferring in a huddle, and then the conductor came back and informed them that he couldn't radio ahead or back to Prince Albert because the radio had been damaged in the fire. They would have to wait, he said, until the station at Lake Claire became concerned and sent a crew to look for them. And they would have to wait outside because of the danger of another train coming along and slamming into them in the darkness. The chances of that happening were next to none, he said, but they would have to wait for help outside all the same. It wouldn't be long. A few hours at the most.

Estella did a calculation in her head. It was an hour and a half from Prince Albert to Lake Claire by train. They had been on the train for most of that time before the fire. They couldn't be far from the village. She could walk the rest of the way, she thought, by following the tracks. It would be impossible to get lost. If another train was coming, she would hear it in plenty of time and get out of the way. She wasn't sure why she wanted to do this, but she did. She knew this place. She was not afraid of bears or other wildlife.

She told the conductor what she was going to do. Less than ten miles, the conductor told her when she asked how far it was, but it was not a wise idea. It would be difficult walking along the tracks. The bush was thick and the rail line was not much more than a narrow path through the trees. What would she do if she did run into a bear on the tracks?

"Be patient," he said. "It won't be long."

"I think I'll walk," Estella said, making up her mind.

"I can't let you do that," the conductor said.

"I don't see how you can stop me," she said.

Beatrice tried to intervene. "Don't be ridiculous, Estella. You heard him. It won't be long before we're rescued."

"I'm not waiting," she said, already tightening the laces on her Red Wings and zipping up her windbreaker. She had a canvas pack with her and she removed her small flashlight before adjusting the pack on her back. She asked the conductor if he had a better light she could take. She wasn't sure how long her batteries would last.

The conductor left, shaking his head, and then he returned with a coal oil lantern and the same porter Estella had sought out for help, whom he insisted on sending with her if she couldn't be talked out of making the trek on foot. The porter's name was Eugene and he had red hair and looked to be about her age, thirtyish, or perhaps a few years younger. He was dressed in his uniform, a dark jacket with brass buttons and red piping, and a matching cap with a brim. Estella thought it made him look like an organ grinder's monkey. The conductor gave strict instructions to the porter to get Estella off the tracks if he heard another train coming.

"I'm not brainless," Estella said. "I know enough to get off the tracks, and I don't need a babysitter. Just give me the lantern and I'll be fine."

"You'll be lucky if you're not killed," the conductor muttered. "But I'm sending my fellow along with a motive other than your safety. Someone needs to tell the station what's happened. It might speed things up."

"I can do that," Estella said. Then she said to Eugene, "Give me the lantern."

"Under no circumstances do you give her that lantern," the conductor said. "She'll set the bush on fire."

The porter looked as though he might be more afraid of Estella than making the trip on foot through the dark woods, but he held on tight to the lantern.

Beatrice begged her one last time to listen to reason, but her mind was made up. She didn't wait for the porter's lead; she set out ahead of him, and he followed her. Once they were out of earshot of the conductor, she stopped and tried to make him return to the train, but he wouldn't go, and he wouldn't give up the lantern. She told him she could just as easily inform the stationmaster in Lake Claire about the fire, but he said that was his job, not hers, and he could be as stubborn as she was.

She could see that more arguing was not going to get her anywhere, so she turned away from him and began to walk. The porter started after her and stayed close enough that the lantern lit the way for both of them. The tracks ahead created a dark tunnel through the forest. Estella tried to walk on the ties, but they were too close together so she tried the gravel, attempting to find a comfortable rhythm between the ties, but she couldn't pace her footsteps in a way that would allow her to avoid tripping on the boards. She tried the gravel bed outside of the ties but it sloped away from the rails and was not comfortable either. She went back to walking on the ties, as awkward as that was, and found a way to step: *tie tie, gravel, tie tie, gravel.* Her footsteps made a hollow sound, and then a crunch. *Thud thud, crunch, thud thud, crunch.* The porter stepped along behind her, trying to do the same. Synchronization seemed important to keep them both from losing their rhythm and tripping up. She could hear every time one of them missed and broke the pattern.

The porter began to talk. At first, he had trouble walking and talking at the same time, but then he figured it out. He was, he said, completing a master's degree in clinical psychology at the university in Calgary. The railroad was a summer job. It paid well, enough to cover his upcoming year at school. He had been lucky to get the job. Before he'd gone back to university he'd worked for a construction company, but he'd hated it. He'd decided he could do some good in the world if he became a psychologist. He liked to write and had even considered newspaper journalism as a career rather than psychology, but he thought the chances of anyone paying him to write were pretty slim and he needed a job. His father wasn't the kind to put up with an unemployed son. Of course, the same might be true of psychology. It would turn out to be a bad choice if that was the case.

Finally he seemed to have run out of things to say, and was silent briefly, until he said, "What do you do? You must have a job. I didn't see a ring on your finger."

Estella ignored him.

Thud thud, crunch, thud thud, crunch.

She did a skip and switched legs just as the porter chose to switch the lantern to his other hand, and she lost the light and almost stumbled.

"Are you all right there?" he asked. She recovered her balance and kept walking.

A raptor of some kind screeched in the air above them.

"What the hell was that?" the porter asked. "It sounded big enough to eat a moose."

She bit back the temptation to answer and tell him that, in fact, it might have been a relatively small bird, or an owl perhaps. People assumed all owls said *whoo whoo*, but that wasn't true.

Then the porter began to sing. *"I love to go a-wandering . . ."*

"Oh, please," Estella said. They were the first words she'd spoken to him since he'd refused to return to the train.

"Finally," he said. "She speaks."

"Do not sing," she said.

He quit, but instead began to talk in a long diatribe about the popular music of the day and how misguided it was that people thought Bill Haley and his rock and roll were going to ruin the minds of a generation. Estella happened to agree with him, but she kept her opinion to herself so as not to encourage him.

Moments of blessed silence except for their footsteps, and then he said again, "What do you do? You must have a job."

Estella stopped walking and the porter almost ran into her. She looked at him then for perhaps the first time, his face lit by the lantern, framed by his ginger hair and topped by his porter's cap. He was not bad-looking even in the eerie light, and she couldn't help but be flattered that he had noticed her and wondered if she was married.

"Never mind what I do," she said. "And what were you doing, looking at my ring finger? I wouldn't have thought you'd have time to be looking at women's ring fingers. And shouldn't that be against the rules of your job?"

"You can't stop a guy from looking," he said. "All men like to look, but it's innocent, at least in my case. And it's a compliment, in case you didn't know that."

She didn't believe him that looking was completely innocent. She'd grown up with four brothers who had been fiercely protective, especially Jack, because they knew what boys were driven by. And there were all those young men in uniform she had danced with.

When she started walking again, the porter hurried to catch up, and this time he positioned himself beside her instead of behind, and she found herself telling him that she was a high school mathematics teacher.

"So you like kids," he said.

"Probably not as much as I like math," she replied.

Then she told him that her family was on the way to Lake Claire for a two-week vacation. That she was not sure she was looking forward to it, even though they were her family and she wanted them to have a good time, but it was *her* lake, and she felt that it was like a piece of music or poetry that only you can appreciate, as though it were written just for you. Once she started talking she couldn't seem to stop, and at some point she stumbled and the porter grabbed her arm to steady her, and then his hand found her hand, and he didn't let go when they started walking again. She didn't pull hers away, even though she thought it was daft, the two of them holding hands like a couple of fatuous teenagers, like something Caroline and a boy she'd met on the beach would do. The air around them had grown cool, and the porter's hand was warm.

Twenty minutes later, they saw the first sliver of light through the trees, and soon after they emerged from the bush and saw the train platform and the small station house with the village of Lake Claire behind it. The stationmaster and the Diamond men were all standing on the platform, pacing around and waiting for the train. When they saw the swinging light emerge from the bush, the stationmaster called, "Who's there?" and Estella realized the people gathered on the platform couldn't see them in the darkness, but she pulled her hand away just the same.

Eugene called out, "Hello, everything's all right, but there's been a little problem with the train."

Just then, they heard something in the distance behind them, and everyone's attention turned to the sound. Estella and the porter stepped off the tracks, he on one side and she on the other, and they watched as the swath of the engine's headlamp slowly approached, and then the train itself emerged from the trees, the passengers in the windows, cheering and waving at the station. The train was limping along, but moving nonetheless, having been repaired at least to the degree that it could make the last seven miles, which was all the distance had been in the end.

Estella had to walk around the train to get to the platform and she watched as the Diamonds and the other passengers spilled out of the two passenger cars, thankful to have arrived and anxious to get to their beds. Oliver and his sons began to ferry the women and children in the Oldsmobile and Allen Foster's car and Lake Claire's one taxi, and they all temporarily forgot about Estella. In her head she was still saying, *Tie tie, gravel, tie tie, gravel.*

The porter had gone into the station, and when he came out again and joined her on the platform she told her teenaged nieces, who were waiting for the next ride, that she was going to walk to the cottages. Without being asked, the porter accompanied her, and she saw her nieces exchanging glances. If they had been younger, they would have chanted, *Auntie's got a boyfriend.*

She easily knew the way, and she and the porter walked to the village and then along the familiar shortcut through the bush—the path that the boy Peter Boone had shown her four years earlier—and when they were into the bush and out of sight they held hands once more, even though the path was really too narrow for two people to walk side by side, and one of them was forced to fall back every ten yards or so by a tree branch. Estella thought how completely out of character it was for her to encourage this man she barely knew, who would have to leave on the train as soon as it was repaired and would not likely return. The train from Prince Albert to Lake Claire ran only twice a week, and it was not his regular route. In fact, he had no regular route, he had told her. As a student with a summer job, they sent him hither and yon, filling in for permanent staff on holiday or away sick. That very week, he was scheduled to travel to Montreal.

When they were near the end of the trail through the woods, Estella led the porter off the path toward the lake, and they found themselves on the sandy beach. There was no moon and the black sky was full of stars. They stood listening to the sound of waves lapping the shore, and she was not surprised when Eugene pulled her to him and kissed her full on the mouth. Before she knew it she was dropping her canvas pack to the ground, letting him unzip her jacket, slip her cotton blouse out of its tuck in her jeans, and slide his hands up her back, against her bare skin. She thought perhaps she should push him away, but then she thought, *What the hell, I'm thirty-one years old, why not?* Instead of stopping him, she pulled his cap from his head and tossed it onto the beach, and then led him into the shelter and darkness of a sand embankment that had been created by the eroded roots of an old spruce tree. She grabbed a tree root above her head to keep from slipping down into the sand as Eugene tugged at her jeans and pressed her up against the bank.

She wanted to laugh—surely this was funny?—but she was too uncertain of the rules to risk it. But it *was* funny, the two of them pretending to be hidden in a spot that she knew was wide open in daylight, doing *this* with the other Diamonds barely out of sight, unpacking and putting children to bed. She hung on to the tree root and tried not to laugh out loud. The little moans Eugene emitted with his thrusts matched the rhythm of their steps along the railway tracks—*thrust thrust, oh, thrust thrust, oh*—and when it all came to a crescendo and he stopped moving, Estella was no longer able to stifle the laughter. She had sand in her eyes, her hair, *everywhere*, and she was clinging to a spruce tree with her clothes half off—her blouse and bra hanging from one arm, and her jeans around her ankles, prevented by her boots from coming off altogether.

Eugene appeared to agree that it was funny. He bumped his head on the root when he tried to stand, and they both laughed at the absurdity as he stood rubbing his head and trying to hike up his pants and his underwear. Then he turned away from her to get himself in order again, and she got her blouse and her jacket back on, and she held her head upside down and tried to shake the sand out of her hair. She zipped up her jacket just as Eugene found his cap and adjusted it on his head.

When they were both out from under the tree and standing on the beach again, he said, "That was a pleasant enough end to a long walk."

She slipped her canvas pack on her back and said, "I doubt I'll forget it, if that's what you mean."

"I guess I should get you back," he said. "They'll be wondering where you are."

She pointed over the embankment toward the cottages and said, "We're just up there. No need to walk with me. My family is a nosy bunch."

He didn't argue. "Well, good night then," he said, and he walked away down the beach. He began to whistle, a song she recognized from the radio, but she couldn't quite think what it was. She watched him go, watched his shadow merge into the darkness until she couldn't see him anymore, hardly believing what had just happened. She'd thought he might ask for her phone number or address or some way to get in touch with her, even though she wasn't sure she wanted him to be in touch. Still, wouldn't that have been the thing to do: ask whether she might like to see him again, whether she might like to do *that* again, because he had enjoyed it, and he wouldn't mind a repeat performance?

Oh, what the hell, she thought for the second time that night, *he's probably married anyway.* She stepped up the embankment away from the lake and cut across the lawn between the beach and the cottages. Once she had thought of the porter being married, it became the most logical explanation. Almost everyone was married by the time they were her age. So, that was that, then. She'd had a very brief fling with a married man.

And that made her want to laugh again. She, Estella Diamond, thirty-one-year-old spinster schoolteacher—the one to whom Caroline had said on the train, *You used to be our fun aunt*—had just had a fling. She was almost sorry that her family, especially Caroline, would never know.

When she was halfway across the lawn, she stopped and looked at the row of cottages that she knew had been reserved for the Diamonds. Her father was sitting on the deck of Emily Carr, his feet up on the railing, smoking a cigar. She saw how contented he looked, so pleased with himself that he had pulled off the feat of getting every single member of his family settled into a Fosters bungalow. She looked back to the beach to make sure he couldn't have seen anything in the darkness, and then she crossed the grass and climbed the steps of the cottage.

Her father took a puff on his cigar and then said, "I hear you walked to the station when the train broke down."

"I figured someone had to," she said.

She half-expected an admonishment, something about worrying her mother, but he didn't say anything more about it. She sat with him for a few minutes and then said good night and went inside, and she guessed correctly in the darkness which of the twin beds Rose would be in. She crawled into her own bed in her underwear, hoping that she would not leave any evidence of her encounter with the porter on the bedsheets.

She was almost asleep when Rose whispered, "Where were you? We were wondering."

She had not known Rose was awake.

"Just walking along the beach," she said.

"That's what your father said. 'We shouldn't worry. Estella will be down at the water.' I so admire you, Estella. You just do what you want."

Estella wondered, was that true? Did she do whatever she wanted? If she did, it was news to her. Otherwise, she would have jumped into bed years ago with a serviceman who thought he could dance like Fred Astaire.

She said good night to Rose and rolled into a more comfortable position, and then they both went to sleep.

ESTELLA AND THE rest of the Diamond family were awakened the next morning by the sound of crows in the spruce trees. They all gathered outside on the cottage decks—some of the women still in their dressing gowns—to see in the morning light where it was that Oliver expected them to spend two weeks every summer for the rest of their lives. Emily Carr was the showpiece of the cottages with its bay window and oversized deck. The other four Diamond cottages were adjacent to it, all of them facing the water.

It was clear to Estella that her father was waiting to hear what her mother thought. He watched Beatrice closely as she leaned on the deck railing and took the measure of her surroundings: the lake, the lawn that Allen Foster had seeded in front of the cottages, the children's play equipment, the picnic tables and park benches placed about the compound, all freshly painted. When she turned to look down the row of cottages at her children and grandchildren on the decks, she said, "Just look at all of us," as though she had not before realized what a big family she had. Then she said she'd best get dressed if she wanted to make the most of this vacation Oliver had planned, and she went back inside.

The sisters-in-law followed her cue, leaving the men in charge of the youngest children, who then spilled from the decks and took over the playground. A family with two young girls approached the swings and waited their turn, but they gave up and went down to the beach instead. When Beatrice stuck her head out the door and said she was making pancakes for everyone, Oliver directed his sons to pull the picnic tables together. They lined five of them up in front of Emily Carr, and the sisters-in-law began carrying plates and cups and cutlery from their cottages.

Estella went back inside and found her mother with two frying pans on the stove, and Rose helping her mix pancake batter. Beatrice's old brass bell was on the counter, the one she'd rung at the bottom of the stairs every morning when Estella and her brothers were still in school.

"I can't believe you packed that," she said.

"Your father's idea," Beatrice said.

Instead of offering to help, Estella went back to bed. There were curtains on the bedroom window—a repeated cherry pattern—but they did not adequately block the light. Half an hour later she was still awake, and her mother was ringing her breakfast bell on the deck outside. Estella gave up on sleep and got dressed, wondering what the non-Diamonds in the fifteen other cottages thought of the bell. She made her bed after brushing the sand out—the only sign she could see of the night before—and went outside to join her family. They were seated around the tables eating pancakes and everyone seemed to be talking at once. Each table was covered with a matching plastic tablecloth, and Estella wondered who had thought to bring them. Gladys, she guessed, who knew how to set a good table, according to her mother.

She sat down on the top step of the deck with a cup of coffee and watched the other Fosters guests walk around the picnic tables, no doubt wondering where this crowd of people had come from. The Diamonds were all talking at once about the near-disaster, or more than one disaster when you considered the train fire *and* the hours stranded on the tracks in the company of wolves and bears and other dangerous creatures. No one asked Estella about her walk through the bush. They were too busy talking about their own adventure.

When Estella had finished her coffee, she picked up a plate and heaped it with pancakes, and then she carried it down to the beach, where she sat in the sand not far from the place where she and the porter had done what they had. In the light of day, the spot under the tree was not hidden at all. What if someone had come down to the beach to see the lake in the darkness? Her teenaged nieces, perhaps, or her father? The thought was horrifying.

When she was done eating, she stashed her plate where she could retrieve it later, and she walked along the lake to the train station, almost certain that Eugene would not still be around. She asked the station attendant about him—"You know, the redhead who walked from the train fire with me last night"—and he said only that another engine had been sent out, and the train was gone, the porter with it, whose name, he thought, was Eustace.

"Eugene, you mean," she said.

She never heard from him again, not that she expected to. She could still hear him whistling his way up the beach in the darkness, and she remembered the song: "Blueberry Hill." It was perfect. He'd found his thrill and then hopped on the next train. She did not think he had used protection—she didn't remember him fumbling with himself or any foil package—but she refused to believe she might be pregnant, and was confident she wasn't when she did the calculations in her head. Even mathematics teachers sometimes got questions that teenaged girls couldn't ask their mothers.

After breakfast, the Lake Claire vacation began in earnest, and it was soon apparent that everyone, including Beatrice, was going to have a good time. The men went fishing most mornings while the women supervised children who refused to get out of the water until they were blue with cold. There were trips to the village for ice cream and hikes in the woods—without fear of bears because the Diamonds were so noisy there was no danger of running into any wildlife at all. Estella tried to go for a swim by herself every day, but there were always others who wanted to go with her. By the end of the first week she made it as far as the north point of the bay with three other Diamonds in the water, and Jack and Rose in a canoe beside them. There was a deserted sandy beach on the tip of the point and they did the swim a few more times with picnics packed in the canoe. On one of these times she saw the boy, Peter Boone, emerge from the trees in running shorts. They'd eaten their picnic and were lying in the sand in the sun before heading back when Peter stepped onto the beach, his thin legs sticking out of his running shoes like toothpicks. He stopped, not expecting to see anyone on the point, and then he gave Estella a shy wave and ran back into the bush.

By the time the two weeks were up, the whole family was talking about returning, as though there had never been a doubter among them, not even Beatrice.

It was in Allen Foster's new office that first year that Oliver was referred to as a "kingpin." He was handing in his family's cottage keys at the end of their vacation and saying his goodbyes to Foster. The Diamonds were waiting outside with their bags, and Beatrice sent Estella in to see what was taking so long, they were going to miss the train. Estella opened the office door just as another man and his wife were checking out, and the man turned to her father and said, "You must be the kingpin of that big family." Oliver laughed and said, "I guess I am," and he shook the man's hand and said he hoped he would see him again next year.

After the man and his wife left, Oliver said to Allen Foster, "That's us, eh, couple of kingpins." Then Oliver noticed Estella standing there and said, "Beatrice sent her messenger. Time to go."

As Oliver and Estella left the office, he said, "Did you hear that? I was just called a kingpin."

"I'm not sure that's a good thing," Estella said. "It makes you sound like a hoodlum or a mob boss."

An hour later, Estella and the others were on the train south again.

———

IN 1959, FOUR YEARS after that first summer at Lake Claire, Beatrice had a stroke. She had been having mini strokes ever since the incident with her book in the kitchen, but she'd dismissed them and they were never properly diagnosed. After the big stroke she could still speak, but she was confused and mostly bedridden. Oliver refused to hear of moving her to a home so Estella took leave for a second time from her teaching job and became her mother's nurse. None of her brothers tried to talk her out of it. They were grateful. Estella insisted that Oliver move down the hall into Theo's and Mathew's old room so he could sleep, saying that she didn't need him having a stroke too, but sometimes Beatrice would wake in the night and wonder where he was, and Estella would have to wake him up to sit with her until she went back to sleep.

Most of the time, Beatrice tried not to be any trouble. She said things like, "Don't bother with lunch, Estella, I'll get myself a sandwich when I'm hungry," or "I think I'll be well enough by Sunday to do a roast for everyone so you can have a rest." At the same time, she didn't argue when Estella brought her meals on a tray. It was as though she knew the truth about her condition even as she asked whether it was laundry day and told Estella to leave the bedding, she would do it herself.

During the day, Estella tried to keep her mother entertained. Sometimes she stretched out beside her on the bed and read to her from the humour sections of *Reader's Digest*, or recipes from

Chatelaine. She didn't try to talk to her about anything of substance because Beatrice couldn't follow the conversation. Estella tried to choose safe topics: the mundane things she'd done that day, the garden, the plans for Theo's daughter Lynn's wedding. There was no date yet but she had recently become engaged.

At the end of the school day, there were always grandchildren popping in for a quick visit. Beatrice would forget their names, or sometimes not remember them at all, and Estella would have to take them aside and explain why. It was upsetting to the children, that their grandmother could forget them. Some days Beatrice seemed to think Estella was still a teenager and she wondered why she wasn't at school. Estella would tell her it was a holiday.

Once, Beatrice said to her, "When you were born your father wanted to name you Sally. Aren't you glad we didn't? I don't like that name at all." Another time, she told Estella, "I think your father might have had an affair with that other woman. But it was a long time ago. Water under the bridge."

Even though Estella knew her mother was not thinking straight, she began to worry that Beatrice meant Salina, and that she had felt, through all the years of her marriage, like Oliver's second choice for a wife. Estella began to feel guilty that she herself used to imagine Salina as her mother. She'd been so obsessed with the letters when she was a girl. They'd been her *Anne of Green Gables* or *Little Women*. She thought it was possible both she and her mother had shared the house with a ghost all these years.

One day her mother mumbled something about a stack of letters, and Estella thought she must have been referring to Salina's letters. She did not seem to be upset, and so Estella asked, "Which letters do you mean, Mom?"

"The ones in the teapot, of course," her mother said, and Estella didn't pry any further.

Another day, she thought to ask, "Where did you meet Dad, anyway? I don't think I know."

Beatrice didn't hesitate. "In a cemetery," she said. "At a funeral."

Estella assumed her mother was thinking about Salina again, but then Beatrice said, "His mother's funeral, in fact. Our mothers knew each other from the church. His father was not a very nice man."

It sounded credible enough that Estella later asked Oliver, and he confirmed that they had in fact met at his mother's funeral.

When Beatrice told Estella once again that she thought Oliver might be having an affair—present tense this time—Estella said it was impossible, that Salina had died. Beatrice looked happy to hear it, even though she said, "That's sad. Perhaps we ought to send a card."

After that, Beatrice never mentioned Salina again. Instead, she became preoccupied with the state of the house. In her mind, a cyclone was blowing bricks from the walls. There had been a cyclone in 1913 that had badly damaged some of the Diamond brick buildings in the city, but Estella assured her that there had been no cyclone since then. Beatrice kept bringing it up and fretting about the house, so Estella finally told her, yes, there had been a cyclone the day before, but Oliver had a man there right now, on a ladder outside, repointing all the bricks. That seemed to satisfy her. Then she began to count out loud, her index finger moving rhythmically through the air.

"What are you doing?" Estella asked, curious about what was going through her mother's mixed-up mind.

"Counting the bricks, of course," Beatrice said. "Will you keep an eye on them, then? When I'm gone?"

Estella wondered if her mother was confusing bricks with four generations of Diamonds, and she was actually counting heads.

"Of course, Mom," she said. "I'm good with bricks."

Then her mother looked right at her, seemingly not confused at all, and she said, "Promise me you'll take care of your father when I'm gone. He's an old man, you know, and I don't want strangers in my house."

"I know, Mom," Estella said. "I promise. I'd swear on a Bible if I had one."

As it turned out, her mother had one in a drawer beside her bed. She made Estella hold the Bible and swear.

Beatrice didn't last long after that.

Estella was in the reception hall at the church after the funeral, looking at her parents' wedding portrait, which had been placed on an easel. She was feeling neither sociable nor hungry for the lunch the church ladies were busy setting out. She had gripped so many hands in the receiving line that her fingers were numb, and she couldn't count how many times she'd heard, "Your father is so lucky to have you." She was wondering how long it would be before they could all go home, when she heard a voice speaking—almost in her ear—and when she turned to see who it was, she recognized a man from the receiving line. She couldn't remember his name. He was saying something about Beatrice and Oliver being a handsome couple. So many wedding pictures from that time, he said, had the new couple looking so stern that one could hardly imagine the marriage lasting a week, let alone a lifetime. Although they did believe in long marriages in those days, did they not? Divorce was not as much an option as it was now, people tended to stick it out.

"Are you suggesting," Estella asked, "that my parents would have divorced if they'd had the chance?"

"Sorry, no, I didn't mean . . . That's a happy couple in the portrait, no doubt."

"I don't follow you, then," she said.

"It was the photographs," he explained. "They had to hold the pose for so long that they didn't smile. That's all I meant. My apologies."

"Oh," she said. "Yes, I see now. Like the Mona Lisa. Well, that's one theory."

"I don't expect you remember my name," the man said then, holding out his hand. "Clarence Angell. My father and yours were business colleagues of some sort. My father would have been here himself but he's not well. He asked me to come in his stead. Which I was happy to do, of course."

"Clarence Angell," she said, taking his hand. "Well, how do you do? Thank your father for thinking of us." He was handsome, a dapper dresser, although she didn't trust a man who spent too much time thinking about what he was wearing. She herself spent very little time thinking about it. Beatrice had told her on more than one occasion that she ought to attend just a little more to her appearance: try a different hairstyle, get a perm, perhaps wear a bit more colour.

Clarence shook her hand firmly and she wanted to pull away, although not for any particular reason having to do with him, she was just tired of people's hands. She was aware that she was speaking with a strange man whom she had just met at a funeral.

Then Clarence Angell cut to the chase. "Let's say we get out of here for a bit," he said. "Go for a drive. Get away from the smell of egg salad. Not that I have anything against egg salad, but some fresh air might do you good."

She turned toward the door without looking back. Clarence followed her, and when they were on the sidewalk in front of the church he took her arm and led her to his car, an Oldsmobile like her father's, but sportier, a pale-yellow two-door sedan, with leather upholstery. He had parked the car on an angle so that it took up two spaces in the crowded parking lot, and although she thought this smacked of pride, she admired the vehicle.

Clarence opened the door for her and rolled the window down against the heat inside. Estella had a scarf in her purse and she considered tying it on her head to protect her hair from the wind, but then she decided she didn't care. She was too old to care about such things. What did it matter if her hair blew around her face?

They drove the length of Albert Street, both directions, and then through the park and around the lake, and when he asked her where she wanted to go next, she said, "Anywhere. Just keep driving." And so he did. Albert Street again. Victoria Avenue to the edge of town and back.

"I brought you out here to cheer you up," Clarence Angell said, because she wasn't talking. "Apparently it's not working."

"I can think of something that would cheer me up," she said, cutting to her own chase. "Let's go to a hotel."

He laughed. "Wow," he said. "You go from zero to sixty in a hurry. You're kidding, though, right? A real card."

"I'm not a card at all," she said. "I'm dead serious."

"All right then," Clarence said, and he drove them to the Plains Hotel on Albert Street. On its roof was a new sign that had everyone talking. The neon tubes were on a narrow tower you could see for blocks and their colour told you what kind of day it was. Today was blue, fair weather. Which was true. It was early spring, but there were tulips blooming all over the city.

Clarence parked his car in the hotel lot, and once again he walked around and opened the door for Estella. A real gentleman, she thought, one who was about to lead her to a rented room on the day of her mother's funeral. He walked with the swagger of a man who figured he deserved his unexpected bit of luck. He booked them a room and paid cash—Mr. and Mrs. Jones, bags to be delivered later—and the desk clerk pointed out the elevator.

This was the first time Estella had been with a man since the train porter. Like the time on the beach, she didn't know what had got into her. She shed her funeral dress and got into bed with Clarence Angell, and she wondered how she could be doing this when she should be back at the reception with the rest of the Diamonds. What kind of woman was she? She knew what kind of man Clarence was because he hadn't tried to talk her out of it, but she had no intention of seeing him again anyway, even though they had met at a funeral.

He used a condom. He had one in his wallet. She was quite a bit more impressed than she had been the first time, and she had no regrets. Afterwards, she got dressed and fixed her hair in the bathroom and then told Clarence he'd better drive her back to the church. She hoped the guests would still be there and she could slip in without being noticed. Clarence was sitting up in bed smoking a cigarette.

"Sure thing," he said. He seemed to be studying her, which was not surprising.

On the way to the church, she asked Clarence what his father did that he had known Oliver, and Clarence said, "Commerce. But he didn't have your father's business sense. He did all right, but he was never rich."

Rich.

It was an uncomfortable word. It was a word Oliver had not liked when it was applied to him. Estella was the same. She thought it was a vulgar word.

"And what do you do?" she asked.

"Sales," he said.

When they arrived back at the church, the funeral home's silver cars were gone but the Diamond cars were still parked out front. Clarence found a parking spot, and then he walked around and opened Estella's door.

"No need to come in," she said.

"Nonsense," Clarence said, and he walked her inside and into the hall, where a group of mostly family remained seated at the tables. They all looked when Estella came in with Clarence, and she wished that they had not been seen together.

"Would you consider going to a movie with me sometime?" he asked while they were still out of earshot of the others.

"Probably not," she said.

She immediately chose a lone empty chair between Fay and one of her nieces, and she proceeded to ignore Clarence Angell, even though he came and stood right behind her chair as though he had some proprietary claim on her, and once again she thought his behaviour was crude, or at least insensitive since he wouldn't take the hint. Finally he went to where Oliver was seated, shook his hand, and then left.

"Who was that?" Fay wanted to know, and Estella said that he was the son of a colleague of Oliver's, and that she was just being nice to him because he hadn't known anyone at the funeral.

"I'm not sure you could have made your lack of interest any clearer," Fay said.

Estella was afraid her niece would start chanting *Auntie's got a boyfriend*, but she didn't. She supposed that it was too out of the ordinary for Estella to walk through the door with a man that could, in fact, be a boyfriend. She wondered why Fay's comment had sounded a bit on the critical side. Did Fay think she should be glad of the attention of any man? And what would she think if she knew that Estella and Clarence Angell had gone to a hotel room?

"He was clinging," Estella said to Fay. "I hate that."

When the family realized that all the guests were gone and they were the only ones left in the hall, Theo suggested that it was time to thank the ladies who were now doing dishes in the kitchen, and take their leave of the place. But they lingered, as though they didn't really want to go home.

Finally Oliver stood, and they all followed his lead. It was distressing to see him walking alone to Theo's car. During her mother's illness, Estella had thought she might apply for a job at an international school when she was free again, or perhaps go to university in another city and finish her stalled degree in mathematics, but she didn't suppose she'd be making much of a change in her life for a while. She couldn't see leaving her father now, promise or no promise to her mother. He'd never lived in the house alone. Clarence Angell could maybe have provided a diversion, but she'd pretty much made sure he wouldn't be calling.

When they got home, Oliver went straight to bed. Estella sat at the dining room table and stared at the white teapot that was still in the same place it had always been. She wondered who had kept it dusted since Beatrice had been unable to do the housework. Not her. That left just her father. She pictured him with a feather duster in his hand, taking care of the teapot.

She thought about going to bed, but she knew she would not be able to sleep. She decided to read the letters again. She had read them many times over the years, but had not done so recently. She reached for the teapot, and when she was lifting it from its place on the corner shelf she dropped it. She waited for the sound of catastrophe, the pot smashing, the lid flying off, but the teapot didn't break. It landed solidly, right side up, between her feet. She stared down at it, her heart pounding, as though she had dropped a sacred object, an urn containing the ashes of a loved one.

She bent down and lifted the lid off the pot and was surprised to see that the letters were gone. The beads were there, inside the jeweller's bag, but that was all. She put the lid back on and picked up the teapot and checked for damage, but there was none. Then she looked up and saw her father standing in the doorway in his grey and red striped bathrobe, just as he had been all those years ago when she had first discovered the letters. She had not heard him on the stairs.

"They're gone," she said. "The letters."

"They've been gone for some time," he said. "I suppose Beatrice finally got tired of them and threw them out. Throw the darn teapot out, too, if you want. It's just a teapot, and not a particularly good one. The spout drips."

"I don't know, Dad," she said. "It's always been here."

"You can have the beads," he said. "I should have given them to you years ago."

Estella removed the velvet bag, and said, "I think we should keep the teapot." She placed it back on the shelf.

"That's what your mother said. I did ask her."

Oliver got himself a glass of water from the kitchen and went back upstairs. Estella took the beads out of the jeweller's bag and unwrapped them, and was glad to see they had survived the fall without chipping. She remembered the story of how Salina had acquired them, by slipping them into her pocket. She tried to think back to the last time she had seen the letters, but she couldn't remember. She was sorry they were gone. She felt as though she had lost two women, both of her father's wives, on one day.

Instead of going to bed, she put on her coat and went outside to the garden. The air had cooled, she was sure it was below freezing. The tulips along the fence never should have bloomed so early, they would all be dead by morning. She sat in her mother's wicker chair and wondered how Beatrice had disposed of the letters. The fireplace was her best guess. Who knew why she had let the beads remain, but perhaps she believed they were valuable.

In the morning, Estella could see the tulips from the kitchen window, still blooming, as she made her father's breakfast.

A month later, she went back to her teaching job, just as she had after Jack mended. When an application for international school positions came in the mail she didn't bother filling it out. She continued to do the cooking and cleaning because she didn't see the need to bring a new person into the house, at least not yet. She felt as though she were biding her time, waiting for an opportunity to present itself, one that would extricate her from the indifference she was feeling to her own life.

It was two years before Clarence Angell came calling. They ran into each other at the dry cleaner's and he reintroduced himself.

"We met at your mother's funeral and we went for a drive in the park," he said.

"Right," she said, "I remember," although she wanted to say, *It was a little more than a drive in the park, as I recall.*

When Clarence was on his way out the dry cleaner's door with his suits draped in plastic, she said, "Would you like to come to the house for dinner on Sunday?"

Gladys and Theo were there when Clarence arrived, and it was obvious that they couldn't believe Estella had invited a man to dinner. They did not remember Clarence from the funeral. Estella could just see Gladys planning the teacup shower as she looked him up and down and tried to figure out how this could have happened without her knowing. Estella supposed that Gladys now saw her as one of those middle-aged women who had given up on having a home and family of her own. In fact, Estella was not especially taken with Clarence Angell, but when she'd seen him at the dry cleaner's she had decided not to ignore the family history of auspicious meetings at funerals. And she was bored, even with herself.

They had a pleasant enough dinner. When Oliver asked Clarence what he did, he said he worked in advertising for the daily newspaper. Estella thought he had told her "sales," but she supposed advertising was sales.

After dinner, he left at a respectable time and did not hang around waiting for something more. Once he was gone, Oliver said, "I can't expect to have you here forever, can I."

Estella said, "Dad, it's nothing like that."

The next weekend, Clarence took Estella to a nice restaurant, and after dinner they went for a drive through the park, and she wondered what she would do if he decided to pull over in a secluded spot and make a dive for her. She felt nothing like she had the day of the funeral: madcap and reckless, and tired of being the family spinster. But Clarence made a completely innocent loop through the park, and then he drove her home and walked her to the door, and he did not even try to kiss her or invite himself inside.

"Do you like boxing?" he asked before he left. He said he was a boxing fan and there was a club on Railway Avenue that had Saturday night bouts. Strictly amateur, but it was something to do if you had an interest in that sort of thing.

Estella said she had no idea whether she liked boxing or not. The only thing she knew about boxing was what Peter Boone had told her years ago at Lake Claire when he was just a boy and he'd talked about his training program, the one she'd assumed he'd ordered from the back of a comic book.

The next weekend Clarence took her to her first boxing match at the club on Railway Avenue. It was hard to imagine Peter Boone, who had not grown into anything close to stocky, committing himself to such a brutal sport. She hoped he had given it up.

She wasn't entirely sure how it happened, but Saturday evenings with Clarence became a regular thing. They went to dinner, or to a movie downtown, sometimes to the same dance hall she'd gone to during the war, although it was no longer filled with servicemen. Sometimes Clarence took her to a boxing match. He was a serious fan, and often carried a magazine called *The Ring* around with him. She was not especially interested, but she was happy enough to go along.

They began to end their dates, by mutual agreement, in a hotel room. Clarence gave her an excuse to start spending a bit of her teacher's salary on better clothes. She'd always been a frumpy dresser and had never cared about what was in style, or what colours might look good on her. She discovered a ladies' boutique in a strip mall not far from her school and the owner helped her choose a few attractive dresses and pantsuits. Olive green, she was told, looked especially good with her complexion. She even bought a black dress and a Chanel suit that was far too expensive. Clarence never failed to notice when she wore a new outfit. They were, without a doubt, an odd couple. Estella knew she was not in love with Clarence, and she was pretty sure he felt the same, in spite of their trysts at the Best Western or the Travelodge.

Her nieces began to ask if she and Clarence were going steady, always with an amused tone, as though it were an impossible turn of events. Her sisters-in-law wondered when she thought this Clarence fellow was going to get around to popping the question. That's how they phrased it, *popping*, like popcorn, as though it were a lighthearted thing, a man asking Estella to marry him.

"Wouldn't you like to know," she would always say, trying to hide her resentment that everyone seemed to think it so entertaining that she finally had a man in her life. She didn't even try to explain that she had no intention of marrying Clarence.

After they'd been Saturday night regulars for almost three years—long enough that even Estella wondered why Clarence had never raised the topic of marriage—she did something she had a hard time explaining. They were out for dinner and she'd had more wine than she was used to—they were into a second bottle—and she was watching a pair of lovebirds at another table in the restaurant. They were younger than her and Clarence, and couldn't take their eyes or their hands off each other. After watching them for some time and wondering what it felt like to be so besotted, Estella impulsively leaned across the small dining table they were seated at, and she kissed Clarence full on the lips. Then she sat back on her own side of the table.

"Oh," Clarence said, obviously puzzled, and then, "Well, well." He lifted his napkin from his lap and wiped his mouth with it. He might even have frowned, it was hard to tell in the dim lighting.

That was not exactly the reaction Estella had been expecting, but the truth was now pretty obvious: Clarence didn't love her any more than she loved him.

What were they doing, then? They really ought to end it, she thought. They had a good enough time together, but they weren't young. If either one of them wanted to meet someone else, this was just getting in the way. She considered breaking it off that very evening, but she worried she was being hasty and the wine had gone to her head. Clarence took her home without going to a hotel first, which was happening more and more frequently, but when he walked her to the door he said, "See you next week," as though nothing was wrong.

She closed the door and made the decision to end it, she was too old to continue out of apathy or inertia.

The next weekend they went to a boxing match. There was a café a few doors down the block from the club called the KO Diner, and Clarence liked to go there for hamburgers before the bouts. There were sometimes questionable types at the lunch counter who looked as though they might happily steal a wallet or a purse if the opportunity presented itself, but mostly the place was a regular diner that had been in the neighbourhood for years and served families and working men and even a few students from the College.

As she prepared in her head for *the talk* she and Clarence would have later, they went to the KO Diner for a meal. They were early enough that Railway Avenue was pretty much empty. They pulled up to the curb in Clarence's sedan, and Estella knew he'd be pleased to have a spot where he could keep an eye on the car. He parked carefully, watching out for the whitewalls, and he walked around the car to open the door for Estella. A couple of what looked to be students passed by on the sidewalk heading for the diner, and Estella heard through the open window some kind of political discussion. Clarence had obviously not heard because he didn't mention it. He had no use for politics or students.

He opened her car door and she stepped out onto the sidewalk. She was wearing a new summer dress, green with a pattern of bright-red flowers. The dress was probably too young for her, but it was the fashion, and she'd loved the colour when she'd seen it in the Eaton's window downtown. Clarence had wolf-whistled when she'd come to the door in it, and she'd almost turned around and gone back to her room to change, but at the same time, it meant the dress looked good on her so she hadn't. She was getting vain, she thought. She never used to care.

After Clarence locked the car, they walked up the block toward the diner. Estella now felt conspicuous in the colourful, sleeveless dress. It was warm for the first week of May and she hadn't brought a sweater, knowing it would be warmer still inside the boxing club. She wished she could cover her arms.

They passed the club's entrance and Clarence stopped to look at a poster that described the night's card. Estella glanced at the names along with Clarence, not expecting to see one that she recognized. But she did see a familiar name: Peter Boone's. He was one of the two boxers vying for the light welterweight championship. So he was still at it, she thought. She'd lost track of him several years ago when he left Lake Claire.

"Look at that," she said, pointing. "Peter Boone. He's in the championship bout."

"The nobody, you mean," Clarence said. "Some kid from Prince Albert."

"He's not a nobody," Estella said, offended on Peter Boone's behalf. "He's someone I know, from the lake in the summer."

"Really? Well, my bet's on the other guy."

"Then we're betting against each other."

"Since when did you care enough to have an opinion?" Clarence asked, putting his arm around her waist and squeezing. The squeeze felt like an affectation, like something he'd seen in an old black-and-white movie. "Anyway," he said, "ladies don't bet."

Ladies don't bet. The wolf whistle. She couldn't believe she had managed to spend as much time with this man as she had. She resolved to bet a whole lot of money on Peter Boone, just to show

Clarence that some ladies do whatever the hell they want. She thought of the old home economics teacher at her school, the one who gave the girls a lecture at the beginning of every year on the difference between "ladies" and "women." Everyone in the school had been waiting for her to announce her retirement so they could hire someone who lived in the twentieth century.

A train passed just then behind the diner and the boxing club, and Estella and Clarence had to stop talking. Clarence took Estella's arm and guided her up the street to the diner as the train rumbled slowly by. She thought about Peter Boone, the boy who had trained on his own in the hotel where he'd lived with his mother. How old would he be now? In his twenties, twenty-three or twenty-four. Perhaps he was married. She was amazed that he'd apparently stuck with his childhood passion. She'd never imagined that a young man built like a jockey would have any kind of future in boxing.

When Clarence opened the door to the diner and Estella stepped inside, she saw a man who looked as if he might be an assassin staring back at her. He was seated at the counter, and his eyes followed her as she and Clarence walked all the way to the back of the diner to an empty booth. Estella thought Clarence might say something—*Put your eyes back in your head*—but he didn't notice. She slid into the booth and tucked her dress under her legs, hiding as much as she could. There was no hiding her bare arms or the deep V of her dress, though. The man let his eyes roam from her ankles under the table up to her neck, and then he turned back to his plate of fries.

"Best burgers in town," Clarence said, picking up a menu from the Formica tabletop.

"Didn't you see that?" Estella asked.

"See what?"

Estella shook her head with disgust. "Surely there are other places with good burgers," she said.

"This one has atmosphere," Clarence said. "Don't you like it here? I thought you did."

"I don't really," she said, but she opened a menu anyway. They were bickering, she thought. Or at least, she was.

They ordered burgers. There was a newspaper on the bench seat beside Clarence and he picked it up and found the sports section.

As Estella waited for her burger and Clarence read the paper, she thought again about Peter Boone, and hoped he would not lose as badly as Clarence seemed to think he would. She wondered if she'd be able to talk to him later in the evening after his bout. She wondered whether he'd even recognize her. She had certainly never worn anything like this dress at the lake. At the lake she wore shorts over a bathing suit and tied her hair back.

The man at the counter paid his bill and left. Another train went by. Estella could see that cars and trucks were beginning to pull up and fill the empty spots on Railway in front of the boxing club. Soon they'd be parking around the corners on the side streets. The waitress brought their burgers and slid them onto the table, and Clarence folded up the paper and put it back on the seat.

"Anything else I can get ya?" the waitress asked. Her name tag identified her as Peggy.

"Thanks," Estella said. "I'm good."

"So, who's going to win the title tonight?" Clarence asked the waitress.

"Don't ask me," Peggy said. "I wouldn't know a boxing glove from an oven mitt." She was looking at Clarence, waiting for him to tell her whether he wanted anything else. She had a pencil tucked into her hair.

"We have everything we need," Estella said, and Peggy left.

Clarence took a bite of his hamburger and savoured it. Beef fat dripped onto his plate.

They watched a big Cadillac cruise slowly past, driven by a woman, a bottle-blonde. She was no doubt looking for a place to park.

"Should have come early, Blondie," Clarence said.

Irritation again. Calling the woman Blondie. Acting so pleased with himself that he'd found a good parking spot so he could keep an eye on his car.

But why was she being so ungenerous? Now she couldn't tell if she was cranky with herself, or with Clarence. She was as bad as her high school students. She picked up her hamburger and ate it, taking care not to drip anything on her new dress.

When they'd both finished, Clarence left a dime by his plate and went to pay the bill at the counter. Estella slipped some more change onto the table. Another point of irritation: he was a cheap tipper. She caught up with him and they left the diner, the bell on the door clanging again as they opened it to step outside onto the cement. Music was now coming from the boxing club, a radio station playing popular music through the sound system.

Clarence shadow-boxed as they walked up the street. He was enjoying himself. A spring robin was singing like mad in an elm tree about to leaf out, competing with the music coming from the club. There was no breeze at all. It was going to be hot inside.

If it hadn't been for Peter Boone, she'd have asked Clarence to take her home.

At that moment a taxi pulled up across the street from them. The windows were down, and Estella saw a small man hand the driver a bill over the back of the seat and then open the street-side door and step out. He hauled an enormous gear bag out of the car after him and hiked it onto his shoulder. As he started across the street toward them, Estella saw that it was Peter. He appeared to recognize her at the same moment. She stepped toward the curb, lifting her arm to wave at Peter, when the same Cadillac that had cruised by earlier came flying around the corner, fishtailing this time, and ran right into Peter Boone, who was now in the middle of Railway, looking at Estella, heading for her and the boxing club.

Estella tried to warn him but it was too late. Peter was instantly separated from his gear bag, and he and the bag flew in front of the big car, which came to a sudden, screeching stop. Peter and his bag hit the pavement twenty feet in front of the Cadillac. He lay there, not moving. A pair of boxing gloves bounced out of a rip in the bag, which was still sliding down the street, and one of them landed by Peter's head. It was sickening, the way he lay there in the street. Everything seemed to come to a halt, everything but the music.

The woman driving got out of the car and started to scream, "Where did he come from? I didn't see him. Where *the fuck* did he come from?"

Estella ran toward Peter. Clarence followed and tried to grab her arm and stop her, but she shook him off. One of Peter's legs was at the wrong angle, and blood spilled from a terrible gash above his temple. The bloated boxing glove lay beside him, as though it had delivered a blow and then quit. The taxi driver, who had not yet moved, now suddenly pulled away from the curb and left as though he did not want an accident that he'd had no part in to interfere with his evening's fares. He didn't even look. He pretended that he hadn't seen a thing.

"Call an ambulance," Estella shouted, but no one moved. She was kneeling now beside Peter, and Clarence stood behind her looking as though he might keel over, his face drained of colour.

"Clarence," she said, trying now to sound calm. "Go into the diner and tell them to call an ambulance. Now. Right now. And then the police. Call them, too."

He finally did as she told him.

A man with grey hair who had apparently got out the passenger side of the Cadillac was now stuffing the blond driver into the back seat, and Estella used her teacher voice and yelled at them: "Don't you dare leave. And don't move that car. I have your licence number." She didn't, but they must have believed her because they stayed put. The man got into the back seat of the car too, and the two of them sat there.

When Clarence returned, she made him take off his suit jacket—she had to practically pull it off him because he resisted—and she draped it over Peter. She didn't know if he was dead or alive. People started filing out of the diner and the boxing club, and then a man from the club came running and said he was a doctor. He was carrying a leather bag, like doctors in the movies. Estella supposed boxing matches had doctors in attendance. She stood up and let him check Peter as best he could. Someone else started directing traffic around the accident scene. The doctor said they couldn't move Peter without a backboard. There was one at the club, and someone went to get it, but then the ambulance came, and then the police, and Estella and Clarence had to get in the back of the police car and tell them what had happened while the attendants took Peter away in the ambulance, lights flashing. Clarence kept asking about his jacket, could he get it back, and the policeman said, "In time." Estella could see Clarence looking up the street where the ambulance and his jacket had disappeared as she told the policeman what had happened.

"It was my fault," she said. "He saw me and he wasn't watching."

"How could it be your fault?" Clarence said. "We were just standing there on the sidewalk."

"Let the lady talk," the policeman said. "Your turn will come."

"That car came flying around the corner," Estella said. "And I mean flying. Fishtailing. I wonder if she was drunk. The driver. Do you check for that? I saw the look on her face. She looked terrified. Maybe they were fighting. Maybe that was it."

"You're jumping to conclusions," Clarence said.

"Clarence, shut up," Estella said.

"Right," said the policeman, giving Clarence his own warning look.

Estella tried to slow down then and tell the rest of the story just the way it had happened. Peter getting out of the taxi and crossing the street. The car hitting him. The taxi driver leaving, even though he had clearly seen what happened.

When it was Clarence's turn, he simply said, "What she said. She's better at details than me."

"You're sure?"

"Yeah. The guy got out of a taxi and was crossing the street. The Caddy came around the corner and hit him. Blondie was driving, even though the guy is probably going to try and tell you he was. The Caddy stopped. The taxi left. That's about it. Can we go now? I need to get my jacket." Estella thought he was pouting because she'd told him to shut up.

"I know his name," she said. "Did I tell you that?"

"No," the policeman said.

"Peter Boone. From Lake Claire, north of Prince Albert. At least that's where he grew up. His mother still lives there. She works at The Travellers Hotel. He was here for the fight tonight."

The policeman wrote it all down, and then Clarence and Estella got out of his car. Another policeman was in the Cadillac talking to the driver and the grey-haired man. Peter's gear was still scattered in the street, and Estella thought she could see blood where his head had lain. More policemen were blocking the road to traffic and placing orange cones in the street. A crowd was gathered on the sidewalk in front of the boxing club. They knew by now that the accident victim was on the evening's card.

"I wonder why they took my jacket," Clarence said.

"Stop worrying about your damned jacket," Estella said. "I'm sure we can collect it at the hospital."

"At the hospital?" Clarence said.

"Yes," Estella said. "We're going to the hospital now. Unless you think the other contender—the one you said was the favourite—is going to fight with himself for the title. If so, you can stay and watch and I'll go alone."

"You're upset," Clarence said.

"Of course I am," Estella said. "I know that man. Now are we going or not?"

"Yes, we're going," Clarence said.

The Grey Nuns' Hospital was just around the corner so they

assumed that Peter had been taken there. They went to the emergency entrance and asked if he'd been brought in and were told yes, but that was as far as they got. They sat in a waiting room. There were others there—a man who had been stabbed, a crying child with a fever, a woman who appeared to be having an allergy attack—but they were all waiting for treatment, and Estella and Clarence were the only ones waiting for word on the condition of someone else. And they were certainly the only ones there in any kind of evening attire. Estella once again felt self-conscious about the colour and the neckline of her dress. Clarence kept going on about his jacket, and she wished he did have it so she could ask him for it to cover up her bare shoulders. At the same time, she wanted to tell him to be quiet, his missing jacket was not the most important thing about the evening.

When Estella inquired at the counter for the third time, a nurse finally told her that Peter was stable for now.

"So he's not dead?" Estella said.

"He's not dead," the nurse said. "He has broken bones. He's stable for the moment. That's all I can tell you. You aren't family."

Clarence convinced the nurse to get his jacket back, and she did, perhaps just to get rid of them, and he checked it over carefully, for blood, Estella thought, growing more and more annoyed with him.

They went home.

Under the street lamp in front of her parents' house, after they'd spent hours at the hospital and it was at least midnight and Estella was exhausted, she could see that Clarence had something to say. She assumed he was about to break it off with her, and she wanted to speed things up and tell him it was all right, she agreed, they should stop seeing each other, no hard feelings.

She had it altogether wrong, though, and Clarence did not want to break it off. Instead, he asked her to marry him. He reached into his jacket pocket and took out a ring, and he proposed marriage.

Estella couldn't have been more shocked, and at the same time she wanted to laugh, because that's why Clarence had been fussing about the missing jacket, he'd had an engagement ring in the pocket. She remembered herself pulling the jacket off him while he resisted, and it was farcical, like a situation comedy on television, *I Love Lucy*. And then she thought maybe he was joking and it wasn't a real ring, it was a prize from a box of Cracker Jack. That would have happened to Lucy, wouldn't it? Ricky would have lost the real ring, and given her a toy one.

But of course the ring was real. Clarence Angell was really asking her to marry him on the very night that it had become absolutely clear to her that there was no point continuing with their relationship, whatever it was. It wasn't love. Not on her part, and she didn't believe on his, either. She had no idea why he wanted to marry her.

The ring sparkled under the street light. It looked expensive. Clarence was looking impatient. He clearly hadn't expected her to take so long to say yes.

"I'm sorry," she said. "I can't marry you. I thought . . . well, I don't know what I thought, except that we don't love each other, not like that." She was thinking about how annoyed Clarence had been when his jacket had gone in the ambulance—well, okay, she could see why he was worried about the ring, but if it hadn't been for the ring, she was sure he would have foregone the trip to the hospital and stayed for the fights instead. She remembered how she had felt at the hospital, how what she'd really wanted was for

Clarence to leave so she could wait out the uncertainty of Peter's injury by herself. Peter Boone was of no interest to Clarence. It was wrong that he was there.

Clarence's face said that he'd fully expected Estella to say yes to his proposal. He was left holding out the ring, a diamond of a pretty good size, until Estella finally reached out and closed the lid on the case and then slipped the box back into his jacket pocket.

"Is it the boxer?" Clarence asked. "Are you upset about him? Because the nurse said he's stable. That's good news."

"It's not that," Estella said. "And there's not really any good news yet, Clarence. They don't know anything. He could still die, or end up with brain damage."

"He's not going to die," Clarence said. "He'll be back in the ring before you know it. What's he to you, anyway? Small-town scrappers are a dime a dozen in boxing."

And that did it. That one thing, that one phrase—*dime a dozen*—confirmed to Estella what she had known but had not wanted to admit to herself: that she didn't even like Clarence Angell.

"Clarence," she said, "I don't want to marry you. I don't think of you in that way. I thought you knew that. In fact, I thought you felt the same way."

Clarence's confusion turned to anger.

"Is that why you're wearing that dress?" he asked. "To impress someone you don't think of 'in that way'?"

Estella looked down at her dress, the one she'd felt uncomfortable in all night and should never have bought. She had others like it, wrap dresses in good fabrics with white piping or covered buttons, sophisticated shoes to go with them. She regretted that she'd ever indulged herself. It must have had something to do with her age, her mother's death.

"You've never told me I meant anything more to you than a friend would," she said.

He laughed in a way that wasn't funny, and then he said, "So what kind of whore does that make you? All those visits to the midnight hotels, you know them all now, don't you. Maybe you knew them before you met me."

That's when she slapped him, right there under the street light for anyone to see who happened to be looking out a window, although it was late enough that the houses were in darkness and she hoped no one was.

He stood there rubbing his cheek.

"I certainly thought we were moving toward marriage," he said, "but I guess I got it wrong. You're not who I thought you were."

"Clearly, since I turned out to be a whore," Estella said.

Then, before she could say anything else, Clarence grabbed her roughly and kissed her on the mouth, one hand on the small of her back and the other behind her head, his tongue working to find its way between her lips. She tried to push him away, but then his hands slid down to her hips and he pulled her to him harder, almost violently. He was breathing heavily, out of anger, not passion. "Is that what you want?" he said. "I can give you that, but I thought you were a better sort. Although I suppose I should have known, considering the first day we met."

"What in the name of God are you thinking?" she said, struggling to shove him away from her. "I've never said that I loved you. I don't love you, and you don't love me, either. I don't know why you want to marry me, but get a hold of yourself."

"It's not enough," he said, angry now to the point that she would have been frightened of him if they hadn't been standing in the street in front of her house. "You owe me more than that."

Owe? she thought, anger now growing in her as well. She didn't owe him or any other man anything.

"Fuck you, Clarence," she said. She turned around and walked away from him.

"You are middle-aged, and you live with your father," he shouted. "You might as well be an old spinster who rides a horse to a one-room school every day."

"That's enough," she said. "I'm sorry this is ending so badly. We've had some good times together." She thought she saw a curtain move in the neighbour's front window, and imagined gossip up and down the street.

"Maybe *you* have," Clarence said.

She stopped. "What does that mean?"

"Just what I said. You've had a good time dining out on my money."

Why, oh why, had she kept up this charade for so long?

"And that's why you asked me to marry you?" she said. "Because I owe you money? Well, send me a bill. I'll put a cheque in the mail."

She was almost at the front steps, but she stopped, and looked at him again.

"Oh my God," she said. "You want money, that's why you're asking me to marry you."

Clarence shook his head.

"For a mathematics teacher, you are a stupid woman," he said. "You think you're the daughter of bloody royalty."

"And you think I'm a catch because of my father's money. You see that my father is old, and you think there's bound to be a will with a pretty substantial bequest. Is that why you came to my mother's funeral in the first place? If so, I have to hand it to you.

You're patient, but then I hear that's a trait of a good con man."

Clarence was no longer standing under the street light; he had moved toward his precious yellow sedan, and Estella couldn't read his face. "I don't need your father's money," he said. And then he got in the car and drove away.

Estella was relieved that he was gone. She was angry, but only at herself now, for having such bad judgment, for giving Clarence Angell even the time of day.

She hardly slept that night between disgust with herself and concern for Peter, and fear that everyone on the block was talking about her.

In the morning at breakfast she studied her father and thought that her mother had been right when she'd said he had turned into an old man. Since Beatrice's death, he'd had at least one fall that he would admit to, and Estella suspected there had been others, and she was beginning to worry about the staircase. He'd recently run his car into the ditch on his way out to the plant and Estella had insisted he give up his driver's licence. He'd reacted as though she'd just asked him to check himself into a home, and ever since, he'd been short-tempered with her. The word cantankerous came to mind, which he had never before been.

She thought about telling him that she was done with Clarence Angell, but she was afraid of what he would say, that he would find a reason to blame her for not being able to hang onto a man when she finally had one. She decided he didn't need to know about Clarence, and she told him instead about Peter Boone's accident.

"You might remember him from the hotel at the lake," she said. "His mother works there. He's the young man who's always wanted to be a boxer."

Her father nodded, perhaps remembering the boy who picked up dishes in the restaurant.

"I wonder if anyone has thought to be in touch with his mother," she said.

After breakfast, she went to the hospital, where she learned from an admittance clerk that Peter had been moved from emergency to intensive care. He was still listed as stable. She found the ICU but the doors were locked and a sign read "Authorized Personnel Only." The nurses' station was inside the doors and Estella couldn't get anyone's attention. She went back to the admittance desk and spoke to the clerk again.

"Do you know if his mother has been notified?" she asked. "Would the police have called her, or someone here?"

"I can't say. I don't have that kind of information."

"Has anyone else been up to see him? Someone from the boxing club, a trainer? Anyone at all?"

"There's nothing I can tell you except that he's in the ICU."

Estella decided she'd better call Peter's mother in case no one else had. She found a pay phone and got a number for the hotel in Lake Claire from directory assistance, and then loaded the phone with coins and called. It was a good thing she did. Peter's mother didn't know anything, and so Estella was the bearer of the news that there'd been an accident and her son was lying in a hospital bed. She thought he was in a coma, although she didn't know that for sure.

"He was knocked out, then," Peter's mother said. "In the ring."

"No, not in the ring." Estella then repeated the story, because she realized the woman was having trouble taking it in. "Not knocked out in the bout last night, Mrs. Boone," she said. "He was hit by a car. In front of the boxing club. It was before the fight. He was just arriving when a car came out of nowhere. I'm so sorry to be telling you this."

"And you're calling from the hospital?" Peter's mother said. "You're a nurse at the hospital?"

"I am at the hospital," Estella said, "but I'm not a nurse, and they won't let me see him." Then she gave her name again and explained that she had witnessed the accident because she'd been going to see the fight. She knew Peter from Lake Claire, she said, and explained that her family rented cottages every summer, that she had first met Peter when he was just a boy.

"Oh, yes," his mother said. "I know now. The Diamonds. There are a lot of you. I don't know which one you are. I'm sorry."

"That's okay," Estella said. Then she said something impulsively. "If you want to come and see your son, why don't you stay with us? We have a big house. We would be happy if you stayed with us, and I can drive you up to the hospital every day. It's not that far from where we live."

She imagined her own mother approving—*It's the right thing to do*—and then Estella gave Peter's mother their phone number and said to call from the bus depot.

Shirley Boone arrived the next day. Estella picked her up at the bus depot and took her right to the hospital to see her son. It had been a long trip, Shirley said, avoiding the question of her son's current status. A two-hour wait in Prince Albert, then another transfer in Saskatoon. She'd gone for a walk after having a sandwich at the lunch counter there, and had become lost and had to ask a stranger for directions. She'd worried she'd gotten on the wrong bus and might end up in Edmonton and was relieved when she saw a highway sign that told her she was on the right road.

When they got to the hospital, Estella took Peter's mother to the admittance desk, and this time the clerk found someone who would let her in to see her son. Estella delivered her to the locked doors and a nurse came and opened them. She would have let both of them in, but Estella didn't think it was right, not until Shirley Boone spoke to someone and found out what was going on. She went for coffee in the cafeteria and told Shirley she would wait for her there.

Two hours later, Shirley sat down across from her and reported that Peter would be kept sedated until the swelling in his brain went down. He had a dislocated shoulder and a broken leg, and his jaw was wired shut. Shirley was the picture of self-control, Estella thought, sitting across from her at the long white cafeteria table, but when Estella asked her if Peter was in pain, she broke down. Estella found a package of tissues in her purse and Shirley pulled one out as she told Estella that they had her son on morphine, so she didn't think he was in pain.

"Will he be addicted?" Shirley asked. "He wouldn't want that. He's never had a drink in his life because he thought it might affect his training."

"I'm sure he won't be addicted," Estella said. "The doctors will know how to manage that." She was thinking that Jack had come home from the war addicted to morphine, and what a hard time he'd had weaning himself off of it.

Shirley Boone stayed at the hospital that night, and then the next day she asked Estella to drive her back to the bus depot. Estella objected and tried to convince Shirley to stay with them, they had lots of room, but Shirley said she had to get back to work. There was only her, she said, running the hotel at this time of year. There was no else to do it. She would lose her job if she stayed away. Estella drove her to the bus depot and promised that she would visit Peter, and she would call her every day and let her know how he was doing.

She requested another leave from school, just a few weeks this time, she said, to care for a nephew who'd been in an accident. She'd just had an interview for a vice-principal's job and she worried it might interfere with her chances of getting it, but she went ahead anyway. She knew it wasn't necessary for someone to sit all day by Peter's bed, but she felt responsible, and she thought of Jack, who had been the same age when he'd come back from the war nearly twenty years ago. She'd hoped then that Jack had had someone by his bedside during his time in the French hospital—a nurse, or a volunteer, or some French soldier's mother—but there had been so many wounded soldiers they were probably lucky to have even a bed.

She remembered reading to Jack, so she took *The Collected Works of Robert Service* to the hospital and read poems to Peter. Sam McGee and Dan McGrew and "The Spell of the Yukon." She did other things she'd done with Jack: rubbed his feet, brushed his hair, and trimmed his fingernails. She wondered if she was trying to do a better job than she had with Jack, because she had not managed to fix him and he was still broken, even though he and Rose now had two sons.

A week after the accident, the medical staff woke Peter up and got him breathing on his own again. He knew where he was, and the doctors were happy with his responses when they poked and prodded. Estella immediately phoned Shirley and gave her the news. Peter took himself off morphine as soon as he found out he was on it. He had a rough few days, but he was insistent that he didn't want to be on any drug that he didn't need to stay alive. He was in the city for another week before he was moved to Prince Albert to be closer to home.

All that week before he was transferred, Estella continued to sit with him, but it was different now that he was awake. He was a young man she did not know well and had not spoken to since he was a teenager helping his mother at The Travellers. It was hard for them to talk because of his wired jaw. Although he had recognized Estella right away, he had no memory of the accident and couldn't figure out how she knew he was in the hospital, even though she explained several times.

When one of the nurses told him that it had been Estella who'd been keeping him clean-shaven, he grew embarrassed. The nurse made it worse by saying, "I guess she thinks you're too handsome to lie here looking like Robinson Crusoe."

After the nurse left the room, Estella picked up his hand and patted it. She understood. It would not be easy for a young man to realize he'd been cared for in such a personal way by a woman who was neither a nurse nor his mother.

"Don't worry," she said, "I grew up with four brothers. You remind me of my brother Jack. You might remember him from the lake."

The day Peter was transferred to Prince Albert and the ambulance was on its way to collect him, she went up to the hospital to say goodbye. He looked so much better than he had just a week ago, even with the wires in his mouth and the shaved head and the cast on his leg.

"I'm grateful for everything you did," he managed to say through the wires.

"I really didn't do much," she said. What had she done other than keep him company? Especially since she believed the accident to have been at least partly her fault.

There was only a month left until the summer break but she returned to school anyway after Peter was gone, because she didn't want to jeopardize her chance at the job she'd applied for. She fell back into her old routine, although without Clarence on Saturday nights. Her father didn't seem to notice when she stayed home, and she didn't tell him Clarence was no longer in the picture. She dreaded telling any Diamond that she'd broken it off, and imagined the looks of pity that would come because Clarence had been her last chance and now she truly was a spinster. She wondered what his version of the story was, and what words he was using to describe her when he told it.

A few days before the end of the school year, she was summoned from the classroom to take a call from a Mr. Willis in central office. The school secretary handed her the phone and then went to supervise her class. Mr. Willis informed her that she was not being offered the vice-principal position because her teaching record had too many interruptions when she'd taken leaves to care for her brother and her mother and, just recently, the nephew.

"All that is admirable, Miss Diamond," Mr. Willis said. "But you have a lot of responsibilities outside of school, and we therefore don't think you are a good fit for our administration cohort." He then went on to say she was not to take this in any way as a reflection of their opinion of her as a teacher of mathematics, and that she had their full confidence in that regard.

"And on a personal note," said Mr. Willis, "I hear congratulations are in order. We wish you all the best on your engagement."

"Engagement?" Estella said. "Excuse me?"

There was silence, and then Mr. Willis recovered and said, "I'm
sorry, perhaps we were misinformed."

"Is that the reason you're not offering me the job?" Estella asked.
"Because you thought I was getting married? It's 1965, in case you
hadn't noticed. And I'm too old to be popping out babies."

It took him a few seconds to recover his voice, but he managed
to say, "That would never enter into the decision. As I said . . ."

She didn't wait for a repeat of the official reason.

Estella had been back in charge of her students for just minutes when one of the other women teachers knocked on her
door and called her out to the hall. She told Estella she'd seen
one of the older boys with a set of brass knuckles and she wasn't
sure what to do, since the neither the principal nor the vice was
in the school.

Estella didn't know why it was up to her to handle it, especially
given that she was apparently not fit for school administration,
but she went looking for the boy. She found him with a younger
student, whom he'd backed up against a locker and was jabbing
in the chin with the brass knuckles. Estella grabbed him from
behind, pulled him away from the younger boy, and told him that
if she ever caught him in any act of torture again, she would beat
him senseless.

"Give me that weapon right now," she said.

He handed over the brass knuckles.

"Now get out. And don't come back. I don't care what your parents say. You aren't welcome here next year. Find yourself a job.

Do something useful the world might eventually thank you for."

The boy started to say that she couldn't talk to him that way.

"No sense telling me that," she said. "I don't care. Now get out." He left.

Later, when the principal was back in his office, she handed him her letter of resignation in a sealed envelope and informed him that he might have to deal with the boy's parents if they cared enough to call and complain. In fact, he might want to call them now and get ahead of it.

"The year's almost over, Estella," the principal said. "Let's just forget about it."

She pointed at the envelope and said, "I'm resigning, in case you're interested," and left the office before he could talk her out of it.

"I hope you've been keeping an eye on your car in the lot," he called after her.

Her car.

She went to check, and of course all four tires were flat, and the driver's side window was broken.

She made the obligatory report to the police, and then called a tow truck and had them haul the car to the Ford dealership. It was a five-year-old Falcon and she'd been planning to replace it anyway.

As she waited for a salesman, she looked around the showroom at the new cars and a shiny white one caught her eye. She'd never seen a car like it. There was a horse in mid-flight on the grill, and an emblem on the passenger side identified the car as a Mustang. A mounted poster propped on the hood showed a picture of a woman in a bride's dress, looking as though she was on the run, like the horse, apparently making her break from married life. Was that her? Estella wondered. By the time a salesman was available, she had already convinced herself to buy the car. It was a stupid thing to do considering that she had just quit her job, but she bought it anyway.

She felt something akin to freedom as she pulled off the lot, even though she knew she was not likely to be driving into the sunset anytime soon.

EVERY YEAR SINCE he'd discovered Lake Claire, Oliver had travelled there in his own car, always a roomy Oldsmobile sedan. He hadn't driven anything else since the Depression, and his current Oldsmobile had never been farther than the brick plant without him behind the wheel. When he'd given up his driver's licence, Estella had promised him that they would continue to travel in his car, even to the lake, and he could issue orders from the passenger seat. When she announced that she had changed her mind and they were going to the lake in her new Mustang— which Oliver called her "toy car"—he said that had not been the agreement and he refused to travel with her.

"What does it matter which car you're in?" Estella said. "I'm the one driving."

"I want to get there alive," he said.

Then he decided he was taking his new La-Z-Boy armchair, and he argued that it would only fit in the trunk of the Oldsmobile. If there was no one to drive it, he'd drive it himself, with or without a licence. Estella normally bent over backwards to avoid fighting with him, but this time she refused to change her mind. She had a new car and she wanted to take it. Oliver told her she had become stubborn in middle age, and she replied that she had got it from someone and it wasn't her mother.

In the end, Mathew and Fay said they would drive Oliver in the Oldsmobile. They agreed he was being difficult, but Estella was getting as bad as he was, could she not see that? Why couldn't she have driven his car to keep the peace?

"Why is keeping the peace my job?" she asked, even as she wondered why she didn't just placate her father and go in his car.

On the Friday of the July holiday weekend, Mathew and Fay came for Oliver and then collected a woman named Lorette whom they'd hired for the two weeks they were to be at the lake. Lorette had been Gladys's idea. She was thinking ahead to Estella getting married and moving out, because Estella had still not told them she was done with Clarence. Gladys knew that nothing would ever convince Oliver to leave his home when Estella wasn't there to look after him, so she proposed a trial run with a private nurse.

Estella agreed. She was curious to know what her father would think of hired help.

Once Oliver was away with Mathew and Fay, she locked the house and headed out in her new car. Besides the car, she had in her suitcase one other post-Clarence item of vanity: a two-piece bathing suit with a bright geometric pattern resembling a Mondrian painting. She'd never before worn a two-piece. In spite of Clarence Angell calling her a whore, she was modest when it came to public displays of her body. She was the only one of the Diamond women—with the exception of her mother and the significantly older Gladys—who had never displayed her midriff on the beach.

As she drove, she cranked up the radio and sang along. She was hardly out of the city when she was stopped for speeding.

"What's New Pussycat?" was blasting and the young officer had to ask her to turn the radio down. She told him that she was a teacher and she was so relieved school was over for the year that she'd forgotten herself. He didn't give her a ticket. When she got to Prince Albert, she stopped at the A&W and ordered a burger and root beer, which were delivered on a window tray by a carhop. Her new car was a bit of a sensation in the drive-in lot.

Once she was back on the highway again, she realized the sedan in front of her was her father's Oldsmobile. The trunk lid was tied down with ropes because of the armchair, and she could see Oliver and Lorette's heads through the back window. She considered passing but Mathew was driving exactly the speed limit, so she settled in behind them and avoided the temptation to step on the gas.

When they finally turned off the access road into the village, they found it packed with people, there for the long weekend. The drive along the main street happened in starts and stops as families and groups of teenagers crossed back and forth between the beach and the shops. Estella followed Mathew and ignored the gawkers— mostly young men, not wives on the run—who took an interest in her car. She noted all the changes that had taken place over the fifteen years since she'd first seen Lake Claire. There had been no Dot's Beach Hut then, no motel next to The Travellers, no Beach Café, no tackle shop or bicycle rental kiosk, no concession stand at the marina, where a dozen people were now lined up to order hot dogs or onion rings. Something new at the marina caught her eye, a party boat of some kind with an awning that covered the upper deck. She wondered what that was about.

When they finally negotiated their way through the crowds

and past the three-way stop that marked the end of the village, they made their way to Fosters and parked in front of the office. Estella and Mathew went inside for their keys, and found Allen Foster behind the counter, waiting for them. He too was now a middle-aged man with grey in his hair. He showed them the list of the cottages they'd booked, and which Diamonds had already checked in. When Estella looked at the names, she realized they'd forgotten to cancel the cottage for Harold and Astrid, Theo's son and daughter-in-law, who had stayed behind with their newborn premature baby. She wondered if she might take it for herself, but she knew she shouldn't leave her father alone with Lorette. She and Mathew discussed whether they ought to keep the key, just in case Astrid and Harold were able to come with the baby for a few days, and they decided they should. Everyone was hoping they would make it so they could set a new record for the most Diamonds at the lake. They'd planned for forty-three, but then Astrid had gone into early labour. Estella didn't understand the fuss over the number and thought forty-one Diamonds was probably plenty.

Before they left the office, Allen told them all about the new paddlewheeler. The owner of the marina had purchased it from a man who had previously toured it up and down the Missouri River in Montana. It had been renamed the *Claire de la Lune* and could hold up to fifty passengers on deck or below, depending on the weather. You could book the whole boat for a lake cruise, or purchase a ticket for the sunset tour every evening. Estella knew the marina owner practically lived at the golf clubhouse and she said it was hard to picture him touring cottagers around the lake.

"He's hired someone," Allen said. "Peter Boone, remember him? He was in a bad accident in the spring but he seems to be alright."

Estella didn't tell Allen that she knew exactly how bad the accident had been. Telling him she'd witnessed it would have meant
telling him more, all the details of what she'd been doing in front
of a boxing club, so instead, she said simply that she'd heard about
the accident, and was glad to learn Peter had been able to go back
to work. As she and Mathew left the office with their keys, she
thought that Peter must have recovered a lot faster than Jack had.
Noise still sent Jack to a dark room with an ice bag for his head.

"Tell Oliver I'll drop by after supper," Allen called after them.
"We've got a year's worth of breeze to shoot."

Estella parked next to Emily Carr, as usual, and Mathew pulled
up behind her to unload Oliver's chair and his suitcase. By now,
Oliver had figured out why Lorette was there and he wasn't happy.
She was a woman in her fifties who looked like she'd seen it all
before, and she was unfazed when Oliver brushed her away and
refused any help as he made his way up the steps. Because he
insisted he was going to sleep in his armchair in the living room,
Estella took the big bedroom and gave Lorette the one that had
always been hers. They unpacked the bags while Oliver sat on the
deck and watched his sons appropriate the picnic tables, as they
did every year.

Later, they all gathered outside for a barbecue. At sunset,
the new paddlewheeler made its way across the bay with patio
lanterns glowing orange and yellow under the awning. Music
played through the sound system, Roy Orbison singing "Only the
Lonely." The Diamonds all went down to the beach with their
Dixie cups to watch the boat pass, even Oliver.

At bedtime, Estella had to negotiate with her father over what
Lorette was allowed to do. He had to let her help him in the

shower, she said. There were no bars to hang on to and they didn't want him to have a fall. She reminded him that he'd had a close call the year before when he'd slipped on the tiles stepping out of the shower. She tried to lighten the fact of his new need for assistance by saying, "You and Allen should have thought about your old ages when you designed the bathrooms."

Lorette tried to help by telling him she understood his issues about privacy, and that she was a professional and he didn't have anything she hadn't seen before, but that only made it worse. In the end, he refused to have a shower.

After Oliver was finally settled for the night in his armchair, Estella put on her new bathing suit and went for a swim in the dark. The surface of the water was black and she couldn't see the lake bottom, but after so many years she could have walked in with her eyes closed. The water was warmer than usual because the weather in June had been so hot. Still, the air was cool, and when she got out she dried herself quickly and went back to the cottage for a hot shower.

She found her father still asleep in his chair, and Lorette browsing through a magazine with a tiny reading light clipped onto it. Lorette had come prepared, Estella thought. Probably more prepared than she would ever be for this new version of Oliver Diamond.

THE NEXT MORNING Estella walked to The Travellers for breakfast, hoping to run into Peter so she could see for herself how he was doing. She expected his mother to be waiting tables in the restaurant but she wasn't there. Estella asked the teenaged girl

who took her order if Peter was around, and she said, "He sometimes goes fishing in the morning. Or he might be at the marina
working on the boat."

On her way out, she saw Shirley Boone at the hotel registration
desk. She waved at her when she went by but she wasn't sure that
Shirley recognized her. She was busy with guests so Estella didn't
hang around.

She went down to the marina to see if Peter was there, but it
was deserted except for some teenaged boys fishing off the pier.
She walked out to where the paddlewheeler was moored and had
a look at it. It was perhaps thirty feet long, and *Claire de la Lune*
was newly painted on the side. A pair of foam fenders protected
the boat from the pier as it bobbed up against it. A sandwich board
propped on the pier gave the sunset cruise details.

She returned to Fosters along the old trail through the trees
and sat with her father on the deck. Her teenaged nephew Paul—
Andrew's youngest—was sitting by himself on a lawn chair,
smoking a cigarette. He was wearing a black leather jacket even
though it was too hot for it.

"What's wrong with him, anyway?" Oliver said. "He looks like
a hooligan."

"He's a teenager," Estella said. "It's the style." She was thinking
about the incident at school with the brass knuckles and hoped
Paul wasn't turning into one of those boys.

"His father was overseas when he was not much older," Oliver
said. "I don't imagine he was thinking about style when he was
fighting the Germans."

"I know, Dad," she said, "you're right." She agreed with everything he said, trying her best to leave the arguing to Lorette.

That evening they watched the paddlewheeler cross the bay, Roy Orbison once again playing on the sound system, "Crying" this time, and then "Running Scared" on the way back to the marina.

"Surely they're planning to change the music," Fay said. "Or is the entire village going to be subjected to Roy Orbison every night?"

Later, Estella swam alone in the dark again. This time she struck out across the water toward the point at the far end of the bay, even though she knew she ought to swim parallel to the shore.

The next night she went farther still before turning back.

The night after that she made it all the way to the point.

On the way back she grew aware of a sound in the water. She stopped swimming and tried to see in the darkness where the sound was coming from, and she saw someone paddling behind her in a canoe. It was Peter Boone. When he saw that she had stopped swimming, he laid his paddle across the gunwales and let the canoe drift alongside her. He said he'd been at the point and had seen someone approach in the water and worried about a swimmer alone in the darkness.

She said she didn't think daylight or dark made any difference, if you got into trouble alone you were likely going to drown.

He said, "I meant a motorboat could come along and run over you."

Something she hadn't thought of.

She was still treading water and starting to feel the cold, but she said, "I hear that's you playing Roy Orbison on the paddle-wheeler every night. Don't be too offended if my family suggests you change the music."

Then she said she was too cold to talk and she began to swim again. Peter followed her all the way, into the shallow water in front of Fosters. He beached the bow of the canoe in the sand while Estella got out shivering and wrapped herself up in her beach towel. Peter seemed to be waiting in the canoe for her to head up to the cottages. She searched in the dark for her plastic beach sandals, and shoved her feet into them.

Then she said, her teeth chattering, "Thanks for the warning about the motorboats. I should have thought of that."

He stuck his paddle into the sand and pushed himself off, and she watched the canoe disappear in the darkness. Then she practically ran up the embankment and across the grass.

When she got back to the cottage her father was smoking a cigar on the deck in his pyjamas and Lorette was inside, sitting on the couch. Estella could see the back of her head through the window.

"I thought you'd be asleep," she said.

"I don't like that woman," Oliver said.

"You don't have to like her," Estella said. "Just let her help."

She dropped her wet towel and hung it over the deck railing and was about to step inside the cottage and get into a hot shower when her father said, "Always thinking about yourself, aren't you."

"Dad," she said, turning back to him. She was now in her wet bathing suit without her towel, and her teeth were chattering so hard she could barely talk. "It wasn't my idea. The others thought we could use an extra hand."

"I don't see you doing much," he said. "You don't have children to put to bed, do you?"

She never snapped at her father but she did now. "It's been a long year, Dad," she said. "I need a break once in a while, and that includes from you. Anyway, I can't argue. I'm freezing."

Once again she went to open the door to the cottage, but he wasn't done.

"I want you to move that damned car in the morning," he said. "Move it up to Mathew's cottage and bring the Oldsmobile back to its proper spot."

"What's got into you?" she asked.

"I could ask you the same thing," he said. "What kind of bathing suit is that for a grown woman? It's a good thing your mother isn't here."

She had no idea what had got under his skin besides Lorette, but she was too cold to fight with him. She went inside and grabbed her nightgown and housecoat from the bedroom, and then sent Lorette out to get him. She turned on the shower and got in, and let the hot water run over her goosebumps.

When she had finally stopped shivering, she turned off the water, and she could immediately hear Oliver yelling at poor Lorette. She quickly dried herself off and got into her pyjamas, thinking she would run to Theo's cottage and get him, but by the time she came out of the bathroom, the shouting had stopped. Oliver was in his armchair and Lorette was arranging a pillow behind his head. Lorette put her finger to her lips and motioned for Estella to go to her room, so she did. She sat on the edge of her bed and listened, waiting for the yelling to start up again, but it didn't.

An hour later, when all was quiet, she slipped out to check. Her father appeared to be asleep and Lorette was under a blanket on the couch. She gave Estella a thumbs-up. Estella brushed her teeth and tiptoed back to her room.

IN THE MORNING, it was as though the whole episode hadn't happened. When Estella got up, her father was eating a boiled egg at the table. She sat down with him and he remarked that it was going to be hot, over eighty degrees, and they should keep the cottage shut up if they could. It was as though he had no memory of his tantrum the night before. Estella tested the water by saying, "I thought I might switch the cars, move the Oldsmobile from Mathew's today and park it here, where you can see it. What do you think?"

"Suit yourself," he said. "But I don't need to see it. I know where it is."

She spent the day with the women and the younger kids at the beach in front of the cottages while the teenagers walked up to the big public beach and the men went golfing. That night, she went for her swim, parallel to the shore this time instead of out to the point, and she didn't see Peter in his canoe. As her arms cut rhythmically through the water, she remembered the time her mother had put her book in the cooking pot, and how that had preceded her stroke. Did these mood swings of her father's mean something more than old age?

When she got back to shore, Peter was waiting under the spruce tree. There was a walking cane beside him in the sand. She wrapped herself up in her towel and sat down beside him.

She still had the key to Harold's cabin, Tom Thomson, and she wondered if she should get it so they could move inside where it was warmer, but she thought better of it. How could she suggest it without Peter jumping to an awkward conclusion? Instead, they sat in the sand under the tree and talked. He told her much more than he had been able to in the hospital. He had moved to Prince Albert five years ago and had been working on his journeyman's papers as an electrician before the accident. He'd decided to put that on hold, he said, because he could see his mother needed his help. He thought he'd do odd jobs in Lake Claire for a while, see how things went. Now that it was such a popular spot there was plenty of work for a man who was handy with tools. He didn't mention his future in boxing and she didn't ask. They talked for an hour, and then he said good night and picked up his cane and walked home on the bush trail.

The next night, Peter was there again when she finished her swim, and once again they sat by the water and talked. She began to take a pair of sweat pants and a warm sweater down to the beach with her, to pull on over her wet bathing suit. Peter was sometimes there and sometimes not, but she was always happy when she stepped out of the water and saw him sitting under the spruce tree. There was never anyone else on the beach, with the exception of an older woman who took a black lab for a walk at the same time every night. They said hello when she passed, and then went back to talking, their voices low so they wouldn't carry. As she sat in the sand with Peter, Estella thought she understood what was missing from her life: the chance to talk to someone who was not her increasingly difficult father, and was not, in fact, even a Diamond.

One night when Estella got back to the cottage, her father was still sitting on the deck and he wanted to know where she'd been for so long.

"You weren't swimming all that time," he said.

She lied and told him she had been. When Lorette came out and asked if Oliver was ready to go to bed he went in with her, but then immediately had a tantrum over nothing.

Estella followed them inside and wondered where Lorette got her patience.

ESTELLA AND THEO would sometimes have a mid-afternoon cocktail together while the others were still at the beach or the golf course. Theo was almost sixty years old by this time and he said the heat bothered him. Oliver typically had a nap in the afternoon, so they sat on Theo's deck, next door to Emily Carr. They were there one day with their usual gin and tonics when they noticed a man in a Winnebago motorhome with Ontario plates cruising slowly among the cottages, as though he was inspecting them for future reference, or perhaps looking for someone. They watched as the motorhome stopped across the road and the driver got out and walked toward them. He introduced himself as Miles Kingwell from Thunder Bay, and asked if their name was Diamond. He might be a relative by marriage, he said. He and his family were on their way to Jasper in the mountains, he explained, but they'd taken a diversion off the Yellowhead Highway to Lake Claire. They'd heard in the campground about the big family of Diamonds that always stayed at Fosters, and the name Diamond had caught his attention. He'd left his family at the campground and driven to Fosters to introduce himself.

Estella imagined the family stranded in the campground without the motorhome. The mosquitoes were notoriously bad in the trees.

"Your family is from Ontario originally?" Miles Kingwell asked. "The Ottawa Valley?"

Estella told him yes, but they didn't know any family there.

Miles said the connection was through a first wife. He didn't know much about her or the marriage, just a vague story.

Estella thought immediately of Salina, but Theo shook his head and said there was no first wife in their family. He said, "Our father had a brother. George, I believe. He moved to the States many years ago, something to do with the car industry. He and our father lost touch. I suppose George could have been married more than once."

"I don't think that's it," the man said. "But the Diamond name, for sure, from Byrne Corners. I believe the first wife was my great-aunt."

Estella could see that Theo was ready to send this man on his way. He was not convinced of the connection, and they'd not been raised to believe there was family anywhere else that mattered. Estella, though, wondered if her father might want to meet Miles Kingwell. She tried to think quickly because she didn't know whether Theo was denying Salina's existence, or if he genuinely didn't know their father had been married before Beatrice. That would have been astounding if true, but then again the first marriage had never been discussed. If she hadn't found the letters in the teapot and been there for that brief conversation her father had had with Allen Foster, she wouldn't have known he'd been married twice.

She felt she had to say something before Theo did, so she invited the Kingwells to join them for a barbecue that evening, and then she asked Miles what his grandparents' names were.

"Not that they would mean anything to me," she said.

Miles said that his grandfather's name was Burt Kingwell. His grandmother was Roseanne, but he couldn't remember her maiden name. His father's name was Amos.

From the letters, Estella knew of Roseanne as Salina's sister, and Amos as her nephew. These were indeed Salina's relatives.

After Miles Kingwell left, Theo looked at Estella as though he disapproved of what she'd done, invited strangers to supper, but she said, "What can it hurt? Let's see what Father thinks of them."

Later, when Oliver was awake and seated on the deck with his rum and Coke, Estella told him that guests were coming to dinner. She didn't mention who she believed them to be, and said simply that the Kingwells claimed to be relatives by marriage, from Byrne Corners. Theo was there, and he said that maybe they were descendants of Oliver's brother, if they were relatives at all.

When Miles Kingwell arrived in the Winnebago for supper with his family—his wife, a teenaged daughter, and a younger boy—the burgers were already on the barbecues and the Diamonds were sitting at the picnic tables or on the many folding lawn chairs they always brought with them. Theo introduced the strangers to Oliver as being from Ontario with a connection to Byrne Corners, without reporting their claim to be relatives. Then he tried to introduce them to the others but they hardly noticed because they were all so wrapped up in their own stories of the day: one of the kids had got a fish hook stuck in his palm; a couple of the teenaged girls were giddy over a boy they'd met who said he was the provincial junior tennis champion; Paul had gone into the village several hours ago and hadn't yet returned, and should someone go looking for him? Miles tried to break in and explain the family connection through a first wife, and Theo said again that perhaps Oliver's brother had been married more than once, although they wouldn't know anything about that, and then the burgers began to come off the barbecues, and a huge pot of boiled corn appeared on the table. Theo got the

Kingwells drinks from a cooler and told them to help themselves to food.

When Estella went to hand her father a plate of food, she noticed that he was staring at the Kingwells' teenaged daughter, a girl named Cheryl, who was talking to one of the other girls. She was perhaps sixteen years old, and she was dressed in shorts and a T-shirt with flowers on it. She had blond hair cut in a bob curled under, and was wearing stylish pale-pink lipstick. Even when Estella handed her father a plate of food, he didn't take his eyes off the girl.

"Dad," Estella said, tapping him on the knee to get his attention. "Don't stare."

She wondered if this was another sign of impending dementia, some new obsession with young girls, until she had another thought: if the Kingwells were related through Salina, perhaps the daughter looked like her.

After supper, they heard the sound of the paddlewheeler crossing the bay, and Mathew's son Greg reminded everyone that they had the boat booked for a private tour the next evening. They'd hired a photographer from Prince Albert to come along and take a Diamond family picture on deck.

"Too bad there are only forty-one of us," Greg said. "We would have set a new record if that baby hadn't decided to come early."

Estella was sick of hearing about the record.

Oliver hadn't yet gone back to the cottage, even though he usually gave up on the lawn chairs before everyone else and headed for the comfort of his armchair. He was still noticeably staring at Cheryl off and on, and finally Estella said to Miles, by way of explanation, "Dad's seeing a family resemblance in your daughter."

Greg jumped on it right away and said, "Say, if you people are relatives, why don't you come along tomorrow? That'll make forty-five, and we've got our number."

· Just then Paul appeared from wherever he'd been, wearing his leather jacket, and he noticed Cheryl, a new girl, and plunked himself next to her.

Oliver had been watching Paul walk toward them, and he was now giving him some kind of evil eye. Estella grew worried about what her father might be about to say, so she called Lorette and said, "I think Dad is ready to go back." Lorette set down her drink and came to help, but not before Oliver said, "Keep him away from her." Estella managed to get her father headed in the direction of Emily Carr before he could say anything else.

She wanted to talk to her father alone. Lorette helped him into his nightclothes and got him settled in his chair, and then Estella suggested she go back to the group outside. She could hear that Greg's wife, Iris, had gotten her accordion out.

"I don't suppose you like campfire singalongs?" Estella asked Lorette.

It turned out that she did, and she also sang in a church choir, so Estella told her to go save everyone from Iris and her accordion.

When she was gone, Estella said, "Dad, these Kingwells claim to be related to us by marriage. Do you think they could be Salina's relatives?"

He said, without showing any concern that Estella had spoken Salina's name, "Without a doubt. The girl looks just like her."

Then Estella said, "I'm pretty sure Miles is the grandson of Salina's sister. His father's name is Amos. I believe Salina's sister had a boy named Amos."

It was the strangest thing to be talking about Salina as though she were any other family ancestor.

"That would be it, then," her father said.

Then Estella asked, "Is it like seeing her again? After all these years?"

As she spoke, she realized she had gone too far, and was asking something that was none of her business. "Never mind," she said quickly, and she gave her father a quick kiss on the cheek and then turned off all the lights but his reading lamp.

She could hear campfire singing coming from outside, and then it quit, and she saw the lights of the motorhome leaving. Shortly after, Lorette returned.

By this time, Oliver was asleep.

"You might as well sleep in the bedroom," Estella whispered, but Lorette insisted on settling on the couch next to Oliver's chair in case he needed help in the night. Estella didn't think it was necessary for her to take her job quite so seriously, but she was more than thankful she was there.

At breakfast, everyone was talking about what a good voice Lorette had. They were doubly impressed that she knew the words to the songs so they didn't have to sing the choruses over and over. They all agreed Lorette should join them at the lake every year from now on.

IT WAS STILL hot as the Diamonds got ready the next evening for the boat tour and the family photo. The teenaged girls all decided they were wearing their bathing suits, and they set off toward the marina in bare feet and bikinis. Paul, still in his leather jacket, managed to get Cheryl Kingwell's attention again, and the two of them walked with a few other cousins. Estella wore her bathing suit under her shorts and a button-up shirt because she was planning to swim back to the cabin after their tour of the bay. She drove to the marina in the Oldsmobile with her father and Lorette. Miles Kingwell drove the Winnebago full of Diamond children who wanted to see what the house on wheels was like. The others walked along the lakefront, following the teenagers.

The photographer met them in the parking lot, a man named Bob from Prince Albert. Peter Boone was waiting for them on the pier, having already installed the gangplank and turned on the patio lights. A sign draped over the sandwich board said "Cruise unavailable due to private booking." Estella hardly had a chance to talk to Peter, he was so busy getting the forty-one Diamonds and four Kingwells onto the boat and seated on the upper deck. He had his cane but he soon ditched it because it was in the way. There were hard-backed benches built in under the gunwales on both sides of the deck, and several more benches lined up facing the bow. The patio lights swung with the rocking motion of the boat on the water. There was a self-serve bar on the deck and the countertop was stocked with trays of Vienna sausages on toothpicks, cheese and crackers, and strawberries and grapes. Peter loosed the boat from its mooring once everyone was settled with their drinks, and then he seated himself in the wheelhouse and the boat left the marina. The sun was beginning its dramatic descent and Roy Orbison sang as they crossed the bay, the paddlewheel making slapping sounds in the water at the stern of the boat.

When they were out in the middle of the bay, the photographer asked Peter to drop the anchor so he could get his photos before they lost the light. He got his equipment set up, and then he started arranging people in three rows, the first seated on a bench and the other two standing behind. Oliver was on the bench in the middle, and the smallest children were seated on the deck at his feet. Estella was about to take her place in the second row when she lost her balance and spilled Coke all down the front of her white shirt. She caused a bit of consternation when she took it off to reveal her Mondrian bathing suit top underneath, but there was too much commotion for anyone to care what she was wearing in the photo.

After lots of rearranging according to height, the photographer got his shots. Estella put her shirt back on and wondered if she'd made a mistake she would regret every time she looked at the photo. Peter found more crackers under the bar and they sat in the bay drinking beer and listening to Roy Orbison.

Andrew proposed a toast.

"Ten-year Lake Claire anniversary," he said. "Too bad Mom's not here."

They drank up and left it at that. Lorette adjusted the pillow she'd brought along behind Oliver's back, and not long after he fell asleep.

There was a ladder leading onto the bow of the boat, and Jack and Rose took the children up to look over the water. Peter was still in the wheelhouse. Estella joined him and handed him a soft drink since she knew he didn't drink alcohol. She asked if he had anything but Roy's "Greatest Hits" to play, and he said that Roy Orbison was already a tradition. He'd tried Johnny Cash one night and got complaints.

Through the window of the wheelhouse, she could see Jack

and Rose and the kids on the bow. Jack was leaning against the railing, looking into the distance toward the beach, and Estella wondered if he was thinking of that other beach, the one in France. It was hard to believe twenty years had passed since the end of the war. It bothered her that they weren't close anymore. She believed it was because of the year he'd had to let his sister care for him as though he were a child, but she also believed it was more than that. What had happened to him in the war set him apart from the rest of the family, even Andrew, who had fought but returned unscathed.

Theo called up to the wheelhouse and said they should be getting back. Jack herded the children down from the bow, and Estella went back to her place on the deck and waited for the sound of the diesel engine, but something was wrong and it wouldn't start. Peter had to radio for help, and a motorboat soon came toward them across the water. It was the marina's owner. They got the engine going again, but by the time they did it was pitch-dark. Cheryl and Paul had disappeared below deck, and the girls in bikinis were complaining about being cold, and several adults at once said, "Serves you right." They finally made it back to the marina, and just as they docked Cheryl and Paul appeared from below looking, Estella thought, as though they'd been up to something. They were all glad the Kingwells' motorhome was there to transport at least some of the Diamonds who had walked up the beach earlier.

Estella saw Rose step up into the motorhome with the two boys, but Jack started out walking by himself. Instead of sending her clothes with Mathew in the car and swimming back, Estella decided to walk too, and she hurried to catch up to Jack.

"Headache?" she asked as she fell into step with him.

"Why does everyone seem to think I always have a headache?" he said.

The wind was coming up and it felt like it might rain for the first time since they'd arrived. They walked along the beach instead of taking the path through the bush.

She said, "You look like you're in pain sometimes."

"Isn't everyone, sometimes?" he said.

She thought about it and said, "I suppose you're right. But you're my brother. I worry."

"Don't," he said. Then he added, "Nelly."

He hadn't called her Nelly since they were teenagers.

"You know I didn't actually hate that," she said.

"I know," he said.

They walked the rest of the way in silence.

THE AFTERNOON FOLLOWING the boat trip, Estella returned from the beach to find that her new car was gone from its spot beside the cottage. She assumed her father had told Mathew to move it and make room for the Oldsmobile, and she was annoyed that Mathew would help himself to her keys instead of asking her to move it. But when she went to his cottage, she saw that her car wasn't there, either. She walked around Fosters looking for it but didn't see it anywhere. Then a police car pulled up with the news that the hood of a white Mustang was now wrapped around a tree in the village, and that a young man named Paul Diamond had been driving, and claimed that Estella had given him the keys. He had a girl with him, Cheryl Kingwell. Neither of them was badly hurt, although Cheryl had a scrape on her cheek and Paul had jammed his knee on the steering wheel shaft. They were lucky Paul had not been driving faster than he was.

She found Andrew to tell him. As he and Harmony and Estella all drove into the village in the Oldsmobile, Andrew tried to make excuses for his youngest son by saying you can't really *steal* the car of a relative, and they should likely tell the police that he had borrowed it.

Estella was having none of that. She had dealt with too many parents who'd refused to believe their darling children were up to no good.

"No, Andrew," she said. "Your son took my car without permission. If you're asking me to tell the police I gave him the keys, no, I'm not going to. Forget it."

They found Paul and Cheryl sitting on a bench near the crash. Estella was sick at the sight of her new car crumpled into a tree, and furious with Paul. He said that he'd wanted to take Cheryl for a drive and he'd thought Estella would probably say no.

"Of course I would have said no, you idiot," she said, and Andrew had to ask her to tone it down, she might be right, but save that for later.

Just then Miles Kingwell came up the main street of the village in the motorhome looking for Cheryl, since she hadn't returned in the half hour he'd given her to go for a drive with Paul. He slammed to a stop when he saw the Mustang and the Diamonds gathered around, and then he saw his daughter with blood on her face and he ran from the motorhome to see what had happened. When he realized they weren't badly hurt, he flew into a rage at Paul for being irresponsible. He said he had let Cheryl go for a drive with him, but he shouldn't have. How could he have believed for even a minute it was a good idea when Paul looked like a delinquent in that jacket? Then Andrew stepped up to defend his son, and Estella thought a fight might break out between them. Once the police had them separated, she said it would be nice if someone—Paul, Andrew, Miles, anyone—could maybe show just a bit of concern for her car.

Cheryl said she was sorry and started to cry, and Estella had to tell her she had nothing to be sorry for except bad judgment, by which she meant Paul.

Since the police already had a statement from Cheryl and it was clear she hadn't stolen the car, they said she was free to go. The Kingwells were planning to move on to Alberta that after-noon, and Estella imagined they'd be doing so as quickly as Miles could get his family loaded into the motorhome. Neither Estella nor Andrew asked him for his contact information before he left with Cheryl.

Estella eventually agreed to say that Paul had not stolen her car to keep him from getting hauled off to the detachment, although she thought that might teach him a lesson. Andrew and Harmony drove him into Prince Albert to get his knee checked out at the hospital while Estella waited around to watch her car get towed away. The guy driving the tow truck told her he thought it was likely totalled. She walked back to Fosters through the trail in the bush thinking that Andrew had better keep Paul away from her for the rest of his life.

When she got to the cottage, she put on her bathing suit and swam to the point and back without stopping.

THE DAY BEFORE the Diamonds were to leave once again for home, Estella received an invitation from Shirley Boone. Shirley had left a message for her at Fosters saying she was to come for supper that evening. Estella assumed that Shirley wanted to say thank you. She didn't expect to be thanked, but she imagined that if she were in Shirley's place she would do the same.

When she got to the hotel at six, she was directed upstairs to Shirley's small apartment. She could smell fried chicken. The table was set for two, not three. Peter must have gone to the marina already, she thought.

Shirley asked Estella to sit at the table. She was soft-spoken, just as Estella remembered her from the hospital. It was hard to picture her managing a bunch of rowdy fishermen who'd had too much to drink and were set to trash their hotel room. She brought two plates of chicken and mashed potatoes from the small kitchenette and then sat down across from Estella. It was awkwardly quiet as Estella waited to hear what she had to say. Maybe she wouldn't say it, and Estella would be relieved of having to blather about it being nothing. She told Shirley the story of Paul and her car to break the silence, leaving out the part about him stealing it. Shirley had heard about the car crashing into the tree, everyone had, and she said she was glad no one had been hurt. Estella said the chicken was delicious, there was an art to fried chicken and she hadn't learned it. Shirley said the secret was cornflakes in the breading. It was the cornflakes that made it extra crisp. Her recipe was from *Chatelaine*.

Finally Estella said, "I'm glad Peter is doing so well. And that things will work out for him here until he's fully recovered."

Shirley put down her knife and fork.

"There's something I feel I should say."

"Oh," Estella said. "No need. As I said, I'm just glad he's done so well."

"You don't understand," Shirley said. "I appreciate what you did. Otherwise, he would have been alone. But I'm asking you to keep away from him."

Now Estella didn't understand. Keep away? She was hardly following him around.

"I'm not sure what you mean," she said.

"I think you know what I'm talking about."

"No, I really don't."

"Then let me spell it out. You're twice his age. Have you not noticed that? Or are you one of those women who imagines she's twenty-nine forever?"

Estella had handled more than a few distraught or angry parents over her years as a teacher. She tried to stay calm as she defended herself.

"Mrs. Boone, I don't know what you think happened, but you've got it wrong."

"I don't think so," she said. "I know my son. And I know you took leave from your job to sit with him for hours on end. I certainly didn't ask you to do that, so I ask myself, why?" Then she looked at Estella with eyes that were chillingly flinty and said, "I know about women like you."

Now Estella could see her with the fishermen. They wouldn't have a chance.

She stood up and said, "I'm sorry. Somehow you've skewed my desire to help into something it was not. Lake Claire means a lot to my family and Peter was a boy from Lake Claire. That's all it was. I'm going to go now. Thank you for supper."

She left her half-finished plate of chicken and walked calmly to the staircase, and then down, through the lobby, and out the hotel's front door.

When she got to the bush trail, she began to shake and had to sit on a tree stump. It was half an hour before she was able to stand and walk the rest of the way home. The paddlewheeler went by in the bay just as she arrived back at Fosters.

She did not see Peter Boone again before they packed up, booked the cottages for next year, and left for home. She did not know what Shirley Boone thought, but it clearly involved her being a predator who liked to get her talons into young men. She went over and over the time Peter had spent in the hospital and she could think of nothing she had said or done that was improper and might have got back to Shirley. And yes, she and Peter had spent time in the last two weeks talking on the beach at night, but how would she even know about that? There was the dog walker, but that was a person neither she nor Peter knew. She had no explanation for what Shirley was thinking, but she was more than thankful that she had not invited Peter to the empty cottage.

That night, she did not go for her usual swim, and instead packed her bathing suit away in her suitcase.

ON THE WAY home from the lake, Mathew drove and Estella rode in the back seat with her father and Lorette. They stopped in Prince Albert to look at the photographic proofs, which Bob had processed as a rush job. Estella and her father chose what they thought was the best one. Oliver was in the middle of the photo, and the Kingwells' daughter Cheryl was beside him. Had her father engineered that? Estella had not paid attention because she'd been fussing with the spilled Coke on her shirt. She was thankful that she was mostly covered by those in front of her and you could imagine she had worn a sundress for the photo rather than a bathing suit.

"We ordered copies for the Kingwells, right?" Estella asked her father. "Although I don't think anyone got their address before they left. All the fuss with Paul and the car."

When she got home, she spent the rest of the day unpacking and looking after Oliver—first his supper and then bedtime, the long, slow climb up the stairs.

She missed Lorette already.

Once Oliver was in bed, she sat down to go through the mail that had piled up while they were away. Among the bills and bank statements, she found a letter addressed to her. It was from Peter Boone, mailed three weeks earlier, before they'd travelled to the lake. There was a little enamelled pin enclosed, a loon with its red eye and black-and-white-striped necklace, the kind of thing Dot sold at the Beach Hut now that she'd expanded her inventory. There was a note thanking her for visiting him while he was in the hospital.

She dared not write back, not even a thank-you for the pin. She took it up to her room and slipped it into one of her jewellery bags, the same one that held Salina's beads.

A week after Estella received the pin in the mail, the eight-by-ten prints arrived from Bob in Prince Albert. She circulated copies to the family and then framed one and set it on the china cabinet. Not long after, she found Oliver in the dining room with the framed photo in his hand and a hammer and a package of brass picture hangers on the table. He wanted to hang the picture on the wall, but had wisely decided he shouldn't climb up on a chair.

Estella hung the photo, with Oliver directing her, in a spot where he could see it from his place at the head of the table. In the months after, he would sometimes stare at it, and she wondered if it pleased him to look at Cheryl Kingwell and be reminded of a time when he was young and had his life ahead of him. Maybe, in a sense, he had introduced his family to Salina that night on the *Claire de la Lune*, and the photo spliced two parts of his life together when he had kept them separate for so long.

On the other hand, she thought, perhaps he didn't remember the Kingwells at all and wondered what the hell strangers were doing in the family photograph. It was possible he understood who they were about as well as Estella understood Shirley Boone's belief that she was preying on her son. In other words, not at all.

Estella never did figure out where Shirley Boone's accusation had come from. She could only guess that the dog walker knew Shirley and had told her about the two of them sitting in the dark after one of her night swims, although why that might be considered a reportable offence she didn't know. When they returned the next summer, Estella learned that Peter had decided to remain in the village, and that Allen Foster had hired him as a handyman. Between that and his job on the paddlewheeler, he had full-time work. Because Estella was so afraid of his mother, she swam during the day, and as a result she and Peter no longer met on the beach at night, although they would sometimes have coffee on the deck of Emily Carr. He was now able to run again, and she would see him cut across the grass in his running shorts and then head into the bush on the trail that led out to the point. He had the habit of addressing the guests at Fosters as Missus and Mister, perhaps from his years clearing tables at The Travellers.

When he began to call Estella Missus, she couldn't tell whether it was a polite mannerism, respectful of her increasing age, or his way of being playful, roguish even. Either way, she played along and called him Mister Boone, as she had when he was a boy saving her from the cold with a Thermos of tea. Missus Diamond and Mister Boone became a tradition, like Roy Orbison on the *Claire de la Lune*. It suited them more and more as they grew older, Estella thought, although she was always a good bit older than he was.

Relatively less as time passed.

OLIVER WAS THE last of the Diamonds that Estella cared for. When she followed through on her resignation and didn't go back to teaching in the fall of 1965, she told the family that, although she was only in her forties, she had retired to look after her father. She also had to tell them that she and Clarence had broken up, and they looked neither perplexed nor pitying, as though they'd known all along it was her destiny to remain single. Not that they weren't glad at this point of her single status and availability for care duty. They'd tried to hire Lorette as Oliver's full-time help after they'd returned from the lake, but she'd said he was too much of a handful and turned down a generous offer.

Over the last year of his life, Oliver grew more and more difficult. His doctor blamed it on memory loss and said he was acting out in frustration. He'd always been a powerful man, and he couldn't accept his new dependence on others. He told Estella not to take it personally.

The rest of the family had no idea how difficult he was because Estella hid it from them. It was obvious to everyone that his physical health was not good, but she didn't want them to know just how diminished he'd become, that he threw temper tantrums when they weren't around, that he ripped at the sheets because they were too tight, or behaved like a toddler and knocked his soup off the table if he thought it was too salty. She tried to adopt the patience of Lorette and come up with a few things every day that he would enjoy, at least for a short time. At night, once he was asleep, she poured herself a glass of brandy and tried to think of a way to improve the situation, but there wasn't one. She didn't have the energy to break in another caregiver, and he would be miserable in a nursing home and the family would blame her for putting him there. They had no idea what went on when they weren't around. When they were, Oliver was on his best behaviour. She forgave him and imagined what she would be like if she lived to be his age. Worse, she thought. Pity the person who got stuck looking after her.

Once a week, she drove her father out to the brick plant. It took the entire afternoon because he moved so slowly. She had to get him in and out of the car, and then hold his arm for the walk to the main building, even as he tried to push her away. It was a precarious business, getting him up the stairs into Theo's office—*his* old office—where he would promptly fall asleep in a chair. She knew that Theo was not completely pleased with Oliver coming out to have a nap, but she assumed he understood that their father did technically still own the plant, and that it was good for him to get out of the house.

One afternoon, while Oliver slept in the chair, Theo looked up from his paperwork and said to Estella, "I don't suppose he'd ever set foot out here anymore if it weren't for you. Why do you think this is such a good idea?"

Estella immediately bristled at what she thought was below the surface: that she should keep her nose out of business at the factory and care for Oliver at home, where they both belonged. She held her tongue and wondered if Theo would be surprised to learn what she thought about as she sat with her brandy at night, namely, the company's succession plan. She was barely over forty. There was no reason why she couldn't learn the business and replace Theo when he decided to retire. With everything she had done when she'd cared for Jack and Beatrice and now Oliver, she believed her brothers should hand her whatever she wanted on a gold platter. Later, she asked her father what he thought about the trips to the plant, and he said he didn't care. She cut the visits to every second week, not because of what Theo had said, but because it was so much work for her to get him there.

And caring for him only grew harder. The less he could do for himself, the more angry he became. Estella had to help him with even his most intimate acts, and she didn't like it any more than he did. When he could no longer climb the stairs, he was forced to sleep in the sitting room and use a commode until she managed to get a proper powder room installed on the main floor. There was no dignity in his life anymore, and he took it out on her. She slept on the couch in case he needed help in the night, and tried not to give in to anger herself. By the time it was agreed that he should be moved to the hospital, she was exhausted, her head empty of thoughts about anything but her father.

When death was imminent, the family gathered in his room. For two days he had not spoken, and he had refused all food and drink. It was hard to believe he was still alive. But suddenly, his eyes opened and he looked fully alert and ready to say something important.

"What is it, Dad?" Estella asked, leaning closer from where she sat at the side of his bed.

He said one word, and then he closed his eyes, and within the hour he was dead.

Salina.

That was what he'd said.

"Who the hell is Salina?" Mathew asked, and instead of telling her brothers who she was, Estella convinced them they'd misheard, and that their father's last thoughts had been of their mother.

The night of the funeral—at which Theo had eloquently delivered the eulogy and the story of Oliver's last word, Beatrice—Estella had a change of heart about Salina. She was finally alone in the house, and she looked at the teapot and decided she did not want to live the rest of her life being the only one in the family who knew Oliver had been married twice. Her brothers and their wives were coming to dinner the following day to help her put a dent in the fridge full of casseroles and desserts from friends and neighbours. When they were all seated at the table she would tell them what she knew, leaving out only Salina's name. They didn't need to know that.

The next day the women arrived at the door after lunch to help her with Oliver's things and sort through the flowers and sympathy cards. The men would come by later for supper. Estella was so tired that she told her sisters-in-law to knock themselves out when they suggested it might be easier for them rather than her to go through Oliver's closet. They could take his clothes home to her brothers or donate them to charity; it didn't matter to her.

"He always had good shoes," she said. "Someone should take his shoes. And his cufflinks and tie clips. Take them all to the boys. They can decide what they'd like to keep."

While her sisters-in-law went to work upstairs, Estella sat in the yard and thought about what was next now that she was on her own. She wondered whether Theo would be willing to find a job for her at the plant so she could learn the business. She assumed nothing had been decided about who would manage Diamond and Sons in the future when Theo decided to retire, but since the five siblings were now equal owners, it was something to be discussed. She was pretty sure neither Jack nor Andrew would want the responsibility of running the business, and Mathew was not far behind Theo in age. Her father had believed her to be naive at seventeen, but she wasn't naive now, and a high school mathematics teacher knew a few things about accounting and microeconomics.

She came to no conclusion about when to approach Theo, other than *not yet*.

She began to feel guilty that she wasn't helping the other women so she went inside to make coffee for everyone. When she had the perk bubbling on the stove, Gladys came into the kitchen with a piece of paper in her hand and a puzzled look on her face, and said to Estella, "Did you know your father was married to someone else before Beatrice?"

Estella almost dropped the tray of cups she was about to carry to the dining room.

Gladys had found a marriage certificate in the bottom of the drawer with the cufflinks. Estella had not known a marriage certificate even existed.

"Did you find anything else?" she asked.

"No," Gladys said. "Just that."

When the brothers joined them for supper, the certificate was passed around. It was clear that none of them had known about Oliver's first wife. They noted that the date of marriage was less than two years before the date of his marriage to Beatrice.

No one brought up Oliver's last word, and Estella was certainly not going to.

"She must have died," Gladys said.

Jack said, "Wasn't there an aunt with a name like that? The one who made that teapot?"

They all stared at the white pot on the corner shelf.

"I don't see how she could have been an aunt," Harmony said.

Then Theo said, "Those people in the motorhome. I wonder."

He got up and took the lake photograph from the wall and they all had a look at it.

"They claimed to be related through a first wife," Theo said. "I suppose it was her."

No one knew how to get in touch with them, or could remember where they lived other than Ontario.

Over the next few days, they looked everywhere they could think of for more information, through Oliver's drawers and his desk and his file cabinets, in the cupboard where Beatrice had kept the household receipts and her own files, but they found nothing that told them more about a first wife. Estella decided her brothers now knew what they needed to, and she didn't tell them about the letters. She wondered whether they might come across them in all their searching, but they didn't, and this confirmed that Beatrice must have thrown them out. After looking everywhere they could think of, they gave up and concluded that they knew as much as they ever would about Oliver's first marriage.

After most of her father's clothes had gone to charity and her brothers had taken what they wanted, Estella was left with the odds and ends. She considered moving into her parents' bedroom, which was bigger than her own, but she decided against it. In the days that followed, she would sometimes go into the room just to open the closet door and look at her mother's favourite white leather purse on the top shelf, or the pair of cowboy boots that remained on the shoe rack, an occasional habit in footwear her father had adopted during his partnership with the Texan, Nathaniel Thick. The purse, the boots, a man's leather travelling bag, Beatrice's silk housecoat—there was something physical about these things that reminded her of her parents more than anything else in the house.

She thought about trying to contact the Kingwells to let them know they'd figured out the connection, but in the end she couldn't be bothered. What was there to be gained, she thought, other than a correspondence with people who were not even blood relatives?

The marriage certificate went home with Theo, and Estella did not know what became of it after that.

———

In 1968, the year Theo turned sixty, Estella decided it was time to talk to him about his retirement plan. She made an official appointment and bought a new plaid pantsuit, hoping it would make her look young enough to be his successor but professional enough to run a business. She drove out to the plant and walked across the yard with grasshoppers flying up at her from all directions. As she climbed the stairs to the office, she loosed a puff of clay dust with each step. Machinery droned beneath the treads.

She pulled a leather chair up close to Theo's desk and sat.

"Theo," she said, "I want to be considered for a position at the plant with an eye to me being your successor when you decide to retire. I think I've earned a place here. I don't need to point out that I put my life on hold three different times for this family."

Theo looked as though she had just asked him to send her to the moon on a rocket ship.

"You don't want to go back to teaching?" he asked her. "Ever?"

"No," she said. "I'd have thought that was clear."

"Huh," he said, and in that *huh* she could hear what was coming. Theo shifted his gaze to a spot on the wall, and she knew he was trying to find words that would have come easily if it had not been her asking for a job.

"We're all getting older, Estella," he finally said.

"You might be," she said. "I'm forty-four. Plenty of time to begin again."

What he said next was a surprise to her, even though it probably shouldn't have been: he had plans to bring his son Harold into the business to assume eventually the role of plant manager. Harold had been working in a bank and had become an expert on business finances. Theo would stay on for several more years, probably until he was sixty-five, and by the time he retired Harold would be ready to take over.

She wanted to ask, *Shouldn't that have been something we all got to decide?* but she knew she had to be careful with Theo, so she said, perhaps a bit too glibly, "So train both of us and we'll see what happens. An heir and a spare, as they say. Anyway, I could work with Harold."

Theo said, a little too quickly, "You might be able to work *with* Harold, but I doubt that you could work *for* him."

The meaning was clear: Harold had already won the competition, if there had been one to begin with.

She said, "I think we should call a family meeting to talk about this, a shareholders' meeting or whatever it's called. I want to know what the others have to say. It's the company succession plan we're talking about, and I think I have a right to at least be considered for your job when the time comes. It's unfair to me that I shouldn't get some training along with Harold in the meantime. It puts me at a disadvantage."

Theo studied her, and when he spoke she learned what had gone on without her knowledge.

"I know what the others think, Estella," he said. "I did not make this decision on my own. We're all in agreement that Harold is the right choice, or at least Mathew and Andrew are. Jack says he doesn't have an opinion, one way or the other, but he voted with us. Has he told you he and Rose are making plans to move to Calgary?"

No. Jack had not told her that.

She said, "What do mean by voting? How could you vote on anything without me?"

He didn't answer the question and instead said, "It wouldn't work to have you and Harold at the plant together. You wouldn't be satisfied keeping the books, and you wouldn't let Harold tell you what to do. You must know this is true. You're like Father, Estella. You have to be the one in charge. Can't you see that?"

In charge? Really? When had she ever been in charge?

Theo said again, as though he'd found the decisive argument, "You wouldn't be happy with Harold making decisions. It wouldn't work."

She said, "I guess I should have just made everyone happy and married Clarence Angell. After I was done looking after half the damn family, that is."

Theo said, "Now you're just feeling sorry for yourself. We all appreciated what you did, and you know it. We thought you were Mother Teresa."

Everything he said was making it worse.

"I'm an owner of this company, the same as you," she said.

"I know," he said, "but that doesn't mean you get to run the plant. That decision isn't yours to make."

"Whose is it, then?" she asked.

"All of us," he said. "We all decided."

"Not quite all," she said. She stood from her chair then, knowing she wasn't going to get anywhere, at least not with Theo. "And just for the record, I didn't *want* to be goddamned Mother Teresa."

Theo gave her a look of disgust. "Mother is turning in her grave," he said.

"Bullshit," Estella said. "She's cheering me on. And I bet Mother Teresa wishes every day she was someone else."

On her way out of the office she said, "I don't care that you think it's settled. It's not."

She drove home in a rage, and when she had calmed down she phoned her brothers. They all said the same thing: that Theo knew what he was doing, and that training someone from the next generation of Diamonds made sense. The most she got was when Andrew agreed she should probably have been there when they discussed Theo's retirement plan, but it wouldn't have made any difference.

She called Jack last.

"You're set for life," Jack said. "Why are you even thinking about this?"

When she asked him if it was true he was moving to Calgary, he said that he was, and he was glad to be leaving the brick business behind.

"Think about it," he said. "Who's going to buy bricks in a few years' time? No one. That progress Father used to talk about? It means something other than bricks now. Be thankful it'll be Harold and not you who has to shut the plant down."

She had not thought of that possibility, that there would come a day when no one wanted bricks. But what did Jack know? She remembered hearing her father tell Allen Foster he suspected Jack had enlisted in the army to escape the family business.

"So you're moving to Calgary, then, and leaving me to sort this out," she said. She knew she sounded childish but she didn't care.

"There's nothing to sort out," Jack said. "It's sorted."

When she hung up the phone, she supposed that was it. Jack had been her last hope for an ally. She had gotten no farther than she had with her father when she was a teenager, even though she was now supposedly an equal owner of the company. Theo had said she was just like Oliver, but if that was true, why had she failed once again to get what she wanted? She thought of her father contriving to get Nathaniel Thick's share of the business, and remembered what Betty Ellen Thick had written in her letter: *"I'll say right here, Mr. Diamond, that I believe it was a dirty trick you pulled up there in Canada."*

She needed a dirty trick of her own, she thought. She wondered if she could sue Theo, or maybe all of them.

At first, she wasn't really serious, but the more she thought about it, the more a lawsuit seemed like the answer. An important decision had been made without her. There had to be a legal recourse. She found her own lawyer and explained the situation, and he talked about technical breaches and the obligation of shareholders to be reasonable.

"Your brothers, collectively, have an 80 percent majority," he said, "but we could argue that it's not being exercised in a reasonable way." Then he said, "I could go through the bylaws and look for breaches, but is that really what you want?"

She said that it was.

He clearly thought it was the wrong decision.

"This is a family business," he said. "I don't need to tell you what the repercusssions will be. My advice is mediation, not a lawsuit. There's not much to be gained by legal action, and there's a lot to lose."

Mediation, Estella said, implied that there were two sides to the story. There was only one. She was a part owner of Diamond and Sons, and she had not been consulted over a decision that concerned the future of the plant. That was it.

"I advise against it," her lawyer said, "but in the end, I work for you."

When Theo learned she was talking to a lawyer, he said, "Really, Estella? Now you have both of them rolling in the grave." He could not believe she would do such a thing as sue her own family. In fact, all of her brothers had a hard time believing it. They ignored the threat and treated her as though she were the sibling they had to put up with, like Iris and her accordion.

When summer came, they all went to Lake Claire as usual, with the exception of Jack, who cancelled his cottage reservation and moved to Calgary. Estella stayed by herself in Emily Carr and felt as if she were being blamed for the strangers now settled smack in the middle of the row of Diamonds. Heavy clouds hung over the lake and by noon every day it was raining. The picnic tables had been pulled together but they dripped with rainwater. The photo on the paddlewheeler, she thought, had been a prescient farewell to the good times. When Peter Boone asked her what was going on with her normally boisterous family, she didn't tell him about her fight with her brothers, and said only that the rain had them all wondering what to do with themselves.

When she got home, she asked her lawyer what was taking so long. She suspected he was stalling to give her time to come to her senses. She told him to hurry things up or she was finding another lawyer, and he filed the suit.

Then came the news that Harold had no wish to be part of a family dispute, and he'd accepted a job with an oil company in Calgary. Estella assumed then that Theo would change his mind and nullify her need to sue, but before she could ask him, he had a heart attack while climbing the stairs to his office. He survived, but his doctor's advice was to retire and find a way to enjoy the rest of his life. The company was now in a crisis with no succession plan.

Theo called a meeting, and this time Estella was included. Jack refused to come from Calagry but said he would join them on the phone if he had to. Estella was ready with her proposal, but when her brothers arrived at the meeting they had a proposal for her: buy their shares and become the sole owner. Otherwise, they were putting the plant up for sale.

At first she thought it was a ruse, to get her to walk away from the lawsuit and let some other nephew take over the plant's management. But they were serious. Unless Estella saw it otherwise, the best decision was to sell the factory. Jack was in agreement; she could call him if she wanted. It occurred to her that they were doing more or less the same thing their father had done with Nathaniel Thick, only backwards. They were forcing her to buy, not sell.

"It's a solution, Estella," her lawyer told her. "If you really believe you can manage the business, go to the bank and see if you can make it work. Either that, or agree to a sale outside of the family."

She didn't need to go to the bank. She knew that, between her own savings and her inheritance, she had enough money. She could not see the Diamond business being sold to someone who was not a Diamond, so she accepted her brothers' offer and bought them out, knowing that Andrew and Mathew would retire rather than work for her, even though they were still in their fifties.

And there was something else she knew: she was being blamed for Theo's heart attack. Gladys said as much, and when Estella talked to Jack on the phone after they'd all signed the agreement, he asked her, "Do you think it was worth it?"

"Was what worth it?" she asked.

"The years off Theo's life."

"You can't blame me for blocked arteries," she said.

"All the hostility, then. Why bother?"

That was a good question, although she didn't admit it to Jack.

On her first day as the new company owner, she climbed the stairs to her father's office, and Jack's question kept coming back to her: why had she bothered? She'd alienated her family and was about to take over a business she had no idea how to run. She looked down over the factory works, and then she pulled the blind on the office door and locked it, and sat behind the desk and cried. When she ran out of tears, she wiped her face with a tissue and made a list of the people she had to talk to: the various factory foremen, the sales team, the accounting firm. After that, she opened the books and began her study of how to run a brick factory.

Six months later, Jack went missing. At first it was assumed he had gone somewhere to be alone—a cabin in the mountains, perhaps—but when a month went by and no one had heard from him, the family had to believe the worst. Estella was beside herself, but there was nothing she could do other than phone Rose, which she did every day until Rose asked her to stop. Andrew travelled to Calgary so many times to help with the search that he and Harmony finally decided to sell their house and move. Two of their children were already there anyway, one of them married. Andrew sent regular updates but there was never any real news. Jack had simply disappeared.

In the year that followed, a mass exodus of Diamonds occurred. Theo and Gladys were the next to move to Calgary, and before the year was out all four of Estella's brothers had abandoned her, one way or another. It didn't take long for their families to follow, lured by opportunities in the oil industry and the Diamond family inclination to stick together. The first Christmas that everyone was gone, Estella received an invitation from Mathew and Fay, but when she got there, she wished she had stayed home. She was a fly in the ointment, she thought, even though her sisters-in-law— all but Gladys—tried to pretend nothing had changed.

And there was no Jack.

It was the last time she travelled to Calgary, and the last time she shared a dinner table with her brothers.

ESTELLA'S LIFE BECAME the brick plant. She kept the company running well beyond Jack's prediction concerning the obsolescence of bricks, partly by introducing a new brick veneer that sold well for a time. Eventually, cheap products from China did spell the end of Diamond bricks, but by then Estella was in her seventies and ready to retire.

When she made the decision to close down the plant, there was no sentimental backlash because there was no one left who cared about Oliver's legacy. Her brothers had all died, and the only Diamond in the city was her great-niece Lydia. Estella had a hard time thinking of her with any magnanimity because she was just like her father, Paul, the nephew who had wrapped her car around a tree.

For fifteen years after the plant closed, Estella would sometimes drive out to the property and wander around the deserted buildings, which looked for some time as though the workers had just walked away. There were overalls hanging on hooks, a pair of dusty steel-toed boots inside the main entrance, even a black lunch box left open on a work counter. At first there were unsold bricks stacked in the storage sheds: a few pallets of the original yellow Diamond face bricks, more of the industrial firebrick they'd produced since the war years, a few remaining stacks of the brick veneer that had been Estella's last attempt at keeping her product in the marketplace. Eventually, the leftovers from ninety years of production disappeared as people raided the storage sheds for souvenirs or for free DIY materials. Every year, another kiln fell into disrepair and more shingles blew off the sagging factory roof. There were pigeons and barn swallows living in the rafters, and once Estella scared off a coyote that had come inside to hunt mice. The day she arrived and saw that the wooden staircase to the office had fallen in was the last day she visited the plant. Although she had been mostly pragmatic about the demise of the factory, it was agonizing to see her father's glass aerie suspended and inaccessible above her head. She made the decision to have the plant demolished to avoid a kiln or a roof collapsing on some unfortunate trespasser.

On the day of the demolition, Estella sat alone in her back garden with a snifter of brandy even though it was only noon, knowing that all traces of the family business would be gone by the end of the day. She had given the order to bulldoze even the Diamond and Sons sign, which she had never replaced. She had an offer on the land from a farm equipment manufacturer and she was planning to accept it. As she imagined the destruction—dry timber splintering, bricks tumbling as bulldozers knocked the kilns apart, clay dust rising like smoke from a fire—one of Jack's old questions came back to her: Had it been worth it?

She considered it. She had run the plant well, and in the end that had been her vindication. But there was a caveat. When she was a child, she'd thought of her life as before the teapot or after the teapot, but now she realized her life was before and after Oliver's death. Before was the Diamond family. After was the fight with her brothers. After was the Diamonds fleeing en masse to Alberta. After was her drinking alone on the last day of the existence of

Oliver's factory, with no one else to even raise a glass with her.

Then she began to feel sad, about the plant, about Jack, about everything, and she decided she was too old to be drinking brandy in the middle of the day. It had not been a good idea.

When she heard the phone ringing in the house, she rose to answer it in case it was the contractor she had hired for the demolition. She impulsively threw her empty glass into the garden, where it smashed on a paving stone. She'd heard they threw dishes at Greek weddings, although what this had to do with a Greek wedding she didn't know.

It probably hadn't been worth it, she thought, but it was years too late for regret. And there was no one to admit regret to, so what was the point?

When she got to the phone it had stopped ringing.

Her call display was lit up with an Alberta number.

3

The Other Diamonds

Estella's decision to hire a housekeeper for the first time in her life was a pre-emptive move to keep herself out of the home care system. She found a woman named Emyflor Santos who had come alone to Canada from the Philippines to earn money for her children's education. Emyflor worked full-time as a care aide in a seniors' residence, and she lived in an apartment with three other Filipinas. She was always looking for more hours and she agreed to work for Estella three half-days a week. She was trying to get permanent residence status so she could send for her family, she told Estella. She hadn't seen her kids in eight years except on Face-Time or WhatsApp. They had just begun school when she'd left and now they were teenagers. She had to explain to Estella what FaceTime and WhatsApp were.

Estella was happy to hear the Internet was good for something other than online dating, which was her great-niece Lydia's new way of finding boyfriends. Maybe even a husband, she said, but she was being fussy this time. How fussy could you be, Estella wondered, when you advertised on the Internet? She had not thought it funny when Lydia threatened to set up what she called a "profile" for her. It was the same kind of teasing as *Auntie's got a boyfriend,* and she had been happy to hear the end of that as her nieces outgrew it.

The threat of home care had reared its head after an unfortunate mishap in the grocery store, when Estella had fainted in a slow cashier's lineup with a heavy bag of navel oranges and several cans of soup in her basket. It had been a hot day and the store's air conditioning wasn't working, and she'd begun to feel light-headed. She was attempting to gauge whether backwards or forwards was the better way to escape the lineup and make a break for fresh air when the heat got the better of her, and the weight of the basket pulled it right out of her hand so that it landed on the foot of the young man in line behind her. She remembered that he said, *Ouch! Watch it, lady!* as though she'd dropped the basket on purpose, aimed it right at his oversized white sneaker, and she thought, *How rude.* Then she too landed at his feet, and he redeemed himself by calling an ambulance on his cellular phone when he realized what was happening.

By the time the EMTs arrived, Estella was sitting in a chair someone had found for her. She hated that everyone in line was staring at her. A few of the cashiers knew her and they were fussing, flapping store flyers in her face and asking each other if anyone knew how to use a defibrillator. Estella was relieved when she saw the ambulance pull up, thinking the EMTs might be saving her from death by defibrillator rather than a heart attack.

"I don't need to go to the hospital," Estella tried telling them. "I feel much better. It was a just a spell. Have you not noticed the heat in here?"

"How about you let us decide," said a young female EMT who looked as though she didn't take guff. "Let's just slide you over onto the royal litter here and we'll run you to the hospital, just to be sure."

"Don't patronize me," Estella said, but she moved onto the stretcher all the same and let the woman lift her feet as she lay back, because her head still felt light, and she wasn't sure her legs would get her home.

"No patronizing, gotcha," the woman said as she expertly tucked a flannel sheet around Estella, and then they were off, through the automatic doors and into a blast of even warmer air.

"You do know it's a hot day," Estella said, freeing her arms from under the sheet.

"Ah, but the gold carriage is air conditioned."

"You find me amusing, do you?" Estella said as she was jacked up and zoomed into the back of the ambulance.

"Sure, why not?" the woman said, climbing in after her.

Her partner drove them out of the parking lot. No siren, Estella noted. So she wasn't dying, then. The EMT tried to unbutton her blouse to attach a portable ECG machine but Estella slapped her hands away.

"I'm not amusing," she said. "I'm difficult. And I don't want to go to the hospital. Just drop me at home. It's on the way."

"Jeez Louise," the EMT said. "We're not a taxi service. You're going to the hospital, even if it means the world will be blessed with your presence for another twenty years."

Estella didn't argue any further because she didn't actually want to drop dead alone in her house.

They kept her at the hospital for several hours hooked up to a heart monitor, and they half drained her blood supply before deciding there wasn't much wrong with her, at least nothing that was going to kill her tomorrow. In the end, they decided to send her home with an order to stay hydrated on hot days, and a requisition for a home care assessment.

Estella was furious when she saw that.

"I have all the help I need," she said to the nurse who was discharging her. "I have a niece, great-niece, to be exact."

"Will she be picking you up, then?" the nurse asked, looking at Estella over her reading glasses, her clipboard on her lap.

Estella was reluctant to call Lydia but she didn't know how else she would get home.

The nurse was still looking at her, waiting for an answer.

"Tell me the number," she said. "I'll dial for you."

Estella gave her Lydia's work number, and the nurse punched it in and handed her the receiver. She braced herself, because you could never count on Lydia. She was too much her father's daughter. She'd gotten married right out of high school to a junior hockey coach and the marriage had lasted less than a year. When it ended, Lydia was pregnant and the hockey coach was claiming the baby wasn't his and refusing to pay child support. Paul and his wife had by this time left the city, having moved to Fort McMurray, so Estella stepped in and rented Lydia an apartment, and then got her through a bookkeeping course at the technical school after the baby was born, a daughter she named Mercy. Lydia raised Mercy mostly as a single parent with a couple more husbands making brief appearances, and then Mercy grew up and went away, and a year ago she'd returned with her seven-year-old autistic son, Lonny. Lydia, to her credit, took them in.

The nurse handed Estella the phone when Lydia answered, and she tried to explain succinctly why she was calling. She was at the hospital—not to worry, she was fine, but she needed someone to pick her up.

"You want me to come and get you?" Lydia said. "Now?"

"Yes," Estella said. "If you don't mind."

"And you're all right?" Lydia asked. "You're not sick or anything?"

No, Estella assured her, she was not sick.

"Then I think you should call a taxi," Lydia said. "I'm at work. I can't just leave, can I."

Actually, she could, Estella thought. She was always talking about how her boss was hardly ever there, and it sounded as though she spent half her workday in the downtown mall.

"Never mind, then," Estella said, and she handed the phone back to the nurse.

"She's at work," Estella told the nurse. "She can't leave."

"And there's no one else? No other relatives?"

"My misfortune to have outlived them all," Estella said.

At that moment the young doctor who had declared her well enough to go home came in to sign her release form.

"Healthy as a horse," he said as he scrawled his signature.

"Is that why you think I need Meals on Wheels or some such nonsense?" she fired back at him.

"And smart as a whip, apparently," he said, which Estella knew was no longer true. The brain wore out with use, in spite of what they told you about keeping it exercised.

The doctor put down his pen and said, "Look. You're over ninety years old. You still live in your own home. You've earned a bit of help now and then." He turned to the nurse and said, "Send that requisition to home care, yeah?"

"I don't want it," Estella said.

"Do you want to go home?" the doctor asked her.

"Of course I do. Is that a threat?"

"No," he said, "but it's my responsibility to see that you go home safely so you're not back here in an ambulance again tomorrow."

And then he left.

"Don't you dare send that in," Estella said to the nurse.

"It's a condition of your release," the nurse said, and Estella wanted to shoot someone.

The nurse called her a taxi and she went home, thinking that if anyone showed up at her door with anaemic-looking roast beef and instant mashed potatoes on a paper plate, she would show them how able she was with a kick to the shins.

Even though she was annoyed with Lydia, she phoned her anyway that evening because she thought she might need her for backup when the home care people came calling. She told her what had happened, and Lydia somehow got it into her head that Estella must have had a mild heart attack, in spite of the ER doctor's diagnosis.

"I don't believe there's any such thing," Estella said. "That's like being a little bit dead."

There was a familiar silence on the end of the line.

"You're on that Internet, aren't you, looking this up."

"It says you can have a mild heart attack without any symptoms. It can still kill you."

"I'd hardly call it mild, then. Anyway, forget whatever you're looking at. I was hooked up to every machine in the place and they found nothing."

Then she told Lydia the reason for her call: that she might need her support on the home care issue—to lie, that is, and say she helped Estella with the house—but Lydia was by now on the Mayo Clinic site, which she said was 100 percent reliable. Estella ended the call in frustration, hoping that the request for backup had registered.

Two weeks after the hospital visit, the home care assessor showed up. When Estella saw a strange woman with a briefcase ringing her doorbell, she almost didn't answer, thinking she might be a Jehovah's Witness, but then she remembered they always come in twos, so she opened the door.

"Hello," the woman said. "Estella? I'm Nancy Segal, from home care. I've been asked to do an assessment, just routine, to see if you're managing okay in your own home."

"And how does that seem so far?" Estella asked.

Nancy Segal didn't skip a beat and said, "Good, so far. But do you mind if I ask a few questions? It won't take long."

Estella noticed that one sneakered foot was moving slowly toward the open door, as though the woman was going to stick it inside and stop Estella from shutting her out.

"Oh, all right then, if it will keep you people from bothering me," Estella said. "But I don't need help, and you can put that in your notebook."

She took the woman to the sitting room and didn't offer her anything. She wanted to get this over with.

"You have a lovely old home," the woman said.

Estella could just see her calculating how much work it would be to keep up. She hoped the woman wouldn't see the layer of dust on everything, and Estella wished she'd been given notice so she could have put the house in order.

"And you do your own cooking, then?" the woman asked.

"Of course. I'm a good cook. Always have been." Which wasn't true. She'd never much liked cooking, but she knew how to fill her belly with all the food groups.

The woman was looking at a form she'd pulled out of her briefcase. "And I see here that you have a niece in the city who helps you out?"

"Yes. She checks on me every day." Another lie, but a convenient one at the moment.

"And your laundry?"

"I do it myself. I like ironing. It's therapeutic. Have you read *The Edible Woman*?"

Nancy shook her head without looking up. "I don't have much time to read," she said, concentrating on her check boxes.

"Well, that's sad, isn't it," Estella said. "Maybe *you* need some extra help."

"There's nothing wrong with your sense of humour, is there?"

"Is there a box for that?"

"I can make a note of it," Nancy said.

Then she got out her "little memory test" as she called it, and began asking questions.

What year were you born?

Do you know your address and phone number?

Who's the prime minister of Canada?

Estella answered them all without hesitation. If the woman had asked her what she'd done yesterday she'd have been in trouble, but that question was not on the list. Only one of Nancy's questions gave her pause.

Do you feel safe in your home?

Did she?

Not when she heard voices in the night she didn't. Not when she woke up and couldn't remember where she was. It was terrifying. But she couldn't admit that or she'd never get rid of this woman.

"Yes," Estella said. "Of course. I've lived in this house my entire life."

"Well, that's all very good," Nancy said.

Estella saw her eyes lingering on the dining table, the breakfast dishes still there, and the ones from the night before. She sometimes saved them up. It was more efficient.

"Do you mind if I have a look at your bathroom?" Nancy asked. "Just to see if it's safe for you. Is it on the second floor?" She was already rising and heading for the staircase, and Estella didn't see how she could stop her without grabbing her. How, she wondered, did this nosy woman have the nerve to wander so freely in someone else's house? She wanted to ask her to leave, but she was afraid of the power she might have. She followed her up the stairs, wondering when she had last cleaned the bathtub. She knew it wasn't recently.

The bathroom was not in good shape. There were dirty towels piled on the floor, waiting for a laundry day. The washing machine was in the basement and Estella didn't like the basement stairs, so laundry days were less frequent than they used to be. The tub needed a good scrubbing, and she couldn't remember when she'd last mopped the tiles. She thought of her mother and what she would have to say about the state of the house.

"You could use some grab bars in here," Nancy said, ignoring the obvious, which was that Estella needed help with the housework. "Everyone should have them."

She was being polite, Estella thought, focusing on her safety rather than the soap scum in the sink. She felt defeated by this woman, because she realized she was right. Estella was now *that* old woman, the one who lived in a dirty house and walked around with tomato stains on her blouse. She wondered if there was any point hoping that Lydia might offer to help out a little more if she knew about Nancy and her forms, the threat of strangers in Estella's business. She hated to risk annoying Lydia. Without her, she'd have no one.

When they got downstairs again Nancy said, "You did fine on the memory test, Estella, and you seem to get around the house without trouble. Wonderful for your age. Such a big house, though, isn't it? I'd like to recommend a bit of help with the upkeep. We do only light housekeeping—no oven cleaning or window washing—just the daily upkeep. It's subsidized, so very affordable. Can I put that through?"

"Go ahead, then," Estella said, "if you must." She pictured a stranger with a bucket full of cleaning supplies. "I'll need resumés and references, of course."

"Resumés?" Nancy said.

"The cleaners," she said. "I'm not having just anyone in my house."

Then Nancy had to explain the way it worked, that the house-keepers were approved by home care, not the clients, and it might not be the same person every time. Home care would manage the schedule.

"No," Estella said, shaking her head. "Absolutely not."

"Excuse me?"

"I won't have it. I'd rather live in a sty. Anyway, I'm tired. You'll have to leave now."

She showed Nancy the door, and Nancy did leave, promising to be in touch, as though this was all in a day's work and Estella had not objected at all to her offer of help.

A few hours later, once Estella had gotten over the immediate problem of Nancy and her forms and checklists, she walked the three blocks to the grocery store with her wheeled shopping bag, hoping there wouldn't be a repeat mishap in the cashier's line or she'd end up locked away in a nursing home. When she got inside, though, the air was cool and she felt fine. She stopped to glance at the community bulletin board and her eyes landed on one ad in particular. She read it over several times, wondering if it might provide an answer to her home care predicament: *Reliable housekeeper/companion for seniors. References provided.*

"Ha," she said out loud, and she ripped off one of the paper tags with the phone number and stuck it in her purse. When she got home, she placed the call, and that was how she found Emyflor. She wondered why she had not thought of hiring a housekeeper sooner, although it was not lost on her that, after caring for everyone in the family, here she was having to hire her own help.

Still, it was a solution, and she liked Emyflor the instant she met her. She wore her black hair pulled back in a ponytail and she always seemed to be cheerful, even though her family was so far away. She spoke with an accent, and she told Estella that her first language was Tagalog, a language Estella had never heard of. She wore a little gold cross around her neck, which Estella took as an indication that she was Catholic.

Emyflor called her "Miss Estella."

"You don't have to call me that," Estella said. It reminded her of a matriarch in the Deep South—either that or the family spinster. "Just plain Estella will do. We've never been much for formality in this house."

Emyflor said, "But you have to be Miss Estella. All my ladies are Miss." She said it as though it were a fact, something you couldn't argue with, like the sky being blue or the grass green.

"Even the married ones?" Estella asked.

"Of course," Emyflor said.

"Oh well then," Estella said.

Lydia didn't like the fact that Estella was paying good money to a stranger, but she let it go when she realized it meant the demands on her were less. Lydia even asked Emyflor once if she would come and clean for her every few weeks. Emyflor said no, she was a caregiver and she worked only for seniors.

Estella enjoyed it immensely that Emyflor had said no to Lydia. She felt that she had earned Emyflor's company by having done her own share as a caregiver.

And by living so long. That too.

IT WAS ON one of Emyflor's days—a Wednesday, and two days before the annual trip to Lake Claire—that the Nicholas Diamonds came from Calgary. Estella's two-week lake vacation had shrunk down to a long weekend, and she thought it had all gotten a bit pitiful: just the four of them—herself, Lydia, Mercy, and Lonny—for three days in a cottage with sixty-year-old beds that needed to be replaced. They were like a Ringling Brothers Circus on its last legs, she thought: one remaining old elephant and a few straggling performers who were short on talent. Still, she was grateful that Lydia was willing to take her, especially after the year before, when Estella had behaved like her father and reacted badly to a misunderstanding. She could not deny that she was getting to be a fair amount of trouble.

When the doorbell rang, Emyflor hollered that she would get it, but she was upstairs so Estella got there before her. When she saw the man on her porch, she almost had a heart attack, and not a mild one, because she thought at first it was her youngest brother back from the dead. The man said his name was Nicholas Diamond, but still she had to grab onto the doorjamb to steady herself, she was thrown for such a loop. He was the spit of Jack.

"Are you all right?" he asked.

"Yes, of course," she said, gathering her wits again. "I wasn't expecting company."

Her mind was working to place him—could he be one of Jack's sons?—but she quickly reasoned that he was too young, and anyway, she had known Jack's two sons as children, Ryan and Don. Jack's grandson, then, which he confirmed when he said Ryan Diamond was his father. She remembered that Ryan was the one who had walked out on his family when the children were young.

"Is your mother Dora?" she asked. The name had come easily. She'd got lucky, or perhaps she had. If he'd arrived an hour sooner or later, it might have been another story. Her mind was like that now. It worked just fine, and then it didn't.

261

"That's right," he said. "She raised us on her own after our father left." Nicholas Diamond then explained that he was on his way from Calgary to Winnipeg with his wife and two girls, and since they were making good time they'd decided to stop on the off chance that she might be home. He apologized for not calling ahead.

Estella looked and saw a new car parked at the curb across the street, a silver sedan.

"Get your family," she said. "Come in. Don't just stand on the porch."

In forty years, this had never happened.

Nicholas beckoned to his wife and daughters in the car. Estella could see the wife was hesitating, but then one of the girls got out of the car and began to cross the street toward them. She was carrying a shimmery little red purse on a silver chain over her shoulder. A dog trailing a leash jumped out of the car after her—a hound of some kind, a beagle, perhaps—and followed her across the street. The girl was soon standing beside her father while the dog did its business on Estella's lawn. Estella noticed that the purse was covered in sequins.

"My oldest daughter, Hannah," Nicholas said.

Then Nicholas's wife and the younger daughter got out of the car. His wife did not look especially happy but Estella could see her composing her face as she walked toward them holding the younger girl's hand, and by the time she arrived on the step to join her husband she looked the very picture of pleasant.

"Hello. I'm Marie," she said. She introduced the younger girl, who appeared to be seven or eight years old, as Paris. Estella thought, *Who names a child after a city?* She was introduced to the younger girl as Miss Diamond. It reminded her of being a teacher.

"Call me Auntie," Estella said quickly. "I haven't been Miss Diamond for many years now."

Nicholas looked confused and said, "You were married?"

"Heavens, no," Estella said. "I taught school. I was Miss Diamond to the students."

He apologized, as though mentioning marriage to a single old lady was the same degree of inappropriate as asking her age, and Estella thought, *People never stop seeing a single woman as unfortunate, no matter how old she is.* In Nicholas's discomfort, he had a boyish look, which somehow made him appear a bit lost, and in that moment he looked *exactly* like Jack. She wanted to reach out and touch him.

She urged them all to come inside. Before they did, Marie took a plastic bag out of her purse and handed it to the older girl, who sighed but then picked up the dog's mess.

"What should I do with it?" she asked.

Estella didn't know. She surely didn't want it in her kitchen garbage can.

"Is there a trash bin in the back?" Nicholas asked, and Estella said there was, and pointed to the path alongside the house. Nicholas took the plastic bag from his daughter and walked around the house. The dog followed him, still trailing its leash, while Estella showed the others to the sitting room.

Emyflor came downstairs shortly after that, and when Estella introduced the company, she said she would make lunch for everyone. Marie looked at her watch and said, "We don't want to be any trouble," but Estella waved off Marie's concern and Emyflor went to the kitchen. Marie made polite conversation—lovely home, such an interesting porch the way it curved around the front of the house, and such a pretty part of town. Estella kept looking at the door, waiting for Jack/Nicholas to come in. The dog was barking at something in the backyard. The older girl, Hannah, took her phone out of her red purse, and her mother shook her head at her.

"You know the rule about phones," Marie said. Then she said to Estella, "Eleven going on sixteen."

"*Lonch* is almost ready, Estella," Emyflor called from the kitchen. She had long since dropped the "Miss," and now she often called Estella "Lola," especially when they were alone. It meant grandmother, she'd explained, and although it was not the same, Lola reminded her of Nelly, what Jack had called her when they were young.

Hannah zipped her phone back in her purse, and Marie said, "Thank you."

Marie was pretty, Estella thought. She was wearing just a bit of makeup, not too much. Her pink lipstick reminded Estella that she had not put on any lipstick that morning, since she hadn't been expecting anyone but Emyflor. She made the excuse that she had to visit the powder room and she collected her purse on the way. She had never worn lipstick in her life until she was an old lady, and now she liked her lips red, and her fingernails, too. Emyflor was good at nails, and she sometimes gave Estella a manicure after she had the housecleaning done. She told Estella that she still had good hands with no arthritic bumps and hardly any age spots, so why not show them off? Estella agreed, why not?

In the powder room, she pursed her lips and applied the red colour that she had come to like so much. There was a brush in the bathroom, and she ran it through her hair.

When she returned to the sitting room, Hannah was slouched as far down on the couch as she could go without falling off, and the younger girl was already asking how long they were staying. She thought both girls were eyeing her warily.

Nicholas came back in at that moment carrying the dog's leash, saying that he had noticed the backyard was fenced, and did Estella mind if the dog stayed there while they visited? Of course she said yes. The backyard was better than the house. But she would have said yes to anything he asked.

He immediately noticed the photo gallery on the dining room walls: Oliver and Beatrice's wedding portrait, family photos taken over the years as the number of children grew, the group photo that had been taken on the paddlewheeler at the lake.

"I recognize this one," he said. "Lake Claire, right?"

She was surprised that he knew about Lake Claire.

He said that his Uncle Don remembered going there, and he remembered the lake holidays as happy times.

"I hardly knew my father," Nicholas said. "Don was the real father to me."

She savoured this fact, this bit of information about the family. There were so many things she didn't know about what had happened after the Diamonds moved to Calgary, after she had become the hard-hearted one with whom no one could get along. She had gotten over that many years ago, although she wouldn't go as far as to say she had made peace with their desertion.

She told Nicholas that she had not missed a summer at Lake Claire in over sixty years.

"I might be the only person who can say she's stayed in a Fosters cottage every year since they opened. We're going in a few days, although I expect things will be different this year. Fosters sold the business over the winter. I don't imagine it will even be called Fosters anymore."

She pointed to Jack in a family portrait and said, "You look so much like your grandfather. Do you see the resemblance?"

Nicholas said he'd been told that all his life. He looked again at the paddlewheeler photo and found his father as a boy, with his brother Don standing next to him. And then he wanted to know where Estella was in the photo. She was disappointed that he couldn't tell, but she pointed to herself, remembering the day the photo had been taken, the spill on her shirt, how she'd slipped it off because of the stain, Gladys's disapproval of her bare midriff in her two-piece bathing suit. Her father staring at the Kingwell girl, and no one understanding why.

"Come see," Nicholas said to the girls. "Here's Auntie Estella. Wasn't she pretty?"

Hannah got up to have a look but she didn't say anything.

"I'd take that as a yes," Nicholas said, and Estella wasn't sure how.

Then he said that he was working on a bit of a Diamond family tree project and he was hoping Estella would have a look. He had a copy of the chart in the car.

The phone calls, she thought. There had been half a dozen since the first one, the day of the plant demolition. Nicholas was gracious enough not to mention that she had hung up on him the first few times he'd called, before she'd stopped answering the phone altogether when she saw the area code. She'd wondered, perhaps foolishly, if the reason for the calls was her will, all those Diamonds she didn't know wondering what she had planned for her money. Lydia was bad enough. She didn't need any more like her.

Emyflor came from the kitchen then carrying a tray of dishes, and Marie immediately got up to help her set the table. Estella looked at her mother's good dishes in the cabinet and wondered if this might be an occasion to use them for once, but she didn't know when they had last been dusted. It was not the kind of thing she asked Emyflor to do.

Marie remarked again on what a beautiful old house it was— the Arts and Crafts architecture, the Queen Anne windows with the coloured panes in the top panel—and Estella explained that her father had copied the design of a house in his hometown in Ontario, and that it had been built, of course, with bricks from the Diamond factory.

Then Emyflor was back again with an omelette that she called a *torta* and a tray with buns and butter and sliced tomatoes. Estella tried to get her to join them for lunch—it was their habit to have lunch together—but Emyflor said she had too much work to do and excused herself. Marie asked where they could wash their hands and Estella showed them the powder room.

The dining room faced the neighbour's yard, and a thick hedge of yellow flowers was blooming all along the foundation of their house. Some kind of false sunflower, she couldn't remember the name. While the others washed their hands, Estella sat at the table and watched her neighbour Kayla deadheading the blossoms. Kayla and her husband had recently bought the house. They had a teenaged daughter whose boyfriend drove a car that sounded like the engine was falling out. It was noisier than Lydia's van, or more correctly SUV. Estella did not know what SUV stood for.

When the family returned she seated Nicholas in her father's spot. The dog began barking in the backyard again. The girls wanted to check on her but Marie said to ignore her, as she sat and placed a paper napkin on her lap.

"Thank you so much for your trouble," she said.

"No trouble," Estella said, which it hadn't been since Emyflor had done the work, and she was thrilled to have guests for lunch. In the days before her mother died, there had rarely been a day when someone from the family didn't stop in for a meal. An invitation was never expected or required.

"Did you know Hannah's middle name is Beatrice?" Nicholas asked. "After your mother."

"Is that so?" Estella said to Hannah.

"Granny name," Hannah said. "I don't love it, obviously."

"Hannah," Nicholas said, looking embarrassed, but Estella waved it off and said, "I believe there's a Princess Beatrice somewhere in the royal family now. That must give it a modern edge."

The girl made it clear with a shrug that she didn't care about the royal family, and then she picked up her fork. Nicholas did the same, and then Marie, and Estella thought it was as though the girl were an actual princess, and she had just given the royal assent to begin eating. She had not been around little girls for a long time.

Estella changed the subject by saying, "So, you're on your way to Winnipeg. A family visit?"

"If that's what you want to call it," Hannah said.

Nicholas and Marie exchanged looks, and then chose to ignore her.

Marie said, "Yes, my parents are there."

Estella wondered what was going on in Winnipeg.

"Is there any salt for the tomatoes, please?" the younger girl asked.

Estella said, "What's a tomato without salt?" and she fetched the salt shaker from the kitchen.

After the meal, Nicholas turned the conversation back to the family tree. He explained that he'd been able to track down a lot of missing information on the Internet, but there were still a few dates he didn't have.

"Would you mind looking at it?" he asked.

Marie said, "Quickly though, Nick. We have a long way to go."

Estella didn't want them to leave. It seemed they had just arrived.

"Let's have a look, then," she said.

Nicholas went to retrieve the family tree from the car while Estella and Marie carried the lunch dishes to the sink. Marie checked on the dog through the window and then offered to do the dishes while Nicholas showed Estella his chart. Before Estella could say she wouldn't hear of it, Marie was putting the stopper in the sink.

She heard Nicholas at the door again so she left Marie and went to see what he had for her to look at. He was carrying a cardboard tube, and he removed a large piece of poster paper and unrolled it on the coffee table in the sitting room. The two girls were by now on the couch, looking at something together on Hannah's phone.

The writing on the chart was very small and the room was dark. Estella pulled one of the floor lamps closer and positioned it so that it cast light on the poster. She saw three names at the top of the page: Beatrice Shaughnessy, Oliver Diamond, and Salina Passmore. Oliver was sandwiched between the two women. Estella's generation of names followed below Oliver and Beatrice, and all down the page more names were carefully written in black pen, her brothers' children and their wives, their children and the ones that followed, spreading out toward the bottom, until there were so many names they formed a tangle of descendants at the foot of the tree. Estella was struck by the stark illustration of her failure to reproduce. She was the only one of the five Oliver Diamond offspring who had not created her own vertical inventory. "Estella Diamond, 1924" was a lonely anomaly at the top right of the page.

"Am I related to all these people?" she asked.

There were certainly more than the forty-five Diamonds in the lake photo, the number they had all celebrated as a record without most of them knowing how four of them were actually related.

Nicholas was pointing to a woman's name on his chart, a descendant of Theo's. "This one became a diplomat," he said. "I think she's in South Africa now. And this family . . . the oldest boy here . . . he went to Australia to learn to surf and married a woman from Sydney. They live there. This one's an air force pilot, so he's all over the place. He was stationed just down the road from you for a time, in Moose Jaw. Apparently there's an air force training centre there. The pilots can learn to fly without any mountains to run into."

"Moose Jaw," Estella said. "I wish I'd known." She was thinking, *So close, and he didn't call.* Well, maybe he had and she'd hung up on him.

Nicholas moved his hands away from the two outside edges of the poster and it rolled itself up again.

"Why don't I leave this with you?" he said. "I have other copies."

Marie came from the kitchen then.

"I wasn't sure where the dishes went so I left them on the counter," she said.

Right away the younger girl jumped up from the couch and said, "Can we *please* go now?"

So this was it, Estella thought. They were leaving.

She tried to think of a way to keep them there just a little longer, ten more minutes, but Marie was making no move to sit again, and both girls were at her side.

Marie said, "Girls, take the leash and get Livvy. We have to go now."

Hannah grabbed the leash and went to the back door.

Paris whispered something in her mother's ear, and Marie said, "You know where the powder room is."

"Come with me," Paris said.

"Oh, for heaven's sake," Marie said. "How old are you, anyway?" But then she went with her.

When Marie and Paris were gone, Nicholas got up from his chair and crossed the room to look in the cabinet by the fireplace. Oliver's first brick had caught his eye. It had been mounted on an oak base, and there was a brass plaque with the date of the plant's opening.

"This brick," Nicholas said. "It must have been the first one out of the kiln, was it?"

As she lifted herself off the couch to open the cabinet door for him, she lost her balance partway up and dropped back down, and was lucky to land on the chair and not the floor. Marie returned at that moment, and she stepped quickly across the room to help her.

"Are you all right?" she asked.

"I'm fine," Estella said, shaking away Marie's hand and sounding grumpier than she'd intended. She hated for people to think she needed help. She struggled again to propel herself onto her feet, and this time got her legs under her, but in the meantime she had forgotten what she'd been about to do. She heard the back door, and Hannah and the dog came in. Hannah had the leash in one hand and her phone in the other. Estella could hear the dog's toenails scrabbling on the hardwood floor as it tugged on the leash.

Marie said, firmly now, "Your aunt is tired, Nick. And Hannah, please put the phone away while we're in company. You know the rule. If you don't follow it, I'm going to confiscate it."

She sounded impatient with Hannah, and Nicholas as well, like a teacher who's had enough.

Nicholas looked torn, not quite ready to give up on what he was looking at in the cabinet.

The brick. That was it. She'd been about to show him the brick.

Paris came back from the powder room then, and Marie hustled the girls toward the door, saying, "Come. Time to go. Thank your Auntie Estella for the lunch." She turned to Estella. "Thank you so much for the visit. You don't need to see us out. Stay where you are."

Well, of course she was going to see them out.

She followed them to the door. Marie and the girls and the dog stepped outside and walked toward the car, but Nicholas lingered. He took a card out of his pocket and handed it to Estella.

"Give me a call if you see any mistakes on the tree," he said. "Or if you need anything."

Estella looked at the card with its many phone numbers. The term *calling card* came to her.

"Thank you," she said, slipping the card into the pocket of her slacks, "but I won't be needing anything. I manage on my own."

"Come on, Nick," Marie called from the street as she opened the back car door for the girls. Estella noticed that they had to climb over whatever was piled on the floor of the car, bags perhaps. The car was loaded up as though they were going on a camping trip. The dog jumped in on top of the bags.

"Girls," Nicholas called. "Take a good look at this house. This is where you came from."

Hannah leaned out the car window with her phone.

"Okay, Dad," she said with obvious sarcasm. Estella supposed she was taking a picture.

"No one has a real camera anymore," Nicholas said. "Everything is digital, in the cloud."

The cloud, Estella thought. It wasn't infirmity that left old people out. It was technology. Pretty soon she wouldn't know how to work her coffee pot.

"You'd better get going," she said with regret. Then she added, "Call me when you get there, so I know you arrived safely."

She heard Emyflor coming down the stairs.

"Emyflor, my nephew is leaving." She loved saying that. *My nephew.*

Emyflor appeared wearing yellow rubber gloves.

"Bye-bye, then," she said, standing halfway down the stairs and waving one gloved hand. "So nice to have visitors. Miss Estella gets lonely."

"Lonely?" Nicholas asked. "Really?"

"She's very kind," Estella said, "but don't listen to her."

Nicholas left then, and Estella watched him cross the street and get in the car. He did a U-turn as they drove away, and she got a good look at Marie, who did not wave at her and seemed to be speaking sharply to Nicholas. She couldn't see what the girls were doing but she imagined them with headphones on, already tuned in to their phones or their music or whatever they had with them.

She closed the front door, and she shook her head and she said, "Gold digger."

"Gold digger?" Emyflor said. "What does that mean?"

Estella didn't know why she'd said it. She must have been thinking of Marie, the way she had admired the house. She explained to Emyflor what a gold digger was, and Emyflor looked horrified. "You mean they want to steal from you?" she asked. "Those people?"

"Not they," Estella said. "She. And don't worry, I've got a good will, and I'm leaving everything to charity. And everything is not as much as people might think it is."

Emyflor still looked concerned and said, "You sit down and rest now, Lola," and she went back upstairs to her cleaning.

Estella returned to the sitting room and saw the family tree still rolled up on the coffee table. She took it to the dining room where the light was better and spread it out again and had a good look at it.

She found Nicholas Diamond's name on the chart and followed the line up to her brother Jack. There was no date of death because his body had never been found. Phyllis's name was there, the first wife, and then Rose, and Rose's other husband, the one she married after Jack. Then Jack and Rose's boys. Don's name had a man's name next to it, Austin. Was that a mistake? Probably not, these days. Ryan had Dora's name next to his, and then a question mark, and Estella wondered if he had disappeared the same way his father had.

She searched for Lydia's name but it wasn't there. She got a pen and found the spot where it should be and wrote it in. Then she realized she had written it in the wrong place, under Jim instead of Paul, so she crossed it out. She found Paul's name and saw that Lydia was there after all. She couldn't remember the names of Lydia's husbands, so she wrote *three husbands*, and then she added Mercy's name, and Lonny's in a direct line from Mercy's.

There, she thought, she had done her part, and Lydia, with her three husbands, was proof that the Diamonds here were just as modern as they were everywhere else. She rolled the paper up again and slipped it back in the cardboard tube, and then put it in her broom closet next to the vacuum cleaner.

She took the card Nicholas had given her out of her pocket and examined it.

Bow River Resources, Nicholas Diamond, Oil and Gas Exploration Services.

Not a calling card. A business card. And not the best business to be in these days. From what she understood, Alberta was no longer the mecca that had lured all the Diamonds across the border. She hoped Nicholas had a secure job.

She stuck the card with a magnet to the fridge door and went out to the backyard to sit in a chair and rest her eyes while the sun was out. But then she saw flowers still blooming along the fence, her fall asters. They looked terrible, past their prime, slumped over with the weight of the blossoms. She retrieved her clippers from her garden shed and chopped them all down. It was October, she thought, and they were going to go soon anyway, so why wait? She began to gather the chopped flowers, but she was overtaken by tiredness so she left the plants where they lay in the flower bed and made her way to her chair on the patio—a new wicker armchair that had replaced her mother's old one—and she sat down heavily and closed her eyes. The chair was in the shade but the sun was shining on her feet. She could feel its warmth.

The only time she ever had a nap in the afternoon was when she was sick. Still, she closed her eyes and fell sound asleep in the chair. Behind her eyelids, she saw a little girl curled up in a child-sized dip in a pink clay gully, like the ones at the plant. She could almost feel the fine dry clay, like flour or cornstarch. Her eyes fluttered open, fighting sleep, and she tried to remember if a child had gone missing at the plant, or if she herself had ever been lost in the hills, but she didn't think so. She closed her eyes again, and slept for another hour, until Emyflor woke her up with a cup of tea.

She had a crick in her neck but her mind was clear. She remembered she'd had visitors, Nicholas and Marie. She remembered the girls, the younger one, Paris, and the sassy one, Hannah. She drank her tea and thought about them, and wondered why they were going to Winnipeg. Something had not been right. After she'd finished her tea, she rose carefully from the wicker chair, and when she noticed the flowers lying in the flower bed—peonies, not asters—she remembered immediately what had happened to them, that she herself had chopped them down.

It was terrible, the confusion. She'd be so certain one minute and then know she'd had it wrong the next. She tried to drag the flowers with a rake from the flower bed into a pile on the lawn, but it was too much work. When she was half done, she found Emyflor putting the lunch dishes away in the kitchen and asked her if she would mind carrying the flowers to the garbage bin in the alley before she left, without adding any kind of an explanation.

"Flowers?" Emyflor said. "What flowers?"

"The ones I cut down," Estella said. Then she added by way of explanation, even though she knew it wasn't true, "They were almost done."

"No, no, no," Emyflor said, looking at the piles of flowers through the kitchen window. "Your beautiful peonies, Lola."

Estella said, "I think the dog must have got into them. I couldn't be bothered trying to stand them up again."

Emyflor said, "Never mind, they'll come back next year."

Later, once the flowers had been loaded into the bin and Emyflor was getting ready to leave, the two of them were standing in the kitchen and Emyflor said, "Tell me again. That word *gold digger.*" She was always trying to improve her English and she knew Estella had been a teacher. She often asked her what words meant, and she kept track in a little notebook she carried in her purse.

"Gold digger," Estella said. "I don't think anyone uses that term anymore."

She felt a little guilty for implying that Marie was a gold digger. Where had that idea come from? Such distressing thoughts invaded her head sometimes, like armies of ill will.

"I think I'm almost out of Ivory," Estella said, looking at the near-empty bottle of dish soap by the sink. "I'll put that on the shopping list, then."

There was a notepad on the counter. Estella found a new page and wrote "dish soap."

Before Emyflor left, Estella said to her, "This is a big house. You should live here. When your family comes, you should all move in."

They talked sometimes about what would happen when the family was able to immigrate: how Emyflor would find a house and a good school for the kids. She wanted them to come before they grew up and started families of their own in the Philippines.

Emyflor laughed at the idea of her kids living with Estella, and said, "You're used to a quiet house."

"This house wasn't always quiet," Estella said. "It had a lot of people in it at one time."

When Emyflor was gone, Estella heated a can of soup for supper and turned on the television. Before she knew it, she was asleep in her chair.

THE TELEPHONE RANG and woke her up. It was dark outside. The call display showed a Manitoba number so she answered it. It would be Nicholas calling to say they had arrived. She sat in her chair with the cordless phone she had finally mastered and listened as he said he hoped he wasn't calling too late, but he just wanted to let her know they were in Winnipeg. The traffic had been good, he said, not too many trucks.

Estella thought it sounded as though he'd been drinking. He was slurring his words.

"Thank you for letting me know," she said.

"I didn't want you to worry," Nicholas said. "Since you asked me to call, and then if I didn't call . . . well, you know."

"Thank you," she said again.

There was silence on the other end of the line. She almost said goodbye and hung up, thinking he'd conveyed what he wanted to, but then he said, "I wasn't completely honest with you this afternoon."

She was immediately wary. The wife, she thought. Marie.

Maybe she had been right that Marie was a gold digger. She had some idea that Estella was a wealthy old lady, and she had her eye on Estella's will.

But that was not what he had called to say.

"I wanted to tell you we've separated," Nicholas said. "Marie is staying here in Winnipeg for the summer. We've just had a meal with her parents, the last supper, I guess. I'm sorry, I've had quite a bit to drink. I don't usually drink, but this is an exceptional circumstance."

She suspected he was still drinking. She could hear the sound of ice in a glass. She didn't know what to say. Was the separation a good or a bad thing?

He made it clear that it was bad.

"I'm losing my girls, Estella. All three of them. Four, if you count the dog. I'm losing everything. I'm supposed to drive back to Calgary alone. How am I going to do that? Get back in my car and leave my girls behind? I don't think I can do it. She claims it's a trial separation, just until the end of August, but I don't believe she's planning to come back to Calgary at all. She'll stay, and the girls will go to a new school, and if I'm lucky I'll see them a few times a year. They'll forget me."

He broke down. She heard a sob, then a catch as he tried to hold back another. A pause and then, "Hannah, she's the one I worry about the most. She's at that age. She's very vulnerable. Marie doesn't seem to understand how vulnerable she is."

This is dreadful, Estella thought. She sat up in her chair and tried to muster whatever capacity she had left to say something useful. Old people were supposed to be wise. What wisdom did she have?

"Nicholas," she said, "this is very difficult, I know, but you have to pull yourself together. For your girls."

She was surprised by her voice, the authority in it. It was her old teacher voice. But she'd said nothing of substance. *Pull yourself together.* What did that mean? "I'm sorry," she said. "I know that sounds inadequate as far as advice goes, but truly, unless you're on death's door, it will get better. The pain is temporary."

"How did I not see this coming?" he said. "I'll tell you how big a fool you're talking to. I thought we were happy. How could I have been so wrong about that?"

"Maybe you weren't wrong," Estella said.

"Oh, I'm pretty sure I was, but here, you tell me. Two weeks ago, Paris's sixth birthday. The poor kid's party had to be cancelled at the last minute because of an outbreak of measles at school, but she was a trooper. She said she'd just as soon go to a movie as long as we bought her a really good present to make up for the missed party, so the four of us got in the car and went to the movie she picked, some superhero cartoon. And what are the odds, it turned out the whole mall had been shut down because of a gas leak. Again, she said she didn't care, why didn't we pick up McDonald's and have a picnic in the park? So we went to McDonald's and got Big Macs and fries at the drive-through, and we went to the river, and we'd no sooner found a picnic table than the sky opened up. We ended up eating our McDonald's in a car in the parking lot, the rain coming down so hard you couldn't see out the windshield. Poor, poor Paris, I thought. How could so many things go wrong on one kid's birthday? And then Paris held up a soggy french fry and stuffed it in her mouth and said, 'This has been the best birthday ever!' Marie burst out laughing, and then Hannah, and me, and we were the Swiss Family Robinson. Lost maybe, but happy. And Paris looked so damned adorable in her purple tutu.

"So yes, anyone watching from outside the car would have thought we were happy. But we weren't, apparently, because Hannah told me so. When I went to her room later to say good night, she was lying in the dark with only her night light on, and I said, 'Wasn't that great that we managed to have such a good day when everything went wrong?' and Hannah said it wasn't a good day, it was a shitty day, and don't pretend I hadn't noticed that she'd faked it for Paris's sake. And then I thought, maybe Marie faked it too. And Paris, maybe even Paris faked it, and I was the only one stupid enough to think we'd had fun. And I wondered, what else don't I know? Hannah's night light, for one thing. Why would an eleven-year-old choose a night light the shape of a human skull out of all the others on the store shelf? Why not a crescent moon, or a banana, or a kitten smiling like the Cheshire Cat? Why had there been no talking her out of that skull?"

Estella tried to picture the night light. It sounded like a Hallowe'en decoration. She could hear Nicholas refilling his glass, and the sound of ice clinking. She wanted to tell him to stop, put the bottle away, pour it down the sink, but he began to talk again.

"After that, I took the dog for a walk. It was still raining, and while we were walking the power went out. I knew the whole neighbourhood was down because I couldn't see any big-screen TVs through the neighbours' windows. Total blackout. Just a few solar garden lights. I decided to head for home because I thought the kids might be scared. I knew there was a flashlight somewhere. Marie would know where it was, I thought, Marie knows everything. And then I thought, Marie probably knows what my future is, too, and she just hasn't told me yet.

"The house was dark when I got home. I found a towel and dried the dog off and stripped out of my wet clothes and wrapped myself in the same towel. I smelled like a wet dog. Then I went looking for a flashlight and I found one in a kitchen drawer, a mini-light on a key ring, but at least I could walk around the house with it.

"I found Marie in Paris's room. Paris was asleep and Marie was on the floor next to the bed, and she did have a proper flashlight, but she had it switched off and was sitting in the dark. Her back was against the bed and she had Paris's tutu in her hands and she was caressing it, as though she had Paris in her lap, sleeping. I switched off my light because I couldn't stand to look. I stood there in the dark until Marie said, 'What are we doing?' I told her that I didn't know, but that if she did, maybe it was time she told me. She started to cry and said that guilt was killing her, knowing that she would never again have my respect. It would have been easier, she said, if I hadn't so readily forgiven her. You can guess what she'd done—an affair, of course, so predictable—but it had been months before and I *had* forgiven her. But I hated her for saying that about the guilt killing her, as though she was the one who deserved sympathy. And then she said she had a plan, and she and the girls would spend the summer in Winnipeg. I found out the next day that she was already packed. She had packed before she bothered to tell me."

He stopped talking, and Estella heard the rhythmic clinking of ice again. Then he swore, as though he'd spilled his drink, or splashed it on the arm of his chair.

"Nicholas," she said, "put the glass down. Put it down right now. You're drunk, and that's not doing you any good. I'm not going to say anything more as long as you have that drink in your hand."

He told her that he was setting it down. It grew quiet on his end of the line.

"All right, then." She took a breath and said, "I don't know you and Marie. I don't know what to say about your future or what you should do. But I do know this: if you live long enough, you'll survive the loss of almost everyone, and then you'll know the meaning of the word loss."

The minute she said it, she regretted it. She was talking about herself, feeling sorry for herself, and what good would that do a young man who was in the midst of his own family crisis? She had probably just made it worse. She was suddenly so tired. She was an old woman. What could she possibly say that would help?

"Nicholas," she said, "I'm afraid I have to go now."

He apologized for calling her then, for having had too many drinks, for burdening her with his problems. He said good night and hung up.

She sat with the phone in her hand and thought, *At one time I was a smart woman.*

She turned off the TV and the lights, and at that moment a car pulled up out front. It was that boyfriend, Kayla's daughter's, and a terrible racket started. Car doors slamming, shouting, a fight, the girl's high-pitched voice. She couldn't make out what she was saying, but the boyfriend was shouting, "Fuck you, then. Fuck you!"

Estella went to the window and drew back the curtains just in time to see Kayla come running out with a broom as though she were about to break up a dogfight, and she chased the boyfriend down the sidewalk with it. Then she grabbed her daughter by the arm and dragged her into the house. The boyfriend looked toward Estella's window, and she quickly let the curtains fall together.

She heard the car drive off, tires squealing on the pavement.

Nothing like that ever happened on this block in the old days, she thought, barring the night she'd broken up with Clarence Angell under the street lamp.

She went upstairs to get ready for bed, hoping the boyfriend wasn't in a gang. When she switched on the bathroom light, she saw that Emyflor had everything polished to a shine. There was a grab bar screwed to the rim of the bathtub now—Emyflor's idea—and Estella didn't know how she'd ever got in and out of the tub without it. As she brushed her teeth, she wondered if Nicholas would phone again in a few days to let her know he was back in Calgary, or whether she had given him such pointless advice that she would never hear from him again.

She spat in the sink and then looked in the mirror and thought what a constant surprise it was to see such an old woman staring back.

SHE WOKE UP when it was barely light thinking she could hear singing in the hallway outside her bedroom door. It was the train porter. He had a tenor voice, clear and melodious. He was singing "Blueberry Hill."

She got up and looked but there was no one there, so she padded back across the hardwood floor in her bare feet and slipped into bed again. She must have been dreaming. She sometimes couldn't tell the difference.

Eugene, that was his name. How had she managed to remember after all these years when she often forgot what day of the week it was? He had not been important in her life, although losing your virginity to a train porter when you were past thirty, practically under the nose of your family, had to be at least notable. The "night of the porter" was one of those memories that had lately popped into her head out of nowhere and seemed not to be clouded by time. It was as though moments of her life were happening all over again, and all at once, and she found herself wondering what kind of life Eugene had had, and whether he'd become a psychologist or had continued working for the railroad. She had known him for all of a few hours and she and Eugene had never been a possibility, but still she wondered what had become of him.

She dozed off, and when she woke up for the second time she didn't know where she was. She lay in bed listening to the murmurs of people talking—a doctor and a nurse, perhaps—and thinking the worst must have happened, that she'd had some kind of fall or illness and Lydia had moved her to a home, and not a very good one, at that. She stared at a strip of wallpaper that appeared to be peeling from the top where it met the ceiling. What an ugly choice of wallpaper, and what a disgrace that it was in such bad condition.

But where exactly was she? It didn't look like a nursing home. Those places were painted pale-green or beige, like hospital rooms. They had easy-to-mop floors, not hardwood and area rugs, and blinds rather than curtains. This appeared to be a room in an old house. The window had proper drapes, although they were dated.

Those drapes look familiar, she thought.

The voices in the hall started up again and she realized they were talking about the Diamonds, saying things that weren't true: that Oliver Diamond had stolen the brick plant from the Texan, Nathaniel Thick, killed him really, because he'd committed suicide in the end. And Estella Diamond. What had she been thinking when she tore the family apart with that talk of a lawsuit?

Estella Diamond.

That was her.

A woman's voice: *Estella was not as lily-white as everyone thought, you know. Clarence Angell knew what she was like, but he would have had her as a wife anyway. He bought her an expensive ring and she threw it in his face. That's how high and mighty Estella was, that she thought she could do better than Clarence Angell.*

Is that so? Estella thought, and she sat up and threw back the covers, feeling more than a little indignant. She marched to the door and opened it, but when she looked out she saw that no one was there. She stared into the hallway and thought it looked just like her own house. The same chiffonier against the wall across from the bathroom, the one that held the tablecloths and napkins. The bathroom door in the same place, and the other doors, three of them, that led to the bedrooms: her parents' room and the other two her brothers had shared. The window at the end of the hallway that looked out over the backyard.

It *was* her house.

She did not know how the people talking could have disappeared so quickly. She did not know how they could have got inside.

There was only one answer.

They had not been there.

She felt tremendous relief that Lydia hadn't stuck her in some dreadful home, and at the same time she feared that she was finally losing her mind altogether.

She went back to bed and lay down again, and as her head cleared, she slowly began to recognize things in the room: a watercolour painting that she herself had done, the dressing table she had moved from her parents' room, the curtains on the window that she had chosen in a drapery shop. No wonder they had looked familiar.

My bedroom, she thought, *that's where I am,* and her eye returned to the painting, which was not very good, and then the wallpaper, the tiny green leaves on a cream background that had finally replaced the sea of pink she'd disliked so much. It was time to paper again, she thought. She could do it herself, with Emyflor's help. She lay in bed for fifteen minutes before she sat up again, and she wondered whether her legs would hold her, but they felt fine. There was a mirror on the dresser, and when she looked she knew it was her looking back, Estella Diamond, and there was not much wrong with her except that she was old.

Her bedside clock told her it was only 5:30. She remembered that this was the day Lydia was picking her up for their trip to Lake Claire, and she had another moment of confusion when she looked around her room and she did not see her bag packed and waiting. Perhaps she had taken it downstairs already, but she didn't remember doing that. She kept a little calendar on her bedside table—the one the bank sent her every year at Christmas—and each morning she crossed off the day. There it was, the last Thursday in June with an X through it, so today was the Friday before the long weekend, the day they had planned to travel to the lake. She picked up the pen beside the calendar and crossed off Friday. Then she got up and looked in the closet, and there was her suitcase. She knew right away when she picked it up that it was empty, but she lifted it to the bed anyway and opened it, just to be sure. Not a thing inside, not even a bobby pin, because she was always very particular about cleaning it out after every trip.

She began to throw things in the suitcase. She didn't need to think about what she was taking because she took the same things every year: shorts, trousers, a velour track suit, assorted T-shirts, underwear and socks, a flannel nightgown because it was always cool at night, a heavy sweater, her walking sandals, and her Tilley hat. She would have liked to have included a second track suit—the nice dark-green one with the little stars down the seams of the pants—but she was conscious of keeping the weight of her bag down. From the bathroom she retrieved her bottle of Aspirin and her Tums and she added them to the suitcase. Then she laid her watercolour supplies on top, all neatly contained in a wooden box. She used them only once a year to paint a Lake Claire sunset or perhaps a forest scene. She'd taken up watercolour painting again when she closed the factory and realized she needed a hobby, but she was still no artist.

Back to the bathroom for her toiletry bag. Sunscreen, deodorant, face cream, toothbrush. She packed the bag and zipped it up.

A bathing suit, she thought, just in case. She hadn't worn a bathing suit in years but she always took one along. She went on a search of her dresser drawers and found her purple one-piece with the slimming panel. A bit of bright yellow caught her eye at the bottom of the drawer, and when she pushed a stack of obsolete T-shirts out of the way, there was the Mondrian two-piece. It had held its colour and the fabric was still good, but the elastic was shot. She studied the gaping waistband and wondered if it was beyond repair. She remembered buying the suit, and how she had loved the colours. She laid it on top of the dresser, not quite able to throw it out, and packed the purple suit.

When she couldn't think of anything she'd missed, she washed and dressed and brushed her hair, and then she made her way downstairs, lifting and resting her suitcase with each step until she reached the bottom. She checked the time and was surprised to see that it was still only 7:30. After draping her rain jacket over her suitcase, she went to the kitchen to have a bite of breakfast. Lydia never arrived before 10:00, so she'd lost no time by forgetting to pack. Last year it had been noon before they'd got away. She hoped Lydia would remember to bring the cooler with the groceries in it. One year they'd packed it at Estella's and then Lydia had forgotten it on the front porch, and they'd arrived home to a cooler full of rotten produce and pork chops with a crow sitting on top as though it were guarding a cache. Lydia had blamed Estella, of course. Estella had thrown the whole thing out without opening it.

After breakfast, Estella took her coffee outside and sat in the wicker chair. Kayla was already in her yard in her gardening gloves and she waved at Estella.

"You're up early," she called. No sign of upset over the daughter's boyfriend the night before last, when she'd chased him away with a broom.

"Off to the lake," Estella said, as though this was another year like all the others and there were many more to come.

"Oh," Kayla said, sounding surprised. "I'll keep my eye on the house, if you like."

"Not necessary," Estella said. "It's just a few days. Emyflor will be looking after the house." Then she lied and said Emyflor would be staying overnight. She didn't want that boyfriend finding out the house was empty.

"I hope you have a nice time," Kayla said.

She approached the fence separating their yards and said, "No need to worry about this now, but we were wondering . . . my husband and I . . . if we might trim the branches on your apple tree for you." She pointed to the branch that was hanging over their side of the fence. "It's creating a lot of shade. The flower bed on our side doesn't get much sun. But like I said, no need to decide now. Just think about it. It's not the right time anyway. In the fall, after the sap is down."

Estella pictured a lopsided tree, flattened on Kayla's side of the fence.

"It's very pretty when it blooms in the spring," she said.

"Oh, it is," Kayla said. "I agree. We're not suggesting you cut it down. Just a trim, on our side only, if that suits you. But I shouldn't have mentioned it when you were on your way. Don't give it another thought."

Kayla began to walk away, but then she hesitated, as though she wanted to say something else, and finally she did, cautiously.

"You know, Estella," she said, "my husband is in construction. Would you like him to have a look at your roof sometime? He'd be happy to give you some advice. The gutters, you see . . . well, they leak in a heavy rain and the water pools around our foundations, both of our houses. Perhaps you've noticed? We've been getting a bit of water in the basement."

Gutters? Estella thought. There was nothing wrong with her gutters.

Kayla must have seen the look on her face because she said again, "Oh, I'm sorry, what's the matter with me? We'll talk when you get back." Then she gave Estella a little wave and walked away, back into the leafy cover of her own yard.

Yes, we will talk, Estella thought. She would tell Kayla to mind her own business, and that she wouldn't have her oaf of a husband anywhere near her roof. She wondered what other plans Kayla and her husband had for her.

She hoisted herself out of her chair and went back inside because she didn't want Kayla spying on her. She sat on the front porch swing and waited, her suitcase by the door where she could see it. She could hear a crow squawking high up in one of the spruce trees. The neighbourhood was overrun with them. Now that would be a job for Kayla's husband, she thought, get a pellet gun and shoot the crows out of the trees.

The day was already hot, even in the shade. She went inside again, and to pass the time she fetched her sewing basket and her old two-piece bathing suit, and she sat at the dining room table where the light was good and did what she could to repair it. She rubbed the remains of the dried-out elastic away from the waist, and then she hand-stitched a channel and threaded a length of cord into it, like a drawstring. The leg openings were another matter. The best she could come up with was to sew a few tucks around the openings on each side. The bra was still serviceable because it tied in the back and behind the neck rather than relying on elastic. She had no intention of ever again wearing the bathing suit. She just didn't want to throw it out. Still, she took the purple suit from her bag and replaced it with the two-piece. Then she sat again on the porch swing to wait.

It was not Lydia's SUV that finally pulled up in front of her house.

It was Nicholas Diamond's silver sedan, and he had the older girl in the front seat beside him. When Estella realized it was Nicholas's car that had parked at the end of her walk, she wondered where the rest of the family was, and what Nicholas and the girl were doing here. She hadn't spoken with him since he'd called her from Winnipeg, drunk as a lord.

"Hello," Nicholas said, stepping out onto the street and waving to her across the top of the car. He didn't look any less like Jack than he had two days ago, and he didn't look like a man who had been on a bender. The girl, Hannah, emerged from the passenger seat and the two of them came toward her up the walk, and then stood at the bottom of the steps. There was no dog this time.

"You look like you're waiting for someone," Nicholas said.

The suitcase.

She didn't know whether she should invite them in. Lydia's SUV was sure to come around the corner any minute.

"Lake Claire," she said. "I'm waiting for my niece. I suppose she'll be late. She always is."

"I'm glad we caught you," Nicholas said. "We were hoping—Hannah and I—that we might drive to Lake Claire too, just to see what it's all about. We don't want to intrude, and we would stay out of your way, of course, but we were wondering what the cabins are called. The ones the Diamonds always stayed in."

Estella couldn't remember the new owner's name.

"It used to be Fosters," she said. "Fosters Bungalows. But they have a new name. I don't recall what it is."

In her head, she was trying to decide whether Nicholas and

Hannah at the lake would be a good or a bad thing. Would Nicholas drink himself blind every night over his marriage breakup?

On the other hand, six Diamonds, not just four.

And then he said, right in front of Hannah, "I really want to apologize for calling you like that the other night, Estella. That is really not who I am. It won't happen again."

That was good enough for the benefit of doubt.

She stood up from the swing and invited them inside, leaving her suitcase on the step and hoping a crow wouldn't claim it. She had the number for Fosters in her little phone book. She assumed the number would be the same. At one time she had known it by heart.

She took Nicholas and Hannah to the kitchen and found her phone book. Nicholas called, and when someone answered he said in reply, "I was trying to reach Fosters. Is this still Fosters?" He listened for a bit—he was getting the explanation, Estella thought—and then he asked for a cabin, just a small one, he said, for himself and his daughter. "Nicholas Darling," he gave as his name, and Estella saw him wink at Hannah, who was standing by the counter watching.

"From *Peter Pan*," Hannah said to Estella.

Estella supposed it was a joke between the two of them, but he should have told them he was a Diamond. They might have given him a better cottage.

Nicholas retrieved a credit card from his wallet and read the number, after which Estella got his attention and said, "Tell them you're related to me."

"I'm a relative of Estella Diamond's," he said to whoever was on the phone. "Can you tell me how close together our cabins are?" There was a pause and Nicholas frowned. "I wonder if there's a mistake," he said. "Can you check again?" He waited, and then said, "I'll speak to her and we'll call you back, just to confirm."

When he hung up the phone he told Estella that there was no cabin booked in her name.

"Marigold Bungalows," he said. "Apparently that's what they're called now. Do you think that might have caused some confusion?"

Estella said she didn't see how since the phone number was the same, but she had best call Lydia. She dialled her number and got Mercy.

"There seems to be a problem with our cottage booking," she said. "Let me talk to Lydia."

"What booking?" Mercy asked.

"For the lake. What booking do you think?"

There was silence, and then Mercy said, "But we're not going to the lake this year."

"Of course we are," Estella said. "Surely she hasn't forgotten. Let me speak with her."

Mercy said Lydia was at work.

"That's ridiculous," Estella said. "We'll be driving in the dark."

There was another silence on Mercy's end of the line, as though she couldn't think what to say, and then she said that Estella must have forgotten, the plans had changed.

"If they have, nobody told me," Estella said. "I've been sitting on the porch waiting for you."

"I know we're not going to the lake, not this year," Mercy said. "Lonny's going to summer camp tomorrow instead. It's that special needs camp. We thought it would be good for him. Remember?"

"I remember no such thing," Estella said, which was not quite true, it was coming back to her. There was something about a camp, Lonny's school had suggested it, and Lydia had asked Estella for the fees because it was expensive. But was that this weekend, the weekend they always went to Lake Claire?

"Perhaps there's been a misunderstanding," she said. "Tell Lydia to call me later, then."

"A mix-up?" Nicholas asked after she'd hung up the phone.

Estella heard herself sigh. "Summer camp," she said. "For my great-niece's autistic grandson."

It was true. Lydia had argued that the camp would be better for Lonny than Lake Claire; they had therapists there, and activities designed for children like him. But was it all an excuse because of what had happened the year before, when they'd said she couldn't be trusted to look after Lonny and she'd lashed out and broken a water glass and sent everyone into a tailspin? The more she thought about it, the more certain she became that they just didn't want to take her anymore. That was the real reason there was no booking.

"They're a pair, like mother, like daughter," she said. "One day it's on, the next it's off."

There was a wooden kitchen chair by the telephone and she sat on it, trying not to worry because she had completely forgotten about Lonny's camp. Nicholas was bound to be thinking she was senile. She herself thought she might be. The chair had been placed to cover a cracked linoleum tile, but she could still see that a chunk of the tile was missing. She remembered the tiles when they were new; she and her father had chosen them not long after her mother died.

"You must be disappointed," Nicholas said.

He sounded genuine, and again she thought of Jack, who had

been the kindest of her brothers, at least until he came back from the war, and nothing after that could be blamed on him. Not even his final act, which had not been kind at all, the way he'd left everyone without an explanation or a goodbye. She reached with her foot to feel the spot where the tile had broken away.

"This needs to be taken care of," she said. "My father was always particular about keeping the house up."

Nicholas said, "I wonder if there are leftover tiles stored somewhere. It would be hard to find a match now."

She thought there very well could be. Her father had kept his odds and ends in the garage, and she had not once looked through his storage shelves in all the years since he'd been gone.

"If there are, the garage is where they would be," she said. She turned to Hannah then and asked her if she'd mind getting her a glass of water.

Hannah found a glass in the cupboard. She filled it from the tap and then handed it to her.

"I know the boy is their priority," Estella said, "but I do think they could have told me." It was a feeble attempt at covering up her mistake.

Nicholas said, "I don't know your niece but it sounds inconsiderate to me. I'll have a quick look for those tiles, then. Is there a key handy?"

Estella thought he was probably just humouring her, feeling sorry for her, but she felt better then, the way he had understood her disappointment without judging her. She pointed toward the back entry, where there was a key rack by the door.

"The one on the yellow tag," she said, "although you needn't bother."

"I'll have a look," Nicholas said. "It's no trouble."

She heard the door as he stepped out on his way to the garage.

She felt her fingers tapping the side of the water glass to the rhythm of "Raindrops Keep Fallin' On My Head." Lonny liked to tap out rhythms, on his thighs, the soles of his feet, the surface of the table at mealtimes. She and Lonny were alike, she thought, half in the real world and half in their own poor heads. Ever since Lonny's bell-ringing class he'd been experimenting with objects other than his hands, trying to find a sound that resembled his bell. Mercy had enrolled him in the class because everyone seemed to think he was musical with all that tapping, but she was now saying it had been a mistake because he was driving her crazy.

"Do you know about handbells?" Estella asked Hannah. "It's a choir of a sort, with bells."

Hannah nodded. "School," she said. "Second grade."

Estella stopped tapping and took a sip of her water and studied Hannah. She didn't know what to make of her. She'd thought she was insolent two days ago, but now she seemed nervous, or curious, perhaps, as though she'd never been alone with an old lady. She had the red purse over her shoulder, but she seemed to have given up her obsession with the phone she carried in it. Estella was about to ask her about phones and what it was that had young people fiddling with them all day long, when Hannah said, "They're splitting up. My parents. Did he tell you that?"

Estella hesitated briefly and then nodded. What reason was there to pretend she didn't know? "I'm very sorry to hear it," she said.

"I don't see why it's all up to them," Hannah said. "They're always talking about the family, you can't turn around without considering the family, and then they go and make a decision like that, and, oh sure, they'll say it's for the best, for all four of us, but that is total crap. You know?"

"I can't say that I do," Estella said, but she was thinking, *Oh yes, I do know that.*

"Anyway," Hannah said, "I'm not sure my dad even believes it, that it's for the best. I suppose he's giving her time." She said it in a mocking tone and put air quotes around *giving her time.*

Hannah fell silent then. She reached for her purse as though she was going to unzip it, but then she changed her mind and let it hang once again from her shoulder.

"You young people and your phones," Estella said. "I don't know what the rules are, but you can get it out if you want. I don't mind." She wondered if using a cellphone was like smoking and you ought to get permission from the person whose house you were in. Then she said, "You don't put pictures of yourself on the Internet, do you? Because I hear it's very dangerous."

After she said it, she wished she hadn't, she might put ideas in the girl's head. But Hannah said, "I know someone who sent a selfie to her boyfriend. Not exactly topless, but close. It was supposed to be private but then he put it on his Instagram. She got him to take it down but, oops, already out there."

Estella hardly knew what to say to that. Topless photos at Hannah's age? Surely not.

"And that was nothing," Hannah said. "There's way worse. Anyway, she was stupid, if you ask me."

"Well, what happens to these girls with the pictures?" Estella asked. "What do they do?"

"Get smarter," Hannah said. "If it's not too late."

She'd said it so nonchalantly, as though this was a fact of life, and Estella wanted to ask her more, but then Hannah said, "Anyway, I don't have my phone anymore. I don't need it."

That was a change from just two days ago when her mother had been unable to keep her off it. Then she realized that Marie had probably confiscated it.

Nicholas came back in just then, saying that he didn't see anything that looked like tiles but there were a lot of taped-up boxes on the shelves that he didn't go into.

"Very kind of you to look, but never mind," Estella said. "My neighbour's husband is a contractor. Perhaps I'll ask him what to do." She wouldn't, but she didn't want Nicholas worrying that he had to fix her kitchen floor.

"Estella," Nicholas said then. "What do you think of this idea? I could call Lake Claire and see if we could switch to a bigger cabin. Perhaps you could come with us. We're just going for the weekend. Three nights. We'd bring you back Monday."

He seemed to be sincere. Sincerely asking her to come to Lake Claire with them.

"I couldn't," she said.

She really couldn't. You didn't go off with strangers, even if the stranger was a Diamond, and looked exactly like your brother, and had his daughter with him. She remembered him slurring his words on the phone, even though he'd said that he hadn't been himself.

"It would be our pleasure," he said. "Wouldn't it, Hannah?"

Hannah said, "I guess."

Estella said, "I doubt they would have any bigger cottages free at this late date." As she spoke, though, the arguments were bouncing back and forth in her head, one way, then another. Even if the offer was completely innocent, which it surely was, she didn't want to be a burden.

But her suitcase was packed. All she would have to do was get in the car.

Then the telephone rang. It was Peter Boone.

"Missus Diamond," he said, "I hear there's been a mistake."

"Mister Boone, it's you," she said. Silly after all these years, but it amused her just the same.

Then he said he'd thought it was peculiar that they had no cottage booked for her. He'd worried something was wrong.

Perhaps, Estella thought, he'd assumed she was dead. He did sound very pleased to hear that she wasn't, if that was the case.

"Just some confusion at our end," Estella said. "You know Lydia."

And then the Lake Claire vacation was back on course, when it had almost been derailed, and she asked if there was a family-sized cottage still available for the weekend. Peter switched Nicholas's booking to Emily Carr, the one she and her parents had always stayed in. She didn't know how he managed it. Perhaps a significant discount was about to come to the family who already had it booked.

After they said goodbye, she heard him say to someone else, "Estella. Oliver Diamond's daughter."

"We'd better treat her like royalty, then," the other voice said before the line went dead.

She couldn't tell what had been meant by that, but she said, "Apparently they're going to treat us like royalty. They're giving us the best cottage of the lot."

She could see that Nicholas was only half paying attention. He said, "I noticed that your car in the garage is up to date with plates."

It was true. She'd renewed the plates so Emyflor could drive her places.

"We could take your car, if you like. I don't imagine it's had a good run on the highway for a while. I remember my father saying a car needs a road trip to blow the carbon out. It might have been his only useful piece of advice."

"My father used to say the same thing," Estella said, and she remembered how he'd always wanted to travel in his own car.

While Nicholas went to switch the cars instead of leaving his on the street, Estella called Mercy and said she had found a ride to Lake Claire for a few days, and that she hoped Lonny would have fun at his summer camp.

Of course Mercy wanted to know who she was getting a ride with, but Estella was vague and said, "Oh, just some regulars."

When she saw Nicholas pull up in front of the house in her car, she went to retrieve her house keys from her purse, and realized she had left it upstairs. Then Nicholas came in and said he perhaps ought to call Marie.

"Why?" Hannah said, but then she didn't wait for an answer and went outside. Through the screen, Estella saw her sit on the porch swing.

Estella lingered at the foot of the stairs so she could hear what Nicholas was saying to his wife. He left a message.

"It's me," he said. "I guess Hannah told you what she did, but everything's fine. I'll bring her back in a couple of days. My phone quit working if you've been trying to reach me. I'll buy a new one today. Okay, so, don't worry. Hannah is in a surprisingly good mood." There was a pause, and then Estella thought she heard him say, "No thanks to you, you cheating bitch. Yeah, that's right,

I know about the sequel." Then he hung up. She wondered if she'd been mistaken about the last part, because the rest of the message had been so ordinary.

When she got upstairs, she found her purse on top of the clothes hamper in the bathroom. Her cane was there too, and she supposed she ought to take it, although pride was tempting her to leave it behind.

She heard Nicholas call up the stairs, "Estella? Ready to go?"

"Be right down," she called, and as she turned away from the mirror, she happened to look out the bedroom window and saw Kayla in the yard next door, and she remembered the apple tree and Kayla's suggestion to trim its branches. It certainly didn't look from there as if it needed a trim. What was Kayla up to? Estella had so many valuable things in her house. It would be easy enough for Kayla to figure out how to get into the house. Or that daughter. Or the boyfriend.

Estella picked up her jewellery box, planning to take it down-stairs with her and put it in her suitcase, but then she remembered the suitcase was jammed full, so instead of carrying the whole jewellery box with her, she opened the lid and took out the velvet bag with the antique clay beads in it, the ones that her father had given her. The beads were valuable, something she'd learned only recently when she'd had her things appraised for the insurance agent. Over a thousand dollars, they'd said, since they were rare and thought to be created by a designer who had become quite famous a hundred years ago. She tucked the velvet bag into her purse, safely away from the light-fingered Kayla and her delin-quent daughter, and then she made her way downstairs, carrying her cane, because good sense won out over vanity.

Nicholas was waiting on the steps with her suitcase in his hand. Hannah was already in the car. Estella was about to lock up when she decided she should call Emyflor and ask her to look in on the house while she was gone. She couldn't remember what she'd told her. She reached her voice mail and left a message with the Fosters number, or Marigolds, as it was called now, in case she needed to get in touch.

She locked the house and walked out to the car. Hannah was in the front seat and Nicholas suggested that she give Estella the front, but Estella told Hannah to stay where she was, she should have the best view since it was her first trip to Lake Claire. They were barely out of the city before Estella was dozing in the back seat.

THEY WERE TALKING about the Diamonds again, those same voices, strangers, saying things that weren't true, spreading rumours about Oliver and the Texan, and about her, how she cheated her brothers, and they were talking about her mother this time, too—her mother, who had never done a wrong thing in her life—saying that Beatrice thought she was really something just because she was married to Oliver, and what an easy ride she had, and never had to lift a finger.

And she calls her living room a parlour. Who does she think she is?

Estella woke with a yelp when her cane slipped from where she had propped it and wacked her in the shins. She wasn't sure where she was at first, but then it came back. She was in her own car, and Jack was driving her to Lake Claire.

She'd been dreaming. A relief to know that, she thought, because she wasn't always so certain.

"What happened?"

It was Jack speaking, trying to see in the rear-view mirror if everything was all right in the back seat. But who was the girl who had her head cranked right around and was staring at her?

Not Jack. Jack had been gone for years.

Nicholas and his daughter Hannah.

She scrambled to get her thoughts straight. "My cane slipped," she said.

"Are you all right?" Nicholas asked.

"Yes, I'm fine. It was nothing."

"Should I stop?" He was already pulling onto the shoulder and slowing down.

"No need."

"Are you sure?"

"Didn't I say I was sure?" she snapped.

An uncomfortable silence.

Estella heard the echo of her own voice. Irritable. Self-centred.

"Sorry," Nicholas said, "it's just . . ." His voice trailed off as he sped up again and steered back onto the highway.

She ought to apologize, but that was something she had never been good at.

"Don't worry about me," she said, trying to sound contrite. "You won't have much fun if you're worrying about me the whole time."

"Just let us know if you need anything," he said, and he looked away from the mirror.

She hated it when her mind was not right. Whenever she was confused, she wanted only to be at home, where everything was known to her and the only surprises were in her head. She didn't want to be on the road with people she didn't know. What if she was mixed up all the while she was away? What if she got lost, or talked nonsense the whole time and made a fool of herself? The fields and sloughs and farmhouses flashing by were familiar, and she knew this was the right road, the road to Lake Claire, the one she had travelled countless times, but all she wanted was for Nicholas Diamond and his daughter to turn the car around and take her home.

Then Nicholas spoke again, and she could tell he was trying to put her at ease. He was talking about family, the Diamonds, his Uncle Don, how Don was the one with the Lake Claire memories. Don spoke of a time when his father was still alive and all the cousins were there, and they went to the beach every day and barbecued every night, and he didn't remember a single day of bad weather, although there must have been some. Nicholas said Don was planning to retire in another year, and he often spoke of making a trip back to Lake Claire when he had more time. He and his partner were planning to spend the winters in Florida.

Had Estella tried that, he asked, winter holidays, snowbirding off to places like Myrtle Beach or Palm Springs in California?

She said no, she'd never taken a winter holiday. Perhaps she had missed out.

The girl began to speak then, about the time they had gone to Disney World in Florida one winter. Remember this, remember that, the Animal Kingdom and the Epcot Center.

The panic began to abate.

She opened her purse to find the roll of mints she knew was in there, and as she rooted around she saw that she had managed to upend the jewellery bag, and the beads were now at the bottom of her purse with her wallet and her dark glasses on top of them. The cloth they'd once been wrapped in seemed to be missing so she slipped them back into the velvet bag without it. As she did so, she discovered an enamelled pin in the bag, a loon. She could not remember where it had come from, or why it was there. It was just a little souvenir pin, but it was attractive. It must have been her mother's. She pinned it to her jacket.

Why had she brought the beads with her? They were too valuable and all she was going to do was worry about them. She removed the beads once more and wrapped them in several tissues before retying the bag, tightly this time.

"There," she said, snapping her purse shut. "That's better."

Nicholas glanced in the rear-view.

"All's well back here," she said.

THE BUMPS ON the lake access road woke Estella up again. She'd slept off and on most of the way with the sun shining in on her. She saw the familiar black-and-yellow signs in the ditch—don't feed the bears, moose on the loose, deer crossing—and she knew exactly where they were, not far now from the village. Sometimes Peter Boone came this way if he was out for a longer run. He was over seventy, but he still ran every day, unless that had changed in the last year. She watched for him in his nylon shorts, his skinny calves in white tube socks that came almost to his knees. Today there were neither animals nor Peter Boone on the road, just traffic, cottagers and campers heading for the lake. A sign she hadn't seen before appeared in the ditch, a hand-painted sign that said "Marigold Bungalows Ahead." Estella was about to remark on it when another sign came into view: "You Are on Treaty 6 Traditional Land. Visitors, Please Enjoy Your Stay." That was new, too.

Then the village of Lake Claire came into sight, and she forgot about the new signs and directed Nicholas down the main street with its usual holiday crowd, past the shops and the public beach, until they were through the village and the traffic thinned.

As they approached the three-way stop, Nicholas asked her which way to go. She told him straight ahead; the road to the right led to a campground. He stopped at the sign and then proceeded just as another car approached from the right and entered the intersection without stopping. Hannah yelled, "Dad, car!" as it came toward them. Nicholas slammed on the brakes, and the other driver did the same. Still, the other car's front bumper nosed up to them on the passenger's side, and they held their breaths and waited, but all that came was a little bump, barely perceptible. The other driver immediately backed away and drove off as though nothing had happened. They watched as his car disappeared down the road to the village. Estella thought he looked familiar.

Nicholas asked if everyone was all right, and then he got out to check Estella's car to make sure there was no damage. When he returned he reported that there was a small dent in the fender.

"It's not much," he said, "but it's there. I'm so sorry, Estella."

"It wasn't your fault," she said. "It was the other driver who didn't stop."

She was wondering who he was and why he had looked so familiar, and then it came to her: he was the weatherman on one of the local cable TV channels.

"I know who that driver is," she said, and she told them, and said perhaps they should report it to the police. You weren't supposed to leave like that, were you? At the very least he should have given them his licence number. She looked around for witnesses but didn't see any.

At that moment they saw another vehicle approaching the intersection, and so Nicholas put the car in gear and carried on. He would have a closer look at the dent when they arrived, he said. He wasn't sure it was a matter for the police.

Then the lake appeared through the trees ahead, and the cottage compound, and in no time they were there, pulling up to the office. It looked the same as always except for a new sign: "Marigold Family Bungalows." There were red clay flowerpots on both sides of the steps with bright-orange marigolds blooming in them. There must have been a dozen.

Estella opened her purse and found her lipstick and comb, and gave herself a quick touch-up. "You wait here and I'll get our key," she said.

Just then, Peter Boone stepped from the office door. He was still not much bigger than a jockey, and his thick head of hair was now white. He'd grown a moustache since she'd last seen him. As far as she knew, he was still living at The Travellers. He'd stayed on in his mother's suite after she died several years ago. He came right to Estella's door and helped her out of the car. The new owner—a middle-aged man with freckles and a bald head—came outside and introduced himself as Gavin Caige, and a great fuss was made over Estella and her long history with the place, and the fact that the cottage bricks had been produced at her father's factory.

"Our pleasure to have you back for another year," said Gavin Caige.

She introduced Nicholas and Hannah, and Peter looked surprised to see two Diamonds that he'd never met before. She explained that Nicholas was Jack's grandson. She couldn't take her eyes off all the marigolds. Gavin saw her looking at the flowers and explained that his wife's name was Marigold.

"I've always told her she should have a country named after her," he said. "She's just that kind of woman."

Estella thought a country named Marigold would have a hard time being taken seriously.

When she got inside the office, she was relieved to see many things were the same as when Allen Foster had been behind the counter: the mounted lake trout on the wall, the laminated map of Lake Claire showing all its bays and islands, the 1955 Norman Rockwell calendar from the business's first summer. And then she began to notice a few things that were different: the big-screen TV, the sign on the counter that said *"We don't accept cheques . . . cash or credit card, please,"* another laminated sign beside it that said, *"I delight in insult and difficulties. For when I am weak, then I am strong. II Corinthians 12:9–11."* Either Marigold and Gavin Caige had a bizarre sense of humour or they were of the evangelical bent. Perhaps both.

She turned her attention back to the sign that said no cheques. She was thinking that, according to the terms of her father's deal with Allen Foster, she would have to pay for a cottage this year since the business had been sold. Gavin saw her looking at the sign and said, "Don't worry, a cheque from you is fine. God is telling me to trust you," and she had the answer to her question.

Gavin retrieved the key to Emily Carr from the drawer under the counter, attached to the same old maroon plastic key ring.

"I'm sure you know the ropes," he said. "I'm still learning them, with a bit of help from Saint Peter here."

Biblical humour at every turn, Estella thought.

At that moment a woman whom Estella assumed to be Marigold stuck her head through the entrance to the living quarters and asked Gavin whether he wanted his plate in the office or was he was coming to the table. She was a small woman with a curly hairdo pretty close to the colour of the flowers that were everywhere outside.

He said he would be right there, that Estella was his last check-in for the day.

On her way out of the office, Estella noticed that the news channel was talking about forest fires in British Columbia. The Interior was dry as tinder. She asked Peter if it was dry there as well, and he said no, everything was fine, they were not prohibiting open fires in the campground, which was always the marker of fire hazard.

Once they were away from the office, though, she began to get the real news, and it did not sound as though everything was fine. As Hannah and Nicholas walked down to the lake for a quick look, Peter unlocked Emily Carr and carried Estella's bag inside. He told her that the Caiges had been notified soon after they'd taken possession of the place that they would be unable to renew their lease when it was up in two years. The First Nation that owned the land wanted it back, and they had their own plan to tear down the cottages and build a year-round hotel and convention centre, or at least that was the rumour. The Caiges were saying they wouldn't have bought the property had they known, and they were blaming it on Allen Foster's son, who had taken over the business from his father and then sold it to the Caiges. He was saying he had not known about the lease being terminated, and that the Caiges had failed to do their due diligence by consulting directly with the First Nation. Everyone was suing everyone, including the real estate agent, and no one knew what the end result would be.

And there was more. The old Beach Café had been torn down over the winter and replaced by a seafood restaurant, and by seafood they didn't mean jackfish. They had an aquarium with live lobster from the East Coast, and they shipped in salmon and shrimp and halibut from the West. They'd served lake trout in the spring during trout season, but that was the only nod to anything local. The fishermen, they said, wouldn't pay good money for what they could catch themselves and cook for shore lunch in a frying pan.

And to top it all off, the *Claire de la Lune* had been declared unsafe and had been retired, because the repairs would cost more than she was worth. She was still moored at the marina, and every night Peter went down and turned on the patio lanterns and played Roy Orbison through the speakers, but she was no longer licensed and her days of crossing the bay at sunset with a boatload of campers and cottagers were over. She was listed for sale on the Internet as an antique, but Peter figured she was worth not much more than a few hundred dollars for scrap. Someone was supposed to be coming to look at her in the next day or so. If he came hauling a flatbed trailer, Peter said, it would be goodbye to the paddlewheeler.

Estella wondered how all this could have happened in just one year. At least Emily Carr, aside from a bit of crumbling mortar and an organic-looking buildup of moss on the shingles, looked more or less the same as always.

Peter's cellphone rang just then and he was summoned to deal with a guest who had locked himself out.

Nicholas and Hannah came back from the lake and they carried their bags in and took the room with the twin beds. Estella took her parents' old room. She tried all the taps and light switches and everything was in working order, and the window screens were all patched to keep the mosquitoes out. She noticed there was a mousetrap under the sink and another behind the couch, which Hannah took exception to, saying they were cruel, so Estella agreed they didn't have to bait them.

There was a little convenience store attached to the office, but it carried mainly last-minute necessities like milk and sunscreen and toilet paper, so Nicholas suggested that he and Hannah walk along the shore into the village and get a few groceries. After they left, Estella sat on the cottage deck, and she couldn't help but picture the grassy common filled up with generations of noisy Diamonds. This was where her father had sat looking out on the action that last year he was alive, smoking his cigars, the disapproving caregiver Lorette his ever-present shadow. In her father's time, there would have been an Oldsmobile instead of a navy Ford Taurus parked next to the cabin. Her new Mustang had been the one exception. That car had been her fifteen minutes of fame, she supposed. Paul had made sure it lasted not much longer than that. She'd replaced it with another Falcon.

From where she was sitting on the deck, she could see the little dent in the fender of the Taurus. There was an old-fashioned pay phone in front of the office, or at least there had been one last time she noticed, and she decided to phone the police while it was on her mind. The pay phone was still there, but of course the person who answered asked for her plate number, which she didn't know, and her name and driver's licence number, and she had to explain that she didn't have a driver's licence but she had not been the one driving. It took ages to finally get to the story, and she gave them Nicholas's name and said no, she didn't have his licence number either. She said the damage wasn't much, not more than a small dent, but that wasn't the point of her call. It was the *idea* that the other driver had left without stopping. And he was a public figure, too, a TV personality. From the response she got after that, she figured there wouldn't be any follow-up.

When she got back to the cottage deck, she saw Peter cross the grass wearing his shorts and white socks and running shoes. His bush trail to the point was so narrow that you might not see it if you didn't know it was there, and he stepped into the trees and was immediately out of sight. He almost looked like *Alice in Wonderland*'s rabbit disappearing in his white socks. She wondered how long it would be before he emerged again, or whether he would come back across the bay in his canoe.

She wasn't sure how long she sat on the deck, but it must have been well over an hour before she saw Hannah and Nicholas coming up from the beach carrying shopping bags. They'd both bought bathing suits at Dot's because they didn't have suits with them. Hannah showed Estella hers, an orange bikini, and Estella was a bit taken aback at how little of it there was. Both Hannah and Nicholas had bought T-shirts with "Lake Claire" on them, and they'd bought one for her, too. It was likely a redundant present, Nicholas said, since she was sure to have a dozen of them.

No, Estella said, she didn't, not one; in all her years of coming here, she had never once bought a souvenir T-shirt. She held it up and examined the picture printed behind the letters on the white cotton: the lake and the paddlewheeler at sunset. They all pulled their T-shirts on over their clothes, and then Nicholas lit the charcoal barbecue and cooked a chicken. They ate chicken and potato salad at the chrome set in the cottage in their matching T-shirts, on the mismatched plates with their chipped rims and faded blue windmills. The chicken was delicious. Estella was surprised that Nicholas was such a good cook, although she wasn't sure why that should have surprised her, perhaps just because Jack wasn't.

Through the window, she saw a canoe out in the bay, coming from the point. It was Peter. Before long he came up from the beach with the canoe balanced on his shoulders, his head underneath somewhere. He could still manage it at his age.

"That's Peter Boone under there," she said.

The canoe passed by the window and then was gone around the corner.

By the time they'd finished supper and had the dishes done, it was getting dark. Hannah and Nicholas went for a swim and Estella could hear them laughing through the trees. She got herself ready for bed and she was under the covers before they came back. It was comforting to hear them speaking quietly in the other room. She thought they were making tea.

After they went to bed, she could hear Peter's music drifting faintly from the marina. She fell asleep to the sound of it.

IT WAS ALL reassuringly familiar in the morning light. The varnished plywood walls of the room, the frosted-glass light shade above the bed, the open closet where she'd hung her rain jacket and velour track suit, the curtains on the window with their pattern of cherries with their stems crossed, a squirrel chattering outside in one of the trees. She lay in bed under the red plaid wool blankets and felt a calm sense of gratitude that everything was as it should be, including herself.

She got out of bed and put on her track suit, since it was still early enough for the air to be chilly. If the Diamonds in the other room had been Lydia and Mercy she might not have bothered to get dressed right away, but she didn't want Nicholas and Hannah to see her in her nightgown. When she found the living room empty, she took care to be extra quiet so she wouldn't wake them up, but then she saw that the other bedroom door was ajar, and the room was empty, the beds already made. She checked the time: it was nine o'clock. She couldn't believe that she had slept so late, and that she hadn't heard Nicholas and Hannah moving around.

She looked in the cupboard to see what they'd bought for breakfast and saw a variety pack of cereal boxes with several missing. She didn't know they still made variety packs. She chose Rice Krispies, thinking that if Hannah was like the other children she had known, she would want the ones with the most sugar. She found a jar of instant coffee and she plugged in the kettle before sitting at the table with her cereal. There was a bowl of fruit in the middle of the table, oranges and bananas, with a note tucked beneath it saying that Hannah and Nicholas had gone for a walk. The window by the table looked out over the deck and the grass. Through the trees beyond she could see the lake glistening in the morning light.

She peeled an orange and pulled it into sections. As she ate them one by one, she flipped open a new-looking sketchbook that had been left on the table. On the first page, she found a pencil sketch of the spruce tree overhanging the beach. She wondered if it was Nicholas's, but then she saw that Hannah had signed her name in tiny letters. She was looking at the pencil markings, and admiring the skill for a girl so young, when strange-looking, big-eyed cartoon creatures began to emerge from between the drawing's branches. For a moment she thought she was seeing things because they were so well-disguised, expertly hidden in the tree. She closed the sketchbook, thinking it was private and she probably should not have opened it.

When she was finished her breakfast, she took her coffee out to the deck. She saw that the bumper of her car had been polished, the dust wiped off. Nicholas must have done that, feeling responsible, she supposed, even though it had been the other driver's fault. She watched a couple walk across the grass with a dog and a small child, a boy. The child kept stopping to pick things up, and then he would hand them to his father, who stuffed whatever they were in his pockets. Estella watched the father fish them out and throw them away again whenever the boy wasn't looking.

Just then Peter walked by wearing his tool belt and carrying a sheet of glass. When he saw Estella he stopped to say hello, and she invited him to sit with her and have a cup of coffee.

"It's instant," she said, knowing that instant was his coffee of choice.

He said he couldn't stop, he was on his way to fix a window in Lawren Harris, but if Estella was still there in half an hour, he would come back. After he rounded the corner and she couldn't see him anymore, a woman stepped out onto a deck several cottages down—the one with all the bunk beds in one big bedroom, De Grandmaison it was called—and she looked right at Estella with her hands on her hips, and then turned away without waving. At one time, that cottage would have housed Andrew and Harmony and their five kids, but it wasn't the best one if you wanted actual bedrooms. She wondered if the woman had been ousted from Emily Carr to make room for her.

Half an hour later, Peter was back, but just to tell her that a shower was leaking in one of the cottages, and he had to get to that right away. She saw him looking at the little enamelled loon she had pinned to her jacket.

"I think it must have been my mother's," she said.

Then she pointed out the dent in her car, and told him what had happened. He gave it a look and said he had a way to get dents out, and he left to exchange his carpentry tools for his plumbing supplies.

It was ten-thirty before Hannah and Nicolas came back up from the beach. They'd walked all the way to the campground, Nicholas said, where a river spilled into the lake, and there were people fishing off a bridge, and a young moose crossed the river right in front of them and then turned around and looked back at everyone.

"I swear he was telling us all to get out of his backyard," Nicholas said.

Then he said he was going to have a quick nap since he hadn't slept very well, and Hannah went to get one of the mountain bicycles they had at the office for the guests to borrow. She had noticed the trail out to the point. Estella was concerned about her going alone and told her to make lots of noise to scare off bears, but Hannah said she wasn't afraid. Estella tried to remember what she'd been like at Hannah's age. There'd been nothing to fear since she'd rarely been without at least one of her brothers.

When Hannah got back an hour later Nicholas was still sleeping. By this time, Estella had moved inside, and Hannah sat down at the table with her and told her she hadn't seen a bear or anything else. Just trees, with a glimpse of the lake once in a while. She kept looking at the door to the bedroom, as though waiting for her father to wake up.

Estella tried to think of things to talk to Hannah about. She wondered if she might ask her about the drawing—there was no doubt the girl had talent—but would she be upset that Estella had looked at her sketchbook? Might she want to walk to the village for ice cream, just the two of them? They could leave Nicholas a note.

Out of the blue, Hannah started to cry.

"Oh my, what's wrong?" Estella asked. It was unexpected, this girl crying, the one who had not been afraid of bears just minutes ago.

Hannah would not tell Estella what was wrong. She dropped her head and hung her hands loosely at her side and sobbed. When she did, she looked so much younger, like a very young child.

Estella didn't know what to do. She didn't know how to comfort a crying girl.

She got up to get Hannah a glass of water and set it down in front of her. Nicholas came from the bedroom then, running his fingers through his hair in an attempt to tame a cowlick. When he saw that Hannah was crying, he went to her as though he knew what was wrong without having to ask, and he wrapped his arms around her.

Estella left them alone and went back outside. She saw that her cane was leaning against the railing, and so she took it and walked across the grass to the old spruce tree. She looked up through the branches and tried to imagine Hannah's creatures and where the idea might have come from, but she saw only boughs laden with cones.

By the time she got back to the cabin, the crisis seemed to have passed, and Nicholas had set a plate of tuna sandwiches on the table. After lunch, they all walked around the compound and Estella told them which Diamond families had stayed in which cottages . . . at least the generations she could remember. She stopped in front of Lawren Harris, where Peter had finished installing the new window and was now painting the trim orange. He told them the Caiges planned to paint the window trim on all the cabins orange, although he wasn't sure there was any point if they were going to lose the lease. Estella told Nicholas that this was the cottage where Jack and Rose had stayed with the boys.

After their tour of the compound, Nicholas and Hannah said they were going for a swim, and Nicholas urged her to come down to the beach with them. He had discovered a beach umbrella in the closet, and he said he could set it up for her so she would be out of the sun.

Hannah went into the bedroom first to change into her suit while Nicholas waited. Estella did not at first plan to wear a bathing suit, but she decided to change, even if only her toes were going to touch the water. She was looking for the purple suit when she remembered that she'd brought the old two-piece instead. As she looked at the makeshift repair job she almost gave up, but she decided it didn't matter since she would be covering it.

She sat on the edge of her bed and got herself into the suit. The top was fine. She was smaller now but the way it tied at the neck made it adjustable. The bottoms were a bit loose in the legs, but the drawstring felt secure enough. She looked in the mirror on the back of the door and was momentarily fascinated by the image of an ancient, sagging body in a vintage swimsuit, like a strangely pornographic photograph, but the fascination wore off when she remembered it was herself she was looking at. She pulled her shorts and her Lake Claire T-shirt overtop, and then she sat on the bed and strapped her feet into her sandals.

Hannah was already waiting in the living room. She was wearing her T-shirt over her suit, too, and Estella could see the orange straps tied behind her neck.

When Nicholas was ready, they all walked across the grass toward the water. Hannah carried a plastic bag with towels while Nicholas carried the chairs and the umbrella. Estella had her cane, even though she did not feel that she needed it. In the last year, someone—Peter?—had installed a set of wooden stairs by the old spruce tree so there was no more clambering down the sandy slope. She descended easily. The water was calm and the narrow beach was deserted, although they could see in the distance that the big public beach was packed with people. A merganser bobbed on the surface close by, jabbing its bill at something.

Nicholas twisted the umbrella into the sand and set the canvas chairs beneath it. Estella sank into one, and immediately undid the Velcro straps on her sandals so she could kick them off and feel the sand under her feet.

"Will you be all right here if we go for a swim?" Nicholas asked.

"Of course," Estella said. "Last one in's a rotten egg."

They peeled off their T-shirts and ran for the water. Hannah shrieked as she hit waist deep, and then she dove under and came up laughing with her long bangs in her eyes. Nicholas too went under and swam beneath the surface, away from the shore. Then they were swimming side by side, out to where Estella knew the bottom dropped off.

"Be careful, it gets deep," she called, like any one of the Diamond mothers who'd sat here day after day, supervising children in the water, surrounded in the sand by towels and snacks and beach toys. She could see that Nicholas and Hannah were both good swimmers, and they swam the way she used to, with even strokes and strong kicks. She was pleased that Hannah was such a good swimmer. When they were out over their heads, they stopped and waved at Estella, and for a while they did somersaults and dolphin dives, and then they turned and swam away, parallel to the shore, just as she once had. She could see their arms rising and disappearing, one after the other, Hannah in front and Nicholas following.

Could she, she wondered, just step into the water and get her feet wet? Swimming—the proper kind—was out of the question, but her body remembered the feel of the water and at that moment yearned for it.

She lifted her T-shirt over her head and then stood and took off her shorts. Her legs were white in the sunlight, and she could see the map of veins under her skin, as though she were translucent. She couldn't imagine whiter skin, and for a moment she forgot what she was doing and stood staring down at herself. The body, she thought, was endlessly intriguing if you could look past it being your own.

She took off her glasses. Without them, she couldn't see Nicholas and Hannah, or tell whether they were still swimming away from her or were on their way back. She stepped down to the beach and stood where the water lapped at her toes. It was warmer than she'd thought it would be. She stepped in, up to her ankles, her knees, and then she stopped and felt the sandy bottom, wiggled her toes, let them dig into the sand. A school of minnows approached and she could feel the tickling on her skin. She reached down and splashed water on herself, trying to decide if she would be foolish to go deeper, to let herself fall forward, swim a stroke or two, put her face in, her neck, and feel that rush of coolness when the top of her head hit the water.

It *would* be foolish, she thought, but she did it anyway. She walked in up to her waist, and she relaxed her knees, lowered herself, and let the water rise. And then she lost her balance and she did fall forward, her face right in the water, and she came up sputtering, but once again on her feet. She lay back and let herself float, looked at the sky, moved her legs just enough to keep them from sinking. The sun was bright overhead, and she had to close her eyes again to keep from being blinded. Even with them closed she could see the sun's afterimage.

She didn't last very long in the water. She began to feel the chill, and as soon as she did, she was desperate to get out. She got her feet back on the bottom, but she found it was a lot more work walking out than it had been walking in. The lake shimmered all around her, and it was hard to judge where the surface was. She held her arms out for balance and still she staggered and almost fell several times, but she finally made it back to the hard-packed sand of the shoreline. When she was safely on the beach, she stood to catch her breath, and then she readjusted her sagging bathing suit bottom. She had a moment of remembering the suit when it was new, and how young she had been, even though she had already resigned herself to middle age, post Clarence Angell. She'd worn the two-piece and briefly driven a white Mustang before becoming, once and for all, the old maid of the children's card game.

She heard someone cough, and she looked toward the sound and saw Peter Boone sitting on the new stairs by the spruce tree. She was immediately self-conscious about the bathing suit, although she tried to not to show it as she walked carefully to her chair and pulled on her T-shirt.

"You scare me, Missus," Peter said.

She knew he wasn't talking about the two-piece, although that was an amusing possibility. He meant that she might have needed help, to be rescued. He spoke from experience because he *had* rescued her the previous summer when she'd thought she'd seen Lonny going into the bush, and she'd gone after him. Peter had found her on her rear end on the trail, unable to get up, after she'd tripped over a tree root. He'd actually carried her out, like some kind of he-man, which he had never in his life been. She'd worried he was going to have a heart attack.

She found her glasses on her chair and put them on, and she saw that he was smoking a cigarette. Although he never touched alcohol, he liked his cigarettes.

"You're the one we should worry about," she said. "You ought to give those up."

She draped her towel over her chair and sat down, and he got up from the steps and came to sit next to her in one of the empty chairs left by Nicholas and Hannah. He ground his smoke out in the sand, and then tucked the butt into his cigarette pack.

"Everybody's got a vice," he said.

The merganser was still there. Estella watched as it darted into a particularly reflective spot on the water and disappeared, as though the glare had made it invisible. She looked down at her bare white feet and saw that they shimmered in and out of her vision like a pair of poltergeists. It would be easy enough, she thought, to lose sight of a person, especially one as small as Lonny, in such bright light.

"There it is, then," she said as the merganser popped back into view.

She had just been handed an explanation for Lonny's disappearance from the beach, an alternative to the prevailing one, which was that she had momentarily lost her mind. When she and Peter had got back to the cottage—after he'd finally put her down and let her walk—Lydia and Mercy were both mad at her and claimed they'd found Lonny alone by the water when she was supposed to be watching him. She tried to tell them that she'd seen him go into the bush but they wouldn't listen. While Lydia berated her, Mercy at least got her a glass of water, but she was so confused and hurt that she slapped the glass out of Mercy's hand, and it hit the edge of the table and shattered. One of the shards hit Lonny's wrist, and a drop of blood immediately appeared and trickled down his hand. Mercy checked and it was just a scratch, but Lydia had to say, "Now look what you've done," and Estella saw the blood and she felt sick. She would never, ever have intended to hurt Lonny.

Peter had taken charge then and sent everyone out on the deck while he got the glass cleaned up. No one spoke. Mercy dabbed Lonny's wrist with a tissue until it stopped bleeding. Then Peter called them back inside and said, "No real harm done. Best sleep on it, eh." As he went to leave, he patted Estella's shoulder. It was a small thing, acknowledgement that he knew she had meant no harm and had only been trying to help when she'd gone into the trees. She tried to halt the tears that she felt coming, but once Peter was gone, she couldn't.

Mercy attempted to give her a hug and she wanted to lean in to her, but instead she pulled away and said, "Leave me alone," so they did.

In the morning, Lonny had a green and red ladybug Band-Aid on his wrist. They packed up and left right after breakfast, even though they still had a day remaining on their reservation. All the way home, Estella felt sick every time she saw Lonny run his fingers over the Band-Aid.

No wonder they'd chosen to send him to camp this year.

No wonder Peter Boone had said to her when she'd come out of the water, "You scare me, Missus." The shimmering sunlight had provided an explanation for why she had not seen Lonny when he was right there, on the beach, but there was no explanation for why she'd knocked that glass out of Mercy's hand.

Peter stood from the chair under the umbrella and said he'd best go, he had work to do. The Caiges were in Prince Albert for the day meeting with their lawyers; they were expecting guests, and he was supposed to check them in. As he walked back to stairs by the spruce tree, Estella saw Nicholas and Hannah returning. When they stepped out of the water and joined her under the umbrella, water dripping from their hair and suits, they were surprised to see her bare legs and the T-shirt revealing a wet bathing suit underneath. She told them she was not good for much more than a quick dip.

Nicholas dried his hair with a towel and asked, "Was that Peter Boone I saw?"

Before Estella could answer, they were all distracted by the merganser running along the surface of the water. It took off in spectacular fashion, with wings flapping and water splashing out in all directions.

NICHOLAS AND HANNAH barbecued burgers for supper that night. After they'd eaten, Estella got out Salina's beads. She told them only that they were an heirloom, and had been given to her by her father. She wanted Hannah to see the figures on the beads because they were not unlike the ones she had drawn in the spruce tree. Hannah picked up the beads and ran her fingers over the tiny faces, then handed them back to Estella without saying anything. Estella put them in the velvet bag and returned them carefully to her purse.

Not long after, Hannah said she was going to bed even though it was early. Nicholas made tea, and he and Estella sat on the deck and watched the sun setting through the trees. Estella had been wanting to ask Nicholas what he knew about Jack's disappearance and now was a good time, with Hannah asleep.

It had been assumed he'd drowned himself in the Bow River, but she didn't know any details. "There must have been talk," she said. "He'd been depressed, we all knew that, but had it gotten worse? Did the family know what he was about to do?"

"I don't think so," Nicholas said. "He just walked away one day."
He told her that most of what he knew about Jack had come from his Uncle Don, who said Jack went to a store called Wong's Lucky Grocery for cigarettes and didn't come back, just like in the movies. He didn't leave a note. He took nothing with him but his wallet. Rose remembered him sticking it in his pants pocket and saying, "Just popping out for fags," and she told him to get a pound of butter too because she was low for baking. She saw his hat pass the kitchen window, and then she never saw him again.

The police interviewed Eddy Wong and he confirmed that Jack had been in the store, and he'd bought cigarettes and butter and some licorice, and then he'd left with a paper grocery bag in his hand. Eddy hadn't seen which direction he'd gone, but he remembered that he'd been whistling. He volunteered the opinion that happy people whistle. The police asked him if he could remember what the song was, because a sad one might mean the opposite. Eddy didn't know. He wasn't familiar with many Canadian songs. He only knew it wasn't "O Canada" or "Happy Birthday."

"They kept the investigation open for a long time," Nicholas said, "but they never came up with a shred of information that went past the moment when Eddy Wong heard him whistling his way out the door of the corner shop."

Estella said that she remembered her brother Andrew travelling to Calgary to help search, before he finally moved there.

"That's right," Nicholas said. "Apparently Andrew would walk from Grandma Rose's house to Wong's, as though retracing Jack's steps might tell him something. He took Don with him sometimes, and when they got to Wong's, he would ask Don, 'Which way would your father go from here if it was a nice evening and he wanted to go for a walk?' Or, 'Is there a bowling alley nearby?'

We used to go bowling in London, during the war.' They would walk whatever route Don suggested, and he remembers Andrew rifling through the bushes along the way. He pictured them finding his father's hat or his wallet, or even his body. He said it was terrifying. And then he remembers one time, after Andrew and Harmony moved to Calgary, when Andrew went to the house to collect him and they went to Wong's and Andrew bought a pack of cigarettes and a bag of licorice Twizzlers. Then they walked to the Bow River and sat on the bank for an hour, smoking and eating licorice. Andrew finally said, 'I think he must have fallen in.' Don wanted to say 'or jumped' but he couldn't bring himself to admit that his father had probably killed himself. Then Andrew said he didn't suppose they'd ever know for sure what happened. And that was the last time Don remembered searching for his father."

Estella thought it was hardly fair of Andrew to take Jack's son with him on those searches. What if they *had* found his body?

When the sun was gone and it was dark, they went to bed, but when Estella got under the blankets, she found that she couldn't sleep. She kept thinking about Jack, whistling in Wong's Lucky Grocery, walking into the river and leaving those two boys behind. What had been going through his head? That he was a disappointment to everyone because he had never recovered from the war? Or the opposite: that the world was a disappointment to him? Jack had become unknowable, and watching him retreat from her—long before he'd gone missing in Calgary—had been the greatest sorrow of her life.

An hour passed and she was still awake, so she got up and put the kettle on, trying to be silent so she wouldn't wake anyone else. Hannah's sketchbook was on the kitchen table. She opened it again to see if she had drawn anything new, and there was a drawing of a bicycle, very carefully rendered and accurate. She thought of her own poor watercolour versions of Lake Claire. Hannah's drawings were far superior. She closed the sketchbook and then found herself sitting at the table crying. She could not understand what was wrong with her, why the tears were so close to the surface.

She heard the bedroom door open and Hannah came out, closing the door carefully after her. She was wearing plaid cotton pyjama bottoms and a T-shirt. She looked alarmed when she saw Estella, and Estella quickly wiped her eyes and said, "Don't mind me. I'm just a weepy old lady."

"Should I get Dad?" Hannah asked.

"No," Estella said. "Nothing's wrong. Nothing at all."

Her kettle was boiling. She went to the stove and made herself a cup of tea. Hannah went into the bathroom and closed the door. When she came out, Estella was sitting at the table, her tea in front of her, and Hannah surprised her by coming to the table and draping an arm over her shoulders.

"I don't much like being old," she said.

"I know," Hannah said.

How could she know? Estella wondered.

"Will you have to go and live in a home?" Hannah asked.

"No," Estella said. "I'd rather throw myself down the stairs."

She immediately thought she shouldn't have said that, not to a child.

"Did I shock you?" she asked.

"Not really," Hannah said.

Estella said, "Anyway, Emyflor will look after me. So that's that."

Then they both went back to bed. Estella left her tea on the table. When she was settled again, she thought not of Jack but of Peter Boone carrying her out of the bush. She'd wrapped her arms around his neck and felt the wiry muscles in his shoulders, the heat coming off his body, and his breath against her cheek.

It had been a long time since she'd felt another human being that close.

She fell asleep remembering.

The bathing suits were hanging near the deck on a line strung between two trees: Nicholas's shorts, Estella's old two-piece, and Hannah's tiny orange bikini. Hannah and Nicholas had been for a swim and were now making lunch in the cottage. A hummingbird kept darting past the bikini as though it couldn't believe it was not in the flower family. Estella was sitting on the deck watching it when Peter came around the corner carrying a bucket of steaming water and a plunger, saying that he was going to get the dent out of her car. She watched with curiosity as he drizzled hot water over the dent, and then sucked it back out again with the plunger.

After he left, she stepped off the deck to run her hand over the place where the dent had been. There was no sign of it. When Nicholas came out carrying a plate of sandwiches, she showed him the spot where the dent had been and told him he could stop worrying about it, thanks to Peter Boone.

Since it was their last day, Estella suggested they go for ice cream in the village. It was blistering hot, so they drove rather than walk. Nicholas was able to find a parking spot on the busy street, a bit of a miracle. Because it was Canada Day, someone had stuck little maple leaf flags on the windshields of all the cars, and the ice cream stand was offering holiday cones topped with red sprinkles and flags on toothpicks. A poster on the order counter announced an all-ages party that evening at the golf course, with fireworks after dark.

There were a few plastic tables and chairs on the grass next to the ice cream stand and they sat in the shade with their cones. They could see that the public beach was crowded, and a steady stream of vehicles passed by on the street pulling boat trailers and golf carts. At the marina, the decommissioned paddlewheeler was still moored. It would be gone, Estella thought, if she ever made it back here again. A drip of red-and-white ice cream was running from her cone down her hand and she licked it off.

Hannah didn't seem to be eating her cone and was instead stabbing her Canadian flag in and out of her ice cream. Then she suddenly got up and dropped her whole cone in a garbage can by the stand, and headed down the sidewalk, back toward the cottages.

"What was that about?" Estella asked.

"She's moody," Nicholas said. "Best to let her be." Then he added, "The separation."

Just then a familiar car parked illegally right in front of the stand and a man got out. It was the man who had run into them at the stop sign. Estella could see right away that she had been wrong, it wasn't the TV weatherman after all, although there was a resemblance. She wondered if Nicholas recognized him, and when she looked at him she saw that he did, and was probably hoping she hadn't.

"Yeah, that's the guy," he said. "But let's give him a break. It's Canada Day, right?"

She agreed. It was too hot for a confrontation.

The man ordered six ice cream cones and then carried them back to his car in a cardboard holder. He pulled out right in front of a big diesel truck towing a long flatbed trailer, and the truck driver honked, which drew everyone's attention.

Estella said, "He's going to get himself killed."

There was a police vehicle behind the truck, an SUV like Lydia's, and Estella thought it might follow the car and ticket the driver, but instead the SUV slipped into the now-empty spot in front of the ice cream stand. A young woman officer parked and got out, and walked back to Estella's car and had a look at the plate. Estella remembered her call from the pay phone. She hadn't given her plate number but she supposed they had looked it up.

"There's free parking on the street, isn't there?" Nicholas asked. "I didn't see any signs." Estella told him it wasn't that, it was because she had called about the accident.

"I ought to tell them not to bother," she said.

Nicholas looked as though he might say something, but he didn't, and Estella waved the officer over. She explained that she was the one who had reported the accident at the three-way stop but she would like to withdraw her complaint, there was no damage, the dent had been taken care of.

"The handyman at our rental fixed it with a plunger," she said. "So, no harm done. Well, not yet anyway. That driver of the other car is a menace." Another creamy drip with a red candy in it ran down her hand and once again she licked it off.

The officer said something about the handyman earning his name, and at that moment Nicholas finished his cone and got up to drop his napkin in the garbage. The officer's eyes followed him.

He wiped his hands with another napkin and then he waited for Estella by the stand.

"Just for my notes, though," the officer said, "who were you were travelling with?"

"My nephew, Nicholas," Estella said. "And his daughter."

"Are you Nicholas?" the officer called to him.

"Yes," he said. "I was driving the car."

"Okay, then," she said to Estella. "That's all I need. We'll cancel that report. You folks have a nice day." She walked back toward her vehicle and got in. Estella could see her writing in her notebook before she drove off.

When she was gone, Estella threw the last of her cone in the garbage, and Nicholas said he thought they should get back and check on Hannah. They stopped at the grocery store on the way and picked up frozen fish and chips for supper. Hannah was not in the cottage when they got there, so Nicholas went looking for her and found her sunbathing on the beach. He put on his suit and joined her.

Estella got out her watercolour box and sat on the deck to do her annual painting. She attempted the spruce tree, the one she had once thought of as the porter's tree, the one Hannah had drawn so adeptly in her book, but she got the paper too wet and the tree turned into a messy green blob. She thought she was getting worse at watercolour rather than better, and she put it away in her room before Hannah could see it.

THE FLATBED THEY had seen in town had come for the *Claire de la Lune*. Peter stopped by Emily Carr after supper that evening and told Estella that a man from Manitoba had bought and paid for the old boat, and was now at the bar in The Travellers.

"Throwing himself a pretty good Canada Day party, I hear," he said.

The two of them were sitting on the deck. Nicholas and Hannah had walked down to the public beach hoping to see the fireworks from there. Estella had packed her bathing suit away, but Hannah's and Nicholas's were on the line again, damp from another swim. The sunset was peeking through the trees.

Peter said, "He'll be in The Travellers all night."

A minute later, he said, "I imagine most of the town will be up at the golf course."

It seemed as though he was getting at something, but Estella wasn't sure what until he said, "What do you think about one last tour on the boat before she goes? I can't see any harm in it."

Estella already knew her answer was yes, but she said, "Are you certain she won't sink?"

Peter assured her that the paddlewheeler was still seaworthy, and Estella retrieved her sweater from the bedroom. The two of them sat on the deck and waited for the orange sky to grow dark. Peter said this was the first night since the beginning of the season that he hadn't gone down to the pier to turn on the patio lanterns and play music for an hour. He wondered if anyone had noticed.

When the sun had gone down and the only light was at the horizon, she left a note for Nicholas and Hannah on the door, and she and Peter walked to his pickup, which he'd left in front of the office. He helped Estella up to the passenger seat and they drove to the marina and parked in the empty lot. They could see The Travellers Hotel beyond the beach, and Estella wondered if the boat's new owner was keeping an eye on his purchase, but she thought it was too far to see in the darkness. Peter took her arm as she climbed the few wooden steps up onto the pier, and she saw that two people were already there, looking at the paddlewheeler. A man and a child. They were talking, and at first they didn't see Estella and Peter, but then the man turned toward them when he heard their footsteps, and they saw that it was Nicholas and Hannah. Nicholas had a shopping bag in his hand, as though they had been to the store on their walk. Estella remembered that they needed milk for breakfast.

Peter had a flashlight with him, and when he switched it on they could see how shabby the boat looked, with paint peeling and the letters of her name faded out.

Nicholas said, "So I guess she's seen her last cruise, then, has she?"

"Not quite," Peter said. He hefted himself from the pier onto the deck and shifted the gangplank into place.

Estella led the way. Hannah and Nicholas exchanged looks, and then Hannah said, "Cool," and stepped onto the deck, and Nicholas followed her. Most of the old benches had been removed, except for the ones built in under the gunwales along both sides. Peter had set blankets out, as though he had been planning this. They settled themselves beneath the awning and Peter pulled the gangplank back on board and then untied the moorings. When they were free of the pier, he went into the wheelhouse with his flashlight and started the diesel engine. It was noisy and blew black smoke into the air while it warmed itself up, and Estella half expected someone to come running and tell them to disembark, but no one did.

Peter steered them slowly away from the pier without running lights. They could see cabins lit up all along the shore, and some-one had a bonfire going. No one spoke as the paddlewheel slapped rhythmically at the stern and they headed farther out into the bay. Estella unfolded one of Peter's blankets and draped it over her knees just as the first of the fireworks exploded at the golf course. Hannah seemed to know a bit about fireworks and she provided a commentary: peonies and flying fish, willows that left long tails as they fell. The finale was a chrysanthemum. She said they weren't much, as fireworks went.

"Come on," Nicholas said. "Not bad for a village," and Hannah agreed, for a village.

When they were at the line between points of land, where the bay opened into the lake beyond, Peter turned off the engine and dropped anchor, and then he went behind the bar on deck and prepared a tray of drinks. He handed Estella and Nicholas plastic glasses of rum and coke, and he and Hannah had cans of orange soda. The lake was so dark it could have been a vast ocean for all they could see of it. A string of car lights on the road meant the party at the golf course was over, at least the all-ages part of it.

"Can we turn the lanterns on?" Hannah asked, and Peter said he didn't see why not. Estella thought there might be a reason why not, but she decided she didn't care about being seen if Peter didn't. When he switched on the patio lights they were suddenly illuminated in patches of red and yellow. Then music began to play softly from the two speakers that hung over their heads. Roy Orbison.

Peter sat down on the bench and lifted his glass and said, "Cheers to the *Claire de la Lune*, eh," and they all said cheers. When Nicholas asked Peter how he selected his music, he said he'd been playing Roy Orbison since 1965. He'd tried to change the music a few times in the early years but there was always a rebellion because Roy Orbison had become part of everyone's Lake Claire tradition. He'd given up and set out instead to find every one of Roy's recordings. Then he'd had to search all over again for CDs when he'd upgraded his sound system.

Hannah was sitting very close to her father, leaning against him. She had her little red purse draped across her body and the sequins caught the light and sparkled. She began to sing with the music, and seemed to know all the lyrics to "Only the Lonely."

"How do you know such an old song?" Estella asked.

Hannah said she didn't know, and Nicholas said, "Yes you do." He explained that she had had a child's karaoke microphone, and she sang oldies karaoke before she was even in school.

"You remember that, don't you?" Nicholas asked.

The song changed, and in answer to her father's question, Hannah used her soft drink can as a microphone and sang along to "Pretty Woman." The sound of her young voice blended with Roy's and carried out over the water.

When the song ended, Estella said, "Oh, but you have a lovely voice."

"Hear that?" Nicholas said. Then he asked, "So, what would you be doing if you were out here with your friends instead of us oldies?"

She said, "I don't have any friends anymore. They're in Calgary, remember, and I'm in Winnipeg."

"Hannah," he said. "Come on. It won't be that bad."

Then Hannah said, "If I did have friends, we'd play Truth or Dare." She barely took a beat before she said, "Truth. I hate her."

Estella guessed right away she was referring to her mother, Marie, but Nicholas seemed not to.

"Who?" he asked.

"You know who. Mom."

"Don't say that," Nicholas said. "You don't mean it."

"I do mean it," she said. "And you should hate her too. Stop pretending you're all Mr. Reasonable."

Nicholas's silence seemed to be an admission that she was right. Hannah reached into the grocery bag that was now at her father's feet and pulled out a big bag of ripple potato chips and ripped them open. As she pulled out a handful, she said to him, "Your turn. Truth or dare."

"I'm not playing," he said.

She turned to Estella and said, "Truth or dare."

Estella didn't know how the game worked.

"Hannah, stop it," Nicholas said.

"It's easy," Hannah said. "Just pick one or the other."

She was being impertinent, and Estella knew it, but she rose to the challenge and said, "Truth."

"Did you ever have a boyfriend?" Hannah asked.

"Hannah!" Nicholas said.

"Never mind," Estella said. "There's a good lesson in my answer. I did have a boyfriend once, and he asked me to marry him, but he was good for nothing in the end and I turned him down. My sisters-in-law were so disappointed. They thought any man was better than none. There. How was that?"

"Good," Hannah said. "You were smarter than they were."

"Exactly," Estella said.

Then Hannah asked her father, "Truth. Did you have a girl-friend before Mom? A serious one, I mean."

"I didn't pick truth," he said.

"Well, you don't want dare," Hannah said. "I'll give you a hint. It involves water."

"Whatever you're doing, stop it," he said.

"Why? You asked me what I would do out here with my friends. This is what we'd do."

She was still eating chips from the bag and she passed it around. Estella was feeling light-headed from the rum and she took some, thinking they might help, before handing the bag to Peter.

Nicholas decided to play along with Hannah after all, and he told them a story about a girlfriend he'd had when he was going to university. He'd been working a summer job in the northern Alberta oil patch and his girlfriend was waiting tables in Calgary. It ended one weekend when he decided to surprise her, urged on by his roommates who told him girls love surprises, and he headed out after his shift on a Friday night.

"In a 1980 rust-riddled Honda Civic with a broken headlight," he said. "I bought it for almost nothing so I'd have wheels to get in and out of Fort McMurray. Eight hours, Fort Mac to Calgary. I left at nine o'clock and stopped only once at a truck stop. The sun was coming up when I saw Calgary ahead."

Hannah interrupted and said, "I bet I know what happened. She had another boy there."

"No," Nicholas said. "That wasn't it. She just wasn't that thrilled to see me. She went to work and I slept all day. Then when I woke up she was home again, and she told me it was creepy, the way I'd driven all night and come without telling her. I didn't think it was creepy, I thought it was romantic. She made me feel like a stalker. I left and drove all night again to get back in time for a Sunday shift. I passed a billboard ad for a jewellery company on the way and it said 'Surprise her with a diamond.' I thought, no damned way, I'm never surprising a woman with anything ever again.

"I spent the rest of the summer trying to avoid my idiot room-mates, which wasn't easy because we shared bedrooms in a flimsy trailer. I took extra shifts so I wouldn't have to spend any time there. I hardly slept. By the end of the summer I had enough money to pay for my whole year of school without a loan. Any-way, my heart mended. It didn't take me long to realize that I'd hardly known her."

"And then you met Mom," Hannah said. "Poor you."

Nicholas said, "Yes, and then I met your mom. And it was not poor me. It was lucky me, because I have you and your sister."

It was quiet again, and the boat rocked on the water, and Estella thought the game was over, ended by a moment of real truth, but then Hannah said, "Your turn, Mr. Boone. Truth or dare, and I advise you to take truth."

"Hannah," Nicholas said, "now you're just being rude."

But Peter played along too, and he said, "Well, the truth is, there's only ever been one woman for me. Miss Estella Diamond here."

They laughed, and Estella wanted to enjoy the moment, but all she could hear was Shirley Boone telling her what kind of woman she was.

Then a sudden breeze hit them and the lanterns began to sway. The boat caught a little wave and the drinks tray slipped onto the deck from the bench, where Peter had set it down. He picked it up and then collected their empty glasses and took them to the bar. It began to spit rain. They listened to the *tap, tap, tap* on the awning above them, and the Roy Orbison disc started over at the beginning again.

Peter said from behind the bar, "I hate to see the old girl go."

Estella recovered from thoughts of Shirley Boone and said, "If you're referring to me, I'm not planning to shuffle off anytime soon."

Not long after, they began to see the lights of vehicles at the marina, and then the blue-and-red flashing light of a police car.

"Are they for us?" Estella asked. "Do they think we've stolen the boat?"

Peter said sometimes kids went out on the pier to drink and the police chased them off, but he didn't sound especially convincing.

"I suppose we should head back," he said.

He winched the anchor back up and started the engine, and then he steered them across the lake toward the marina, with the navigation lights on this time. He turned the patio lights and the music off and there was only the sound of the boat's chugging engine, the *slap slap slap* of the paddlewheel as it churned in the water.

By the time they docked at the marina, there were two more police vehicles waiting. Peter tied the moorings, and then he attached the gangplank and stepped down first, as though offering himself up to the police officers. But they weren't interested in him.

"Are you Nicholas Diamond?" one of the officers asked as Nicholas stepped down onto the pier.

Before he could answer, Hannah said, "No, he's not. He's Nicholas Darling. Dad, tell them. That's not you."

"Are you Hannah?" the officer asked, his voice softening.

Estella caught a glimpse of Hannah's face, and she looked desperate.

"No," Hannah said. "I don't know any Hannah. I don't know who you're talking about."

"Hannah," Nicholas said. "It's okay." Then he turned back to the officer and said, "I'm Nicholas Diamond. This is my daughter Hannah. What seems to be the problem?"

"The problem, Mr. Diamond, is that we were that close to issuing an Amber Alert. Your wife says you took your daughter without her consent or knowledge."

"An Amber Alert?" Nicholas said. "What the hell for? Hannah's not in danger. And I don't need anyone's consent to take my own daughter to the lake for the weekend. It's Marie. Fine, I'll give her a call."

Estella was by now off the boat, and she tried to intervene.

"You must be Estella Diamond," the officer said. "If you wouldn't mind staying back where you are."

"I am Estella Diamond," she said. "And I'm telling you to leave my nephew and his daughter alone."

The officer held up his hand. "Ma'am," he said. "Stay right there." Peter Boone took her arm and held on.

"Okay, Mr. Diamond, I'm going to ask you to come with us. Hannah, you'll go with this officer." He indicated a woman who stepped forward and put her hand on Hannah's shoulder. It was the same officer who had spoken to them at the ice cream stand.

Then Hannah began to kick and fight to get away from the woman, who now had hold of both her shoulders.

"Don't fucking touch me!" Hannah was yelling, and, "Leave my father alone, don't listen to that bitch."

Estella was shocked by the language. Nicholas tried to get to Hannah, but the other police officers held on to him and he couldn't move. Then he started to shout at the officers—"I would never hurt my daughter, for Christ's sake, get your hands off me"—and soon it was complete chaos, and they were dragging Nicholas away toward one of the cars. And all the while Hannah was screaming at them to leave her father alone, he hadn't done anything wrong.

"It was me," she shouted, "I got in the car, he didn't even know I was there." Then she was yelling at her father, that this was all his fault for putting up with it, why hadn't he stopped her? That he just rolled over and let her do whatever she wanted, like fuck around with that idiot on the bicycle.

The female officer was doing everything she could to hang on to Hannah.

Estella had never seen such anger or heard language like that coming from a child. It was as though Hannah were possessed, the way she was screaming and dragging her heels while the officer tried to get her to a police car. She couldn't help but admire the girl, the way she held nothing back, the way she spoke even to her father, who surely did have something to answer for if what the officers said was true.

They were dangerously close to the edge of the pier and the boards were wet from the drizzling rain. The woman who had Hannah was now shouting for help, and Estella felt a new surge of anger herself. She pulled away from Peter Boone and stepped toward them, intending to take charge of a situation that had got out of control. Shouldn't a trained police officer be able to handle an eleven-year-old girl?

"Stop that," she said. "Leave that girl alone."

She saw Hannah's little red purse go flying off her shoulder and land with a splash in the water.

"Hannah," she said, following behind them as the officer tried to get Hannah off the pier. "Calm down. This woman is trying to help." Then she said to the officer, "Let go of her, for heaven's sake, she's a child, not a wild animal. Give her a chance to walk on her own."

Hannah stopped struggling.

"Yes," she said. "I can walk on my own."

The officer relaxed her hold on Hannah's shoulders and they walked toward the end of the pier. When they were close to the steps that led down to the beach, Hannah pulled away and leapt from the pier. Before the officer could grab her, she ran, away from the beach and the village and into the darkness. The officer was so surprised Hannah had got away that it took her a moment to recover, and then she slipped on the bottom step and pitched forward into the sand, and by the time she got herself up and was yelling for help, Hannah was out of sight.

"Oh, Christ," one of the other officers said, the one who seemed to be in charge. "How the hell did that happen?" He motioned to the car in which they had put Nicholas, and it pulled away with its lights flashing.

Estella knew there was nothing in the direction Hannah had gone but rocky outcrops and bush. She was afraid for her: that she might get lost, that she might fall on the rocks and hurt herself, fall into the water. She heard her own voice shouting Hannah's name over and over, until one of the officers told her to be quiet or she'd find herself in the back of a police car.

Peter had been silent, but now he told Estella to hush, to let the police handle it, they'd find her. She listened to his calm voice and she stopped shouting and tried to step down from the pier, but she felt herself sinking. She grabbed one of the handrails and managed to sit on the top step. Peter was telling the officers that he knew how to turn the marina lights on, and he did, and they lit up the beach and the parking lot.

There was no sign of Hannah. In the halogen beams, Estella could see the rain falling. Peter came back and sat down next to her on the step, and they watched as the police tried to decide what to do. Estella suddenly thought of the old train station that had been right where the parking lot was now, and she wondered if it was possible that Hannah had found the tracks and was now walking away from Lake Claire just as she had once walked toward it. She could almost hear her footsteps, *thud thud, crunch*, and she said to Peter, "Do you think she could be on the old train tracks?" and he said, "No, the tracks are gone. It's all grown over now."

"I think we should look anyway," she said. "She'll be frightened when she realizes she's alone in the dark." She thought of herself on the tracks and wondered if she would have been frightened without the porter. She'd been so convinced she had something to prove that she would never have admitted to being afraid.

The three remaining police officers went into motion then, and they walked away in different directions, waving their flashlights around.

"What a goddamned fiasco," one of them said.

Peter took Estella's arm, and she managed to stand with his help.

"Let's get you back," he said. "It's wet out here."

Estella couldn't get her mind off the tracks and the night she had walked out of the bush. She knew that was a long time ago, but at the same time it seemed to have just happened.

"Should we walk along the beach?" she asked, confused about whom she was with. Maybe it was the porter, but what had he done with his buttoned jacket and cap?

"No," Peter said. "It's raining too hard."

He led her to his truck and she didn't argue, and by the time they got back to the cottage, she had her senses back and had calmed down. She still couldn't understand what had happened on the pier, though, and how it had gotten so out of control so quickly. She was worried about Hannah and hoped someone would think to let her know when they had found her.

She put the kettle on and made instant coffee. She told Peter he could go home, she'd be all right, but he wouldn't leave.

At some point she fell asleep on the couch and dreamed that she and Hannah were sitting on a bench along a trail through the bush. They were holding hands.

"You're supposed to stay put if you're lost," Hannah said in the dream. "We might as well save our energy."

"You're wise beyond your years," Estella said.

The wind blew a gust and spread the tree branches, and they could see the lake. It was such a big lake, but following it would surely lead them somewhere.

"Could we not follow the shoreline?" Estella asked.

Hannah thought for a minute, and then she shook her head.

"Let's just wait," she said.

They sat on the bench, catching glimpses of the lake, listening to the leaves rustling, and they waited.

"I don't know where I am," Estella said.

"Here's the thing," said Hannah. "If you stay put, you'll always know where you are."

Estella thought about that until the dream faded.

By morning, the sky had cleared and the sun was out again. The same female officer came to Emily Carr to tell Estella that Hannah had been found not far from where she'd run off, and was now on her way back to Winnipeg and her mother. She asked Estella a few questions and wrote her answers in a notebook while Peter looked on.

No, Estella said, she'd had no idea that Nicholas had taken the girl without her mother's consent. They'd driven her car because it had needed a run on the highway. Yes, he was her great-nephew. She didn't know the wife well.

She didn't let on that she'd met both of them only days ago, although she supposed the police already knew that.

After the officer left, Peter said that he was going home to his room at The Travellers, but he would be back later to check on her. She went to bed and slept for an hour, and woke up thinking about Hannah's purse.

She should try to find it for her.

She put her bathing suit on just in case she had to wade into the water to retrieve it. She pulled her shorts and the Lake Claire T-shirt on over her bathing suit, and put on her shoes rather than her sandals because they were better for walking. She took her cane, thinking she ought to be sensible and not risk falling and having to be carried out of the bush again. She sprayed herself with the can of bug spray someone had left on the windowsill, clipped on her sunglasses, grabbed her hat, and felt confident that she had thought of everything.

She took the same path through the trees that Peter had shown her when he was ten years old. She had to watch each step because there were tree roots everywhere. There were flowers blooming along the path, Indian paintbrush and some kind of white anemone. She could smell the evergreens. She kept looking for a bench like the one that had been in her dream, thinking she would rest when she came to it, but there were no benches. She didn't remember the marina being this far, and she was beginning to wonder if she'd somehow taken the wrong path when she saw the break in the trees ahead that opened to the public beach, and the marina beyond.

She was almost there when she heard footsteps coming rapidly up the path behind her, and she turned with a start. It was Peter Boone, in his running clothes. He stopped when he reached her, barely puffing, which seemed impossible to her, and he said, "Where are you off to?"

"The pier," she said. "To find Hannah's purse. It fell into the water last night."

"Funny, just where I was headed," he said.

Estella thought he was probably lying.

He fell in behind her, letting her set the pace, and they soon stepped out of the bush and onto the beach. There was a new cement sidewalk between the beach and the road, and they walked along it to the marina because it was easier than walking in sand. When they came to a bench, Estella was glad to sit for a minute, her cane propped between her knees.

"I've been wondering," she said, "if there have been any repercussions about the paddlewheeler last night."

"None," Peter said. "Maybe the excitement . . . well, everyone is talking about the other. The fellow who bought her loaded her up this morning. She's gone."

The other, he'd said. She wondered if she would ever see Nicholas and Hannah again.

They sat on the bench for a few minutes and then carried on, and as they approached the marina she could see the big empty space where the paddlewheeler had been moored. The concession stand was open and Peter bought them each a cold drink, and then they went to the spot where they thought the purse had gone into the lake. They looked over the edge of the pier and there it was, lying on the bottom in perhaps six feet of clear water. There was no way either of them could wade in and retrieve it.

There were several boys fishing off the pier and Peter commandeered one of them to help. The boy dropped his hook and dragged it along the bottom until he managed to snag the purse and reel it in. Peter handed him five dollars and the boy immediately headed for the concession stand and came back minutes later with a hot dog.

The purse was waterlogged and ruined. Estella got the silver zipper open so she could see if there was anything valuable inside that ought to be dried out, and she found the jewellery bag containing her beads, which she hadn't known were missing. The wet bag fell apart when she tried to open it. She picked soggy bits of tissue off the beads and checked them for damage, but they all seemed to be intact.

Peter looked at the beads and said they were odd things.

"They belonged to my father's first wife," she said.

In that moment, she decided she was truly tired of the burden of Salina, and she wondered whether she had come to the same conclusion the day before and given the beads to Hannah, even though she didn't remember doing that. She wondered if there was a way she could get them back to her in Winnipeg.

The village taxi pulled up to the pier just then and dropped off a pair of fishermen, and Estella flagged it for a ride back to the cottage. She went by herself while Peter continued on with his run. It was clear, Estella thought, that he was still a good sight younger than she was.

She had no sooner got back to the cottage than Marigold Caige knocked on her door and said there was a phone call for her in the office.

"A woman. I think she said her name was Emmy something," Marigold said. "Emmy Lou? Emmy Lee? Something like that."

"Emyflor?" Estella asked.

"Yes, that seems right, Emyflor. She sounds a bit hysterical."

Estella followed her back to the office wondering what might be wrong, and called Emyflor's cellphone number.

"Oh my God, Lola," Emyflor said. "I don't know what to do. Lydia is here and she's showing your house to some people who saw it advertised on the Internet. They were in the house when I got here. I don't know how they got in. She's selling your house. Did you want her to sell your house?"

"Selling my house?" Estella said. "No. She can't sell my house. Put her on the phone."

She heard Emyflor calling Lydia—"Your auntie is on the phone, she wants to talk to you"—and she heard Lydia saying to Emyflor, "Did you call her? I asked you not to do that," before she took the phone.

"What the hell are you doing, Lydia? Get those people out of my house right now."

"Estella," Lydia said. "I'm doing you a favour. This house is too big for you. Anyway, I'm just seeing what you might get for it."

"Get them out of the house right now or I'm calling 911."

She hung up.

Marigold had been listening.

"Everything okay?" she asked cautiously.

Estella pointed to the Caiges' sign about delighting in insult and difficulty, and said, "I am not at the moment delighted, if that's what you mean."

Then she asked Marigold if she had a computer and could find something on the Internet for her. There was a laptop in the office and Marigold did some searching and, sure enough, there was Estella's house on Kijiji, which Marigold said was like the want ads in the paper used to be, although Estella already suspected that. "Heritage home. For sale by owner." The price Lydia was asking nearly knocked her over, almost a million dollars. She wondered if she would have a house when she got back, but it was too outrageous to worry about. She would call her lawyer when she got home and he would deal with whatever Lydia had done.

As she was leaving the office, Marigold asked her when she would be checking out. "It's just, we have your cottage booked for tonight," she said.

Estella told her she would leave right after lunch.

It wasn't until she saw her car parked by the deck that she realized she had no one to drive her home. She was stranded.

Then Peter Boone came along again.

He wouldn't take no for an answer.

——

THERE WAS A pounding on the front door, as though whoever was there couldn't wait for a response to the bell.

"Hold your horses," Estella shouted as she made her way to the foyer, knowing it was going to be Lydia. Estella looked at her

351

through the latched screen door and said, "Is there something you want?"

"You haven't been answering the phone."

"I wonder why," Estella said.

Peter Boone stood behind her in the hallway. He had her father's old tool belt strapped on because he had noticed immediately that a windowpane by the back door lock was broken.

"We can't have that," he'd said, and he'd gone right to work.

Lydia rattled the screen door when Estella wouldn't open it for her.

"I want to know who these other Diamonds are you went to the lake with," she said. "You could have told me."

"Jack's grandson," she said. "Nicholas, from Calgary."

She was not planning to tell Lydia the rest, how Nicholas Diamond had been taken away in a police car after supposedly abducting his daughter. That had all been sorted. Nicholas had called to tell her that he was back in Calgary, and she'd asked for an address for Hannah so she could send her the beads.

"And what's *he* doing here?" Lydia said through the screen, having suddenly realized that the tradesman standing behind Estella was Peter Boone. And then Emyflor appeared in the hallway, too. The smell of lunch was coming from the kitchen, onions and cheese.

"Lola," Emyflor said, "you want me to wash the sheets today, or maybe wait until next time?"

"Excuse me," Estella said to Lydia. "As you can see, I'm busy."

"Let me in, Estella," Lydia said. Just then one of her heels got caught in a crack in the step. She rescued her shoe and held it up for Estella to see.

Estella looked at the shoe. A chunk of leather had peeled off the heel.

"A shoe repairman can fix that," she said.

"Open this door right now," Lydia said, shaking the shoe at Estella.

"Tell me, Lydia," Estella said, "why would I open the door to a woman who has my house advertised on the Internet? By the way, I've spoken with my lawyer and he's going to be in touch with some kind of cease-and-desist order. Or whatever the legal types call it."

Lydia bent over to put her shoe back on, and when she stood up again she took a breath and said, "Let me in and I'll explain."

"I don't need you to explain," Estella said. "You want to know how much my house is worth."

"You have to move out of the house at some point, Estella," Lydia said, sounding exasperated.

"I don't really think I do," she said.

Then she closed and locked the inside door.

The pounding started up again, and continued for at least five minutes, until it finally stopped and they heard Lydia's SUV roar off up the street. Once she was sure Lydia was gone Estella opened the front door again to catch the breeze. The house was warm from Emyflor's baking.

When they sat down to lunch she said to Emyflor, "Remember that term *gold digger*? You wrote it in your little book. Lydia trying to get my house—that's what it means."

After lunch, she asked Emyflor, "Where could I buy a sparkly purse that an eleven-year-old would like?"

Emyflor drove her to a store called Old Navy. They found a shiny black purse with little skulls on it, and Estella remembered what Nicholas had said about Hannah's night light, and she bought it. When she got home, she put Salina's beads in a small jewellery bag she had and tucked it into the purse. Then she put the purse inside her watercolour box, along with a letter to Hannah explaining that her red purse had not fared well in the water, and once it was dry it had shrunk so much the zipper would no longer work. She also told her the story of the beads, although not that Salina had stolen them. She said they had been made by a woman artist in England, who had taken a big risk to make them in secret because she was not an actual factory designer and was supposed to be dipping teacups in glaze or some such thing. She wanted to assure Hannah that her parents loved her and that everything would work out, but she changed her mind because there were no guarantees. She ended with, "It might not seem like it, but there are many people who love you." She underlined the word *many*.

She signed her letter Estella Diamond and addressed the package to Hannah at her grandparents' home in Winnipeg. Then she wrapped up the first brick from the Diamond plant and sent it to Nicholas at Bow River Resources. It cost her a fortune to mail the two packages.

A few weeks later, a letter arrived from Hannah. Estella took it out onto her back porch to read. Peter was in the yard, setting up a ladder to trim the runners on the apple tree. He seemed to think you could do that at any time of year. She wasn't sure that was correct but she didn't really care about the tree. Her neighbour was right. It had grown too big and shaded the whole yard.

Estella sat in her wicker chair and opened Hannah's letter. She saw that she had enclosed a new drawing of the spruce tree that hung over the bank at Lake Claire, but this time it had the faces from the beads hidden in its branches, peeping over and under like gnomes in a fairy tale.

She set the drawing aside and read the letter.

Dear Estella Diamond,

Thank you very much for the beads. I will take good care of them. My mother asked why you sent them to me and I told her they were a hundred-year-old heirloom and she said she wondered why they were black instead of that "pretty" Wedgwood blue. I think she missed the point. Please find enclosed my drawing of the faces, which I happen to like a lot. The faces, I mean, although I like the drawing, too. Otherwise I wouldn't be sending it to you. Thank you also for the watercolour paints, although I don't yet know how to use them.

Here is what happened, in case you want to know. It was not my dad's fault. Please don't blame him. I want to live with him in Calgary. I'm working on it.

That day we left your house, everything fell apart. The first day, I mean, when we were on our way to Winnipeg. We were all bickering in the car like some terrible family on TV, and Dad finally pulled over onto the shoulder and said he wouldn't drive until we all agreed to be quiet the rest of the way. When we got there we sat down to dinner and Dad drank too much and got really drunk. After dinner, I went to the kitchen to help with the dishes and I heard Nan say to Mom, "You look so tired, but we'll look after you, won't we."

I wanted to tell Nan, "Mom isn't the one who needs looking after. It's Dad. Mom's the one who went and ruined everything." But Nan is her mother so I didn't.

Dad stayed overnight, and then he played with us in the pool all the next day. I knew he was leaving that night, so I snuck into the back seat of his car after they thought Paris and I were asleep. I was on the floor and when he threw his bag in, it almost landed on me. He backed out of the driveway and then we were on the highway again in the dark. He had the radio on an oldies station and was singing along. I was trying to decide when to tell him I was there, when I realized he wasn't singing anymore. He was crying. Did you ever see your father cry? It's pretty terrible. I sat up and scared him so that he nearly drove the car into the ditch. He yelled at me that I had almost got us both killed.

All I could say was, "Dad, stop crying."

He tried to deny that he was crying. I climbed over the console and into the front seat. He was still mad at me. Then he said, "I have to take you back. We can't start out this way. We have to do it right, your mother and I." And he said, "Your mother is not to blame. That's important to remember."

How was it possible that he didn't know?

I said I would text Mom and tell her I was all right, I was with Dad and he'd bring me back soon. But that's not what I texted her. I said that I was going to live with him in Calgary and then I threw my phone out the window.

Dad started the car again and pulled back onto the highway and said maybe we could have a little holiday and check out Lake Claire. In the morning we stopped at a 24-hour pancake place. Dad went to the washroom and when he came back he said he'd dropped his phone in the toilet. I wondered if he'd done it on purpose because we were on the run, at least for a few days.

And then we went to your house, and you know the rest.

Well, not all of the rest. Before we left the parking lot at the pancake house I told Dad that he ought to know Mom had a boyfriend. I wanted him to know. It wasn't fair that he didn't. He wouldn't believe me, so I had to tell him how I knew, which was because we conveniently ran into him and his two boring kids when we were out with Mom for a bike ride a few weeks ago, just before Paris's birthday. We were on the bike

*path and Mom was, like, Oh look, someone from work, and Oh, what
a coincidence, he's got a picnic with him too, so why don't we eat our
picnics together? And we had to sit on the grass in the park with this
stranger while he introduced us to his kids as though that were somehow important, and she had a blanket and fancy napkins and everything else stuffed into that stupid basket on her bike. "How was that
not planned?" I said to Dad. She'd brought the bagels and cream cheese,
and he'd brought the olives and the cookies.*

*So that is all. That is what our family has come to, and Dad is in
Calgary and I'm in Winnipeg. It's not as bad as I thought it would be. At
least there's a pool. It will be okay for the summer. Dad says he will find a
way for us all to be happy again, but I don't know how that can happen.*

*Thank you again for the beads. I will take good care of them and
make sure they do not end up in a lake. I'm very sorry that I took them
in the first place. I don't normally steal things, but my life right now is
not normal, as you can see from what I've told you.*

Yours truly,

Hannah Diamond

So, Hannah *had* taken the beads, which at least meant that
Estella had not given them to her and then forgotten. And even
though Hannah had taken them, she couldn't think of what she
had done as stealing, and she did not regret that she'd sent the
beads to her, because of the letter she'd received in return.

She thought about Hannah's question: *Did you ever see your
father cry?*

Never. Not when her mother died, not when they thought Jack
was dead during the war, not even in his final year when his mind
had failed him. He'd raged in anger, but he'd never cried, at least

not in front of her. She didn't think she could have stood it, seeing Oliver Diamond cry.

She thought also about what Hannah had said about a normal life. She didn't know what a normal life was. She knew only that most of her life, normal or not, had passed.

From the deck, she watched Peter on the ladder trimming the tree. She didn't dare leave him alone up there. *Who's looking out for whom now?* she thought. He had an old transistor radio that he'd found in the garage, and he'd set it in the grass. Music was playing, something classical. He told her he never again wanted to hear Roy Orbison so he was avoiding the oldies stations.

Estella folded Hannah's letter and slipped it and the drawing back into the envelope, and then into her pocket.

From the kitchen came the scent of Emyflor's cooking.

The Diamond House

Estella Diamond died in her sleep. She simply didn't wake up one day. Her papers were in order thanks to the steady advice of her lawyer, and her will revealed that all she had left to Lydia was her Ford Taurus. For Lonny, she'd set up a trust fund to make sure he received the care he needed when he became an adult. At one time it would have been unfathomable that the Diamond estate should go anywhere other than to a Diamond, but Estella did not see one who deserved it more than those she had chosen as her main beneficiaries. She had taken great pleasure in writing her last will and testament. She knew Lydia would think she was entitled to everything, but so be it. Estella's lawyer, who had been her counsel since she'd sued her brothers half a lifetime ago, was certain the will was iron-clad.

Still, before she died, Estella said to Emyflor, "No matter what happens, Lydia is never to get her hands on this house."

"Okay," Emyflor said, confused about what this had to do with her.

Then Estella made Emyflor hold onto the cross she wore around her neck and repeat, *She'll get this house over my dead body.*

"Lydia will get this house over my dead body," Emyflor said. What she was doing felt vaguely profane but she did it anyway, because she was making Estella happy.

Predictably, Lydia challenged the will, asserting that Estella had been completely demented, and that Peter Boone and Emyflor Santos had conspired to influence her. Estella's lawyer knew about Lydia's failed attempt to coerce Estella out of her house with an ad on Kijiji, and Lydia's own legal counsel told her how much it was going to cost her to lose her case, which he assured her was what would happen. She wanted to know if she could at least challenge the charities Estella had left money to—selected according to what had killed her brothers: depression, lung cancer, and a pair of heart attacks—but the answer was no, and she was forced to accept the will as incontestable.

It was during Estella's last days, when she slept on the sofa most of the time, that Emyflor broke the white teapot. She'd been waving the vacuum cleaner nozzle around the ceiling corners, sucking up cobwebs, when it got away on her and, *bang*, there was no question this time that the pot was going to break into pieces. Shards flew all over the dining room. Several large chunks ended up under the table. The spout landed across the room, where it was deflected off the wall and bounced around the corner. The lid somehow hit the window and cracked a pane. Estella heard the crash in her sleep and woke up long enough to say, "What was that?" Emyflor was about to explain when she noticed Estella's eyes had closed again, so she swept up the pieces and carried them out to the bin in the alley.

On her way back inside, Emyflor stopped and admired Peter Boone's repairs to the old house: the new asphalt shingles, the gutters coaxed back into their proper place, the trim painted a shiny white. Now she had another job for him: repairing the cracked window in the dining room. Such a big house for an old lady to live in on her own, she thought. She was thankful Peter Boone was there. She didn't understand his unlikely friendship with Estella, but she could see they enjoyed each other's company. One could brighten the other just by walking into the room.

When Estella died a few weeks after the teapot broke, Emyflor was told the house was hers. She almost tried to give it back to the estate, thinking it was not right for Estella to have left it to her, but then she remembered that promise she'd made—*over my dead body*—and she decided she had to accept the gift. Otherwise, Lydia might end up with it.

When the estate was finally settled, she sold the property because she didn't want the bother of such an old house, or the cost of heating it. Her husband was no Peter Boone with his tools and handyman know-how. When she put it up for sale, she worried that Lydia might try to purchase it, and what would she do then? But a young family bought it, two doctors and their new baby. It wasn't worth as much as some other houses in the neighbourhood because it needed updating—a new kitchen, bigger closets, a double garage—but the doctors said they loved old houses, and they could imagine what Estella's house had looked like when it was new. With the doctors' money, Emyflor bought a practical bungalow in the suburbs, in a neighbourhood where she had friends, and where the taxes were lower and the schools were close by.

After Estella died, Peter Boone returned to Lake Claire because he didn't much like the city. He went back to working for the Caiges, who were still in business for the time being. The Travellers had been torn down during the year he was away, and the Caiges let him rent one of the smallest cottages to live in. It had been winterized several years before when cross-country skiing had become popular, so he was able to stay in it year round. Estella had convinced him to apply for his old age pension, which he had not previously done, and once the cheques started arriving he figured he was a rich man. She'd wanted to leave him some money in her will but he'd asked her not to. He wouldn't know what to do with it, he'd said.

During his year in the city with Estella, Peter had visited the scene of his accident. He'd been surprised to see the boxing club was still there and he'd gone inside and found that the owner of the club was the same man, now a grizzled old-timer. He remembered Peter and the day of the accident, and Peter appreciated hearing the story from someone other than Estella. It wasn't that he didn't believe her version, but she had been a friend, while the boxing club owner was simply a bystander. Talking to him was like finding old film footage of the accident. Morning coffee at the club became a regular thing. The owner was the only person with whom Peter had talked about boxing since the day his career was ended by a Cadillac.

After Peter left and the house was sold, Emyflor began to clean it out so the doctors could take possession and start their renovations. Cleaning was a long, slow process. There were Diamond possessions in every room and in every cupboard and drawer. When she got to Estella's bedroom, she found Hannah's letter in an envelope on the dresser, and she read it with curiosity because she remembered Hannah and her family. After she finished reading, she looked up and saw in the dresser mirror that she'd placed her hand over her heart. That poor girl, she thought. Her life was so much more complicated than it ought to be. Emyflor had a daughter not much older than Hannah and they had lived apart for so long, but always they'd had the knowledge that they would be together again. From the letter, she did not think there was much hope for Hannah's family. She put it back in its envelope and carried it downstairs, where the clutter in the dining room awaited her.

Her mind was on many things at once that day. Her husband's immigration papers had finally come through and she was going home in a month—the first time in ten years—to see her parents and grandparents and fetch her family before the school year started. A friend with a pickup truck was coming by later to take some of the furniture Emyflor didn't have room for in the new house, and after that she had several girlfriends dropping by to collect the linens and towels and curtains she herself didn't need. There was so much, some of it worn but with plenty of life left, a reminder of the large family that had once filled the house.

She stood staring at the china laid out on the dining table, ten place settings with a red-and-black daisy pattern, too old-fashioned and formal for any table she was likely to set. She knew that it had come from Ontario with Estella's mother, and she had been trying to figure how to properly pack it so nothing would get broken. If Estella hadn't told her the china had been a wedding present to her parents, she might have given it away, but now she felt she ought to keep it. She decided she needed better boxes for the china, which meant another trip to the liquor store for the heavy ones. She worried that she was getting mixed up: what to take with her, what to give away, what to throw in the garbage bin in the alley. She had the contents of the house set out everywhere, in the bedrooms, the garage, the basement. She stood in the dining room, Hannah's letter in her hand, and she was no longer thinking of the letter at all, and in fact she had almost forgotten she had it. She was thinking there were so many things to take care of. Would her children like the new neighbourhood? Would they make friends? Was their English good enough for school?

A red-and-black teapot almost the size of a samovar was right in the centre of the table, with the matching plates and bowls and cups and saucers set around it. One cup was on its side, resting on its delicate handle. Emyflor lifted the lid on the teapot and was surprised to see envelopes stuffed inside, yellowed with age, folded to fit the shape of the teapot. She peered inside and thought it was peculiar, letters in a teapot, but she didn't have time to read them. She popped Hannah's letter inside, on top of them, and then put the lid back on and absently set the teacup upright. She thought she might send Hannah a note once she had moved into the new house, and ask her if she wanted her letter back.

At that moment her phone buzzed. It was her daughter on FaceTime, and Emyflor used the camera to show her the china. Her daughter, not surprisingly, wasn't interested in the china. She was calling to ask if the new school had a basketball team. She was in love with basketball. Could they go to Toronto, she asked, to see a Raptors game?

Emyflor assured her that the school had a team, even though she didn't know that for certain, and that Canadians loved basketball, especially since the Raptors had won the championship. Maybe they could visit Toronto sometime. "We'll see," she said.

They talked for a few minutes more and then her daughter said she had to go, she had friends waiting.

"Love you, my girl, see you soon," said Emyflor, and then she hung up and went to get more boxes.

Acknowledgements

I am grateful to the many people who provided comments and answered what must have sometimes seemed like curious questions. I sent one friend into a panic when I asked about induced comas without explaining that I was fact-checking for fiction. Thanks especially to Mac Aldred, Cody Anderson, Travis Anderson, Melanie Daluong, Zach Dietrich, Connie Gault, Marlis Wesseler, the Saskatchewan Military Museum, the Stoke-on-Trent Potteries Museum, and the Victoria and Albert Museum. Mistakes or fabrications post-research are mine. Should anyone be interested in source material on the history of women in the British potteries, I recommend *Potters and Paintresses* by Cheryl Buckley. A 1902 novel called *Anna of the Five Towns* by Arnold Bennett brings to life the early ceramics industry in Stoke-on-Trent, and *A Rudimentary Treatise on the Manufacture of Bricks and Tiles* by Edward Dobson (1850) is a bit of a brickmaker's bible. Thanks to the Claybank Brick Plant National Historic Site in Saskatchewan, a place well worth a visit, for both its history and the surrounding landscape; and to the public funders for their support of this novel: the Saskatchewan Arts Board and the Canada Council for the Arts. Thanks also to the Access Copyright Foundation, and to Cheryl and Henry Kloppenburg for their sponsorship of the Cheryl and Henry Kloppenburg Award for Literary Excellence. Finally, thanks to my husband, Bruce, who knows a thing or two about clay, and to my editor, Jennifer Lambert, and my agent, Dean Cooke, who love novels and work tirelessly to keep them coming.